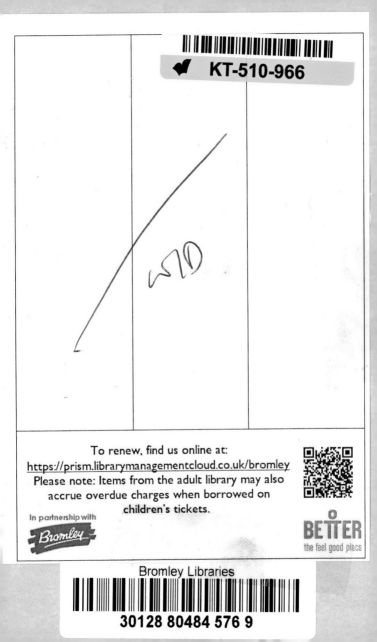

KT-510-966

Discover more at millsandboon.co.uk

A SONG OF SECRETS

JAYCI LEE

MIDNIGHT SON

BARBARA DUNLOP

MILLS & BOON

First Published in Great Britain 2022
by Mills & Boon, an imprint of HarperCollins*Publishers* Ltd
1 London Bridge Street, London, SE1 9GF

www.harpercollins.co.uk

HarperCollins*Publishers*
1st Floor, Watermarque Building,
Ringsend Road, Dublin 4, Ireland

A Song of Secrets © 2022 Judith J. Yi
Midnight Son © 2022 Barbara Dunlop

ISBN: 978-0-263-30323-0

0122

MIX
Paper from
responsible sources
FSC™ C007454

A SONG OF SECRETS

JAYCI LEE

To my lovely father-in-law and mother-in-law.
Your support means the world to me. Thank you.

Prologue

The Neimans' annual dinner was not Joshua Shin's usual scene. He was more accustomed to long hours in the office and longer hours sitting at his piano. But his grandfather wasn't feeling well and had asked him to attend in his place. He couldn't seem to deny his *halabuji* anything. He had hero-worshipped the man since he was able to tilt his head up.

So he'd acquiesced, knowing full well the dinner party was a fundraising event for the Chamber Music Society of Southern California—knowing that there was a chance *she* might be performing tonight. God, it was pathetic. After ten years, he still couldn't think about her without the familiar ache clenching his heart.

As he passed the wrought iron gates of the Beverly Hills estate, a regal Georgian mansion came into view, gleaming with light against the dusk. Joshua maneuvered his Tesla to join the line of high-end cars in the driveway and entrusted his car to one of the valets in white jackets and black ties.

A flute of champagne was thrust into his hand as he walked through the front door. Newly arrived guests mingled in the circular grand foyer before moving on to the ballroom. But the thread of anxiety running through him made Joshua rather antisocial. He nodded politely to the other guests and proceeded into the ballroom, claiming a spot near the rich emerald drapes of one of the floor-to-ceiling windows.

He couldn't stop his eyes from sweeping across the room, searching for a face he dreamed of too often. To his…relief, she was nowhere in sight. It was unlikely that out of close to a hundred musicians with the Chamber Music Society, Angie Han would be one of the performers. Then again, the musicians would've been herded in through the service entrance and relegated to the back rooms, so he wouldn't see her until the performance even if she were here.

Irritation licked at him at the thought of her being treated like a second-class citizen, but he stopped himself short. What the hell business was it of his how she was treated? She'd been out of his life for a decade, and he wanted to keep it that way.

"Mr. Shin," a cool, cultured voice said from behind him.

"Yes?" Joshua turned to find a silver-haired man in an impeccable suit regarding him.

"I'm Timothy Pearce, the executive director of the Chamber Music Society," he said. "I'm surprised not to see your grandfather here tonight. He rather enjoys these small, intimate performances."

"He regrets missing it and sent me in his stead." Joshua didn't volunteer the reason for his grandfather's absence.

"Well, you are very welcome here." He assessed Joshua

with calculating eyes before a charming smile spread across his face. The man was obviously gauging whether he'd be as generous a donor as his grandfather. "We're always thrilled to see the younger generation join in the appreciation of classical music."

"I do share my grandfather's love of music." Joshua saw no harm in reassuring him. He had every intention of donating as his grandfather would have. "Speaking of which, what do you have lined up for tonight's performance?"

"You're in for a treat." Timothy Pearce's smile had warmed by ten degrees with Joshua's reassurance. "The Hana Trio will be playing for us."

He exerted every ounce of his self-control to keep the shock from showing on his face. Angie was the cellist in the ensemble, with her two sisters on the violin and the viola. While he'd been aware of the possibility, the thought of actually seeing her tonight sent his mind spiraling.

"You *have* heard of them, right?" The other man cocked his head to the side when the silence stretched on a moment too long. "They are a phenomenal up-and-coming string trio."

"Yes, of course," he said through numb lips, feigning polite interest. "I'm looking forward to their performance."

"Wonderful. It was a pleasure meeting you, and I hope you enjoy the rest of the evening." The executive director walked off to greet to a jovial older couple just entering the ballroom.

What Joshua said about his love of music was true, but it went much deeper than that. There was once a time when music was his life. Images of sunlight streaming down on his fingers as they flew over the piano and sounds of beautiful music and laughter flitted through his mind. Happiness, sweet and full of hope, filled his soul before reality slashed through it, leaving it in pitiful tatters. She had ruined it all.

Deep in his thoughts, Joshua belatedly noticed the guests migrating out of the ballroom. He followed the herd to an impressive conservatory opening up to a manicured garden, its vastness obscured by the coming night. The string lights on the glass ceiling sparkled against the darkening sky, and the elegant lamps around the room added to the beauty and intimacy of the space.

When the throng of people in front of him dispersed to take their seats, the makeshift stage at the far end of the room came into view. That was when he saw her. *Angie.* Everything else melted away and the only sound he could hear was the drumming of his heart.

In the years they'd been apart, she'd gone from a lovely girl to a breathtaking woman. The black silky hair she used to pull into careless ponytails lay shimmering on her shoulders. The slight slimming of her face highlighted her cheekbones and added an alluring sharpness to her soft features. He couldn't tear his gaze away from her. Fortunately, her eyes were downcast, her slender arms and long, graceful fingers poised over the cello as she tuned her instrument with her sisters.

Before she could glance up and see him, Joshua situated himself by the doorsill, concealed by a tall, leafy plant. Some of the stragglers passing by glanced curiously at him, but they soon took their seats. A hush fell across the room and the concert began.

The first strains of the music sent a shiver through his body and raised goose bumps on his arms. Angie had been a talented and promising musician in college, but her sound had matured into something nuanced and silken that caressed his senses. He'd listened to the Hana Trio's debut album while visiting his grandfather, so he knew they played beautifully…but hearing them live was something else entirely. True to their name—*hana* meant *one* in Korean—they played as a united whole, and the result was exquisite.

He closed his eyes and let the music wash over him, smoothing out the jagged edges of his rampaging emotions. He felt nothing for Angie Han. Not even anger. The fury, pain, and…yearning that filled him were mere echoes from his past. It hadn't been easy but he'd moved on from her long ago. This sentimentality wasn't like him.

It was a fine performance and Joshua clapped along with the resounding applause of the audience. He hated the nervous trip of his heartbeat, wondering what he would do when she saw him. Staying partially hidden behind the plant, he watched as the trio stood and took their bows. He was being ridiculous. She was a musician and he was there as a patron of the Chamber Music Society. If she saw him, he would greet her politely like an old acquaintance and go on with his life. With an irritated huff, he stepped away from the doorsill and joined the rest of the guests in the conservatory.

"Ladies and gentlemen." Timothy Pearce raised his voice to be heard over the excited chatter, and Joshua dutifully gave him his attention. "I want to thank the wonderful Mr. and Mrs. Neiman for hosting this amazing dinner. And I sincerely thank each and every one of you for joining us. You can continue to enjoy and foster beautiful chamber music like tonight's Hana Trio performance by making a generous donation to the Chamber Music Society."

Joshua's sense of someone watching him grew as the executive director continued his smooth fundraising pitch. The pinprick of awareness started at his head and spread all the way down his spine. Slowly, he turned his head to find Angie's wide, horrified eyes on him. She had paled until no hint of color remained on her cheeks, and her mouth was open slightly as though a gasp had just escaped from it.

As their eyes met and held, Joshua couldn't breathe. His body heated up and his hands flexed by his sides as though remembering the feel of her. *No.* He refused to give her even a sliver of his emotions. He held her gaze for a split second longer and gave the barest nod of his head to acknowledge her. Then he looked away from her and faced Pearce again in time to hear the end of his speech.

"You are part of our family. Thank you."

The hearty applause faded and conversation filled the room. Unconsciously, Joshua's eyes sought her out once more, only to glimpse the back of her as she left the conservatory through the door leading out to the garden. Disappointment flitted through him before being replaced by irritation. He didn't regret not speaking to her. There was nothing left to say between them other than forced pleasantries that he had no patience for.

As the rest of the guests headed to the dining room for dinner, Joshua stopped Timothy Pearce to hand him a check. He'd come to the party and stayed for the performance. His grandfather wouldn't mind if he didn't sit through a stuffy meal with a roomful of strangers. When he'd said his goodbyes to the executive director, he made his way across the deserted grand foyer to the door.

"Joshua," a quiet voice said from the corridor.

He spun at the sound of his name. Angie took hesitant steps into the foyer but stopped long before she reached him.

"What do you want?" He grimaced at the simmering anger in his tone—a telltale sign that he wasn't immune to her.

"I… I just wanted to say hello." She wrung her hands before dropping them to her sides and curling them into fists. "I wanted to know that you're…happy."

"Happy?" His bark of laughter tasted as bitter as crushed aspirins in his throat. "You don't expect me to dignify that with a response, do you?"

"I'm so sorry, Joshua," she said, her voice catching on his name.

Something snapped inside him and he stormed across the room until he loomed over her. She was suddenly so close that he could feel the heat coming off her body. The shock of her proximity paralyzed him and all he could do was stare down at her upturned face. Neither of them moved a muscle as awareness swirled around them and their breathing quickened. The tension grew unbearably taut as the seconds ticked by. Faint laughter in the distance ripped him out of his trance.

"You don't get to know if I'm *happy*. You don't get to say you're sorry," he said in a low growl, reining in the desire pounding through his veins. "You forfeited that right when you left me ten years ago."

A vise threatened to crush his heart when a single tear rolled down her cheek, and he hated her for it. He hated her for making him want to wipe away the tear and gather her into his arms. For making him wish for things he could never have again. For making him want *her* again—even for a passing second.

He turned on his heel and walked out of the mansion without a backward glance. She threatened the equilibrium he'd worked so hard to achieve. Never again. Angie Han meant nothing to him anymore.

One

Two months later

After rehearsing with her sisters, Angie hurried to the parking lot of the community college where they rented a classroom for their practices. She had a meeting with Janet Miller, her mentor and the Chamber Music Society's artistic director.

She unlocked her car and opened the rear door—her semicompact didn't have enough trunk space for her cello—while humming a song under her breath. The melody had been stuck in her head for weeks but she hadn't been able to place it. Maybe it was something her mom used to sing for her when she was little. It was such a lovely tune. Once she finagled her instrument into the back seat, angled just right so she could still see through the rear window, she slipped into the driver's seat and steered her car out of the parking spot.

Anxiety ran through her as her thoughts turned to her

meeting with Janet. The Chamber Music Society was struggling to remain afloat after the pandemic. All concerts, fundraising events and in-home performances for their highest donors had ceased with the lockdown, which meant much of their funding had also come to a halt. If it hadn't been for their most dedicated benefactors, the many musicians of the society would've already been without a home. With the new season only a few months away, she was hoping things would eventually return to normal—whatever that meant these days. But the situation could be more dire than she'd thought.

She had her radio set to her favorite classical music station and smiled as Erik Satie's Gymnopédie no. 1 came through the speakers. The French composer's music was her catnip. For some reason, it always made her imagine the world moving in that peculiar way it did in silent movies. The piece infused her with much-needed serenity as she arrived at her friend's office and knocked lightly on the open door.

"My dear, it's so lovely to see you," Janet said, embracing her warmly.

"It's good to see you, too." Angie hugged her back tightly.

There had been times she'd wanted to quit music, believing herself to lack the talent to *make* it. But her mentor had always been there to remind her that she had the talent, passion and drive to succeed as a musician. She wouldn't be where she was without Janet.

"Why don't we sit by the window?" Her friend led her to the cozy seating area and they sat side by side on the plush love seat. "Do you want something to drink?"

"No, thanks. I'm fine," Angie said with a hint of impatience. Her heart picked up pace, anxious to find out what this meeting was about. "Tell me what's going on."

Even before she answered, Janet's resigned sigh confirmed her worst fears. "The Chamber Music Society's financial situation is even grimmer than we'd initially thought. The success of this coming season is crucial to its survival. The board intimated at the last meeting that if we don't pull off the best season we've ever had, it might be the end of the society."

"Just like that?" she whispered.

"Just like that." Her friend looked down at her hands.

Janet's hesitation told Angie there was more to the bad news. "And?"

Reluctance in every line of her face, her mentor said, "And Timothy wants you and your sisters to ask your father for help."

"But…he stopped supporting the society when I cut ties with him," she stuttered, rattled by the request.

"I know. I hate asking this of you, but I also understand where Timothy is coming from. Really, every donation will increase the chance of our survival. And your father used to be one of our top donors."

Angie looked out the window at the streets and buildings baking in the Los Angeles sun. "Let me think about it."

She couldn't refuse her mentor outright no matter how much she wanted to. And the fate of the Chamber Music Society wasn't just about her. Her sisters and all the other musicians would suffer right along with her.

"That's all I can ask for." Janet reached out and gently grasped her hand. "Thank you."

"Of course. I want to do my part in saving the society." She pulled her hand out of Janet's after a quick squeeze. "I'll let you get back to work."

She walked to the parking lot with heavy steps. Her father would never support the society because it was the source of Angie's livelihood—her independence. Even though her sisters had a better relationship with him, he wouldn't budge for them either if it meant helping her, too.

Still, she had to try, didn't she?

Once she got in her car, she pulled out her cellphone from her purse and dialed her father's number before she lost her nerve. He picked up after the fourth ring.

"Let me guess," her father drawled. "You want something from me."

Her hand clenched around her phone as anger and humiliation assailed her. Setting aside her pride, she said, "The Chamber Music Society needs your help."

"And why would I help them?" He sounded almost bored.

"Umma supported them when she was alive," she said quietly.

There was a long pause, then he said in a tired voice, "Come home, Angie. I'll donate to them if you cease your childish rebellion and come back home."

Her throat tightened with emotion—it had been five years since she'd spoken to her father—but leaving home had not been a childish rebellion. She refused to give him the leverage to control her life again.

"That's not my home anymore." She blinked away the tears that threatened to fall. "I'll find another way to help the society. Goodbye, Appa."

She headed home with a heavy heart. Home was a small one-bedroom apartment on the outskirts of downtown Los Angeles. Outdated and located in a not-quite-rough neighborhood, it meant more to her than a mansion could. It was her first real place that wasn't her father's house.

Her mom had fought cancer for five long years, and Angie was glad she'd been at her side. But once her mother was gone, she couldn't stand living with her demanding father and the constant reminder of what he'd made her do. Even his threat to cut her off completely wasn't enough to stop her from branching out on her own. She didn't want his damn money. Not then and not now.

She maneuvered her car into her narrow parking space, then waited listlessly for the creaky elevator to take her to the lobby. After checking her mailbox, she took another cramped ride upstairs and walked down what felt like miles of dimly lit hallway. When she finally arrived at her apartment, she shuffled inside, limp with sudden exhaustion. Even so, she carefully stowed away her cello in her practice corner before she collapsed onto the couch, kicking off the sensible pumps she'd worn into the living room.

"Home." She smiled against a soft cushion.

The old, dated building was what it was, but she had made her apartment as warm and cozy as she could with her limited budget. She might have overdone it a bit with the table lamps and floor lamps, but she loved how brightly lit her place was. With bursts of color from the pillows and throws, and a collection of whimsical posters splashed across the walls, it was home sweet home.

But her smile soon faded. The quiet peace of her meticulously constructed life had been disrupted by the uncertain future of the Chamber Music Society...and a ghost from her past. What happened at the Neimans' dinner invaded her thoughts without warning, and Angie scrunched her eyes shut against the memory of Joshua's fury. Even after two months, her heart still ached at the confirmation of her worst fears. Joshua Shin hated her.

She'd convinced herself that she'd moved past it. That she'd forgotten how she'd broken his heart and her own by leaving him. But seeing him after all these years broke the dam that had held everything in check. Holding back her emotions had been the only way she was able to continue her life without him. But now...

No, what she felt was regret at what could've been. Nothing more. She couldn't still want him. He hated her.

There could never be anything between them. She'd blown that chance ten years ago. She impatiently wiped away the tears on her cheeks and took a shaky breath. She had no time to dwell on the past when the present urgently required her attention.

Her father would only help the Chamber Music Society if Angie agreed to his condition, but she couldn't throw away her hard-earned independence. Besides, his dona-tion alone wouldn't be enough to save the society. What was she going to do? With a heaving sigh, she sat up and said, "Alexa, play KUSC."

She needed the company of classical music tonight. And a nice cup of tea. After a brief trip to the kitchen, she settled back on the sofa with a steaming mug, and em-braced the tranquility the music so generously offered her.

A new piece by the composer known only as A.S. filled her living room. He'd burst onto the classical music scene a few years ago, and the mastery of his work and the mys-tery of his identity made him an overnight phenomenon. Angie tended to like what she heard when his music came on the radio.

In the next moment, the small, appreciative smile on her face cracked and slipped.

"No, it can't be," she whispered, her fingers fluttering to her lips. The part in the piece had already passed, but she was certain it was the melody she'd been humming in-cessantly for the last couple months. But how could that be if this was the first time she was hearing the composition?

She quickly downloaded the piece onto her best-of playlist and frantically fast-forwarded to the part that had jarred her memories awake. She rewound to the same spot and replayed it. Again and again. A shaky sigh shivered past her lips.

Maybe it had to do with seeing Joshua again after all these years. Maybe it had to do with her long forgotten memories flooding her mind. But something had awakened the tune inside her, and she could finally place where it was from. It was his. It was the melody he'd played for her in college, shyly telling her he was working on a cello concerto for her. It was *her* melody.

She'd discovered a secret that irrevocably entwined her with Joshua. Because the same melody he'd played for her back then was coming through her speakers right this minute. He was the genius behind the anonymous pieces. He was A.S.

And now I know.

Angie bolted to her feet. Blood pounded in her ears and her breath came in shallow pants. She knew how to save the Chamber Music Society. And Joshua Shin was going to hate her for it. But what of it? He couldn't hate her any more than he already did.

Joshua spun in his chair and stared out the window, barely registering the sprawling view of downtown Los Angeles from his forty-eighth-floor office. With an exasperated sigh, he shoved his hands through his already tousled hair.

Dozens of reports and proposals awaited his approval, but his concentration was shot. He hadn't slept properly in two months, and last night was no different. He'd drifted from one dream to the next—or maybe they'd been memories. He couldn't pin down whether he'd been remembering or dreaming but he was certain that Angie Han had been the focus.

Just one moment with her—it couldn't have been more than five minutes—and he couldn't erase her from his thoughts. *Goddammit.* How could he allow her to have such control over him after all these years? He couldn't. He wouldn't. She'd already taken too much from him. He'd spent six years of his life not composing music because of her. He'd lost an essential part of himself because it had hurt too much. She wasn't taking another second of his time.

He swiveled back to face his desk, and returned to the report he'd been reviewing. Through sheer bullheadedness, he reviewed four more reports and a proposal before Angie invaded his thoughts again. God, she played so beautifully. He'd once dreamed of writing her a cello concerto, so she could perform his music for the world to hear. *That's enough.* He wasn't a heartsick twenty-year-old anymore.

He was the vice president of operations of Riddle Incorporated, an electronic components company started by his grandfather. He was slated to become its new CEO in a few months. The livelihood of over nine hundred employees rested on his shoulders. There was no time to waste daydreaming about an old flame. And that was all she was. She didn't define who he was.

He turned his attention back to his job and succeeded in keeping it there. His focus only broke when his phone rang. Mildly irritated by the interruption, he hit the speaker button. "Yes, Janice?"

"Sorry to disturb you, but there is a Ms. Angie Han here to see you," his executive assistant said. "I asked her to make an appointment and return another time, but she insists on waiting. She said you two went to college together."

Disbelief filled Joshua. It wasn't enough she'd occupied his thoughts and dreams for the past two months. She had to show up in person. Should he send her away? He didn't owe her anything. He didn't have to see her. But could he stand not knowing why she'd come? *Hell.*

"Please send her in."

He steepled his fingers and kept his gaze on the door. There wasn't anything he could do about the thundering of his heart, but he was determined to greet her with utter indifference.

She walked through the door, her chin held high. With her back ramrod straight and shoulders pulled back, she looked ready for battle. When her eyes met his, they flitted away, but only for a second. She quickly turned her determined gaze back to him and strode up to his desk.

He waved a casual hand at one of his guest chairs, and she sat without a word. He tried and failed to ignore how beautiful she looked in her slim black pants and soft, barely pink blouse. She was close enough that he could smell her sweet vanilla perfume—the same scent she wore a decade ago. His body remembered only too well, and a tremor ran through him. Had she worn it to get to him? And why would she want to get to him? His mind spun and he grappled for equilibrium.

"Hello, Joshua." Her smooth, melodic voice felt like a warm caress.

His lips went numb and refused to form her name, so he demanded, "What are you doing here?"

"After the Neimans' dinner…" She didn't need to go on for him to remember their heated encounter at the party. The same rush of lust and anger stirred in him now. "I knew you wouldn't agree to see me if I tried to make an appointment."

"You haven't answered my question," he said with a hard edge in his voice.

Her eyes fell to her hands—again only for the briefest second—then met his. "I have a proposal for you."

"What could you possibly propose to me? You made it clear you wanted nothing to do with me when you left to protect your precious trust fund." He bit his tongue, and stopped the bitter words spewing from his mouth. These feelings should've faded into an unpleasant memory he could shrug away by now.

"I can't change what happened between us. I wish I could explain..." she said in a near whisper. "But I assure you this proposal is purely business."

"Get out." A drop of sweat slid down his neck. He hated that his body still craved her after all this time when he wanted nothing to do with her.

And what business could she have with him? Was she here on her father's behalf? Their companies had been rivals for decades. That was why her father had threatened to disown her when he found out they were together. Even though recent changes in Riddle's business direction finally ended that rivalry, Joshua couldn't imagine the two companies ever collaborating on anything.

When she made no move to leave, he turned his chair to face the windows, underscoring her dismissal.

"I know who you are." Her voice was so soft, he probably misheard her. Still, his stomach dropped like a stone to his feet.

He slowly faced her again and enunciated with care, "What did you say?"

"I know. I know you're A.S."

"Who the hell is A.S.?" he scoffed, panic slapping awake his befuddled brain. It couldn't be. No one knew. Not even his grandfather. He had to tread cautiously. "I don't know what game you're playing at, but I believe I asked you to leave."

The last thing he expected was for her to sing. But sing she did. She hummed the theme of his latest piece, and like a breeze blowing through the window, his memory returned to him with startling clarity. How could he have forgotten?

It was her melody. The first sapling of the concerto he'd dreamt of writing for her. But that dream had died with his heartbreak. Or so he'd thought. Somehow, it had resurfaced as one of the themes of his latest piece. How could he not have recognized it? Because it was no longer hers. The melody was just a part of one of his works. It had nothing to do with her.

"That's enough," he snapped.

Angie clamped her mouth shut at his rough tone, but there was a triumphant light in her eyes. "You *are* A.S."

He wasn't about to tell a bold-faced lie when they both knew she had him. "And what do you plan to do with that juicy tidbit?"

"Please. Don't take offense." She bit her bottom lip and bright blotches of pink stained her cheeks. Inexplicable satisfaction filled him as he watched her placid demeanor crack. "I just need your help."

"If you're here to blackmail me, at least own up to it," he drawled, cold cynicism hardening his features. "Do you expect me to provide you with something in exchange for your silence?"

"I don't even understand why my silence is worth something to you in the first place," she said, her voice unsteady. "Why do you need to compose in secret?"

Despite his feigned nonchalance, he couldn't breathe properly. At first, he'd kept his identity a secret to avoid conflict with his father, who had never approved of his pursuit of music. But now, his family's legacy was at stake.

If the board of directors found out Joshua was a composer *on the side*, it could affect their decision to appoint him as the next CEO. His competition, Nathan Whitley, would have a field day waving it around as proof that Joshua wasn't as dedicated to Riddle as he was. His grandfather and father would be devastated if the career CEO beat him out on the position.

"That isn't exactly the kind of information I would share with my blackmailer, now, is it?" He leaned back in his chair and let disdain stain his words. "Are you trying to gather more ammunition to use against me?"

"I'm not going to reveal your secret," she said with quiet determination. "But I still need your help."

"And I have no reason to help you without that leverage." He bared his teeth in a jagged imitation of a smile.

"The Chamber Music Society is facing a financial crisis, and this upcoming season can make or break us," she continued doggedly. Her tenacity used to impress him, but now it only frustrated him. He needed her to leave. "I would like to commission A.S. on behalf of the society to compose a new piece for us to premiere on opening night. It'll give us the boost we need to propel the season forward and draw the attention we need."

"You have no intention of revealing to the world that I'm A.S.?"

"No. None whatsoever." She met his gaze and held it, and he believed her. She'd always been honest to a fault. He was fortunate she was unchanged in that regard.

"Then my answer to your proposition is no." He hardened himself against her crestfallen expression. If his secret was safe, then he didn't want to risk having more interactions with her. She was no longer a threat to his heart, but he desired her with an intensity that he didn't want to test. Her presence in his office alone shook him to the core. Spending more time with her was out of the question. "But I'm not without sympathy for the Chamber Music Society's situation. I can make another donation…"

"I don't want your money," she cut him off sharply then clamped her mouth shut. After a deep breath, she continued in an even tone, "The money will only get us so far. But a collaboration between A.S. and the Chamber Music Society will create the kind of buzz we need to make the upcoming season a success. It'll increase ticket sales and garner new donors." She sat forward in the chair. "It'll breathe new life into the society."

"My answer is still no," he said, ignoring the stab of

guilt. He wasn't about to apologize for his decision when she was in no position to ask favors of him.

Angie stood from her seat with quiet composure, and he got to his feet with her. She opened her small purse and drew a simple, elegant business card from it. "That's my cellphone number. Please call me if you change your mind."

He took the card from her and said with finality, "I won't."

She left his office just as she'd come in, back straight and head held high, leaving lingering notes of vanilla in her wake. He'd done the right thing. Getting himself entangled with Angie Han spelled disaster for his sanity. Then why did he feel like such a bastard?

Joshua spent the rest of the day putting Angie out of his mind. The Neimans' party and her visit today were minor glitches. She was out of his life and it was going to stay that way. Then why couldn't he slow down his heart? It was merely a physical reaction to an unexpected occurrence. He would forget all about her by tomorrow.

A part of him wanted to admit defeat and acknowledge that he was worthless at work while his mind was spinning and coming to terms with Angie's visit. But the more stubborn side of him insisted that he could still get more work done, so he stayed at his desk, staring unseeingly at the computer screen until the sun dipped below the horizon.

When his cell phone rang, he was relieved at the interruption. "Hello, Mother."

"Hello, son." She failed miserably at sounding chipper.

"What's wrong?" He straightened in his seat.

"Can't a mother call her son just because?" There was a slight tremor to her voice. Now he was really worried.

"Can't a mother just tell her son the truth without worrying him to death?" he said with a touch of irritation, and was immediately contrite. "Sorry, Mom. Tell me what's going on."

"Don't be too alarmed. It was a minor one and he's stable now but… Halabuji had a heart attack." A sob broke free from his mother. "He's been admitted to the Cedars-Sinai Medical Center. Let's talk when you get here."

Joshua's heart stuttered with fear. "I'm leaving now."

Two

Angie sat soaking in a much-needed bath, her knees drawn above the bubbles to fit into the cramped tub. She trailed her hand up her wet arm, remembering the surreal day she'd had. Had she really barged into Joshua's office, thinking she could blackmail him into helping the Chamber Music Society?

It hadn't taken her long to realize that she didn't have it in her to blackmail someone. Especially the man she had once loved. She'd sworn to herself that she would do anything to help save the Chamber Music Society, but as she sat across from Joshua, his handsome face taut with worry, she couldn't bring herself to do it.

Instead, she had wanted to wrap herself around him and kiss away his worries. Angie sank down into the tub, immersing her head underwater. She must've been out of her mind. But she couldn't help but wonder why it was so important for him to keep his identity as A.S. a secret.

Suddenly feeling restless, she finished washing up

and stepped out of the bath. Just as she wrapped a towel around herself, she heard her cell phone ringing. Her heart slammed against her rib cage. It could be anyone. One of her sisters probably. Then why was she running to her room at breakneck speed?

When she grabbed her phone from the nightstand, she saw that it was indeed her sister. She wished she could unfeel the disappointment that shot through her. "Hey, Meg. What's up?"

"I have a brilliant idea to save the Chamber Music Society," Megan said without preamble.

"What is it?" Angie asked, hope sparking to life.

"We need to get everyone together and do one of those calendars. You know, like the ones firefighters do?"

Her hope fizzled out like a wet candle. "How can you joke about this?"

"No, hear me out. We'll call it the 'Hotties of Chamber Music,'" her sister prattled, "and have our finest pose for the photos."

"Like Arthur, our principal cellist?" Angie randomly named one of her colleagues.

"Totally. He's pretty hot for a man in his sixties, but I'm not sure he'd take his shirt off for the photo shoot."

There was only one reason for this silliness. "How many bags of Sour Patch Kids have you eaten today?"

"Three."

"Full size?"

"Yes." She could practically hear Megan twitching from the sugar high. "What of it?"

"Go eat some real food, and call me when you have a helpful idea." She shivered when a drop of water from her hair rolled down her back.

"Can't we chat for a bit? I'm bored."

"And I'm freezing. I just got out of the bath. I need to put some clothes on." Angie walked to her dresser and pulled out her favorite leggings and a hoodie. "Don't forget. Real food. Bye."

As she poked her head out of her hoodie, her cell rang again. Wrangling her arm through the hole, she answered the call. "We are not shooting the 'Hotties of Chamber Music.'"

There was silence on the other end, and mortification spread through her. She didn't need to look at the screen to know that the caller wasn't Megan. *It's okay.* It would be fine as long as it wasn't Joshua.

"Why not?" a deep, amused voice drawled. "That just might give the Chamber Music Society the boost it needs."

Maybe it was someone else with the same sexy voice as her ex.

"This is Joshua, by the way."

Shit. She scrunched her eyes shut, wishing the floor would suck her in like quicksand. Why the hell was he calling her anyway?

"Joshua? What a surprise," she said stiffly, while pushing her other arm through the hoodie.

"You did give me your phone number," he reminded her.

"And you said you won't be calling me," she countered.

"I changed my mind." The cool arrogance of his tone—as though he had every right to do whatever the hell he wanted—was maddening.

A sharp retort formed on the tip of her tongue, but she clamped her mouth shut. He'd changed his mind? Did that mean he'd changed his mind about calling her? Or changed his mind about her proposal? She sat down on the corner of her bed and forced herself to release the breath she'd been holding.

"Changed your mind how?" she asked.

"I'm willing to consider your proposal…for a price."

"Of…of course. The Chamber Music Society will pay you for the commissioned work…"

"I don't want to take money from a struggling organization," he dismissed. "That's not what I want."

"Then what is it that you want?" Her hands shook with anticipation. "What's your price?"

"It's… I need…" He sighed deeply. "Is there any way we can meet?"

"Right now?" She glanced at the clock; it was close to ten.

"Yes, now."

"Um…where?" The thought of seeing him again made her heart race.

"Wherever is convenient for you. It won't take long," he said curtly, reminding her that this was purely business.

"There's a coffee shop down the street…"

"I'll meet you there. What's it called?"

She told him the name of the café and hung up. They were meeting in half an hour. She loathed to change out of her comfortable sweats and considered showing up wearing them. But this was a business meeting. She wasn't meeting a friend for coffee.

As she blow-dried her long, damp hair, she tamped down the excitement bubbling up inside her. She was about to meet a man who hated her to find out what he wanted from her in exchange for helping the Chamber Music Society. What was there to be excited about?

She put on a pair of slim black pants and a light gray sweater. She didn't have it in her to put on any makeup, so she smeared on some tinted lip balm and pronounced herself presentable.

The café was only two blocks away, and she arrived a few minutes early. She ordered a chamomile tea, and found a table by the window facing the street.

How many times had they met in cozy cafés like this to work on their homework or study for an exam? A wistful smile curled her lips as she remembered the warmth and simplicity of those days. She wished she hadn't taken them for granted. But she'd had no idea their days were numbered. They were supposed to have a lifetime together.

Angie pushed away her crushing pain, startled by its intensity. Over the past ten years, it had ebbed into a dull ache in the back of her heart. Seeing Joshua made the old scars gape and bleed. She didn't understand. Did she still have feelings for him after all this time? That would be foolish. She was confusing nostalgia with reawakened emotions.

Taking a sip of her tea, she stared unseeingly at the dark street outside. They weren't carefree kids in love anymore. Tonight, they were meeting under very different circumstances, so she needed to have her head on straight.

"Did I keep you waiting?" Joshua asked, pulling out the chair across from her.

"Oh." The moment she heard his voice, her heart rattled as though a jack-in-the-box had popped open. Heat rushed through her as she registered his disheveled hair and rolled-up sleeves, revealing strong forearms. His tie and jacket from earlier in the day were gone, and the sight of his chest and biceps filling out his shirt made her mind go blank. So much for straight thinking. "No, not at all. I just got here, too."

"Good." He ran his fingers through his hair, making it stick out all over the place.

Angie liked him better this way. The cold, immaculate man she'd met in his office was a stranger, but she saw hints of the old Joshua in this version. Someone who wouldn't completely shut her out. Maybe they would be able to work something out to help the Chamber Music Society after all.

"Do you want to order a drink before we get started?" Once she forced herself to stop ogling his body, she noticed the tension in the corners of his eyes and the weary downward turn of his mouth. Something was wrong.

"No, it's late." He pinched the bridge of his nose. "I don't want to take up too much of your time."

"So what is this *price* you require?" She wanted to find out what was going on with him. Her gut told her it had everything to do with his sudden about-face.

"My grandfather had a heart attack." His nostrils flared subtly as he took a deep breath. Joshua was hiding it well, but she saw it. He was hurting, and she couldn't do anything about the distress burrowing into her. She fought to keep her expression politely sympathetic, and nodded for him to continue. "I want you to play for him while he recuperates."

Whatever she'd expected, it certainly wasn't that. "You want me to play for him?"

"His doctor believes music therapy will be invaluable to his recovery, and you're the obvious choice for a number of reasons," he said with frustration stamped across his features. While he might believe her to be the logical choice, he wasn't happy about it. "My grandfather is a devoted fan of the Hana Trio, and the cello is my grandfather's favorite instrument."

"If you're looking for a music therapist, I'm sure I could find you some highly recommended ones…"

"Is it below you to play for one old man?" he said scathingly.

"What?" She lowered her voice when a couple of heads turned their way. "It's because I don't think I'm qualified. Music therapy entails more than just playing music, and you could find someone better suited than me."

"I doubt there are many concert-level cellists providing music therapy. My grandfather has a discerning ear, and listening to an amateur play will have the opposite of a restorative effect on him." He sighed harshly. "And there's something about your sound. There's depth and heart to it that can touch people. It's…special."

Her mouth opened and closed several times. "Thank you, but…"

"I want you," he growled. Heat pooled in her stomach even though she knew what he meant. "I don't want a substitute. I want *you* to play for my grandfather. That's the deal."

"You forgot to add, *Take it or leave it,*" she said wryly.

A ghost of a smile came and went. "If you agree to play for my grandfather, I'll compose a new piece for the Hana Trio to premiere during the Chamber Music Society's upcoming season."

What could she say? She still had reservations about her effectiveness as a music therapist, but she would be happy to help his grandfather in any way. And she would be giving the Chamber Music Society a real chance to thrive.

"I remember how close you were to your grandfather," she murmured, gathering her thoughts.

"I still am." He leaned forward on the small table, bringing them closer together. "I can't *not* ask this of you, knowing it's what my grandfather needs. I would do anything for him."

Joshua hadn't wanted anything to do with her the last two times they'd met. From his tense posture and the wariness in his eyes, she could tell that hadn't changed. He just loved his grandfather enough to sacrifice what he wanted and, God help her, that moved her more than anything.

She cleared her throat. "How often would you need me to play for him?"

"I'll need to check with his doctor to see what would be most effective, but twice a week makes sense for now."

"Will you be with your grandfather when I play for him?" She didn't want to interact with him more than necessary. Getting over him had been one of the hardest things she'd ever done.

"I'll be there the first day to introduce you to him, but it's unlikely I'll be there after that."

She nodded, refusing to acknowledge the disappointment that pierced her at his response.

"Do we have a deal?" He studied her face intently as he waited for her answer.

"We have a deal."

Joshua arrived at the hospital earlier than their meeting time, not wanting Angie to lug around her hefty instrument in search of him. He planted himself close to the main entrance so he would be hard to miss.

After they parted last night, he repeatedly questioned his decision to bring Angie into his family's plight. His grandfather's sudden heart attack had sent a shock wave through Joshua and his parents. They were prepared to do anything to prevent it from happening again. When the doctor recommended music therapy as part of his grandfather's treatment, he immediately thought of Angie.

The cello was Halabuji's favorite instrument and he was especially enthralled by Angie's playing. That had to be the reason why Joshua had thought of her... That and the fact that he hadn't been able to stop thinking about her for the last two months. He cursed under his breath. He refused to believe that he'd brought her into this just so he could have her in his orbit. That was the last thing he wanted.

What he'd said about her sound being special was true. It had been true when they were together, and she had only improved with time. Listening to her play would help lower Halabuji's stress level and stabilize his condition. More importantly, it would make his grandfather happy. That was what mattered most.

Joshua hadn't asked Angie to play so he could have her back in his life. He'd asked her *despite* the fact he didn't want her in his life because it was the best thing he could do for his grandfather. That had to be it.

But for this to work, he had to control his unwanted attraction to her. As worried as he was last night, his body had trembled with lust at the sight of her. Her face had been scrubbed clean of makeup and she reminded him so much of her younger self. The one who had been his. He would've kissed that Angie deeply before he sat down across from her. They would've held hands across the table, her warmth giving him solace. And he would've taken her home and made love to her, soaking up the comfort she offered. He no longer wanted any of that, but his body insisted on craving her nonetheless.

"Joshua," Angie said, standing in front of him. Lost in his thoughts, he hadn't seen her come into the lobby.

"Thank you for coming." His voice was huskier than he would've liked. Her form-hugging jeans and light beige sweater emphasized her soft curves, which did nothing to curb his libido. *Goddammit.* He had to get a grip.

"Of course," she said in an all-business tone. If she'd noticed his hungry eyes lingering on her, she was doing a great job not showing it. "Should we go see him?"

He nodded curtly and led them to the set of elevators that would take them to the private rooms. His grandfather's room was almost at the end of the corridor so he wouldn't be disturbed by the elevator or the central hub of the nurses' station. They didn't say a word to each other as they made their way there.

Joshua stole a glance at Angie, who was dragging the tall, wide cello case beside her. He hadn't even offered to help; he'd been too busy lusting after her. Feeling like a jerk, he cleared his throat and asked, "Do you need help with your instrument?"

"Oh, please. I used to lug this baby from one end of the campus to the other. This is nothing." Her smile quickly faded as though she'd realized what she'd just said.

"I remember," he said casually.

He remembered all too well. He used to fuss about it back then, too. But they were in no position to reminisce about the old times. Even as the bitterness rolled in, Joshua kept his lips from thinning into a hard line. The last thing he wanted was for things to get awkward right before she met his grandfather.

When they reached his room, the lights were dimmed and a tall, thin figure lay still on the bed. How could Joshua not have noticed how frail his grandfather had gotten?

"If he's asleep, I don't want to wake him," Angie whispered.

While he felt bad that she had come all this way only to go back, he agreed with her about not waking his grandfather. "I'm sorry—"

"Oh, for God's sake. Stop with the whispering and get in here," the old man said, raising his bed into a sitting position. "I'm sulking, not sleeping."

Smiling with relief, Joshua walked up to his bedside. "How are you feeling?"

"Fit as a fiddle," he boomed as though the volume of his voice was proof of his stellar health. "Why wasn't I discharged? I don't need to be kept in the damn hospital anymore."

"Not according to your doctor," Joshua reminded him. "Besides, you won't be in the hospital much longer. We're checking you into a wellness resort tomorrow."

"Your mother told me about that. Why do I have to go to some hoity-toity retreat?" his grandfather grumbled.

"The doctor said you need absolute peace and relaxation," he said. "If you went home, nothing will keep you from going right back to work."

"What work?" Mr. Shin threw his hands up. "I'm retired."

Joshua huffed an incredulous laugh. "You're still a member of the board of directors, and you know more about what's going on in the company than any of us."

"The CEO appointment is only a few months away. With Nathan Whitley sniffing around, somebody has to keep watch," his grandfather said. "He might already have Richard Benson and Scott Grey in his pocket."

"Leave Whitley to me," Joshua said, his tone straddling confidence and arrogance. He needed to reassure his grandfather. He would deal with losing two board members to his competition later. "The board knows that I'm the best man for the job."

"Even so, you better watch your back, son. Whitley is a wily son of a bitch."

"I got this, Halabuji. You need to stop worrying and concentrate on getting better."

"Easier said than done," the old man sighed then caught sight of Angie standing quietly by the door. "And who might you be? Are you his girlfriend? Tell the boy to stop being a smart-ass."

"No, I'm not his girlfriend." She laughed, walking up to the bed. "And I'm not sure he'll take kindly to me calling him a smart-ass."

"This is Angie Han, the cellist for the Hana Trio," Joshua said, the tips of his ears burning. "She's here to play for you."

"Angie Han? Well, let me shake your hand." He took her outstretched hand with both of his. "It is an absolute pleasure to meet you. Your playing is transcendent."

"That's so kind of you to say," she said, a lovely blush spreading on her cheeks.

"She'll be coming to play for you a couple times a week," Joshua said. "But only if you're a good patient."

"Such insolence," he muttered affectionately before turning his attention back to Angie. "And how did I get so lucky as to have an accomplished cellist provide me with live music?"

"I…" She shot a quick glance at Joshua, and he gave a subtle shake of his head. Even his grandfather didn't know about his work as A.S. "I went to school with your grandson, and he looked me up for this lovely opportunity to play for you."

"The doctor thinks listening to her play will help with your recovery, Halabuji."

"Who am I to argue with the doctor?" His grandfather's twinkling eyes belied his innocent expression.

"Yes, you're the picture of a compliant patient," Joshua said drolly.

Angie watched their exchange with a smile. "Where should I set up?"

He moved a chair to the foot of the bed, leaving plenty of space for the cello. "Is this okay?"

"Yup." She lowered herself into the seat and took her cello out of the case. "Any requests?"

"I'm going to write a full list," Mr. Shin said with a contented sigh. "But for tonight, you pick for me, my dear."

"Why don't you play something short tonight?" Joshua suggested after a brief glance at his watch. "It's getting late. You can start full sessions next time."

"That works for me." After briefly tuning her cello, Angie lowered her bow to the strings. "It isn't a traditional piece but this song always warms my heart."

Joshua recognized it immediately. It was the theme from *Cinema Paradiso*, an Italian film from the eighties. The romance and heartbreak of the story had always made

Angie cry. But the ripe, full sound of the notes vibrating on her cello reminded him that she was no longer the college girl he'd fallen in love with. He couldn't stop himself from wondering who this grown-up Angie really was.

He steered his mind away from the dangerous turn of thoughts and focused on the music that filled the room. The tender affection she infused into the dulcet melody made the piece hauntingly beautiful, and the intimacy of her performance seeped under his skin. The remnants of his anger toward her seemed to drain out of him. How could he stay angry at a person who could create something so lovely?

After a sweeping climax, Angie brought the song to an end. Only then was Joshua able to tear his gaze away from her. His grandfather's eyes were red with unshed tears as he clapped.

"My dear, I think you've stolen my heart," the old man said in a raspy voice.

"Thank you so much, Mr. Shin." Angie's eyes softened with fondness.

"Stop this Mr. Shin nonsense. Call me Ed."

"I can't call you by your first name," Angie gasped as though she was scandalized. Joshua couldn't hold back his grin. "I may be a second-generation Korean American, but respecting elders has been ingrained in me. If my mom were alive, she'd have my hide if I called you Ed."

Her mother had passed away? When did that happen? Angie had been so close to her mother. It must've been hard for her. Joshua's heart clenched as he imagined her loss before he caught himself. *Relax.* It was human nature to feel sympathy for someone's loss of a family member. It wasn't personal.

"Mr. Shin is so stiff and distancing," his grandfather protested. "Call me Halabuji, then."

"Okay… Halabuji." She packed up her cello and came to stand by his bed. "I'll leave you to rest."

"Good night, my dear. I'll be counting the minutes until I can hear you play again."

His grandfather's presence had eased the tension between them, but it returned in full force as they made their way out of the hospital.

"You don't need to walk me to my car," she said, breaking the silence.

"Just humor me." It was dark outside and the few streetlamps hardly lit up the parking lot.

"So…what did you think?" She glanced at him as they walked in step with each other. "Do you think I'll be able to help your grandfather?"

"He hadn't stopped complaining for a single minute since we admitted him to the hospital," he said, shaking his head. "One song from you, and he was nearly weeping with joy. So, yes. I think you'll be a huge help."

"I hope so. He's such a lovely man."

"Only when he wants to be." Joshua grinned. "He can be an utter pain in the ass."

Angie laughed. "Well, I hope I stay in his good graces."

"I don't think you'll have any trouble there," he said softly. He'd forgotten how much he liked the sound of her laughter.

"This is me." To his surprise, she stopped by a small car that was showing its age.

She'd parked under a streetlamp and the soft light shone down on her. She was so beautiful. Joshua's hands suddenly shook with the need to touch her. Was he out of his mind? *He needed to turn around and go to his car* but his feet wouldn't obey, so he continued standing in front of Angie like a rooted tree.

Without premeditation, he stuck his hand out toward her. She blinked in surprise then hesitantly placed her warm hand into his. An electric jolt rocked his entire body and his hand tightened around hers. He swallowed with difficulty. A small tug and she would be in his arms. Temptation sang in his head. He was playing with fire. Gathering every ounce of his self-control, he released her hand and turned on his heel.

It was only when he was driving home that he realized he hadn't even said good-night to her.

Three

Angie marveled at the view of the sun setting over the sparkling azure ocean as she drove to the Malibu retreat where Mr. Shin was recuperating. The stunning sunset distracted her from her nervousness about seeing Joshua again. He probably wouldn't be there anyway. Why would he visit his grandfather at the same time she did? Besides, what was she even going to do if he came? *Ogle him.* She sighed, growing impatient with herself.

Once she arrived at the resort, she walked across the beautifully manicured lawn and signed herself in at the reception desk. Then she was shown to a private cottage a short walk from the main building.

"Angie." Mr. Shin spread his arms out in welcome from a recliner by the window. "Please come in."

"Hello, Halabuji," she said as she walked into the spacious living room.

There was a gorgeous view of the ocean and a hint of lavender in the air. But no Joshua. She quelled the disappointment rising inside her. A music stand and chair had already been set up, so she sat down and pulled out her cello.

Joshua had thawed toward her that night at the hospital, and she was hoping maybe they could… Could what? Be friends? Her heart sank. She realized she wanted him back in her life. But how would that be possible?

"You seem distracted tonight," Mr. Shin said, concern clouding his kind eyes. "Is everything all right?"

"Of course," she quickly reassured him. "I'm just a little tired, but I promise to be one hundred percent focused when I play for you."

"I don't doubt that. You're a professional through and through. But you can play a short piece and head on home. You should get some rest."

"No, I'm fine." She put some pep in her voice. "Joshua sent me your list and I want to get started on it. You picked one of my favorites for the first piece."

Before Mr. Shin could object some more, Angie lowered her bow to the strings. Her heart went into the poignant melody and she lost herself in the music. It wasn't until she finished playing that she saw him leaning against the doorframe.

"Joshua?" Her heart pumped with sudden vigor. He was only there to visit his grandfather. His appearance had nothing to do with her. Still, her heart wouldn't quiet. "I didn't see you there."

"That was the goal. I didn't want to disturb you while you were playing." He pushed himself away from the doorway and walked over to his grandfather. "How are you feeling today, Halabuji?"

"Like I can climb a mountain," Mr. Shin said with a stubborn set of his jaw. "I don't know why you all have me locked up in here."

Angie bit her cheek to stop the laughter from bubbling

up. He had been all smiles when she came in, looking well rested and in good spirits. He was just giving his grandson a hard time.

"You're hardly locked up. Mom and Dad visit almost every day," Joshua said in a gentle voice. Warmth glowed in her chest at how good he was to his grandfather. "And they told me you took a nice long walk today. The grounds here are beautiful."

"I'm trying to make the best of my rotten situation." Mr. Shin sniffed and eased back against the recliner. He was really laying it on thick.

"Rotten situation?" Joshua waved his arm to encompass the lovely room and view. "I wouldn't mind staying here for a few weeks."

"Then you stay," Mr. Shin muttered before yawning loudly. "I'm calling it an early night. Be sure to walk Angie to her car."

"Of course." Joshua spoke before Angie could protest, then stood uncertainly for a moment. "I guess it's good night, then?"

"Good night," the older man said decisively, dismissing his grandson for the night.

"Rest well, Halabuji." She kissed his cheek. "I'll see you next week."

"I can't wait. Your visits make all this nonsense more tolerable." He squeezed her hand once and let go. "Now go and get some rest. You've been tired since you got here."

When Joshua's eyes shot to her, she instinctively let her hair fall forward to hide her face and walked out of the cottage. He fell into step beside her, shortening his stride to keep pace with her.

"Is what he said true?" He glanced sideways at her as they walked past the main building.

"Practicing and performing at endless functions is exhausting," she said with a shrug. It was the truth, but she also had no intention of revealing that the source of her distraction wasn't exhaustion but him. "But performing in person is a privilege, so I can't complain."

"Are you sure you're not overdoing it?"

"Overdoing it?" She arched an eyebrow. "Thank you for your concern, but I'm fully capable of deciding how much and how hard I work. It's my career and my life, after all."

"I'm not trying to overstep any boundaries," he snapped. "I just don't want you to worry my grandfather like you did tonight."

"Worry him? Of all the arrogant, overbearing…" She clamped her mouth shut and took a deep breath. He was worried about his grandfather, but she refused to let him accuse her of causing harm to Mr. Shin. "Your grandfather is a wise, astute man who has the insight to understand that people sometimes get tired in this modern world. He won't worry himself over my occasional yawns. But if you think I'm a harmful influence on his health, then I'll stop coming to see him, and you can reconsider your *price*."

Joshua rubbed his face in frustration. "I never said you were a harmful influence on him."

"Then what *are* you saying?" She stopped walking and turned to him.

"I'm saying it will benefit everyone if you took better care of yourself," he said in a softer tone, taking a step toward her. "You used to get so lost in your music, you wouldn't even eat until I reminded you."

"Well, that was a long time ago," she said, the animosity draining from her. "I'm a grown woman and I can take care of myself."

Something flared in his eyes at her words and he took yet another step toward her. A shiver ran down her back, and her pulse quickened. The heat from their argument turned into heat of an entirely different nature. Panic and anticipation rose in her, and she couldn't decide whether to step away from him or toward him.

"You're right." His voice was a husky drawl and his fingers grazed her cheek as he tucked a strand of hair behind her ear. "You are a grown woman."

She fought the urge to press his hand against her face and breathe in his scent. Ripping herself out of the trance, she spun away from him and resumed her trek toward her car. After a pause, Joshua was by her side, walking in step with her. To both her relief and disappointment, they arrived at her car much too soon.

"I scored a parking spot super close to the main building," she babbled, flustered by her reaction to him.

"What happened to your sexy red Boxster?" He cocked his head to the side and looked at her semicompact curiously.

Her heart lurched and she frantically searched for an answer that wouldn't reveal her independence from her father. She couldn't divulge that to Joshua without him asking more questions, because she'd led him to believe that she left him so her father wouldn't cut her off.

Couldn't she just tell him the truth? Tell him that her father had pressured her to leave him, using her mom's cancer diagnosis to guilt her into compliance? No, she couldn't. How could she tell him that after all this time? What would be the point? It wasn't going to change what happened. Besides, he probably wouldn't believe her. She would only humiliate herself.

"It was a childish indulgence," she said, steadying her cello case against the car door. "That thing was a gas guzzler. Very environmentally irresponsible."

"Hmm," he murmured, clearly not sold on her excuse.

"Why are you here tonight?" Angie blurted to change the subject. "I thought… I thought you visited your grandfather in the mornings."

"I had an early-morning meeting today, so I wasn't able to visit him earlier."

"Oh, I see," she said in a small voice, feeling like a fool for being disappointed. What had she expected him to say? That he'd come tonight because he wanted to see her? "Then I guess I won't be seeing you for a while."

"Why do I get the feeling you're relieved?" he said with a crooked smile. "Maybe I'll schedule more meetings in the morning so I can come visit my grandfather in the evenings. I think listening to you play will do me some good as well."

He was teasing her. Maybe even laughing at her. Did he enjoy seeing her flustered? Or had he guessed the reason behind her discomfort? Well, she wasn't giving him the satisfaction of seeing how much he affected her.

"Suit yourself." She shrugged.

They stood awkwardly for a moment, neither of them speaking. She wondered if he was about to offer to shake her hand like the last time. Angie hadn't been able to stop thinking about the warmth of his touch and the jolt of awareness that had run through her that night. It wasn't wise but she wanted to touch him again.

She stuck her hand out to him, her chest rising and falling quicker than warranted for an offer of a handshake. "Good night, then."

He stared down at her outstretched hand for a moment too long, his expression unreadable. Angie was about to pull her hand back as mortification welled in her when his hand shot out to envelop hers. Her eyes locked with his. He still didn't say a word, but she shivered at the intensity of his gaze. Lust, raw and wild, pooled at her center, and she stepped toward him without thought until she stood within inches of him.

"Joshua," she whispered, not knowing what she was asking for.

His arm circled her waist and pulled her flush against his body. Her breath left her in a rush and his eyes—hungry and wild—dropped to her lips. Time stilled and the world around them faded. All that mattered was being in his arms with her hands pressed against his hard chest with the feel of his thundering heart beneath them.

But as suddenly as he'd embraced her, he released her and stepped back—once then twice. She searched his face but the impenetrable mask had slid back in place. After another moment, he spun on his heel and left her by her car. Bewildered as she was, all she could think was whether he would always walk away from her without saying *good-night*.

Joshua stared unseeingly at his computer screen as his thoughts turned to the other night at the wellness resort. Once again, he hadn't said good-night to Angie. Why was it so hard to remember to utter two damn syllables? In his defense, he'd needed to get away from her before he pushed her up against her car and ravished her. How could he have lost his mind like that?

Without him realizing it, the hurt and anger of losing her all those years ago had receded into the background to be replaced by a desperate need to know her. To discover who she was all over again.

But he would be a fool to trust her. In a way, Angie had irrevocably altered the course of his life when she left him. In college, he had spurned his family's legacy and dedicated himself to music—all but severing his relationship with his father. But after everything he'd sacrificed, he had lost his music when he lost her. It was as though he had ceased to exist.

It had taken him six long years to be able to compose again. By then, he had joined Riddle Incorporated, following his father's wishes. He learned the true value of the legacy his grandfather and father had built, and knew he would never turn his back on Riddle.

So he decided to compose in secret as A.S. to save his father from the unnecessary worry that he might choose music over Riddle again. Especially since Joshua didn't know whether he would make it as a composer—his confidence was shot after being unable to compose for six years. He and his father had only begun to mend their relationship…he didn't want to risk another rift over something he might ultimately fail at.

But now, his secret hung over him like a dark cloud, threatening his family's legacy. With the CEO appointment so close, it was more vital than ever to hide his identity as A.S. to keep Riddle out of Nathan Whitley's reach.

And ever since Angie came back into his life, he hadn't been able to compose a single note. This time felt different from when he'd lost her, though. Back then there was only cold silence but now the music was just jumbled up inside him, looking for a way out. Could his conflicted feelings toward her be stifling his creativity? Did he need to distance himself or get closer to her to free himself of his creative block?

Joshua dropped his head toward his desk and squeezed the back of his neck. He'd visited his grandfather this morning so he wouldn't be tempted to return in the evening—when Angie was there—but he couldn't get any work done. Foolish or not, all he could think about was seeing her again. He couldn't run from this. From her. They needed to talk about what was happening between them like adults, even though he still had no idea what to make of it.

He pushed away from the desk and strode out of his office. He glanced at his watch and tapped his foot as he waited for the elevators. It was past seven o'clock and the parking structure was nearly empty. With his heart hammering inside him, he drove his car onto the street. When he realized he was pushing eighty miles per hour, he eased his foot off the pedal and took a deep breath through his nose. He was rushing to the wellness resort as though he couldn't wait to see her. He needed to stop acting like some lovesick kid.

When he arrived at his grandfather's cottage, Halabuji gave him an all-knowing smirk. "To what do I owe the honor of this second visit today?"

Joshua picked up a meditation book from a side table and flipped through it. "I've been so busy with work lately. I figured I can use some music therapy, too."

"So you decided to crash my therapy session?" He chuckled. "Why not? Let's make it a music therapy party."

"We're having a party?" Angie asked from the doorway, her gaze lingering on Joshua for a second. "I'll be happy to provide the music."

"Welcome, my dear," his grandfather greeted her happily.

"Hello, Halabuji." She came up to him and placed a light kiss on his weathered cheek. "How are you feeling today?"

"Fine. I always feel fine." The old man patted her hand. "But with you here, I feel great."

"Flatterer," she said with a teasing smile then turned to Joshua. "I didn't expect to see you today. Another early morning meeting?"

His grandfather jumped in before Joshua could come up with an excuse. "No, this is his second visit of the day. He thinks he needs music therapy, too."

"Is that so?" she murmured, glancing at Joshua from under her lashes.

He tugged his tie loose and cleared his throat. "There's nothing like good music after a long day."

"Hmm." She cocked her head as though she didn't quite

believe him. "I'll gladly play for both of you. What's next on your list, Halabuji?"

His grandfather pulled out a piece of paper from his back pocket and put on his reading glasses. He traced the list with one finger, muttering as he read.

"Ah, yes," he said at last. "Today's piece is the Allegro in Dvorak's Cello Concerto in B Minor. I'm very excited for this one."

Joshua's gaze shot to Angie and their eyes met. It was the piece she had played for him the night they first made love. From the deep blush staining her cheeks, she was remembering that night just as he was.

"It's one of my favorite pieces, too," she said with a touch of huskiness in her quiet voice. "But it isn't the most relaxing piece. Are you sure this is the right song for you right now?"

"Absolutely. It'll be like an extra dose of vitamins to invigorate me. I hope you won't tone it down on my account."

"I won't be able to even if I tried." She smiled, raising her bow. "You'll get the real deal. Don't worry."

She played the piece with her entire body, making strands of long hair slip out of her ponytail. Even when she opened her eyes, Joshua didn't think she saw the room or its occupants. She was completely absorbed in the performance, and her strength and passion pulsed through the music.

It was beautiful. She was beautiful. And he wanted her.

It wasn't wise. No, it was downright reckless. They'd been down this road before. She'd cast aside their love to secure her trust fund. No matter how much he wanted to know this grown-up Angie, he couldn't trust her. She had her priorities and he wasn't one of them. Not only that, but her presence in his life was interfering with his ability to compose. He couldn't risk losing his music again.

His grandfather's resounding applause snapped Joshua out of his frantic thoughts, and he belatedly applauded Angie for her amazing performance.

"I'll never forget tonight's performance," the old man said when she came to stand next to him. "You are a gift to the world and to me."

"Thank you, Halabuji," she said, the corners of lips wobbling. "All I want is for you to get well. I hope my music is helping you feel better."

"It is. I haven't felt this alive since I was a young man."

"Good. Just keep that up while we go through your list, okay?"

"I will, my dear." He clasped Angie's hand and squeezed. "Thank you."

"It is my absolute pleasure," she whispered with a catch in her voice.

Joshua stood watching the scene with his heart in a vise, and he couldn't help but think about what could've been. Would they have gotten married? Would Angie have been his grandfather's granddaughter-in-law if she hadn't left him? He impatiently brushed aside the thought.

"It's time for you to rest," he said, placing a hand on his grandfather's shoulder.

He covered Joshua's hand with his. "I will. I promised Angie I'll get better soon."

"You bet you did." Angie smiled and glanced at Joshua. "Are you leaving?"

"Yes, I'll walk you to your car," he said. "Good night, Halabuji."

They left the cottage and walked across the lawn in subdued silence. The resonance of the song and the memories it brought to the surface still clung heavily to him. But now that he had her to himself, he couldn't think of anything to say.

"Do you want a cup of coffee?" he blurted when they got to her car. He wasn't ready to let her go. "There's a decent coffee shop a couple blocks from here."

She hesitated for a second before giving him a small smile. "Sure. That sounds nice."

He grinned so broadly in response that his cheeks cramped. He had no idea where this was headed, but he would settle for her company. That was enough. For now.

Four

Joshua still hadn't kissed her. He hadn't even mentioned their near kiss. She was fine with that. If he wanted to pretend that nothing happened, so could she.

She watched him from beneath her lashes as she sipped her coffee. He often visited his grandfather in the evenings, which led to more trips to the coffee shop and interesting conversations. Like tonight. They mostly talked about music. He still shared that passion with her and sometimes sounded wistful about not being able to fully dedicate his time to it.

Angie enjoyed these interludes with him, but she didn't know what to make of their current situation. Were they friends now? He might think they were headed down that path, but she didn't necessarily feel friendly toward him. Beneath their light conversations, the undercurrent of their attraction swirled wildly, growing stronger each time they were together. And she wanted to kiss him. So badly.

She wasn't sure if she could stop wanting him. Did

she have to, though? He didn't seem to hate her anymore. Maybe he would be willing to listen to why she really left him, and maybe even forgive her. But then what?

"Will you be open to that?" Joshua asked.

"What was that?" She'd completely missed what he'd been saying.

"I think it'll be exciting to write this new piece with the specific performers in mind. I'll work off the Hana Trio's strengths and what makes each of your sounds your own," he said, leaning forward on the table. She got a whiff of his woodsy scent, and she almost lost her concentration again. "So would you mind if I sit in on one of your practice sessions?"

"No, I don't mind…" She wrapped her hands around her mug.

"But?" he prompted.

"But we need to keep your identity a secret from my sisters, right?"

"Right."

"How are we going to do that?" She worried her bottom lip. "I don't want to lie point-blank to my sisters."

"Hmm." He sat back with his chin in his hand. "How about if you tell them that you have an eccentric donor who wants to observe one of your rehearsals? You won't be lying to them. I did donate to the Chamber Music Society."

"And you happen to be very eccentric," she teased. It was strange to feel comfortable enough to joke around with him. It certainly wasn't like the *old days*, but they'd built an unexpected rapport.

He chuckled, and she stared at the way his eyes crinkled at the corners. Laugh lines were beginning to form, and she loved seeing the evidence of his happiness on his face. No matter how much she'd hurt him in the past, he'd had a happy life. He certainly had smiled and laughed a lot in the past ten years.

"So will you set something up?" he asked expectantly. "Will next Wednesday morning work for you?"

"I'll make it work." He grinned widely at her, and her heart did a little flip-flop.

To cover her reaction to him, she took a sip of her coffee and promptly choked on it.

"Are you okay?" He came to stand beside her and moved his warm hand up and down her back in soothing strokes.

"Yes, I'm fine," she gasped, blinking back tears.

"Sure, you are."

He didn't stop his ministrations until her cough subsided. Although she wanted Joshua's continued touch, she gently pushed away his hand for the sake of her sanity. When his eyes darkened at her lingering glance at his lips, she was tempted to throw caution to the wind. He was still leaning over her, near enough to kiss. She could just grab him right here and now. Before she did something she would regret, she pushed back her chair, forcing him to step back.

"I should be getting home," she announced and stood awkwardly as Joshua continued to stare at her.

After what felt like an eternity, he murmured, "Let me walk you to your car."

"So who is this mystery patron?" Chloe demanded as soon as she stepped into the practice room.

"All she told me was that his name was Joshua Shin." Megan brought their little sister up to speed, having arrived a few minutes earlier. "She won't spill anything else about him."

"Because there isn't anything to spill." Angie threw up her hands, getting flustered by her sisters' curiosity. "He just wants to watch us practice. He's going to sit some-where in the corner and disturb us as little as possible."

"Like watching endangered gorillas in their natural habitat," Chloe chortled.

"We're on exhibit every time we perform. What's the big deal about having someone sit in on one of our re-hearsals?" Angie said.

Yeah, what's the big deal? Why was she so nervous about having Joshua at their practice? Well, she hated keeping secrets from her sisters. But it wasn't only about keeping A.S.'s identity a secret—she couldn't let them find out about her history with Joshua, either.

If Megan and Chloe ever discovered that their father had made Angie choose between their dying mother and Joshua, it would completely disillusion them about their father. It was one thing for her to be estranged from their father, but that didn't mean she wanted him to be iso-lated from all his children. He hadn't been the same since their mother died. He needed her sisters, and they needed him, too.

And there was something else. Joshua watching her practice was much too intimate. She didn't want to show him too much of her real self—her frustration over miss-ing a note, her triumph at playing a section perfectly for the first time and her interactions with her sisters, whom she loved so much. She couldn't say why, but she had a feeling that it was very important to keep a part of her-self hidden from him.

"It actually isn't a big deal...for us," Meg said shrewdly, "but something is going on with you, because you don't even get this anxious before a concert."

"But it's kind of fun watching our perfect older sister lose her cool for once," Chloe interjected.

"I am not losing my cool," Angie said through clenched

teeth. She *was* losing her cool, and her sisters were getting more suspicious by the minute.

Just then Joshua walked into the room, wearing an impeccable gray pinstripe suit and a royal blue tie. There was a stunned silence as both her sisters—and she—absorbed the impact of his presence.

"Hello, ladies," he said with a hint of a smile.

"Hel-loooo, Joshua Shin," Chloe said with a cheeky smirk aimed at Angie.

"Chloe," Megan whisper-screamed. "That is so inappropriate...but I feel you, sister."

"Welcome, Mr. Shin." Angie walked up to him with her hand outstretched before her sisters embarrassed her any further. "We're so happy to have you here. May I introduce you to my sisters? This is Megan Han, our violinist."

"Nice to meet you, Mr. Shin," Megan said formally.

"And Chloe is our violist," Angie continued.

"That's me." Their youngest sister waved cheerily.

"It's a privilege to meet you both," Joshua said with a charming smile. "I'm a fan of the Hana Trio. And I'm thrilled to be a fly on the wall at your rehearsal."

"Do you and Angie already know each other?" Chloe glanced back and forth between them.

"Yes, we went to college together," he stated matter-of-factly.

Angie wanted to groan out loud. Her sisters were going to bombard her with more questions once the practice was over. "Mr. Shin is not here to chitchat with us. He came to hear us practice, so let's practice."

"Mr. Shin? Why so formal?" Megan asked. "I thought you were college buddies."

"We were *not* buddies," Angie said, taking her cello out of its case. It was the truth. She and Joshua had been lovers, not friends.

Her sisters exchanged a glance that she didn't trust at

all, but they both took their seats and prepared their instruments. Joshua lowered himself into a chair in the corner of the room. They were practicing a relatively new piece and still had a lot of kinks to work out. Angie fleetingly wished they were working on a more polished piece, but this was a practice session not a performance.

She quickly tuned her cello and played an open A for her sisters. Her eyes flittered once or twice to where Joshua was sitting, but she forced herself to focus on the rehearsal.

"From the top?" Megan asked as she raised her bow.

"Yes, we need to work on the opening bars," Chloe said with a determined look on her face.

They practiced the opening for the next hour, playing the same few bars again and again. They weren't delivering a unified sound, and they grew more and more determined to get it right. This rehearsal probably wasn't exactly what Joshua was hoping for. But when her worried glance met his, he gave her a reassuring smile.

When she and her sisters finally got the opening down, the music flowed more smoothly and they ended the practice on a high note.

"Chloe, you were busting our ass today," Megan said, beaming with pride.

"The opening is so important with this piece. I wanted us to get it just right." Chloe smiled shyly.

"And we did it, girls." Angie high-fived her sisters.

The sound of applause interrupted their celebration. They'd been so absorbed in their practice that they'd forgotten Joshua was in the room with them.

"That was amazing," he said, walking up to them. "Thank you for allowing me to observe. It was an honor."

"Wow, thank you." Chloe clasped her hands over her chest and mouthed to Angie, *Oh, my God.*

"Yeah, thanks. Come back *anytime*," Megan said magnanimously, earning a warning glare from Angie.

"Let me walk you out, Mr. Shin." Angie didn't give him a chance to respond before ushering him out of the room—away from her incorrigible sisters.

"Sorry about my sisters," she said once they were standing in the parking lot. "They're usually more professional, but the practice room is kind of our safe space where anything goes. I guess it's hard to turn on the professionalism in there."

"I enjoyed meeting them." Joshua smiled warmly at her. "The three of you seem close."

"We are close, and I love working with them," she said, returning his smile. "I don't know if listening to us play the same few bars over and over again helped, but I hope you got what you needed from our rehearsal."

"I did. It was incredible watching you and your sisters work together to find the perfect sound."

When he reached out and took her hand in his, it felt like the most natural thing for her to squeeze it.

"Thank you," she whispered.

"I should let you get back to them," he said, his thumb skimming the top of her hand. "I'll see you tonight."

"Yeah." Her heart fluttered helplessly inside her. "See you tonight."

He released her hand reluctantly, his fingertips lingering on her skin. Without thinking, she grabbed his arm before he could walk away. His eyebrows rose in surprise and he searched her face. Whatever he saw there made fire light in his eyes. With a muttered curse, he crushed his mouth against hers.

This was what she wanted. She sighed a long-held breath and invited him in. His tongue dove into her mouth, drawing a deep moan from her. His kiss was full of hunger, bewilderment and desperation, and she answered in kind. They shouldn't be doing this, but she had missed it so. She rose on her toes and pulled his head down, wanting him to kiss her harder. He obliged with a guttural groan, fisting a hand in her hair to tilt her head to the side.

She pushed her hands inside his suit jacket and spread them flat on his chest, reveling in the feel of him. His arms came around her back and pulled her flush against him, trapping her hands between them. His hard length pushed against her stomach and made her melt into him.

"Angie." Longing saturated his voice, turning her name into the single most intimate word he could utter.

Then she froze. She wanted to take him with an urgency that made her light-headed. But they were in the middle of a parking lot in broad daylight. She belatedly heard the snickers and whispers of passersby and blushed to her roots.

Joshua sighed against her lips and drew back. He gently brushed a strand of hair away from her face and gave her a rueful smile. When she glanced down at her toes with an embarrassed laugh, he lifted her chin with his finger.

"As I was saying," his eyes gleamed with promise, "I'll see you tonight."

The evening traffic in Los Angeles was at its most obnoxious. Joshua leaned back in his seat and drummed his fingers on the steering wheel in time with the music. He didn't mind enjoying the anticipation humming through him a while longer. He was going to see Angie soon.

The kiss they shared earlier today had been nothing like the sweet, tender kisses they'd shared before, even in the throes of passion. It had been raw, frantic and hot as fuck. He remembered with vivid clarity the feel of her lips crushed beneath his and her tongue sparring with his. And God, the little whimpering noises she made had driven him wild. Desire flared through his body at the memory and his blood rushed south.

He shook his head to clear it. The chemistry between them was undeniable but he couldn't forget her betrayal. The more time he spent with her, the harder it was to remember that she had once broken his heart. He couldn't make himself vulnerable to her again no matter how much he wanted her.

Then there was his music. Watching her practice with her sisters this morning had been remarkable. Their single-minded determination to reach the truest sound had sparked inspiration in him and he'd begun to hear the whispers of music in his mind. It had still been formless and scattered, but he'd sensed the start of something beautiful. But now all was quiet. The conflict between his desire and mistrust for Angie twisted his insides and suffocated his creativity. Even if he could risk his heart again, he couldn't risk his music.

But despite it all, he couldn't forget how right she'd felt in his arms and he grew impatient to see her. It was madness but he was helpless against her pull on him. His cell phone rang as he dragged his fingers through his hair. Panic constricted his chest when he saw that it was the wellness resort. He brushed aside his irrational reaction and answered the call.

"This is Joshua Shin."

"Mr. Shin," said a woman in a too-tranquil voice. It made him clench his jaws tighter. "Your grandfather was having trouble breathing and was just transported to the emergency room."

"Which hospital?" he asked as dread seeped into his veins.

His mind remained stark and empty with fear as he rushed to the hospital. He screeched into the first park-

ing spot he found and shot out of his car. He ran the last
stretch to the emergency room.

"Angie?" He came to a stop when he saw her pacing
in front of the entrance.

"Joshua." She reached his side with hurried steps.

"Where's my grandfather? What's happening to him?"
He walked past Angie and spun around the waiting area
as though his grandfather was hiding somewhere.

"The paramedics were taking Mr. Shin away when I
arrived at the wellness resort. I followed them here, but
they won't let me see him since I'm not family." She came
to stand beside him and gathered his cold hands between
her own. "I let them know you were on your way."

He stalked to the front desk. "I need to see Edward
Shin *now*. I'm his grandson."

The receptionist smiled sympathetically at him even
though he was acting like a brute and typed into the computer. "I believe a doctor is attending to him at the moment. We'll update you as soon as we know more, sir."

He blew out a frustrated breath and pushed his fingers
through his hair. Before he could make more unreason-
able demands, Angie appeared at his side. "Why don't
we go sit down?"

Joshua suddenly didn't know what he should do and
turned lost eyes to her. She took hold of his hand again
and found seats at the back of the crowded waiting area.
His thoughts ran in circles and the only thing anchoring
him was the firm pressure of Angie's hand holding his.
They sat and waited like that for over an hour.

"Edward Shin's family?" The woman at the front desk
scanned the crowded room. "Edward Shin's family?"

Joshua shot to his feet and bounded up to her. "Yes.
I'm here."

"Your grandfather has been moved to the ICU. The
doctor there will be able to tell you more."

"The ICU? What does that mean?" he demanded. "I need to know…"

"Thank you," Angie interjected, putting a calming hand on his arm. He clamped his mouth shut and inhaled through his nose. "How do we get to the ICU?"

After thanking the receptionist once more, Angie started walking and he followed her without question. They stepped outside into the evening air, then eventually entered an adjacent building.

"Let's go sit in the waiting room," she said after they checked in at the nurses' station. He nodded numbly.

She guided him into a long, rectangular room with cushioned chairs and watercolor paintings adorning the walls. When she stopped in front of some chairs in the corner, he sat down, his posture rigid. His grandfather was ill. He shouldn't be sitting. He should be *doing* something.

"There's nothing you can do right now," Angie said softly as though she'd read his mind. "Try to rest a little."

"I should call my parents." Or should he? They were in New York for their anniversary, and he didn't want to disturb them. But if their positions were reversed, he would want to know as soon as possible.

Angie nodded and stepped out of the room, leaving him alone. Despite his decision to call them, his fingers wouldn't press the dial button right away. It had required much convincing for them to take the trip. They were too worried to go far from Halabuji, but he'd been doing so well lately. This call was going to worry them, but he hoped they wouldn't feel too guilty. Muttering a curse under his breath, he pressed Dial.

"Joshua." His mother answered after two rings even though it was past midnight there. "Is everything okay?"

"Mom." He paused to swallow the lump in his throat. "Halabuji is in the ICU."

"Oh, my God. I knew we shouldn't have left him," she said, panic rising in her voice.

"Please don't blame yourself. You couldn't have known. And I'm here," he reassured her. "I'm waiting to speak with the doctor, so I'll let you know when I know more. For the time being, try not to worry too much."

"Who is that? Is something wrong?" Joshua heard his father murmur by his mother's side.

"Honey, it's your father. He's in the hospital," she said to him.

There was a flurry of noise on the other end of the line. His father must have jumped out of bed.

"Your dad's on the phone with the airline. We'll book a flight out of here as soon as we can," she said. "How are you holding up?"

"I'm just impatient to speak with the doctor." He sidestepped her question. "Halabuji is strong. He'll pull through this just fine."

"I know he will," she said with quiet conviction. "I'll see you soon."

"Fly safe, Mom."

Joshua sat alone in the waiting room for a few minutes before Angie returned holding two paper cups.

"I went down to the café and got you a decaf green tea." She handed him a cup. "I figured you didn't need to add caffeine into the mix."

"Thank you." He offered her a small smile. He didn't know how he would have made it through this without her. If it wasn't for her calming presence, he might still be rampaging around the hospital demanding to see his grandfather.

"Of course." She settled down next to him.

"You know, you don't need to stay with me," he said, hoping she wouldn't leave.

"I know." She sipped her coffee and made no move to go.

His shoulders slumped in relief, and he leaned back against his chair. But the reprieve was short-lived as his mind churned with anxiety and frustration. Was his grandfather fighting for his life in there? Then he should be with him. His grandfather shouldn't be in there alone. The vise clenched around his heart squeezed harder.

He started when Angie placed her hand on his knee. Despite everything, instant heat spread through his body at her touch. Lost for words, he raised his eyebrows in question.

"Your knee was jumping around so hard that it was creating a small earthquake. I was afraid I might spill my coffee." Her lips curved upward in a gentle smile, and her eyes were warm with sympathy.

"I'm sorry. I'm just…" He looked down at her hand, which was still resting on his knee.

"Getting more worried by the minute," she finished his sentence. "Where is the damn doctor anyway?"

"I'm actually right here." A fit, middle-aged woman with salt-and-pepper hair stood at the doorway with a congenial smile. "I apologize for the delay. I assume you're Edward Shin's family?"

Angie drew her hand away from Joshua's knee and he stood up to greet the doctor. "Yes, I'm his grandson. How is my grandfather?"

"He's stable for now. The good news is he didn't have another heart attack, but his heart rate was erratic and much too fast when he was brought into the ER. At one point, we had to perform emergency procedures to resuscitate him."

"Are you telling me that his heart stopped?" Joshua's voice shook.

"Yes," the doctor said bluntly. "We believe the scars

from his previous heart attack contributed to his ventricular fibrillation—his irregular heart rhythm."

"How do we prevent this from happening again?" Joshua's panic receded to be replaced by determination.

"Once he recovers his strength, we need to discuss more-invasive surgery."

Joshua nodded once. He appreciated the doctor's straight talk. He didn't think he could take some roundabout, sugarcoated explanation without losing his shit. So far they had decided against invasive surgery due to his grandfather's age, but they couldn't let him go through this again.

"Can I see him?" he asked.

"He's asleep and needs absolute rest tonight. I'll allow visitations tomorrow."

"I won't wake him. I just want to see that he's all right."

"Okay." The doctor relented. "Just for five minutes."

Joshua glanced at Angie and she smiled. "Go ahead. I'll wait for you here."

The doctor showed him to his grandfather's bed and said, "Remember. Five minutes."

Joshua nodded, his eyes glued to the old man. Other than his slight pallor and the oxygen tube in his nose, Halabuji looked just as he had the night before. The fist clenched around Joshua's heart loosened its hold as he watched his grandfather's peaceful slumber.

Once he stepped out of the ICU, exhaustion rolled in. He wasn't ready to lose his grandfather. When he opened the door to the waiting room, Angie put aside the magazine she'd been flipping through and quickly crossed over to him. She put her arms around his waist and held him close, and the sob lodged in his chest almost broke free. He wrapped his arms around her and pulled her tighter against him.

"Are you okay?" she whispered against his chest.

"Yes…no. Actually, I'm not okay," he said, his voice raspy with fear and fatigue. "I'm not ready to lose him."

"Oh, Joshua. I'm sure he's not ready to leave you, either. He'll fight his way out of this."

Her warmth, her sympathy and the comfort she offered kept him from falling apart. He needed this. He needed her.

"Come home with me, Angie."

Five

Angie couldn't refuse. She didn't want to. He was hurting and she would give him all the comfort she could. Their kiss in the parking lot had lit a spark of hope inside her, but tonight wasn't about her. He needed her and she was there for him. It was as simple as that.

Joshua's condo was nothing like she'd imagined. The earth-toned walls of the living room were lined with overflowing bookshelves. There was a well-worn but welcoming beige leather sofa, and the low coffee table looked like the perfect place to rest your feet on.

But the grand piano was the centerpiece of the room. It was situated by a large window, and she could imagine Joshua looking up from it to gaze at the view of the city beyond, while thinking up the next notes of his composition.

This wasn't some sleek bachelor pad. It was his home. The space was so warm and intimate, she had a feeling that not a lot of people were invited in. When she turned toward him, he was looking intently at her.

"What do you think?" he asked with almost imperceptible hesitation. "Do you like it?"

Did it matter to him whether she liked his condo or not? A jolt of pleasure ran through her. "I love it. I'm glad you have such a wonderful place to come home to."

"Thank you." Joshua cleared his throat and pulled his tie loose. "Make yourself at home."

"Thank you," she said and sat down on the couch.

It was as comfortable as it looked. She wanted to lie down on it and take a nap. But she wasn't there to nap. She was there to… What exactly was she there to do? The answer to that question made heat rush to her cheeks.

"Would you like a drink?" he asked. "Scotch?"

"Scotch sounds good."

He swiftly disappeared into the kitchen behind the living room. Before she could wonder whether he was hiding from her, he came back carrying two glasses of amber liquid. He handed her a glass and sat down on the other end of the couch. After a deep gulp, Joshua set his glass on the coffee table and ran his hands over his face. She put down her untouched drink and scooted closer to him to rub his back.

"Hey," she said softly, "I know tonight has been a lot, but everything is going to be okay."

"I know," he said, meeting her gaze with sad, lost eyes. "But knowing and believing are two different things. And a part of my mind won't stop screaming in fear."

Her heart ached for him and tears prickled at the back of her eyes. She had no more words of comfort that could change the way he felt, so she leaned forward and gave him a feather-light kiss. When he stared at her with parted lips, she kissed him again, deeper this time.

With a growl, he opened his mouth wider and traced

the inside of her bottom lip with his tongue. Heat unfurled low in her stomach, and Angie struggled to get closer to him. Joshua lifted her onto his lap and deepened the kiss, tasting her like she was sweet nectar.

She whimpered in protest when he broke the kiss but was appeased when he trailed his lips along her jawline and up to the sensitive spot behind her ear. He gave her a lingering kiss there and blew softly on it. She shivered and a low, sexy chuckle rumbled in his chest. He remembered. That was the exact spot that had made her weak-kneed with lust when they were together.

"Joshua," she breathed, running her hands down his firm chest and stomach. His muscles jerked in response to her touch and it was her turn to smile. He wanted her as desperately as she wanted him.

He kissed her rough and hard, moaning against her lips, and any reserve she might have had melted away. She shifted on his lap and moved her leg across his thighs to straddle him. He groaned as though he were in pain when she swiveled her hip over his erection.

His chest rose and fell quickly as her hands explored his body. Unsatisfied with touching him through his clothes, she impatiently undid one button after the next until she spread his shirt apart, revealing what lay underneath. He was magnificent. She'd loved his beautiful lean body when they were together, but the new grooves and ridges of his carved torso begged for her touch.

As though in a trance, she traced her finger along his well-defined abs, trailing it lower and lower to where the hair darkened and disappeared into the waistband of his pants. Desperate to see the rest of him, she reached for his belt buckle, but his hand shot out to grasp her by the wrist.

"Wait," he said in a choked voice. "You don't...you don't have to do this."

The wild fire in his eyes told her how much he wanted this, but he sat absolutely still as he waited for her answer.

"I want to do this." She leaned forward until her lips were a breath away from his. "I want you."

He wrapped his hand around the nape of her neck and kissed her with unleashed passion. His lips didn't leave hers as he stood with her in his arms and carried her to his bedroom. Then he laid her gently on his bed and lowered himself beside her.

"I want to look at you," he said, his voice husky.

She nodded and reached for her blouse but fumbled with the buttons. He squeezed her hands before bringing them down to her sides. With fast, proficient fingers, he finished unbuttoning her blouse and pushed it off her shoulders. He drew in a sharp breath and leaned down to kiss the tops of her breasts spilling out of her bra. Frantic for his touch, she unclasped her bra and threw it to the side.

"You're beautiful," he said, cupping her breast with one hand. His thumb drew soft circles around her areola until she writhed beside him. "Do you like that?"

"Yes," she hissed.

"Do you want more?"

"Please."

Sweat was beading on his forehead. It was as hard for him to hold back as it was for her to wait. So she pulled his head down to her breasts and he succumbed with a guttural groan, sucking one nipple, then the other, into his mouth.

When she reached for his belt this time, he didn't stop her, and she quickly unclasped the buckle and unzipped his pants. He assisted her by lifting his hips off the bed and she roughly stripped his pants off, leaving him in only his boxer briefs, with his arousal straining against the fabric.

He returned the favor, taking her pants off along with her panties. He froze for a moment as his eyes roamed her naked body. Her skin felt electrified under his gaze and she moaned when his warm hand connected with her skin.

His kiss was gentle and almost reverent as his hand trailed down her side to her ass. He cupped her cheek and squeezed before he resumed his exploration of her body. With maddening slowness, he reached between her legs.

"You're so wet for me," he rasped when he finally touched the juncture between her thighs.

His lips were no longer gentle against hers as his tongue thrust into her mouth with urgency. He parted her folds with his fingers and rubbed her hypersensitive bud, making her head thrash from side to side.

"Joshua, I need… I need…"

He thrust his index finger inside her and her back arched off the bed. "Is this what you need?"

"More," she moaned.

He drew his finger in and out while his other hand continued circling her clit. She nearly came when he added a second finger inside her.

"So close. So…close…" she whimpered as she rode his hand.

"That's it, sweetheart. Come for me."

She finally fell apart at his rough command, and wave after wave of ecstasy washed over her. After laying a gentle kiss on her lips, Joshua stood and removed his boxer briefs. Even though she was still limp from her orgasm, she eyed his hard length with growing desire. When he returned to her side, sheathed in a condom, she spread her legs to welcome him.

He kissed her hard and fast as he positioned himself at her entrance, and she wrapped her legs around his waist.

"Joshua, I need you inside me."

He plunged into her, thrusting again and again until

his full length was inside her. They moaned in unison, a sound of relief and satisfaction. This felt…right.

She had never experienced this *wholeness* with anyone else. But she pulled herself away from her thoughts. This might be a one-night thing. She couldn't let herself get carried away. It was just amazing sex. That was all.

"God, Angie. You feel so good," he growled as he set a slow rhythm that threatened her sanity.

She lifted her hips off the bed and urged him to quicken the pace. Looking straight into his half-hooded eyes, she panted, "I want you hard and fast."

All pretense at control shattered, Joshua drove into her, pulling himself nearly all the way out, then plunging into her again. Delicious tightness grew between her legs until she couldn't stand it anymore. Sensing she was close, he tilted her hip to create friction where she needed it most.

"Oh, God. Don't stop. Please …" she begged.

Angie didn't know how Joshua was keeping up this demanding pace, never slowing down, grunting with each push. But she didn't relent, either. She rode him hard, reaching frantically for her climax and crying out incoherently when her orgasm finally slammed into her.

Joshua continued thrusting wildly until he shouted with his own release. He collapsed on top of her, panting and slick with sweat. She could hardly breathe but she didn't care. She liked his solid weight on her, still connected to her. Before it became too much, he lifted his head, pushing onto his elbows to bear the brunt of his weight.

"Are you okay?" he asked, running the back of his fingers down her flushed cheek.

"Yes. Better than okay, actually." She stretched languidly.

"Is that so?" A cocky smile lifted the corner of his lips. "How much better?"

"I feel wonderful."

He leaned down to kiss her temple and said against her ear, "Good."

Joshua rolled off her and lay by her side. He grew quiet as he stared at the ceiling, his mind most likely traveling back to his grandfather. She laid her head on his bare chest, and wrapped her arm around his waist, pressing her body into his side.

With a long, heavy sigh, his eyes slid closed. She soon drifted off beside him, hoping he wouldn't hurt so much tomorrow. Hoping she wouldn't hurt, either. Tonight might be all she had with him and she had to be okay with that.

Joshua didn't think he would be able to sleep, but with Angie's soft, warm body curved around him, he fell into a deep, dreamless slumber. The next time he opened his eyes, dawn was peeping in through the curtains, and he couldn't recall where he was. All he had was a sense of peace and contentment.

He pulled the woman by his side closer to him, knowing she belonged right there. He smiled and sleep nearly lured him back, but his damn mind ruined it all by blasting the events of the night before into the center of his thoughts.

Angie was in his bed. His arms tightened around her without conscious thought. When they made love last night, he'd expected familiarity and comfort, but what he'd found was fierce, thrilling passion. It was something he'd never experienced with any other woman—not even with Angie in the past.

It was beautiful and…it couldn't happen again. He forced his arms to relax and slowly disentangled himself from her, not wanting to wake her. Feral possessiveness flashed through him as he watched her serene, sleeping face, but he pushed aside his feelings with cold swiftness.

He shouldn't have asked her to come home with him

last night. But he'd wanted her for so long…and after the kiss in the parking lot, he didn't have the strength to resist her, especially with his world crumbling around him. And being the sweet, generous woman she was, Angie had made love to him as though she really wanted him. As though he meant something to her.

It was a mistake. This only complicated his already chaotic emotions. The very emotions that prevented him from composing. Losing his music meant losing his identity. No matter how right it felt to have her in his arms, he couldn't do this again.

He stepped into the shower and let the hot water wash over him. He was confused and…panicked. Yes, he wanted her, but if she could affect him like this with just one night together… He couldn't allow her to mean something to him again.

What was last night to her? Was it just pity sex? A one-night deal? The thought left a bitter taste in his mouth even though he'd just been telling himself that it couldn't happen again.

He dried himself off and quickly got dressed, being as quiet as possible to not wake Angie. He wasn't ready to speak to her yet. And if she woke up and so much as called his name, he would take her again. Although sneaking out made him feel like a first-rate jerk, it was for the best.

Joshua scribbled a quick note—"I have to head out. Stay as long as you need."—and placed it on his pillow. With her hair falling across her bare shoulder and her lips softly parted, she looked both beautiful and sexy as sin. If he stayed a second longer, he would kiss her awake. Drawing on the deepest reserve of his willpower, he spun on his heels and left for his office.

It was too early to visit his grandfather, so he might as well get as much work done as possible before heading to the hospital. Besides, if he wanted to put his night with Angie out of his mind, he needed to keep himself busy. Even though he'd taken a shower, her fragrance still seemed to linger on his skin and the scent of vanilla assailed his nostrils.

Enough of this nonsense. He repositioned his hands on the steering wheel and tried to focus on the road. Luckily, he'd left so early this morning, there wasn't much traffic. He made it to work in record time and lumbered into his office.

All the lights were still off because he was the first one in, but he didn't mind the dim stillness. It suited his current mood. Joshua needed to lose himself in his work. That was the only way he was going to get through this morning with his sanity intact.

He didn't realize how much time had passed until Janice peeked into his office.

"Good morning, Joshua," she said, walking up to his desk. She was wearing one of her bright floral dresses with her signature chunky jewelry. "Have you been here long? Have you had your coffee?"

"A few hours. And no coffee, thank you. I'm going to be with my grandfather for the better part of the day, so I needed to get some of the urgent work out of the way."

"Is everything okay?" Concern drew lines across her still-smooth forehead. No one would guess that she was a grandmother if it weren't for her mother-hen ways.

"He had a rough day yesterday, but things should be better today."

"Well, don't worry about a thing here," she said briskly. "I'll reschedule all your meetings for today."

"Thank you, Janice." He stood from his chair and pulled on his suit jacket. "I'll be back tonight but you'll already be gone by then, so I'll see you tomorrow."

"I wish you could take some time off to be with your grandfather, but I know you have to stay on top of things with the CEO appointment coming up. That Nathan Whitley will do anything to get an edge over you." She clucked her tongue. "Well, the board of directors aren't made up of fools. Anyone can see that you're the best man for the job."

"You might be a bit biased," he teased even as he prayed she was right. He couldn't let Whitley usurp the decades of hard work his grandfather and father had dedicated to building Riddle Incorporated.

"Maybe, but that doesn't mean I'm wrong," she said. "See you tomorrow, and don't forget to eat."

Joshua hurried to the parking structure and drove his car onto the road. Now that he didn't have work to distract him, his chest tightened with worry for his grandfather. His jaws clenched and his knuckles turned white on the steering wheel. Los Angeles traffic was never fun, but he had a hard time keeping his temper in check this morning.

When he got to the hospital, he rushed to the ICU nurses' station. "I'm here to see Edward Shin."

"Are you family?" asked the nurse, looking at him through glasses perched on her nose.

"Yes, I'm his grandson."

"Okay. Put yourself down on the visitor's list, but you'll have to wait half an hour for visiting hours to start. We have a waiting room around the corner."

"Thank you," he said, suppressing a wave of impatience.

He entered the waiting room and sat down in an empty seat. Everyone was either staring at their phone or reading a magazine. It was hardly a place for light conversation.

Joshua pulled out his phone, finding fifty new work emails as he'd expected. He passed through the unimportant ones and responded to the urgent ones. It took him a while to notice his knees bouncing and he forced himself to sit still with difficulty. He remembered how the weight of Angie's hand on his leg had quieted him. And the memory of his night with her rushed through him, leaving him warm and frustrated.

"Joshua," a quiet voice said in front of him.

He lifted his gaze to find the woman who refused to leave his thoughts all morning. He stood from his seat and cleared his throat. "What are you doing here?"

Something like hurt flitted across Angie's face, and he wanted to kick himself. "I had a feeling you might be here. I came to make sure you're okay and to hear news about your grandfather."

"He's stable enough to have visitors. I'm going to see him in a few minutes," Joshua said brusquely. "There was no need for you to come."

"No," she said, jutting out her chin. "I didn't *need* to come."

She came because she was worried about him, and he was being a complete asshole.

"Do you want…last night…" he blurted, but Angie stopped him with a hand on his arm.

"I already told you why I'm here—" she lowered her voice "—and discussing last night isn't one of the reasons. You have more pressing concerns."

"I…" He didn't know what to say…or what he wanted.

That wasn't entirely true. What he wanted was to pull her into his arms and hold her. But what if he didn't want to let go? He couldn't risk that. After what last night showed him, Joshua had to keep his distance from Angie.

"Please tell your grandfather to get well soon," she said softly and walked out of the waiting room.

Every instinct told him to hold on to her, but the last time he'd asked her to stay, she'd walked out of his life. The old hurt and anger shot to the surface as though it had never gone away. He couldn't forget her betrayal and what it had cost him. He had gone nearly six years without composing. He had lost a vital part of himself for far too long.

So he let her go. It was the only way to protect himself.

Six

"Mmm... I love *soondubu*," Chloe said after a big spoonful of the steaming hot tofu soup.

"Who doesn't?" Megan said, feasting on her own pot of soup. The individual rock pots kept the tofu soup boiling hot to the last drop.

Angie and her sisters' favorite *soondubu* spot was jam-packed as usual. They'd had to wait twenty minutes to get a table, but it was worth it. The warm, savory comfort food made her feel a little less forlorn.

Days had passed without a single text from Joshua. He obviously regretted spending the night with her, but he could've at least kept her apprised of his grandfather's condition. She held back a sigh as she stirred her soup. That wasn't fair. He and his parents were probably worried sick about Mr. Shin. Joshua couldn't be expected to worry about her right now. She just hoped he wasn't hurting too much.

Even so, she had a cold, hollow spot in her heart that

refused to go away. It wasn't because they'd made love that night. She had wanted him for a long time, and when she saw he needed comfort, there'd been no reason to hold back. After all, it was only sex. It was the best sex she'd ever had in her life, but it was just sex nonetheless. Then why was she feeling this way?

"The Chamber Music Society is so excited about getting the new piece from A.S.," Chloe said, securing a piece of marinated cucumber with her chopsticks. "I can't believe he's writing a string trio for us."

"How did Janet even manage to commission him?" Megan asked. "He's in such high demand, and the man isn't exactly easy to find."

"She's been in this business for a long time." Angie dipped a spoonful of rice in her soup, avoiding her sisters' eyes. No matter how guilty she felt about keeping secrets from them, she had to protect them from the truth about their father's past interference in her relationship with Joshua. "Between Janet and the rest of the board, someone was bound to have a way to connect with him."

When she told Janet about A.S. agreeing to compose a brand-new piece for the Hana Trio, her mentor had read the plea in Angie's eyes and hadn't asked any questions. She accepted the good news with delight and promised Angie not to let anyone know she had a part in getting the A.S. commission. The fewer people who knew about A.S.'s identity the better, especially when it came to her connection to him.

"I heard Claudia, the second violin, telling some of the orchestra members that she had a part in finding A.S." Chloe shared this piece of gossip, shaking her head with disdain. "But I don't believe a word she says. She once implied that she had a *thing* with Joshua Bell, but he didn't so much as nod at her when he performed with us."

"You never know…" Angie said with a careless shrug.

As ridiculous as Claudia's claim was, she was relieved she wasn't the one drawing the attention.

"No, it's not Claudia," Megan said. "But it really could be any of the musicians."

"I highly doubt that." Angie took a big gulp of her *bo-richa*. Luckily for her, the barley tea had cooled down to room temperature. "The important thing is that the Hana Trio is going to have the honor to perform A.S.'s new piece. We have to be in top form not to let the Chamber Music Society down. Not to mention what it could do for our reputation. It's make-or-break time, girls."

"Don't worry, *Unni*," Megan said with a cocky smirk. "We're going to slay it."

Angie and her sisters fist-bumped each other across the table. This was the opportunity of a lifetime, and they had never been more ready. She was so proud of them.

As they finished their lunch, her phone dinged in her purse. Her sisters and she had a no-cell-phone policy during mealtimes, so she just ignored it. Or at least she tried. She couldn't help wondering if the text was from Joshua, and the rest of lunch passed in a bit of a blur.

As soon as she got in her car, Angie dug out her phone from her purse and checked the text.

Grandfather is out of the ICU. He wants you to come. He misses you.

Angie's heart pounded so hard she thought it might burst out of her chest. *He misses you.* Did Joshua miss her, too? She shook her head to dispel the silly thought. She needed to respond to him. Should she ask him how he was doing? Or should she pretend that nothing had happened between them like he seemed to be?

Nah. That might have worked with the kiss, but this was different. They couldn't sweep this under the carpet.

Their coffee dates had been fun, but from the way Joshua was behaving, their trips to the café were obviously at an end. Besides being sort of friends with him had been confusing as hell. They needed to discuss this like two adults and clarify whatever they had between them. She typed a quick response.

I'll see you at eight. We can talk after I play for your grandfather.

Angie found Joshua standing in the hospital lobby, waiting for her. When she walked up to him, his eyes roamed her body with such fire that she sucked in a sharp breath. But he blinked and the fire was gone.

"I'll show you to my grandfather's room," he said stiffly.

Without another word, he stepped toward the elevators, so she followed, tugging along her cello. They got off a floor earlier than before and walked down the corridor on the other side of the building.

"This is it," Joshua said, breaking the silence.

"I see. Thank you," she said politely. This was getting ridiculous. Was it going to be this awkward between them from now on? "May I go in?"

"Yes, he's waiting for you." He extended his arm toward the door and she walked past him into the room.

"Halabuji," she said, blinking back tears.

She rushed to the bedside and picked up the patient's hand. The hospital lights accentuated his pallor and his hospital gown hung loosely around his thin figure. He seemed so frail…it broke her heart. Without meaning to, she glanced over her shoulder at Joshua, her eyes full of sympathy.

"Ah, my child. You come to me at last," Mr. Shin said,

squeezing her hand. His voice sounded stronger than he looked, and Angie sighed in relief.

"You gave me quite a scare. Please don't do it again," she said firmly, tugging down her eyebrows in an exaggerated frown. "You promised me you'd get better."

"And I'm a man of my word." Some color rose in his cheeks as he chuckled. "When I get my strength back, I'm going to get the old ticker fixed once and for all."

"We decided to go forward with the heart bypass surgery," Joshua explained.

"It's for the best," his grandfather said resolutely.

"And you'll be as good as new." Angie smiled at him despite a flutter of nerves. He was strong. He was going to pull through the open heart surgery. "I've been brushing up on some of the pieces on your list. Let me play for you."

"Nothing would make me happier."

Joshua hurried to his grandfather's side and raised the bed, helping him sit up. After making sure Mr. Shin was comfortable, he pulled a chair close to the bed and sat down heavily. He seemed bone weary.

Although she'd planned on playing another piece, she impulsively decided on Bach's Cello Suite no. 2 in D Minor. It was one of Joshua's favorite pieces, and it also happened to be on his grandfather's list. Angie played, infusing her concern and sympathy into the piece, hoping they would take solace in the music.

His grandfather watched her as though mesmerized, a soft smile on his lips. Joshua closed his eyes, and the tight lines of worry around his eyes and mouth smoothed away. Angie felt her own soul relax and heal as she threw herself into the music. She played the rest of the piece with her eyes closed, and only opened them once the last vibrations of the cello melted into the air.

Joshua clapped and his grandfather held out his hands to her. She put aside her cello, and clasped them in her own.

"Thank you, my dear."

"My pleasure, as always." She squeezed his hands before releasing them. "Now you really need your rest."

Joshua rose from his seat to walk her out. "I'll be back after I walk Angie to her car."

"No, you won't. You've been here for over an hour. I need a break from looking at your tired mug," his grandfather said gruffly. "Get some rest, my boy. Worrying about you doesn't help me one bit."

When Joshua opened his mouth to argue, Angie put her hand on his arm. "You're going to burn yourself out. Listen to your grandfather. He'll rest easier."

"Smart girl," the patient said with a wink.

Joshua gave her a curt nod, then helped his grandfather get settled before following her out into the hallway. They retraced their steps to the elevators and strode out into the evening air. Angie couldn't stand the uneasy silence that fell between them as they walked to her car. In that instant, she knew what she needed to do.

When they stopped in front of her car, Joshua dug his hands into his pockets and cleared his throat. "Thank you for coming."

"Of course. I have no intention of not keeping my part of our deal." She crossed her arms over her chest, tired of his distant politeness. "Besides, I love playing for your grandfather."

"So…you'll come see him again soon?"

The vulnerable tilt of his head diffused some of her frustration. In a gentler voice, she said, "Yes, I'll visit him twice a week as we agreed."

Huffing out a sigh, Joshua dragged his hand through his hair. "About the other night—"

"It happened," she swiftly interrupted. Then she took in a deep breath for courage. "And… I want it to happen again."

Joshua's eyes snapped to hers, shock and something like hunger crossing his face. "What are you saying?"

This awkward limbo they were in was insufferable. Their agreement bound them together and they had to find a way for whatever they had to work. In order to do that, they had to be honest with themselves and each other. They had to stop fighting their attraction.

"Let me see your phone," she said, holding her palm out.

"Excuse me?" He arched an arrogant eyebrow.

"Your phone, please."

Joshua shrugged his broad shoulders and handed her his phone. She quickly typed something into his map app and returned it to him.

Before he could ask, Angie explained, "That's my address. We need to talk."

"You want me to come over to your place? Tonight?"

"Yes and yes." She squared her shoulders and issued a challenge. "Will you?"

He studied her with an inscrutable gaze for long enough to make her want to fidget. Before she succumbed to the urge, he said, "Yes."

She was both relieved and panicked. *Now what?*

Joshua had figured from her address that she didn't live in the most stellar neighborhood, but the run-down facade of her apartment complex made him pause. He circled the block several times before he found street parking. Angie was waiting for him inside when he reached the entrance to the building and opened the door for him.

"I hope it wasn't too difficult to find parking," she said apologetically.

"Not at all." He glanced around the dim, tired lobby and couldn't hold back a frown. He would never have imagined her living in a place like this.

"This way." She led him to the elevators, and pressed the button.

The cramped elevator ride to the third floor took longer than it should've, and Joshua wondered when the elevator was last inspected. It was none of his business but he couldn't help but worry about Angie's living situation. After a short walk down a narrow corridor, she stopped and turned to him.

"This is me," she said, unlocking the door and leading him inside.

Her apartment was small, but it was surprisingly warm and charming. It was her home, and many of his misgivings about her living situation melted away when he saw it.

"Nice place," he said, removing his shoes on the floor mat in front of the door.

"Thank you." She set her cello by a music stand in the corner of the living room. There was pride in her voice when she said, "It's not much but it's mine."

"I assumed you still lived with your father." He didn't want to pry, but he couldn't help but wonder. Even if she'd wanted her own place, why did she choose this neighborhood to live in?

"I had a falling-out with him after my mom died," she said vaguely. She walked toward the kitchen and he followed.

"A falling-out?" he said in a deliberately moderate tone. After she shattered his heart and soul for her precious trust fund, she'd just up and walked away from everything? He fought his confusion and rising anger. Their relationship was in the past. What she chose to do with her life after she left him was none of his business.

"Wine?" she asked, holding up a bottle of red.

"Sure." He picked up the wine opener from the counter

and held out his hand. With a shrug, she passed him the bottle. He opened it and poured out two glasses.

She reached for her glass and raised it up. "Cheers."

"Cheers." He tapped his glass against hers, still distracted by what she'd said. Did her falling-out with her father have anything to do with her mother's death? *It wasn't any of his business but he couldn't stop himself from saying,* "I'm sorry about your mother. I remember you were close to her."

"Thank you." Angie circled the rim of her glass with her fingertip. She was quiet for so long that he didn't think she would continue. "It was breast cancer. She fought like a warrior—full of grace and strength—but lost the battle after five years."

It seemed to hurt her to talk about it, so he laid a hand on her shoulder to comfort her. So much had changed since they'd been together, he shouldn't jump to conclusions about her independence from her father.

"Let's go sit," she said with an unsteady smile. She walked out to the living room and sat on one end of the sofa, tucking her legs under her. He took the other end, resting one arm on the back of the couch.

She glanced at him from under her lashes. "I miss our trips to the café."

So did he, but he couldn't go back to pretending that he didn't want her. Memories of their night together refused to be quieted, and he hungered for her even now. "Angie…"

"It almost felt like we were becoming friends," she mused, swirling her wine.

"We can't be friends," he said bluntly. He wanted her to the point of distraction. A platonic relationship with her would be impossible.

He thought he could stop thinking about her by staying away from her but that wasn't the case. Not at all. And distancing himself from her had done nothing to help him compose. He didn't have a single note written for the Hana Trio. It was as though his overwhelming desire for her held his creativity hostage. Maybe the only way to free it was to let his attraction run its course.

"I don't want us to be friends," she replied with a wry quirk of her lips. Although he was the one who'd said it first, her agreement made his stomach clench with disappointment. "I want you too much for that to be possible."

"Where is this going?" he asked even as his blood rushed below his belt at her bold admission.

"Well, that depends." She took a sip of her wine and licked away a wayward drop from the corner of her mouth. "Do you want me?"

Did he want her? Frustration and desire flooded him. His voice was a near growl when he said, "You know I want you."

"Do you plan on doing something about that?" A sultry smile spread across her face.

This Angie, a sexy-as-hell siren, was the woman he had made love to the other night. The woman he couldn't resist. He hardened his heart and steeled his resolve. "I can't make you any promises."

Her smile faltered but returned full force a split second later. "I have a confession to make. I don't have much time to date, and that night with you was the best sex I've had in a long, long time. Simple as that. The attraction between us is undeniable, and I think we should let it run its course. I don't expect anything beyond that."

"It can only be sex," he said, more to convince himself than her. If he acted on this dangerous attraction, he had to make sure his feelings didn't get involved. He couldn't risk another heartbreak.

"Scorching hot, earth-shattering sex." She raised her

arm to the back of the couch and tangled her fingers through his.

He tightened his hold on her hand despite his hesitation. She was telling him everything he wanted to hear, but there was still a chance that she could get hurt… He tipped back his wine and put the glass down on the coffee table. Who did he think he was? Angie was a grown woman who had a right to make her own decisions. It wasn't his responsibility to protect her from himself.

"The best sex, huh?" Shifting on the sofa, Joshua took Angie's glass from her hand and placed it beside his.

"Well, didn't you think so?" she said, lifting her chin.

"Yes." He reached out and tucked a strand of hair behind her ear, and she shivered at his touch. "It was incredible. *You* were incredible."

Her cheeks flushed even as a triumphant smile lit her face. "So what's holding you back?"

"What's holding me back from amazing, uncomplicated sex?" He leaned in until their breath mingled. "Nothing."

He kissed her gently, tasting the fragrant wine lingering in her mouth. Then he traced his lips along her jawline and kissed the sensitive spot behind her ear. As he expected, a shiver ran through her. Yes, he knew her body, but he was more than happy to get reacquainted with it. He lifted her shirt over her head and ran his hands down her torso from the sides of her breasts to her narrow waist. Her curves had grown lusher since college. His greedy fingers dug into her skin, but he forced himself to relax his hold. He wanted to take his time with her tonight.

She fisted her hands into his hair and dragged his lips back to hers. But he drew away after a while and said against her ear, "Slowly. We have time."

"Slowly?" She stared at him with a slightly glazed look. "You can't be serious."

"It'll be worth it. I promise," he drawled in a low, seductive voice. She pouted in response.

Joshua rose from the couch and stood just out of her reach. As he began unbuttoning his shirt, Angie's eyelashes fluttered and her lips parted. Once he was done with all the buttons, he shrugged his shirt off his shoulders and let it drop to the ground.

"Your turn. Take your bra off," he said in a gravelly voice he hardly recognized.

A provocative smile spread across Angie's face as she ran the back of her hand down her throat and lower, through the valley between her breasts to her navel. She gathered her hair over one shoulder and reached behind her to unclasp her bra. The breath he'd been holding rushed out in a whoosh when she cast it aside and proudly faced him.

He was shaking with the need to touch her, but he held himself back. He unbuckled his belt at a leisurely pace that belied his desperation, and pushed his pants past his hips. Angie sucked in a breath, as she took in his aching erection still trapped by his boxer briefs. He smiled wolfishly as he kicked away his pants. Making sure her eyes were on him, he reached down and squeezed himself, groaning at the jolt of pleasure.

"Is it my turn?" she asked in a husky voice.

Holding his gaze, she cupped her bare breasts and sucked in a hard breath when her thumbs brushed her hard peaks. She bit her lower lip and tilted her head back as she rolled her nipples between her fingers. *Fuck*. He broke and lunged for her. She planted her hands on his chest and held him off.

"Uh-uh," she said breathlessly. "Slowly. Remember?"

"To hell with slow," Joshua growled, laying her down against the arm of the sofa. He captured her hands above her head and crushed his mouth against hers.

"About damn time." She freed her hands from his grasp and scraped her fingers down his back.

He shuddered against her touch and dipped his head to capture her nipple in his mouth. She moaned and writhed against him, and he sucked her harder. Needing to touch and see all of her, he roughly pulled down her skirt, and her panties soon followed.

"God, you're beautiful," he whispered.

He reverently kissed the inside of her thigh and then let his lips travel upward. He gently opened her up and placed a lingering, openmouthed kiss on her center.

"Joshua," she moaned.

"Yes, Angie?" He licked her with the flat of his tongue.

"Please." She gasped and buried her hands in his hair.

"Please what?" He flicked her nub with his tongue, then pulled her into his mouth. "Is this what you want?"

"Yes. More." Her hips rose off the couch.

"More? Like this?" He pushed her back down and swirled his tongue, easing a finger inside her.

"Oh, God, yes." She was close and it was driving him wild.

He continued tasting her as though she was a decadent dessert, and she buried her fingers in his hair, holding him against her. His tongue matched the speed of his fingers and he didn't relent until she arched her back with a hoarse cry.

Once he covered himself with a condom, he pulled her toward him. She straddled his thighs and lowered herself onto his throbbing cock. He arched his hips off the sofa and thrust deeper so she cradled all of him.

"God, you feel so good," he groaned.

Angie planted her hands on top of his shoulders and increased her speed to a maddening tempo. He was so turned on, he didn't know how long he would last.

"I need you to come for me." He gripped her ass and

thrust hard into her, growing desperate as he felt his climax approaching. "Come for me. Please."

Sucking in a sharp breath, she rode him fiercely. As her moaning grew louder, he reached between them to rub his thumb against her swollen clit. They came together with a ragged cry, and Angie sagged limply against him. He cradled her head against his chest and held her close, reluctant to let the moment end.

"That was amazing," Angie murmured, her words slightly slurred. "Let's take a catnap and do it again."

Joshua chuckled and kissed the top of her head. "Anything you want, baby."

Seven

Angie lay warm and satiated beside Joshua as he drew lazy circles on her sweat-slick back. Most evenings, they came to his condo after visiting his grandfather because her bed was too small to fit his tall, broad frame. But the point had been moot until now, because tonight was the first time they actually made it as far as his bed.

Aside from the spectacular sex, there was an added bonus to them being together. Since they weren't trying to hide their attraction from each other, their conversations became easy and comfortable. They sometimes lost track of time and talked late into the night.

But as she grew closer to him, the secret she kept from him weighed heavily on her. She had to tell him why she left him ten years ago. Her excuse that it wouldn't make a difference felt shallow and cowardly now.

She wasn't looking to change what they had between them. A small voice inside her protested, but she shut it out. They might not be in a real relationship but she still owed him the truth. She just hoped she could restore some of the trust he'd lost in her. It hurt her to think that he still believed she had cared more about her trust fund than him. The longer she put it off, the harder it would be for her to tell him, so she jumped in head first.

"There's something you need to know." She raised herself on her elbow and looked into his eyes. "I didn't leave you because I was afraid of my father cutting me off. I didn't give a damn about my trust fund."

His hand froze on her back and his eyebrows rose high on his forehead. "What?"

"I lied to you so that you would let me go." She drew in a shaky breath and the words tumbled out of her. "My mom was diagnosed with cancer, and my father said that if I didn't end things with you, he would never allow me into his house again. I know my mom would've found ways to see me, but the stress of a feud between me and my father would've broken her heart. She needed all her strength to beat the cancer, not to worry over me."

His mouth opened and closed several times before he spoke. "You didn't think I would understand if you told me?"

"I was afraid you would fight for me." A sob broke free. "If you had so much as asked me to stay, I wouldn't have been able to leave you. I thought the only way you would let me go was to break your heart so completely that you would never think of me again."

"All these years, I believed you left me because money meant more to you than I did." There was so much pain and anger in his voice. Even after a decade.

"You meant *everything* to me." She sat up, holding the sheet against her chest.

"Yet, you still left me," he said with a bitter laugh. He swung his legs off the bed and reached down to pick up his pants. "Do you realize what that did to me?"

"I'm sorry I hurt you." She impatiently wiped her wet cheeks. She didn't want to burden him with her tears "I didn't know what else to do."

"You should have trusted me," he bit out, swinging around to face her.

"I was only eighteen and heartbroken over my mom's diagnosis," she beseeched him to understand. "I realize now that I could have done things differently, but I did what I thought I had to do back then."

Joshua paced the floor, frustration and regret shifting across his face.

"As soon as my mom passed away, I left my father's house," she continued. "He cut me off completely, but I didn't care. I couldn't forgive him for what he did to us."

"What happens if your father finds out about our current...arrangement?" he asked with a sardonic twist of his lips.

Arrangement. He couldn't even make himself call what they had a relationship. It didn't matter. She hadn't told him the truth to gain something out of it. She told him because he deserved to know.

"Nothing," she said, lifting her chin. She didn't know where their *arrangement* was headed, but she would never allow her father to factor into it again. This was between her and Joshua. "He has no say in what I do with my life anymore."

He stared unblinkingly at her for a long moment then stalked out of the room with a muttered curse.

She clamped her hand over her mouth to stop a sob from escaping. She didn't think telling him the truth would be easy, but she wished Joshua didn't have to hurt. After taking a shuddering breath, she gathered her clothes off the floor and got dressed.

Angie found him in the living room, staring out the window. The city lights twinkled beautifully below but she doubted he saw any of it. He looked so alone standing there with his back toward her. She walked up to him and hugged him from behind.

"I wish…" He sighed and placed his hands over hers. "I wish we could turn back time, so neither of our hearts got broken."

"I'm so sorry." Hot tears streaked down her face and wet the back of his shirt. Joshua stood still, smoothing his thumb over the back of her hand until the floodgates closed.

For the past ten years, a part of her had been tied up with cold, hard chains that bit into her soul, but those chains finally fell away, allowing her to take a true full breath. But how did Joshua feel? Would he forgive her now that he knew the whole story? And where would that leave them?

"You know what we need right now?" he said, turning around to face her.

"What?" she asked with a tremulous smile.

"Cookies." He grinned boyishly. "We need loads of cookies."

Warmth spooled in her heart and her throat tightened with emotion. He must still be reeling from her confession but he was trying to comfort her. He knew cookies were her ultimate comfort food.

"Let's bake some," he announced.

"I'm sorry." She blinked in surprise. "Are you telling me you bake?"

"No, but I'm very good at following instructions. We'll just look up a recipe online."

"I hope you're not planning to rely on me." She eyed him sideways. "I've never baked before."

"Come on." He grabbed her hand and tugged her toward the kitchen. "It'll be fun."

"If you say so." Images of burnt cookies and a smoke

filled condo crowded her head. She could almost hear the wailing of the smoke alarm. "Do you even have ingredients for cookies?"

"I don't have chocolate chips or anything like that, but maybe there's a simple recipe for sugar cookies."

Standing at the kitchen island, they scrolled through the search results with their heads bent over the tablet. Then something caught her eyes and she pointed to the screen. "Look. It says the world's simplest cookie recipe."

"That sounds promising," he murmured, opening up the page. "They're peanut butter cookies."

"Ooh, I love peanut butter cookies." She leaned in for a better look. "Look how short the ingredient list is. You should have everything."

Joshua rummaged around his kitchen, opening and closing cabinets and drawers. Then he turned to her with a grin. "What do you know? I actually do."

"Lucky us." She smiled back at him. His excitement was contagious. "This recipe really is super simple. I think we can do this."

He brought out his measuring cups and spoons and stared bemusedly at them. Then he held up a quarter-teaspoon measuring spoon. "These look like toys."

She laughed. It did look like something from a play kitchen in his big hand. "Have you ever used them before?"

"No."

"Well, you're the one who suggested this, so let's get started." She read through the recipe twice to make sure she understood what she was supposed to do. "Okay. It says to add one and a half cups of flour. And you need to level it."

"Level it?" He scooped up some flour with the one-cup measuring cup and slid a chopstick over the uneven surface to smooth it out. "Like this?"

"I think so," she said, watching him repeat the process with the half-cup measuring cup. "We need to do that with all the dry ingredients."

"We? So far, it seems like I'm the only one getting my hands dirty." He already had some flour on the bridge of his nose.

"Not only your hands." She reached across and wiped the flour off his face. "Anyway, I do better giving orders than doing the actual work."

"You're not getting out of this that easily." Joshua reached out and ran his flour-covered hand down the side of her face. "That's better."

"Hey." She tried to wipe the flour off her face but based on his laughter, she apparently only managed to smear it more. "You're going to pay for that."

She grabbed a fistful of flour and threw it at him. He swerved to the side and it mostly missed him, but his hair was dusted with it.

"It's war, then," he said.

When he picked up the entire bag of flour, she ran out of the kitchen with a yelp and planted herself in the middle of the living room.

"You can't throw around flour in the living room," she warned. "You'll ruin all your furniture, not to mention your piano."

"Cheater."

"Being a brilliant strategist does not make one a cheater." She cocked her hip to the side and placed her fist on her waist. "Anyway, I'm really invested in making those cookies now, so stop messing around. Truce?"

"Fine. Truce." He pointed at his eyes and then at her. "But I'll be watching you."

Once they were back in the kitchen, she checked the tablet to see what they needed to do next. "Okay. You keep putting together the dry ingredients, and I'll work on the wet ingredients."

The butter needed to be softened, so she cut it up into small cubes and microwaved it for a few seconds. That probably wasn't the way to do it, but she had to improvise. Then she added the butter and sugar into a mixing bowl and whisked it by hand since Joshua didn't own an electric mixer of any sort. After a few minutes, her arm burned like she had done two minutes of plank.

"Do you need help?" Joshua asked.

He scooped out a bit of the mixture with his finger and licked it off. Angie watched with her mouth open and forgot what they were talking about. With a knowing smile, he leaned in and kissed her with his butter-and-sugar-flavored mouth. She pulled back before they forgot all about the cookies.

"Yes, please." She cleared her throat and handed him the whisk and bowl. She became mesmerized by how amazing his arm looked as he whipped away, but to her disappointment, he made quick work of the creamy mixture. "That looks ready. Now I'm going to add the dry ingredients a little bit at a time."

Her favorite part of the recipe was flattening the scooped dough with a fork to give it the classic criss-cross look of a peanut butter cookie. "Ooh, look how fancy these are."

Joshua chuckled and continued scooping out little mounds of cookie dough onto the baking sheets. They worked in cozy silence until all the cookie dough was laid out on the trays and ready to be baked.

"Will you do the honors?" he asked, gesturing at the oven.

"I would love to." Biting her lip with nervous anticipation, she put the first batch of cookies in.

They stood in front of the oven, ready to watch the

cookies the entire nine minutes it took to bake them. She leaned her head against him and he wrapped his arm around her waist. Baking with Joshua and enjoying the warmth of the sweet-smelling kitchen felt like the most natural thing to do. She sighed happily.

Then she caught herself. Cute domestic situations weren't part of their arrangement. Just because he knew the truth about their breakup didn't mean that he suddenly wanted a real relationship with her. She couldn't let herself get used to moments like this—moments when it felt as though she and Joshua belonged together. She stepped away from him and began wiping down the counters. But he came up behind her and wrapped his arms around her.

"Hey, what's wrong?" His hot breath tickled her ear and an involuntary shiver ran down her spine.

"Nothing. I wanted to help clean up this mess before I left," she said lightly, hoping he would buy her act. Or maybe a part of her hoped that he would ask her to stay the night. Now that she'd confessed, the proverbial ball was in his court.

"Don't worry about it. Leaving the mess behind is one of the perks of being a guest." He gave her a swift peck on the cheek then gathered up the used bowls and utensils to place in the sink. "I'm just going to stick these in the dishwasher after you leave."

She squashed the sting of disappointment and forced herself to smile. "I think the cookies are ready."

Joshua hurried to the oven and took out the cookies, and placed another sheet of cookie dough inside. The cookies looked and smelled perfect. But when he reached out for one, Angie slapped his hand away.

"We need to let it sit for five minutes."

"Bossy," he said, rubbing his hand.

In the end, they only managed to wait for three minutes before they each grabbed a cookie off the baking sheet.

"Mmm," they moaned in unison and laughed.

The warm, soft cookie was just the right amount of sweet, salty and nutty. In her opinion, it was even better than the ones she got at cafés. A corner of her heart still felt hollow but the sugar rush was helping her mood. She was content with her relationship with Joshua. It didn't have to mean something or last forever. She was happy with the now.

When all the batches were done, Angie filled up a good-sized plastic container with her half of the cookies. She wouldn't be spending the night with Joshua, but she had her cookies to keep her company.

Eight

Angie leaned back in her tub and sank her head under water. She was done with practices for the day and had time for a leisurely soak. But she kept her hands out of the hot water, so they wouldn't get pruney and desensitize her fingertips.

When most of the bubbles fizzed out and the water turned lukewarm, she unplugged the tub and stepped out of it. She toweled herself off, thinking about her date with Joshua in a couple of hours. *A date.* She pursed her lips as she cinched the belt of her bathrobe.

Other than their trips to the café before they…well…before, they had never been on a date. They met. They had sex. They talked—they always talked. But that was it. They didn't go out and do things that real couples did. Like go on dates.

She walked listlessly to her room and fell back on her bed. She shouldn't read too much into it. It was just a date. It probably had nothing to do with her confession.

The cookies from that night were long gone but her disappointment that he didn't invite her to stay lingered. She didn't know what she'd expected to happen after she told him the truth but *nothing* wasn't it. Maybe this date meant…*something.* She flopped onto her stomach and buried her face in her pillow.

He was cryptic about the plan, saying something about a dinner and a concert. She should have asked him what kind of concert it was—the ripped jeans kind or the formal dress kind or something in between. Grabbing her phone from her nightstand, she shot him a quick text.

What's the dress code for this mystery dinner and concert?

She put her phone back down and sat up in bed. It was time to face the truth. She was no longer content with their *arrangement.* She wanted more. It was foolish, especially since Joshua didn't want anything more—he'd made that clear from the beginning—but she couldn't stop herself from caring about him and wishing that he could come to care about her, too.

That didn't mean she was willing to do anything about it. Angie sighed and got to her feet. She opened her closet door and stared at her many dresses. Most of them were for performances; they had full skirts with room to cradle her cello between her legs. She could also wear them on the rare occasions that she went to watch someone else play. She sometimes wished she had dresses that hugged her curves—something sexy and flirty. But she couldn't buy dresses for fun on her budget.

Her intercom rang, which meant that someone was outside. A deliveryman? *Odd.* She hadn't ordered anything recently.

"Who is it?" she asked, picking up the receiver.

"I have a package for Angie Han," a man answered. *Hmm.* "Okay. Come on up."

The box was big—the size of a sheet cake but taller. She thanked the delivery guy and closed the door with her butt, juggling the box in her arms. She plopped it down on the sofa and took off the card attached to it.

I want you to wear this so I can peel it off you to-night.
Joshua

Angie couldn't stop the excitement that coursed through her. A gift like this had to mean something, didn't it? Or maybe he just didn't want his date to look like a frumpy matron. It didn't matter. It was a gift and she was going to enjoy it.

She opened the box with trembling hands and gasped with delight. Apparently he was taking her to a formal concert tonight. She held the gold-sequined, strapless dress against herself and rushed to the mirror hanging on her closet door. The floor-length mermaid gown was something she could never wear to one of her performances. It was absolutely impractical and ridiculously expensive—based on the designer label—but she didn't care. She loved it.

Stripping off her T-shirt and shorts, Angie slipped on the gown and zipped up the low back. It fit her like a glove. *Wow.* Were those really her curves? She was far from a pin up, but damn… She had some *va-va-va-voom* in her. After twisting around in front of the mirror for ages, she reluctantly stepped out of the dress. She didn't want to mess it up while she did her makeup and hair.

She painted on dramatic cat's-eye makeup and pouty red lips to complete her bombshell look. She didn't exactly look like a different person, but she definitely was a different version of herself. Someone bold and adventurous.

She was ready five minutes before Joshua arrived. With her heart beating faster than usual, Angie opened the door for him and froze. Joshua was wearing a classic tuxedo that emphasized his broad shoulders and narrow waist. He looked so gorgeous that she forgot to breathe for a second. But her favorite part was his expression—eyebrows high, eyes wide and mouth hanging open. She either looked stunningly hideous or beautiful enough to make him speechless.

"Hello, handsome," she said, finally finding her voice.

Fire lit Joshua's eyes as they roamed her body from top to bottom and back again. "Let's stay in tonight."

She tilted her head back and laughed huskily. "Not a chance. You promised me dinner and a show."

"After that," he said in a low growl, "I'm going to get you naked."

Her breath quickened and lust flared inside her. "Promise?"

"Let's go," he said.

She raised her eyebrows at his brusque tone.

"We need to leave before I bend you over that sofa and take you from behind."

"Oh," she breathed.

She quickly stepped out and locked her door. Despite her body's protestations, sex would have to wait until after their date. She was dying to know what he had in store for her tonight.

Luckily for her stiletto-clad feet, Joshua had found parking close to her building. Once they were settled in and on their way, Angie couldn't hold back her curiosity.

"So where exactly are we going?" She turned in her seat to face him.

"You'll see when we get there." He shot her a playful grin, then returned his eyes to the road.

"Why are you being so secretive?" She lightly socked his arm.

"Hey," he said, rubbing his arm. "No abusing the driver."

"Just tell me," she pleaded. "Please."

"You used to love surprises. What happened?"

"I still love surprises," she said. "So tell me where we're going so I can be surprised."

"Nice try." Joshua chuckled, shaking his head. "But you'll find out soon. It's not too far."

She slumped back in her seat with a huff. Then she sat up and leaned forward to look through the windshield. They were headed downtown. That narrowed the possibilities a bit.

"Wait. We're going to L.A. Live?" She furrowed her brows. L.A. Live was an outdoor mall on steroids with hip night clubs, restaurants and…a bowling alley. "We're not dressed like this to play glow-in-the-dark bowling, are we?"

"We sure are," he deadpanned. "I thought you'd get a kick out of it."

"If you make me bowl and I hurt my hand, I'm telling your grandfather."

He finally turned onto a smaller street and pulled into a parking structure across from the Staples Center. After handing the keys to the valet, he came around to her side and held out his arm. "Shall we?"

Taking his arm, she grinned triumphantly at him. "So the concert is at the Staples Center?"

Joshua smiled blithely in response and led her to the building's elevator.

"Why are we getting on the elevator here?" she asked. "The Staples Center is across the street."

"You'll see." Joshua pressed the button for the top deck.

The elevator doors opened to reveal throngs of people standing around red, orange, green and blue cocktail tables below crisscrossed string lights. Geometrically-shaped topiaries dotted the whimsically decorated outdoor space, which led to the biggest event tent she had ever seen. Accent lights splashed against its entrance.

"Okay. I'm definitely surprised," she said. "Where are we?"

"This is the Children's Hospital's charity gala," Joshua said a little sheepishly. "I didn't really mean for it to be a surprise, but you were so adorably curious, I couldn't help teasing you. I hope you're not disappointed."

"Why would I be disappointed? You're obviously here as a donor." She leaned in close and said, "Frankly, I'm a little smitten with you now. Helping those children is such an amazing cause."

He scratched the back of his head and the tips of his ears turned pink. "I'm just doing what I can."

"And so modest," she teased.

Joshua led them down the red carpet with a possessive hand on her back, and they posed for the photographers. She felt a little like a star at a movie premiere but the night's excitement was about raising funds for sick children, not the latest blockbuster. She pushed aside the prickle of unease that her sisters might see these pictures—it wasn't like they read through the society pages.

When a server passed with a tray of champagne, she plucked off two flutes. "Here. Let's toast. To the children."

"To the children." He clinked his glass against hers and brought it to his lips.

After drinks and hors d'oeuvres, they were ushered inside the tent. Angie gasped. It was lit up in vibrant purple, and giant versions of the colorful Children's Hospital logo were stamped on the ceiling. The logo reminded her of both a butterfly and a flower, filled with hope and spirit.

They sat down at a table occupied by two older couples, who smiled warmly at them. The server came around to offer them wine, and she chose the white to go along with her scallop entrée.

"It's nice to be a guest at one of these events," she whispered, taking a sip of her chardonnay. "I feel so pampered."

Joshua chuckled. "You deserve it. And rather than performing yourself, you'll get to watch Katy Perry perform."

"Shut the front door." She slapped Joshua's arm. "Katy Perry is singing tonight?"

"Don't believe me? Read the program."

Angie grabbed her program and scanned through it. Her face split into a huge grin when she looked up. "This is so much fun."

"I'm glad you approve." Joshua smiled and pressed a sweet kiss on her lips.

Her heart stuttered, and her breath left her on a soft whoosh. Truth be told, every moment she spent with Joshua was special to her, and she was dangerously close to losing her heart to him once more.

Joshua pulled Angie tighter against him in bed. Her obvious delight at the gala had been contagious, and he had enjoyed the evening. But if he'd had his way, he would have left early and brought her home sooner. The dress had looked spectacular on her, and he'd steadily lost his mind, wanting to tear it off her. Finally getting her naked had been well worth the wait, though. They were desperate and hungry as they made love, and now they lay spent in each other's arms.

He placed a lingering kiss on her bare shoulder, and she snuggled closer to him. Having her in his arms and in his life felt…right. He couldn't put it any other way. Even when he'd found music again, he couldn't free himself from the piercing discontent that haunted him. With Angie back beside him—and knowing the real reason she'd left him—he felt as though he'd been mended. But she wouldn't stay by his side for long. Not when he couldn't love her like she deserved. Still, his arms tightened around her. She was his for now, and he was going to cherish every moment of it.

Angie pecked him on the lips and untangled herself from him.

"What are you doing?" he asked, pulling her back into his arms.

"It's getting late." She pushed her hands against his chest but he didn't give an inch. "I should head home."

"Stay," he said simply.

He was the one who had insisted on a purely physical relationship but that wasn't enough anymore. He wanted her to need him. He wanted her to trust him. *How about you? Will you be able to trust her? To need her?* He selfishly pushed aside those questions.

She grew still in his arms then slowly raised her eyes to meet his. "You want me to stay?"

"I do."

"You made it clear that a real relationship was out of the question. It'll be the best for both of us to keep things as simple as possible."

"To hell with simple." What was he doing? He must be out of his mind.

"Is this because I told you the truth about why I left you?" she asked quietly, something like hope flaring in her eyes.

"No. Yes. I don't know." He blew out a long breath and tried again. "All I know is I'm not satisfied with just having your body. I want to spend time with you and laugh with you. I want to wake up with you in my arms. Even if it's only for a short while, I want to *be* with you."

"I want those things, too," she said in a whisper.

"I…" He swallowed with difficulty. "I still can't make you any promises—"

"And I'm not asking for any." She lifted her chin but couldn't stop one corner of her lips from wobbling for a second. "I just don't want either of us to get hurt."

His chest clenched with fear and he felt a moment of panic. But wouldn't they be safe from heartbreak as long as they didn't fall in love? He reached out and cupped her cheek. "Let's take things slowly—day by day. Our hearts were broken when we were young because we expected a lifetime with each other. As long as we don't give into such unrealistic expectations, neither of us will get hurt."

He thought he caught a glimpse of bleakness in her eyes, but it was gone when she blinked. "You're right. We'll go into this with our eyes wide open and our hearts safely locked away."

He nodded vigorously to dislodge the sense of loss her words wrought inside him. He leaned toward her and nudged her nose with his. "Does that mean you'll stay the night?"

"Yes, I'll stay."

He held her close as relief and happiness rushed through him. Angie was so quiet for a while he thought she'd fallen asleep.

"I've been meaning to ask," she said hesitantly. "Why do you compose in secret?"

He paused to consider how much he should share with her. She would beat herself up if she found out he couldn't compose for years after she left him. And he didn't want to worry her by telling her about the threat Nathan Whitley posed.

"I don't want my father to worry that I might turn my

back on Riddle to pursue music full-time," he offered her a truncated explanation.

"Is that what you want? To compose full-time?"

"No. Riddle means too much to me. Besides, I've been doing this for years now. I know I could successfully run Riddle *and* compose."

"I'm glad," she said. After a pause, she came up on one elbow. "By the way, how is your composition going? When do I get to see it?"

It was the question he dreaded. He was still without a single note after crumpling numerous false starts. But now that his conflicted emotions were becoming untangled, maybe he would be able to compose again.

Even so, he couldn't keep it from her any longer. The Hana Trio and the Chamber Music Society were counting on him, and she deserved to know his lack of progress.

"I have nothing to show you," he said.

"What do you mean you have nothing? Are you not ready to share it with me? Because I would totally understand."

"No, I mean I haven't written a single note." He sighed. "I'm blocked."

Angie propped herself up on her elbow and the sheet slipped down to reveal her creamy breasts. He was immediately distracted and reached out to cup one of them. She slapped his hand away.

"Focus, Joshua. The season is opening in less than two months. That means you have a month at most to finish the piece. My sisters and I need some time to practice, too."

Instead of filling his hand with her glorious flesh, he raked it through his hair. "I know all that. But I can't help it. I'm still blocked."

She swung her feet down to the floor and stood, picking his shirt up off the floor and shrugging into it. She haphazardly buttoned it and tugged his hand. "Get up. I'll help you through this."

"I don't think I'll be able to compose any better with you distracting me. You don't know how sexy you are in that shirt." He didn't budge from his prone position. "Come back to bed, baby."

"All you need is a little inspiration. Once you get started, everything will flow smoothly."

When she pulled harder, putting her back into it, Joshua got out of bed and slipped on his pants. "I'm up. Now what?"

"We brew some coffee and sit at the piano." She headed straight to the kitchen.

"And stare blankly at the keys," he added morosely as he joined her. After grabbing a couple mugs from the cupboard, he started the coffee. "Just so you know, I've tried that already."

"You need to psyche yourself up."

"Psyche myself up?"

"Yeah. When I get stuck on a phrase, I can't get past it without making the same mistake over and over again. The longer that goes on, the more stuck I become. Sometimes, starting a few measures back and playing at a ridiculously fast pace helps me spit out the phrase."

"Interesting." He nodded but couldn't hide his skepticism.

Angie rolled her eyes. "Just trust me. It's all about not overthinking things."

When the coffee was ready, she filled the mugs and carried them out to the living room. She handed him his cup when he came to stand next to her. After a few sips, she waved her hand toward the piano.

"Sit," she ordered.

He put down his mug on a side table and sat at the piano. "I'm sitting. Now what?"

"When you think about the Hana Trio, what's the first word that comes to mind?"

"Fluid," he said without hesitation. Their unified sound reminded him of a calm, spring river—the water flowing freely without obstruction.

"Don't think too hard on this. How best can you translate that into music?"

He imagined the flowing river and played a single strain on the piano with his right hand. His heart thumped. He used his left hand to add layers and played the strain again.

"That sounds amazing," Angie whispered, her eyes wide. "Run with it, Joshua."

And he did. The sky was clear and blue above the river and the dense forest surrounding it was teeming with life. He heard the violin, cello and viola painting the picture of this river in the depth of a secluded forest. He felt the beginnings of the string trio take form in his mind.

He grabbed a blank piece of music paper from the top of the piano and scribbled notes onto it with a stubby pencil. He alternately wrote and played until he had pages of music spilling over the piano.

A soft sigh brought him out of his frenzied composition. Angie was sitting quietly on the sofa, watching him with a tender light in her eyes.

"Angie… I'm sorry. I got carried away." He extended his arms over his head and stretched his back. "How long have I been inadvertently ignoring you?"

She turned her head to read the wall clock behind her. "Oh, it's only been about an hour."

"You must be tired." He pushed the piano bench back. "Let's go to bed."

"I'm a big girl. I can tuck myself in." She walked up to him and placed a hand on his shoulder to stop him from getting up. "You're not tired at all. I know how you work for hours on end when something grips you."

Even as they spoke, more notes danced in his mind and he was eager to jot them down. "Thank you. I'll join you in a bit."

She placed a lingering kiss on his lips and turned away before he had a chance to tug her down beside him. He watched his muse walk away clad only in his shirt, her shapely legs bare for his perusal. He almost chased after her, but he held himself back. His music demanded his full attention now.

Nine

It was just Angie and Edward Shin this evening at the Malibu wellness resort. Joshua was held up in a meeting, so she'd decided to stay a bit longer after she played for his grandfather.

"Are you nervous about the surgery?" she asked, placing a hand on his arm.

"Not nervous. Just impatient to get it over with." He sighed wearily. "I'm tired of this place—and don't get me started about the hospital. If it wasn't for your visits, I'll probably fly the coop."

"Hang in there for a bit longer. Your surgery is only a few days away. Then you'll be able to go home."

"Thank you, my dear." He patted her hand. "You're an angel."

She smiled warmly at him. She'd grown so fond of the kind, spirited man.

"I haven't seen Joshua this happy in such a long time," he said, watching her closely.

"Oh?" The sudden change in topic froze her smile on her face.

"You're good for him."

"Well, you know what they say. Music is chicken soup for the soul," she blabbered.

"I'm sure your music helps, too," he said knowingly.

"Halabuji, I'm not sure what you're implying, but Joshua and I are just friends."

"My child, I may be old and sick, but I'm not blind. I see the way you look at each other." He chuckled. "And I know my boy. He's head over heels in love with you."

Angie laughed nervously, which turned into a hiccup. *Joshua. In love with me.* Her heart curled into itself, fighting against the hope that threatened to bloom inside.

"And I think that you're a hopeless romantic," she said affectionately. Standing from her seat, she leaned down to kiss his cheek. "I should leave you to rest."

She spent the entire drive home trying not to think about what her charming patient had said. Then she showered and dried her hair, not thinking about what he'd said. And when the thought *What if?* bubbled up in her mind, she popped it without mercy.

If she considered the possibility that Joshua might love her even a little, then she would have to face her own growing feelings for him. Angie cherished every moment she spent with him. Every smile and every touch made her heart swell with...*like*? Her instinct for self-preservation brought her thoughts to a screeching halt. She couldn't do this.

They had already discussed where the relationship was heading, and commitment wasn't part of the plan after what had happened between them before. How had Joshua put it? *Our hearts were broken when we were young because we expected a lifetime with each other. As long as we don't give into such unrealistic expectations, neither of us will get hurt.* She swallowed the emotion rising up in her throat.

Tea. She needed some tea. What good would it do to wonder about what happened next? When either of them decided to end things, that would be that. And everything would be fine because *unrealistic expectations* like love and forever weren't part of the equation, right? Hot water splashed on the counter as she poured some into her mug. Her hands weren't quite steady.

Grabbing her cup, she settled down on the couch and reached for the remote control. She scrolled through the Trending Now titles on her streaming service without much interest when her phone rang. It was Joshua.

"Hi," she said breathlessly. *No, you don't sound love-sick at all.* "Are you done with your meeting?"

"Yes, I just got home." Silence stretched on a moment too long. "I miss you."

Her hand tightened around the phone and her blood pounded loudly in her ears. Even if it wasn't forever, their relationship was real. And it was perfectly natural for them to miss each other.

"I miss you, too." Inexplicable tears prickled behind her eyes.

"Come over," he said, sexy and demanding.

"I can't." Her emotions were too close to the surface. If she made love to him tonight, she might do or say something she would regret. "I have an early rehearsal tomorrow."

"Then can I keep you on the phone a little longer?"

Why was he making this so hard? Despite her best intentions, her heart turned into mush. "Of course. I'd love to keep you company."

"I wrote some more last night," he said. "Do you want to hear it?"

"Absolutely." Her stomach fluttered with excitement.

She heard him pull out his piano bench. "I'm going to put you on speaker now."

Then he played a lovely strain for her. She could almost see the music dance in her mind's eye. It was fanciful, yet vulnerable. His talent took her breath away.

"That's exquisite," she said softly.

"Thank you." He sounded a bit embarrassed by her praise, and it was adorable. "But I'm not too sure about the next phrase."

"Do you think it'll help if you heard it on the cello?" she said, eager to help.

"That would be fantastic."

She put her phone on speaker and placed it on her music stand to take out her instrument. When she was ready, she said, "Play it for me again."

He did, and she mimicked him on the cello.

"Huh." He sounded pleasantly surprised. "How about this part?"

He played a slightly different phrase, and she repeated it. Soon they got into a rhythm where he played a phrase of music on the piano and she played it back on her cello. It was exhilarating to witness his creative process and be a part of it.

"I might need to use you for every composition from now on," he finally said.

Angie's heart clenched. He said that as though they had a future together. She steadied her breathing and said lightly, "Well, I better start charging you for it."

He laughed and she felt it down to her toes. Then neither of them spoke for a moment.

"Are you sure you can't come over?"

"Joshua," she said sternly.

"Yes?"

"It's almost midnight." She didn't know how much

longer her willpower would last when all she wanted was to run to him.

"I want you, Angie," he said in near growl, turning her knees into Jell-O.

"Stop tempting me." She meant to sound firm but it came out as a plea.

"I can come over to your place," he persisted.

"And what? Sleep on the sofa? You know we can't fit on my twin-size bed together."

"We'll curl up real tight." His voice grew low and seductive.

"I want you, too," she hardened her resolve, "but I have to wait until tomorrow night to have you, and so do you."

"I'll be up all night thinking about you."

Her heart lurched and butterflies took flight in her stomach. How did he expect her not to fall in love with him when he acted like this? Anger suddenly stirred inside her. It wasn't fair.

"Why don't you try some warm milk?" she said with saccharine sweetness.

"That's cold," he grumbled.

She had to laugh at that. But before he could deplete her willpower, she said, "Good night."

"Good night, Angie," he finally relented. "I'll see you in my dreams."

Joshua stood in front of his full-length mirror and adjusted his tie. As he'd predicted, Angie had haunted his dreams all night. When he woke up this morning, his eyes burned and his head felt heavy, but he was happy because he was going to see her tonight. She spent several nights a week at his place, but that wasn't enough. He wanted her in his bed every night. It felt wrong to wake up alone.

He callously swept away the voice that told him he was wandering too close to the flames. This wasn't love.

Yes, he cared about her and burned for her, but it wasn't the all-consuming thing that they'd once shared. It could never be that. They already had everything they needed for a satisfying relationship—affection, passion, respect. Love was an unnecessary risk. Because in the end, she'd left him even though she loved him. He wouldn't gamble his heart and music on something that had no guarantee. Not again.

But how long would he be able to keep her without a commitment? A year? Two years? He was the one who said expecting a lifetime together was unrealistic. He pushed his door open with more force than necessary and headed for his car.

The reminder that their relationship couldn't last twisted him up. He brooded over the thought as he made his daily commute. He didn't have to lose her just because he couldn't promise her love and forever. What they had could be enough. Doubt and restlessness were clawing at his chest by the time he arrived at his office.

"Good morning, Joshua. Would you like some coffee?" Janice said cheerily.

He grunted noncommittally.

"I'm going to take that as a yes."

He slung his jacket on the coatrack and dropped heavily into his chair. This was ridiculous. He was working himself up for no good reason. Things were going well. He was seeing her tonight. But tonight seemed too long of a wait. He needed to see her sooner and assure himself that everything was fine. After checking his watch to make sure he wasn't disrupting her rehearsal, he texted her.

I want to take you to lunch.

To his relief, he saw ellipses appear on his messaging app right away.

You couldn't wait till tonight? J

No, as a matter of fact, I couldn't.

This time there was a longish pause before she responded.

Where do you want to meet?

Are you okay coming downtown?

I'm fine with that.

They agreed to meet at a seafood restaurant near his work—he glanced at the clock—in about three hours. Satisfied with the arrangement, he was finally able to concentrate on the work piled on his desk. His plans for Riddle's growth were ambitious and aggressive. He usually worked twelve-hour days to meet the demands of his job but he'd fallen a bit behind since Halabuji's heart attack. He couldn't afford to let his personal life distract him from his work.

He was making good progress when his phone rang, breaking his concentration.

"Yes, Janice?" he said impatiently while he finished typing out an email.

"Clarice Wong is here to see you."

His hands paused over his keyboard. Why was the chairperson of the board of directors here to see him?

"Please send her in." He went around his desk to greet his guest.

"I'm sorry for showing up unannounced." She shook his hand firmly. "But I had a meeting nearby and thought I'd drop in to see if you had a minute."

"I'm glad you did." He motioned for her to take a seat on the couch and sat down across from her.

"How's your grandfather?" she asked with genuine concern. She was a close family friend.

"He's a fighter," Joshua said. "He'll come back stronger than ever."

"I'm sure he will." The softness in her expression disappeared as she got down to business. "I trust the Nexus contract is progressing smoothly."

"Without a hitch," he said with confidence. "Is there reason for concern?"

"Whitley." Clarice blew out a frustrated breath. "He's been implying that you're distracted with your grandfather's illness and that Nexus might not be renewing their contract with Riddle at the end of the year."

"That's funny. A few days ago, the COO of Nexus assured me that she had every intention of renewing Nexus's contract with Riddle." Joshua crossed his legs and leaned back on the sofa. "I hope no one on the board is buying Whitley's bullshit. Other than Richard Benson and Scott Grey, that is."

"Benson is apparently a business school buddy of his but Grey is still on the fence. The problem is there are a few others that are on the fence," she said. "The Nexus contract aside, Whitley's best offense is that you're young and unproven."

"My grandfather started Riddle when he was my age." His voice grew cold with anger. "And my track record as vice president of operations more than proves my competence."

"But you can't afford to make any mistakes at this point. Remember Whitley is a formidable opponent."

"Thank you for your advice," he said sincerely. "I assure you there won't be any mistakes."

By the time Clarice left, he was late for lunch. He

sprinted the two blocks to the restaurant and when he reached Angie's table, he was out of breath. He dropped a kiss on her lips and sat across from her. "I'm sorry I'm late. A meeting took longer than I expected."

"Don't worry about it." Her smile was open and warm, and Joshua's heart skipped a beat. "I was just looking over the menu. It always takes me forever to make my decision."

"That's good." He didn't bother picking up his menu. "I always get the same thing here."

Lunch service was quick and efficient. His lobster roll and her grilled salmon were ready within minutes.

"How was practice?" he asked, his eyes roaming her beautiful face. Just being with her eased some of the tension from his meeting with Clarice.

"Megan seemed a little distracted today. It took us a while to come together," she answered between bites. "We're eager to start practicing A.S.'s new piece."

"I think he's close to finishing." The tables were pretty close together, so he had to watch his words. "With his muse's help, he should be able to wrap it up this weekend."

"I can't wait to get my hands on it. The Chamber Music Society launched its publicity campaign for the upcoming season—highlighting the premiere of A.S.'s new work. They're already getting so much positive feedback."

"I'm glad it's helping them," he said with a smile, but his chest tightened with worry.

The heightened publicity was going to fuel the search for A.S.'s true identity. It happened every time a new piece premiered or a record launched, but the stakes were too high this time. It would be a disaster if his identity as A.S. was revealed so close to the CEO appointment. Like Clarice said, he couldn't afford any mistakes.

"The salmon is great," Angie said, drawing him out

of his dark thoughts. "Here, have some. I'll trade you for your fries."

She reached across the table to place a perfectly grilled piece of salmon on the corner of his plate, and grabbed some fries while she was at it. For some reason, the simple act of eating off each other's plates made the uncertainty gnawing at him disappear. He was on solid ground again. There was a familiarity and intimacy to it that marked them as a real couple. He wasn't going to lose her.

It was Saturday morning and Angie was fast asleep. She'd gone to bed around two o'clock, but having her near had centered Joshua as he stayed up all night to finish the string trio. It was a fine piece but it didn't feel like the right one for the Hana Trio—for Angie. He wanted to create something truly unique and moving for her.

But maybe he wouldn't be happy with anything he wrote for her. Nothing might ever be good enough for her in his mind. *Why was that?* He ignored the voice in his head. Angie played with soul and her unique sound deserved something equally unique. That was all.

He stood from his seat and stretched, twisting this way and that with his arms raised over his head. He sighed in relief as some of the tension left his stiff neck, back and shoulders. Careful not to wake up Angie, he tiptoed to the kitchen and got the coffee going. Then he rummaged around his fridge and gathered the ingredients for a cheese omelet. It was close to nine. She would be hungry when she woke up.

He cracked the eggs into a bowl and briskly beat them with a couple tablespoons of ice water to make the omelet extra fluffy. Once the pan was hot, he poured in the mixture and carefully folded the eggs with a fork then added the cheese near the end. When the food ready, he arranged the plates on the tray and went to his bedroom.

Angie's shiny black hair was fanned out on the white sheets, and her milky shoulder peeked out from under the covers. She was sleeping on her side with her hands softly curled in front of her face. Her beauty made his heart clench and emotion clog his throat. Belatedly remembering to breathe, Joshua set their breakfast on top of the dresser and gingerly climbed into bed beside her.

He leaned down and kissed her shoulder. Her vanilla scent was sweet and welcoming, and the feel of her warm, smooth skin made desire engulf him. Her eyelids fluttered open and she glanced over her shoulder with a sleepy smile.

"Good morning," she murmured.

And because he couldn't help himself, he turned her to face him and kissed her deeply. With a little whimper, she pressed herself to him as she grasped the nape of his neck and kissed him back. He barely held himself in check and slowed down the kiss. With one last featherlight press of his lips, he drew away.

"Good morning," he said in a husky voice. Her lips, plump and red from kissing, formed a hint of a pout, and she tried to pull him back to her. He chuckled and stood up. "Hold that thought."

When he carried the tray over to the bed, Angie sat up, holding the covers against her perfect breasts. "You made me breakfast in bed?" Surprise and happiness colored her voice.

"I hope you like cheese omelets."

"Ooh, that sounds delicious." Tucking the sheets under her arms, she scooted back against the headrest to make room for the tray. He carefully positioned the food in front of her. "But we're finishing what we started after we eat."

"I'll try to keep that in mind." He swept his gaze over her body, not bothering to disguise the desire in his eyes. Turning a lovely shade of pink, she dug into her omelet, twirling her fork to wrap the strings of melted cheese around it. As she took a bite and chewed, her eyes widened. "Oh, my goodness. This is delicious."

"You don't need to sound so surprised," he teased, sitting down on the edge of the bed beside her.

"I just never knew you were such an amazing cook," she said, taking another bite.

"I can only cook a handful of dishes." He laughed, ridiculously pleased that she was enjoying the omelet. "But I'm glad you like it."

"Why aren't you eating?" She blew on her mug before taking a sip of her coffee.

He'd been pushing around a piece of his omelet, and he put down his fork. "I finished it."

"What?" She put the tray on the other side of bed and enveloped him in a bear hug. "Congratulations, Joshua."

"Thank you," he said into her hair, his arms tightening around her. Finishing a new piece of music had never been more rewarding.

She pushed at his shoulders and he loosened his arms to let her back away a few inches. "Can I see it?"

He tugged her back into his arms, and buried his face in the crook of her neck. "In a minute."

Angie understood what he needed and burrowed against him, the sheet pooling around her waist. It had been a fight, but with her help, he'd finished the string trio, and at last, she was going to perform his music. They took the long way around, but they finally got here. He dismissed his prior misgivings that the piece wasn't right for her. He would never feel that anything was perfect enough for her.

He allowed contentment, sweety and heady, to flow through him. He didn't need any guarantees about the future. She was in his arms now. That was enough. They were enough.

Ten

Angie checked her phone for the umpteenth time, and sighed forlornly.

"My dear, is everything okay?" Janet asked, taking off her reading glasses. She had been reading the sheet music for A.S.'s string trio. Angie had brought it to her office today.

"Mmm-hmm. Everything's fine. I'm just a little distracted."

Mr. Shin was in surgery right now, and Joshua had promised to update her with any news. She didn't know if the surgery was supposed to last this long. More than anything, she wished she could be by his side, providing her support and comfort. But he was with his parents now, as he should be. They would support each other.

"Does it have anything to do with your…composer friend?"

"No, no. It's nothing like that," Angie said in a rush. This was the first time her mentor had alluded to her relationship to A.S. Janet never pried into how she knew the composer and even managed to keep Angie's name out when she informed Timothy about the commission for the string trio. Angie owed her an explanation but it wasn't her secret to share.

"Janet, I wish… I'm…" What could she say? "I'm sorry."

"Don't be. I know you have your reasons." Her words held no judgment. "But I'm here for you if you ever need anything. Don't forget."

"I won't. Thank you for understanding," Angie said, blinking back tears. She sniffed and shook her head to clear it. "So what do you think? Does A.S.'s new work live up to your expectations?"

"This is simply marvelous. He has to be one of the most talented composers of our generation," Janet gushed, hugging the music to her chest. Recovering her composure, she slipped the pages back into the folder. "I can't wait to hear you girls play it."

"We start rehearsals tomorrow." Angie's heart pounded loudly in her ears. She was both thrilled and anxious. What if she couldn't do Joshua's music justice?

"Are you nervous?" Her mentor knew her well.

"Very," Angie admitted.

"Your playing is reaching new heights. A.S. should be honored to have you and your sisters premiere his piece."

"And I think you may be a bit partial to the trio," Angie said with a warm smile.

"That doesn't make me wrong."

"Thank you, Janet." She stood from her seat and went around the desk to hug her friend. "Your faith in me fills me with courage. I'll make you proud."

"I know you will." Janet squeezed her tight and patted her back. "You always do."

"I'm going to let you get back to work. I know you're busy preparing for the maestro's circle event next week."

"Yes, it's for our biggest donors. I have to give a rousing speech to make them itch to write very generous checks." Janet laughed about the part of the job that was most difficult for her. Asking people to hand out hard-earned money was never easy even when it was for a good cause. "Are you and your sisters preparing for the performance?"

"We're practicing Bach's *Goldberg Variations.*" They had sounded pretty great at their rehearsal this morning. She remembered the sense of accomplishment that had filled her. She loved being a musician. "We'll warm up the crowd for you."

"Good, good. And I think the excitement over our collaboration with A.S. will make for an exceptional evening."

"I'm glad." Angie smiled, happy to see how valuable Joshua's help was to the Chamber Music Society. "I'll see you then."

Angie rolled her cello case out, greeting some of her fellow musicians on her way to the parking lot. There was a palpable energy and excitement in the air. They were finally resuming live performances. This season was going to be remarkable. She could feel it.

Some of her enthusiasm dimmed as she drove home, worried about Joshua and his grandfather. Her small apartment usually welcomed her like a warm hug, but it felt oddly cold as she let herself in. Feeling too listless to make herself a real meal, she boiled some instant ramen for dinner. She ate in front of the TV, watching a quirky reality show about an antique shop. But even her favorite comfort food and a fun show did nothing to help her relax.

She took her half-eaten ramen to the kitchen and dumped it out in the sink. After she did the dishes, she made herself a hot cup of tea and sat back down on the couch. Giving up her attempt to take her mind off her worries, Angie reached for her phone yet again. There was still no word from Joshua.

Despite her resolve not to bother him—he had enough to deal with—she texted Joshua.

I'm going to wait for you at your place.

He'd given her a key to his condo just in case, and tonight was the perfect time to use it. She changed into a pair of jeans and a light blouse, and headed to the parking lot. She hit the tail end of rush hour traffic and got to Joshua's a bit later than she'd expected. After checking her phone again, she hurried inside. She doubted he was home, but her heart still raced at the prospect of seeing him.

The condo was dark. Disappointment flooded her even though she knew it was a long shot that he'd be home. He would probably text her from the hospital with news about the surgery before he came back. She walked around, switching the lights on, so Joshua wouldn't have to walk into a dark house.

She sat in front of the piano and ran her fingers over the keys, hoping to feel the warmth of his fingers on them. Her urgency to see Joshua multiplied. Why was she so desperate to see him? Sure, she was worried about him and his grandfather, but that couldn't be everything.

Then she understood. Joshua was finished with his composition, and Mr. Shin would be going home once he recovered from his surgery. Joshua didn't need her to help him through his creative block, and she didn't need to play for his grandfather anymore. Circumstances had necessitated their frequent meetings and brought them closer together. But those circumstances were now resolved. Would this relationship continue even when he didn't need her anymore?

There was still the premiere left. He would want to watch her introduce his new music to the world. What then? Wouldn't it make sense for Joshua to neatly wrap up their brief affair at the conclusion of everything they'd been working toward? After all, he didn't love her. They weren't meant to last.

A sob lodged itself in her throat, and her heart cracked open. Despite telling herself that she couldn't fall in love with Joshua because he would never love her back, she'd gone and done just that. Maybe she had never stopped loving him. She'd hidden from her emotions, her heartache, because she knew she would never have him again. But meeting him at the Neimans' dinner had awakened her dormant feelings for him.

She could've swallowed her pride and gone back home so her father would help the Chamber Music Society. There had been regret in his voice—he missed her. But she chose to involve Joshua because she couldn't stay away from him. She was searching for a way to be in his life again.

But soon there wouldn't be any reason for her to stay in his life. She stood from the piano and crumpled onto the sofa. What was she going to do? Wait for him to end things, then quietly walk out of his life?

Her phone chimed and she grabbed it off the coffee table. It was a text from Joshua.

The surgery went well and Grandfather is stable. I'll be home soon.

She slumped back down on the sofa. *Oh, thank God.* She was so relieved and happy that his grandfather was going to be all right. But she was terrified of how much hope the words *I'll be home soon* created inside her. She wanted to be home to him, because he already was her home.

She loved him and wanted to be with him. *Even if he doesn't love me back?* Maybe her love could be enough for both of them. But she'd promised him to keep love out of the equation…to not complicate things. Didn't she owe it to him to keep her promise? Whatever her reasons, she'd left him. He had every right to protect his heart from her. She couldn't ruin what they had now by telling him she loved him.

"Angie?" Joshua's deep voice snapped her out of her fog. She'd been so lost in her thoughts that she hadn't heard the door open.

She ran to the entryway and into his arms. He tucked her head under his chin and stood holding her for a long while. Finally, he pulled back and dropped a soft kiss on her lips. "Hey."

She kissed him back. "Hey."

"Thank you for coming," he said softly.

"I wanted to make sure you were okay." She cupped his cheek in the palm of her hand. "Are you okay?"

"I'm so relieved the surgery went well, but it was hell waiting." He pulled her back into his arms. "There were some complications and I was scared out of my mind."

"Now it's over and your grandfather is recovering. Everything is going to be okay."

"I know." Joshua dragged in an unsteady breath and blew it out, ruffling her hair. "I know."

"Have you eaten?" She stepped out of his embrace and tugged him toward the living room by his hand. "Do you want me to make something for you?"

"No." At some point, he was the one tugging her to the bedroom. "I just want to hold you."

Once they reached his bed, she helped him undress

with tender care and pulled the comforter over his naked body. Then she went to her side of the bed, undressed and slipped under the covers with him. He immediately gathered her into his arms until the entire length of her body was pressed against his. She drew her hand up and down his back, burrowing her cheek into the crook of his arm. The tension seeped out of his body and his breathing evened out.

"I like coming home to you," he murmured, his words slurred by the pull of sleep.

Hope sprung to life inside Angie, piercing her defensive walls. It took all her willpower to smother the hope before it overtook her whole being. His soft snore of exhaustion saved her from answering. It was for the best.

She'd broken his heart once. She didn't deserve another chance.

The music center's lounge hummed with life and excitement as the maestro's circle event got into full swing. Men and women in glittering formal wear mingled and laughed, sipping expensive champagne. The Chamber Music Society didn't skimp when it came to pampering their highest donors.

Joshua gulped down the rest of his champagne, letting his gaze take in the horde of people. He was once more attending as his grandfather's stand-in. Halabuji was recovering speedily from his surgery and wouldn't need his services much longer. Meanwhile, Joshua obligingly mingled with the other patrons at the gathering while stealing glances at Angie. He wanted to get her alone for a while, away from prying eyes. Sneaking around might have been fun when they were in college, but he didn't have the patience for it now. Even so, they couldn't be seen as more than casual acquaintances in front of her sisters.

She wanted to keep their relationship a secret from

them. That way, she wouldn't have to lie outright to her sisters to protect his identity. Joshua understood and appreciated how carefully she guarded his secret, but he had a feeling there was more to it. And he couldn't deny the sliver of hurt that burrowed into his heart. He didn't intend for their relationship to be a brief affair. Not anymore. How long could she hide their involvement from them? Or did she still believe that what they had was a fleeting interlude?

This longing and possessiveness had grown and solidified into a constant obsession since the night of his grandfather's surgery. Walking into his condo and finding her waiting there for him had almost brought him to his knees with gratitude and happiness. And the way she wrapped herself around his body and lent him her strength filled him with a sense of wholeness he'd never felt before. He'd fallen asleep in her arms believing that everything was going to be all right.

Angie looked stunning in her black strapless gown with her hair swept up into a loose chignon, revealing the graceful line of her neck. The Hana Trio had performed beautifully earlier this evening. She still had the afterglow of a successful performance, and his body flooded with heat every time he looked at her.

The musicians stayed for drinks with the patrons to answer any questions they might have. Angie had been speaking for a while with a silver-haired man with a smarmy smile, and the worm's eyes had never strayed far from her breasts. Joshua quashed the urge to give this guy a good shove. When he met Angie's gaze across the room, her eyes said *Save me*. That was all the encouragement he needed.

"I'm sorry to interrupt," Joshua said as he approached, not sounding sorry at all.

"Well, now… I…" the older man blubbered, suddenly torn away from his ogling.

Joshua turned to face Angie, half blocking her from the other patron. "I wanted to congratulate you on your performance tonight. You and your sisters sounded sublime."

"Thank you, Mr. Shin. You're too kind," she said with a grateful smile.

"May I walk you to the bar for a drink?" He offered her his arm.

"That sounds lovely." She linked her arm through his and turned to the silver-haired ass. "Thank you for your support of the Chamber Music Society."

"It's my pleasure, Ms. Han," the man tried to say graciously, but his pout ruined the effect.

Once they were out of earshot, Angie leaned toward him and whispered, "Thank you for rescuing me. I was seconds away from dumping my champagne over his head to make him stop staring at my cleavage."

"Happy to assist," Joshua said, grinning down at her. When they reached the bar, he handed her a fresh flute of champagne.

She took a sip, her nose wrinkling adorably. "I'm like a kid. I love how the bubbles tickle my throat."

"You look all grown-up to me," he said in a low voice.

A deep pink blush stained her cheeks. "Joshua, behave."

"I don't think I will," he whispered with a wolfish grin. "Meet me up those stairs in five minutes."

"What are you…?"

He walked away from her before she finished. After a quick glance around the crowd to make sure he wouldn't be noticed, he climbed the stairs to the next floor. And five minutes later Angie joined him.

"What is even up here?" he asked, looking down an austere corridor.

"More importantly, what are we doing up here?" she said. "The executive offices are up here, as well as a small library."

"Let's go to the library." He grabbed her hand and tugged her down the hall.

"We should get back." Even so, she ran along with him until she dug her heels in and stopped. When he looked askance at her, she opened one of the doors. "This is it. Were you so desperate for a tour?"

"I am desperate." The private library was small but stacked floor to ceiling with books. The rich crimson-and-gold carpet and the wooden shelves gave a rich, intimate feel to the room. He locked the door behind them. "But not for a tour."

"Joshua," she said sternly.

He pushed her up against a shelf and kissed her deeply, drawing a moan from her. He bent his head and eased her strapless dress down so he could kiss the sweet mounds of her breasts. She buried her hands in his hair and pressed herself against his lips.

A low chuckle escaped him, and a thrill slithered down his back. He loved how responsive she was to his touch and how her passion burned as hotly as his. He knelt at her feet and rose again, drawing her skirt up to her waist. He wanted her and he couldn't wait a second longer. When he looked in her eyes for acquiescence, she gave a quick nod and grabbed his lapels to pull him in for another searing kiss. He tasted champagne in her mouth as her slick tongue tangled with his.

He pushed aside her panties and slid his hand down to her core, and she jerked against him.

"God, you're so wet," he growled, inserting a finger inside her warmth.

"I want you inside me, Joshua."

With trembling hands, he reached for his wallet and

sheathed himself before driving into her to the hilt. Angie began to scream and he clamped his hand over her mouth.

"Shh. We need to be quiet."

Slowly, he began pumping into her, her back against the shelf and her legs wrapped tightly around his waist. Her deep moan was muffled behind his hand. When her tongue flicked out and licked his fingers, he groaned quietly and pushed his index finger into her mouth. She sucked on it, pulling it in and out with the rhythm of their coupling.

He was so damn close. He didn't know how much longer he could last.

"I can't hold on…" He shifted her hips and thrust deeper, harder. "Baby, come for me."

Her internal muscles clenched around him and she bit her lips to quiet her cry. All his control broke and he drove wildly into her before collapsing against her as his own climax claimed him.

They stood still until their panting evened out. She spoke first. "I think I quite enjoy being ravished."

"Do you now?" He grinned with satisfaction as he pulled away from her.

"I do." She primly smoothed out her skirt and adjusted her bodice. "How do I look?"

She was flushed and her chignon had come loose, but it wasn't readily apparent that she'd been ravished. "You look beautiful and professional."

She reached out and smoothed his hair. "And you look handsome and rich."

"Good." He chuckled. "Let's go downstairs and resume our roles."

"I'll go downstairs first. You could come down a few minutes later, okay?"

"Sounds like a plan." He spun her around and patted her bottom to urge her along.

With one last smile over her shoulder, she slipped out of the library. With his heart pounding inside him, he knew he would remember that smile for the rest of his life.

Eleven

Angie focused on the road and attempted to shake off the sense of impending doom that everything was coming to a close. It was a good thing that Mr. Shin would be discharged tomorrow. She was so happy that he was well enough to go home. But tonight would be the last time she performed for him at the hospital. Then her brief stint as a music therapist would come to an end.

She parked her car a good distance away from the main entrance of the hospital. It was silly. But it would be the last time Joshua walked her to her car like this… she wanted it to last as long as possible. She gave her head a firm shake. She was acting as though this would be the last time she saw him. Just the thought alone was enough to make her heart tear and bleed.

Her trek to the entrance was a slow crawl and her cello felt double its weight. She needed to stop feeling sorry for herself. She wanted to give Mr. Shin a performance he wouldn't forget. With her chin held high, she walked into the lobby and froze to the spot.

Joshua was waiting for her, typing furiously into his phone. She guessed it was an urgent business matter because two deep grooves had formed between his eyebrows, which always happened when he was intensely focused on something. She didn't want to disturb him, so she stood where she was until he lifted his head.

The smile that spread across his face made her heart soar. She ran the rest of the way to him and flung herself into his arms. With an "oof," he caught her in a tight embrace and lifted her off her feet, chuckling low in his chest.

"I missed you," she whispered.

His laughter quieted and his arms tightened around her. "I missed you, too."

Both joy and a boundless sadness filled her. She was his for now. That was all that mattered, but her heart screamed that it wasn't enough.

What is it that you want?

She wanted everything. But he'd once entrusted her with his heart, and she shattered it to pieces. What right did she have to ask him to trust her again? To love her again?

And if she ever got his assurance that this was more than a short-lived affair, she would have to tell her sisters the truth about her relationship with Joshua. Telling them that he was A.S. wasn't the problem—she trusted her sisters to keep his secret safe—but how could she tell them about their past? She would have to break their hearts by revealing a side to their father they would be better off not knowing. Their father might lose the closeness he shared with her sisters when they were all he had. She didn't wish that on him even if she couldn't forgive him for taking Joshua away from her. Maybe it was really better this way—this way no one got hurt. Except for her.

She pulled back from his embrace and linked her free hand with his. "So how's your grandfather doing?"

"He says he's feeling like a million bucks." Joshua grinned at her, smoothing his thumb back and forth over the back of her hand. "He's excited to be going home tomorrow."

When they arrived at the older man's hospital room, he welcomed Angie with open arms. She hugged him tight, emotion clogging her throat. She hadn't seen him since the surgery and she was grateful he was doing so well.

"You look well, Halabuji," she said, grasping his hand.

"What did I tell you? I told you I'll get better." He laughed and patted her hand. "I'm a man of my word."

"Is it selfish of me to be a little sad that I won't be able to play for you anymore?"

"I'm going to miss you, too, my dear." He glanced between her and Joshua. "But I have a feeling I'll be seeing you often."

Her cheeks burning, she sneaked a peek at Joshua, who smiled affectionately at his grandfather. "Stop teasing her, Halabuji. She's not here to be pestered by you."

"Insolent boy," his grandfather said mock sternly. "But you *are* here to play for me and there's nothing else I'd like better."

"There are a few pieces left on your list…" She sat down and positioned her cello.

"It's too hard to decide. You play everything so beautifully. I honestly could listen to you play scales all day."

"You sweet-talker." She laughed. "Why don't we make it a medley?"

"That sounds like the perfect solution," the patient heartily agreed.

Joshua watched the exchange with an amused smile.

When their eyes met, he gave her a playful wink. "Classical music lovers sure know how to rock it."

With her heart close to bursting, she played some songs sure to please, like "*My Favorite Things*" and "*Over the Rainbow*," but she ended the medley with a beloved classical piece, "The Swan," by Saint-Saëns.

Joshua and his grandfather clapped resoundingly, and the hospital staff gathered outside the door joined in. Angie blinked in surprise when one of the nurses entered and handed her a small bouquet.

"For me? I don't know what to say." She buried her nose in the flowers and breathed deeply.

"Ed was an absolute delight to have in our ward, but you coming to play for him was an extraspecial bonus for us," the nurse said earnestly.

"Thank you so much," Angie said, turning toward the door to include the other staff.

The nurse who gave her the flowers was the last to leave the room after checking on the patient.

"It looks like you provided music therapy for more than just me," Mr. Shin said in a pleased voice.

"I'm happy so many people got to enjoy my music."

"And more people will be able to listen to you play once the season begins." Joshua's grandfather scratched his chin. "Everyone seems to be aflutter over the premiere of that fellow A.S.'s new string trio."

She almost sprained her eyeballs to keep her gaze from flitting to Joshua. "Yes, the Chamber Music Society is very excited as well."

"I'm not so sure about him. He's a little bit too modern for me," A.S.'s grandfather declared.

Angie pressed her lips together to hold back her laugh, but one look at Joshua staring valiantly at the ceiling almost made her lose it. She cleared her throat. "Give him a try. He grows on you."

After they said their good-nights, Angie and Joshua walked out to the parking lot. The night air was cool against her skin, but her briefly forgotten doomsday mood overtook her again. This was their last walk to her car... Her steps were heavy but Joshua matched her pace and walked slowly beside her, not seeming to mind.

"He grows on you?" He bumped her with his shoulder.

Despite herself, she laughed. "What? I just wanted him to give you a chance."

"My own grandfather." Joshua shook his head with a wry smile.

"Do you plan on telling him someday?" she asked.

"Maybe, but not now." His expression turned somber. "I don't want to worry him."

"Worry him?"

He hesitated for a moment before he answered, "The board of directors is appointing Riddle's new CEO soon but... I have competition."

"I overheard your grandfather mention something about that..." she said. "But what does that have to do with you being A.S.?"

"If I told my grandfather right now, he might worry that my competition will find out about my identity and use it against me to win the CEO seat."

"Use it against you?" Alarm snaked through her. "How?"

"He'll try to convince the board of directors that I'm not committed to Riddle."

"But that's not true. There is no reason why you can't compose *and* run your company."

"I'm not sure what the board will believe with Nathan Whitley twisting the facts." Joshua sighed. "That's why I can't afford to have anyone find out who I am."

"Why didn't you tell me any of this before?"

"The same reason I haven't told my grandfather that

I'm A.S." He offered her a crooked smile. "I didn't want you to worry."

"Oh, Joshua." It hurt her to think he'd been carrying this burden all on his own.

When they reached her car, he kissed her deeply until they were both breathless. "Come home with me."

"After that kiss, I'm not going anywhere else." She stared wide-eyed at him.

"Then I'll be sure to kiss you like that every night." His smile was all male pride and arrogance.

Every night? She steeled herself against the burst of hope. He didn't mean anything by it.

They drove in separate cars to his condo. As usual, Joshua got there first and was waiting for her in the lobby. When they got into the elevator, he pressed her up against the wall and kissed her until she was burning up inside. Luckily, no one interrupted them.

As soon as the door to his place closed behind them, Joshua lifted her into his arms and headed to the bedroom. They tore at each other's clothes and tumbled onto the bed in a mad rush. She pushed him onto his back and straddled him. He held himself still and waited for her to make the next move, but his fingers dug into her hips.

"God, Angie," he growled. "I want you so much."

"And I want you," she said huskily.

Heady with power, she slowly lowered herself onto him, rocking and swerving her hips, until a tortured groan left his lips. For a while, he let her set the pace, but soon he gripped her hips and surged into her faster and harder. As they reached their climax together, they shouted each other's names, then collapsed onto the bed, wrecked and winded.

Once she caught her breath, she said, "Are you sure you want to kiss me like that *every* night?"

"Every fucking night," he said in a satisfied drawl and kissed her bare shoulder. "I can't get enough of you."

Joshua wanted her. But how long would that last? When the first flush of desire faded, what would they have left? No matter how hard she tried to deny it, a relationship built on a flitting attraction wasn't enough for her. Not anymore. She loved him and wanted forever with him.

She wouldn't let fear hold her back. If she had shared everything with him ten years ago, they might never have parted. She had to tell him how she felt about him—tell him that she loved him. Maybe he would be able to trust her with his heart again.

But what about her sisters and their father? Her sisters were strong and she trusted them to make the right decisions. All those years ago, she chose her mom over Joshua—over herself—and sacrificed their love. This time she was going to choose him no matter what. She was going to put their love above all else.

She deserved another chance. *They* deserved another chance.

Joshua stepped out of his condo the next morning, feeling a little off. Nights spent without Angie had that effect on him. She had gone back to her apartment last night because of an early morning rehearsal.

After pushing the button for the elevator, he pulled out his phone to take it off silent mode. He blinked at the screen. It seemed as though every notification possible was crowding his screen—emails, messages and phone calls.

Five of the phone calls were from his assistant, Janice. And there was also a text message from her.

Please give me a call before you come into the office.

The elevator doors opened but he stood where he was and dialed his assistant's number.

"Joshua." She answered on the first ring.

"What's going on, Janice?" He looked impatiently at his watch, wondering if he would be late for his morning meeting.

"It's…the news…" She had nerves of steel and was never at a loss for words. An ominous sense of wrongness settled over him. "They know who you are. Well, we all do now."

"You're not making any sense." His blood pounded in his ears and his fingers tightened around the phone. "Start from the beginning."

"The news is everywhere." She took an unsteady breath. "They're saying that you're the anonymous composer A.S."

Joshua's stomach dropped to the floor and he widened his stance to steady himself. After several attempts, he got his voice to work. "What's the situation at work?"

"It's not quite nine yet, but several board members have called and a couple executives have already come by. Once the workday starts, I have a feeling the phone is going to be ringing off the hook and there'll be a line outside your door."

"Janice, thank you for letting me know…and for not asking any questions. I'll tell you everything once I get into the office."

With his mind in a cloud of panic, he went back inside his condo on autopilot. Then he stood in the middle of the living room not knowing what to do…not knowing what to think. He hadn't meant to keep his identity a secret indefinitely, but he'd wanted to reveal it on his own time—on his own terms—after the CEO appointment.

But his worst fears had come to pass. He might lose his chance to become Riddle's next CEO. His family's legacy might be lost because of his choices. What must his parents think? And Halabuji…he didn't need this shock so soon after his surgery.

How had this happened? No one knew his identity. He'd made sure of that. No one other than… Angie. His heartbeat picked up and he began pacing. He shouldn't jump to nonsensical conclusions.

But s*he'd betrayed him once. Why wouldn't she do it again?* No, that had been for her sick mother. She had no reason to betray him. How could he even suspect her? He shook his head to clear it. She'd helped him through his creative block to compose the new string trio. She'd helped his grandfather's recovery with such generosity and kindness. And what about their relationship? They might not be in love, but what they had was real. Wasn't it?

"Joshua?" Angie's voice rang out from the hallway. It didn't occur to him to answer. He just stood where he was as she ran into the living room looking left and right. "Joshua."

She wrapped her arms around his waist and pressed herself against him, burying her face in his chest. He pulled her close and soaked up the solace she offered despite his splintered thoughts. He needed to calm down and think logically, but he was spinning out of control without anything to anchor him.

"I saw the news." She leaned back and stared up at him with concern and soft sympathy in her eyes. "Are you okay?"

"I… I don't know…" His mind spun in a blur of confused thoughts.

"We'll figure something out. It's going to be okay." She searched his face. "Do you know how this happened?"

"I have no idea." His gaze flitted away from her. "You're the only person who knows."

With a warm hand on his cheek, she turned him to face her again. "You know I would never reveal your secret, right?"

"Ri…right." He hesitated for the briefest second but

the blood drained out of her face. "Of course. Of course, I know you wouldn't."

She stepped out of his arms and retreated to the opposite side of the living room. "But you considered the possibility."

It wasn't a question. He couldn't even deny it. "I…"

"Did you believe it?" Hurt and anger snapped in her eyes. "Even for a second?"

"I don't…know," he said haltingly. Had he believed, however briefly, that she had betrayed him again? "Like I said, you're the only person who knows I'm A.S."

"You didn't answer my question. Did you believe that I leaked your secret?"

"I said I don't know." He threw his hands up in the air, suddenly defensive and scared. "Maybe you needed to drum up more media attention for the Chamber Music Society… The upcoming season is so important…"

Her sharp gasp stopped his blabber. "You thought I betrayed you for the society?"

"It's not important. It was just a passing thought." He ran his hand down his face. Where was she going with this? "I told you I know you weren't the one who revealed my identity."

"No, it *is* important because it shows you still don't trust me," she said, her voice breaking. "It's important because I love you, and…and I need you to trust me."

"You love me?" His heart hammered as joy threatened to take flight in his soul but he immediately crushed it.

"Yes," she whispered through pale lips. "I never stopped loving you."

"But we agreed to keep love out of our relationship." His accusation lingered in the air between them.

"I lied to myself so I could hold on to you as long as possible." Silent tears rolled down her cheeks.

"I told you I couldn't make any promises." Love was dangerous. Love could break him.

"I know." She wiped her tears away with both her hands. "I did this to myself."

She was hurting and he was the one hurting her, but he couldn't stop. He couldn't tell her what she wanted to hear. "You shouldn't have fallen in love with me."

"And I'm sorry I can't be here for you." Fresh tears filled her eyes and spilled down her face. "But now I know I wouldn't have been much help to you. You need someone you love—someone you trust—by your side. And I'm neither of those things."

"What are you saying?" His body shook with fear that began at his core.

"I'm saying I love you—" she took a shuddering breath "—but I can't be with you."

"You can't or you won't?" He clamped his mouth shut when she flinched. "What we have is good enough. We don't need love to complicate things."

"It's not good enough for me," she said with quiet strength. "Goodbye, Joshua."

"Please." He reached out for her but she was already turning her back to him.

When he heard the quiet click of the door shutting behind her, he stumbled onto the sofa because his legs couldn't hold him up. It wasn't supposed to hurt like this. Why did he hurt like this when he didn't love her? The answer was glaringly clear but he refused to face it. He laughed, a barren and hopeless sound. It was over. She was gone.

Numbness overtook him, and he welcomed it.

Twelve

Angie had to concentrate on the road. She couldn't let her emotions breach the dam she had erected until she was in a safe place. *Gas, blinker, brake, stop. Check the mirrors, change lanes, gas, brake.* She parked a bit too far from the curb, but it was the best she could do.

She got out of her car and walked to the intercom on unstable legs. *Please be home. Please be home.*

"Who is it?" Chloe asked through the intercom.

"It's me," she said shakily. Hearing her sister's voice almost undid her, but she had to keep it together until she was off the street. She had to hang on tight just a bit longer.

"Angie? Come on up."

She put one foot in front of the other until she got to Chloe's door. She knocked erratically. When the door opened and her sister's lovely face appeared in front of her, Angie fell into her arms, and the tears she'd held back poured out of her in a torrent of grief.

"Shh. You're okay." Her sister patted her back and held her tight. "You're okay."

When Angie's knees buckled, Chloe grabbed her by the waist and swung her limp arm over her shoulder to support her. Together they swayed and tripped as they made their way to the sofa. Luckily for them, Chloe's cozy graduate housing didn't require them to travel far.

Her baby sister laid her down on the couch, putting a pillow under her head and pulling a blanket over her. "I'm going to call Megan, then make you a nice cup of tea."

Angie tried to nod but all she could do was blink. With another worried glance, Chloe hurried to the kitchen, tapping on her phone. Her kitchen was only ten steps from the couch, but her muffled voice sounded far away. "Megan, it's me. I think you should come over."

Her sister's voice faded away and was replaced by Joshua's hard words. *You shouldn't have fallen in love with me.* Angie placed her hands over her ears and shut her eyes, but she still heard his voice and saw the accusation chiseled into his face.

The hope she'd been cradling in her heart dimmed and flickered out. She was cold. It was a brittle, biting cold that tore jaggedly into her bones. And she was so very tired. The fatigue slowly, slowly weighed her down, and she let the oblivion of sleep erase the nightmare in her mind.

"She wasn't even like this when we lost Mom," Chloe whispered.

"She was trying to be strong for us," Megan said. "I heard her sob night after night when she thought we were all asleep."

"But how could someone so strong crumble like this? What could've happened?" Her youngest sister's voice trembled slightly.

"Don't worry, Chloe. She'll tell us what happened when

she's ready, and we'll be here for her. Whatever it is, we'll help her get through it."

Megan's calm reassurance dulled the pain that threatened to engulf her once she let her consciousness return fully. She couldn't sleep forever. She needed to come back to her sisters even if she bled from the pain.

"I think she's awake." Chloe was jumped to her feet and was by her side in an instant.

With her baby sister's help, Angie pushed herself up into a sitting position. Then Megan and Chloe sat down on either side of her, each grabbing one of her hands.

"I don't know what happened, but we're here for you, Unni," Megan promised.

"And if you need us to beat anyone up, I'll happily kick some ass," Chloe said, trying to draw a smile out of Angie, but she didn't know if she would ever smile again.

"I love him." Her words left her dry mouth in a hoarse rasp. Chloe handed her the cup of water she had ready at the coffee table. Her sisters sat quietly and waited for her to continue. "I'm in love with Joshua Shin."

They looked at each other with wide eyes, then back at her.

"But the state you're in…does it have something to do with him being A.S.?" Megan gently prodded when Angie stopped to stare off into space.

"A part of him believes that I leaked the secret," Angie murmured. A strange kind of numbness was seeping into her. "He doesn't trust me."

"You already knew he was A.S.?" Chloe squeezed her hand. "Unni, you need to tell us from the beginning so we can understand."

The beginning. The first time she saw Joshua, he was laughing in the hallway of the music building. His head was thrown back and the strong column of his throat worked as laughter flowed out of him. He was so beautiful, he took her breath away. He was the first boy who had made her feel that way. If his eyes hadn't met hers across the hallway that day, would she not be hurting so much today?

She needed her sisters. Their love and support had helped her overcome her grief over their mother's death. She needed them to survive this. They had to know everything, so she started from the beginning.

Other than to squeeze her hand and wipe away her tears, her sisters let her talk without interruption. She broke down a few times while telling her story, but at last she got it all out. Then she cried. She let go of the last of her control and sobbed brokenly, mourning the loss of love and hope. And she hurt for Joshua. She hurt for what they could've been...so very much.

Her sisters hugged her from each side, and they sat quietly like that until her tears ebbed and her shaking eased. Angie felt hollowed out, but the burning pain in her heart had numbed with exhaustion.

"I had no idea Appa did that to you. I'm so sorry, Unni." Chloe's voice broke on the last words.

Out of the three of them, she was the closest to their father and he cherished her, his baby girl. Hearing how he'd treated Angie had to be shocking and painful for her.

"Chloe, you shouldn't let what happened between Appa and me to influence your relationship with him." Angie took a deep breath and continued, "He was distraught with Mom's diagnosis, and he didn't trust Joshua. Maybe he thought Joshua was only using me to get information about our company... I don't know. But I believe in his own way, Appa was trying to protect me. I think I'm beginning to forgive him."

Megan scoffed angrily but didn't say anything.

"Don't worry about me," Chloe quickly added. "Are *you* going to be okay?"

"I don't know." Tears filled her eyes again. Megan rubbed her back and made soothing noises as Angie cried quietly into her hand.

She didn't put on a brave face to protect her sisters. There was a crack in her soul that was growing bit by bit, and soon she would split in two. Her sisters had to help hold her together.

"I should've told him how I felt about him before this happened. I wanted to… I was going to…but I kept making excuses about the timing." Angie tore little pieces off the ball of tissue she was holding. "If I'd been braver, I would've told him and our relationship might've had a real chance."

"Or you could've lost what you had together," Megan said, tucking a strand of Angie's hair behind her ear. "He was adamant that he didn't want love and commitment from your relationship. Who in their right mind would find confessing their love easy in that situation?"

"The right thing to do is sometimes the hardest thing to do," Angie murmured.

"Even at a time like this, she's dropping nuggets of wisdom. Our older sister, ladies and gentlemen," Chloe quipped, linking her arm through Angie's.

Angie's watery laugh turned into a hiccup. "And I did the right thing today."

"But you love him…" Chloe said, the rims of her eyes turning red.

"I do." *With all my heart.* Angie swallowed the sob welling in her throat. She had to be strong. "But holding on to hope will destroy me. He'll never love me. I have to accept that and move on. That's the only way I can survive this."

Joshua left his condo with enough time to have an hour to spare before the board of directors' meeting. He had spent the last few days pouring over the arguments he intended to present to them. Nathan Whitley was reacting exactly as anticipated, bringing into question Joshua's ability to lead Riddle Incorporated when he had such an involved "hobby" on the side. The board members who already doubted his competence because of his age might be swayed by Whitley's baseless claims. To distract himself from his frustration, he turned on the radio to a local news station.

He listened with half an ear to the weather and traffic update. Then the public radio station thanked its supporters and sponsors before moving on to the latest news.

"Joshua Shin, the heir apparent to Riddle Incorporated, a thriving electronic components company in Los Angeles, has been revealed to be the famed composer, A.S. Despite the success of his work, Shin kept his identity as the composer a secret. The question is why? What had—"

He impatiently switched to his favorite classical station. He'd forgotten that he *was* the latest news for the time being. When the music ended, the host of the morning show introduced the upcoming piece.

"Next is a work by A.S., or shall we say, Joshua Shin—"

He turned off the radio altogether and sat through the traffic, drumming an agitated beat on the steering wheel with his fingers. He had to tune out all that noise. The media could speculate all they want. All that mattered was convincing the board of directors that appointing him as Riddle's next CEO was the best thing they could do for the company.

He had to focus on that and only that. He'd shut the door on everything else. Joshua fought to hold back his dammed-up emotions. He would collapse from their weight if he gave in.

Janice was waiting for him with a stack of files when he got to his office.

"Is everything ready?" he asked, heading straight for his desk.

"Yes, I made copies of the key graphs and charts for your presentation. The board members will have it right in front of them when you drive the point home."

"Thank you, Janice."

When she shut the door behind her, Joshua focused his attention on preparing for the board of directors meeting. He was still the best man for the CEO position. Being A.S. didn't change that fact. The board members needed reassurance of his competence and commitment to the company. Especially the ones who were already on the fence about his appointment. He intended to give them that reassurance.

A quick glance at his watch told him that it was game time. He fixed his tie, put on his jacket and walked out of his office, ready to get the job done. Once the meeting was called into session, Joshua went to stand at the head of the table and met the eyes of each of the board members. His father and grandfather weren't among them. They hadn't come. A muscle jumped in his jaw.

He'd visited his parents and grandfather the evening after the news broke. Despite their shock, his grandfather and mother were willing to listen, but his father just stared at the wall in front of him—not even acknowledging his presence.

Joshua had explained that music was a part of him and suppressing it would suffocate his soul—it was who he was. But he also reassured them that over the past few years, Riddle and its employees had come to mean the world to him. He wanted to continue his grandfather's and father's legacy. And he had no doubt that he had it in him to succeed at both music and business. They just needed to trust him.

Their absence was their answer. They didn't trust him. It felt like a physical blow and he gripped the edge of the table for support. But he had to pull himself together. He still had a job to do.

Just then, his father and grandfather entered the conference room. Other than the cane he was leaning on, Halabuji looked every bit his formidable self. And his father, the current CEO, walked in like he owned the room. They took their seats in the sudden hush.

Then his father met Joshua's eyes from across the table and gave him a firm nod. A pressing weight lifted from his chest and Joshua faced the board members with renewed determination.

"Let's skip the preamble and get to the crux of this meeting. I've been Riddle Incorporated's vice president of operations for the last three years, and the company's corresponding growth is irrefutable." Joshua's voice rang with confidence. "I've gathered some data for your review."

He clicked through the slides, pointing out key projects and contracts that contributed to the company's growth.

"I realize the news that I'm A.S. comes as a shock to many of you, but if you take a step back and reflect on it, you'll see that my competence as Riddle's future CEO shouldn't come into question." He paused for a moment. "The fact of the matter is I've been composing as A.S. the entire time I've been Riddle's Vice President of Operations." Murmurs rippled through the room. "Being a composer has not and will not hinder my ability to lead this company. You all have just seen concrete evidence of this fact."

"The CEO position isn't only about competence. It's about commitment," Richard Benson spoke up. "It's obvious music is your passion. Riddle Incorporated is just an afterthought for you."

"Riddle has been in my family for three generations. My love of music doesn't diminish the fact that I would do anything to protect my family's legacy," Joshua said with utmost sincerity.

"And is it Nathan Whitley's *passion* that has him moving from corporation to corporation every three, four years?" his father asked. "Or is the fattest compensation package driving his migration?"

"This meeting isn't about Mr. Whitley." Scott Grey loudly cleared his throat and addressed Joshua. "Have you ever thought about the impact your *other job* could have on Riddle?"

"The positive or the negative?" his grandfather interjected. "This presentation provided cold hard facts that being a composer hasn't negatively impacted his effectiveness as an executive of Riddle. As for the positive, I believe the media is quite captivated with the idea of Riddle's future CEO being a true Renaissance man."

"I'll be sure to explore that marketing angle in the future, Grandfather," Joshua said, making a show of jotting down the idea in his notebook. "If there are no more questions, I'll conclude my presentation. Thank you for your time."

"Thank you, Mr. Shin. I'm sure everyone here agrees that our questions have been satisfactorily answered. We'll vote for Riddle Incorporated's new CEO," Clarice Wong looked over at Joshua and held his gaze for an unblinking moment, "at the next regularly scheduled board meeting. This meeting is adjourned."

Joshua had done everything he could to make sure he was still in the running for the CEO position. He hoped it was enough. Several board members shook his hand before going on their way. As the conference room emptied out, he walked up to his father and grandfather.

"Thank you for trusting me." His voice was thick with emotion. "I won't let you down."

"I know you won't," his father said simply.

"And Angie was right about your music." His grandfather coughed, his eyes red with unshed tears. "A.S.'s music does grow on you."

Joshua looked at the two men he looked up to most in this world and smiled. He could face anything with them by his side.

"Now, get back to work." His father stood from his chair. "I'm still the CEO of this company. Don't let me see you slacking off."

Joshua returned to his office and fell into his chair. Along with the relief from his successful presentation, exhaustion rolled in, threatening to flatten him. He'd hardly slept since the news broke, and most of his energy had been spent on protecting his family's legacy and keeping his emotions at bay.

He lasted until the end of the day by losing himself in work. His feet felt like they were encased in cement as he made his way to his car, and cold sweat broke out on his forehead as he drove home.

A few steps away from his condo, he stumbled and caught himself against the hallway wall. He walked the rest of the way with his hand on the wall, then leaned against the door as he unlocked it with unsteady hands. He took a step inside his condo, then another before he fell to his knees.

He had no strength left in him to stem the tide of emotions that crashed into him. Regret. Grief. Loss. More than anything, loss tore away at him. *Angie.* She was gone.

Joshua pushed himself off the floor and grabbed a bottle of Scotch from the bar. He slumped down on the sofa and took a long swig straight from the bottle. Heat burned down his throat and settled in his stomach. He took another swig. He couldn't get drunk fast enough.

It hurt. It was too much to bear. He'd lost her once and it had broken him. This time, he'd sworn he would guard his heart so she wouldn't be able to hurt him. But he was the one who had hurt her, driving a knife into his own heart in the process. He'd lost her again. He tilted back the bottle and drank, hoping the Scotch would help dull the pain. It didn't.

Had he truly believed for even a second that she'd betrayed him? He huffed a humorless laugh. Not even for a second. Then why couldn't he have just told her that? Because he was a coward. For a decade, he'd believed that she left him because she cared more about money than him. And when they met again, he feared that she would walk away from him any time it served her better. Even after learning the truth—that it broke her heart to leave him—he was so afraid of getting hurt again that he'd pushed her away. He'd let her believe that he didn't trust her.

Oh, God. She loved him. She'd offered him her heart and he'd thrown the beautiful gift back in her face. It gutted him to imagine how much he'd hurt her but he couldn't let himself drown in the pain. He had to fix this. He had to make things right and win her back because…he was in love with her.

Joshua had been too afraid to face his feelings because he didn't think he could survive another heartbreak. But what he really couldn't survive was living a lifetime without her.

Even if it was too late—*God, don't let it be too late*—he wanted her to know that he loved her more than anything in the world. That he trusted her with his heart and soul. He was willing to risk everything if it meant having her. Fear would not hold him back anymore.

Thirteen

"Knock, knock," Angie announced herself as she walked through the open door of Janet's office.

Her mentor pulled off her reading glasses and stood up to hug her. "Hello, my dear. How are you?"

"I'm fine," she said automatically, even though it wasn't true. It had been close to a month since she left Joshua but her wound still felt raw. "How about you?"

"Working my tail off for the season opening. It's exhausting but exhilarating at the same time."

"I have to confess I'm a little nervous." Angie settled herself in one of the guest chairs. "You usually don't call me into your office unless you want to talk business."

"Well, this could be good news or bad news, depending on how you look at it," Janet said enigmatically.

"That's not helping. Please just tell me."

"A.S. came in to see Thomas yesterday afternoon with a proposal," her mentor said. Angie's heart dipped as though she was speeding down a roller coaster. "He wants the music he wrote for the Hana Trio to be returned to him."

"What? No." Devastation crashed into Angie.

Did Joshua resent her so much that he would risk the Chamber Music Society's survival to punish her? Didn't he understand it would've hurt her too much to stay with him knowing that he didn't trust her? That he didn't love her?

"He wants it returned because he had a sudden inspiration for a new piece that was perfect for the trio." Janet gazed steadily at her. "He hopes you agree once you see the music."

Angie was speechless. The roller coaster was making a slow climb and she didn't know how far the fall might be. Why would he write another piece? What did he want?

"I know that only leaves you with a couple of weeks to practice it, but you girls can do it," her mentor soothed, thinking her silence was a sign of her concern.

"Of course," Angie said with more confidence than she felt. "We'll make time for extra practices and get the piece ready for opening night."

"I never did ask you how you knew A.S.," Janet began gently, "but I can't help but think that there's some history between the two of you. In addition to writing a new piece for the Hana Trio, he offered to conduct one of his own pieces with the chamber orchestra on opening night. I think his eagerness to help the society has to do with his dedication to you."

"I... I can't..." Angie stuttered. Why was he doing this? She was barely starting to function again. She couldn't do this. She couldn't hope. "I'll tell you someday, but I can't right now."

"As I told you before, you don't need to tell me anything you're not ready to. Just know that I'm always here for you." Janet handed her a folder of sheet music. "Here's the new piece. Let me know if you need anything."

Clutching the folder to her chest, Angie bid a hasty farewell and headed for the parking lot. Once she was sitting in her car, she opened the folder and pulled out the music. Despite her turmoil, she couldn't wait to see what he'd done. Maybe he'd written a new piece because *they* had worked on the other one together. Sadness threatened to overwhelm her, but she pushed it aside. No more feeling sorry for herself.

Her eyes flitted through the notes, and she felt her excitement grow. It was brilliant. Truly brilliant. Joshua's talent was a gift to the world. Despite everything, she was so proud of him.

She headed straight home. Her fingertips were tingling with the urge to play the new piece, and her foot grew heavy on the gas pedal. For the first time in weeks, a flutter of excitement touched her heart, and the world lost some of its dull, gray cast.

Angie loved coming home, but today it felt as though she had reached an oasis after wandering in the desert for days. When she let herself in, she quickly slipped her shoes off and ran to open the curtains to let in the afternoon light. Then she went to her practice corner and placed the new string trio on her music stand. She removed her cello from its case, and took a deep breath to quiet her mind. From the moment her bow touched the strings, she was sucked into another world. It was a world where only music existed and she was part of the music.

Through the flowing melody, she saw the first sparks of attraction between her and Joshua as they fought to deny it. Then the fire caught, making it impossible to ignore the attraction. The fire spread and grew into a bonfire just as their passion had caught and burned between them. They couldn't get enough of each other. It was a thirst that couldn't be quenched. The notes grew strong and powerful and her body moved with the music.

Then the fire settled into a smooth, flowing form— still hot and fiery—but calmer. That was when their relationship grew into something more, and her feelings for Joshua grew. Every moment they shared was warm and precious, and her heart blossomed with the glow of happiness. The music became rich, more melodic. It was beautiful.

She had anticipated what would come next. The storm. The sky tore open and rain pounded on the fire. The smooth flames twisted in agony, steam floating off the dying embers. The deep, dark strains of the music became frantic, tragic. She didn't know when she started crying but tears streamed down her cheeks. Her heart clenched and she couldn't take a full breath. The rhythm grew faster and faster, then screeched to an abrupt halt.

There were three bars of rest but the quiet was filled with the beating of her heart. Then poignant, tender notes filled the silence, and she heard the sound of hope. Against all odds, the next soft, gentle wave of music coaxed the fire back to life. And the piece ended with a last hopeful note hanging in the air, like a tendril of smoke rising into the sky.

Angie put aside her cello and buried her face in her hands. Sobs wracked her body. The new string trio touched her to the core of her soul. She saw her love for Joshua in it, and improbably, his love for her. Why would he do this to her? What did he want from her?

Maybe it had nothing to do with her. This brilliant music might've been born out of his newfound freedom. With his identity revealed, his creativity had been unleashed. This piece might be telling a completely different story from what she heard. It had to be. She would be a fool if she believed it could be anything else. She was meant to play the music and she would do that. And that would be all.

She purposefully walked over to the side table for some tissues and blew her nose. Enough crying. Even though it was the music that had made her cry, it was also because it reminded her of Joshua and their relationship. Well, no more crying over him. She had to move on.

Then she cried again in the shower. She felt a bit rebellious about it by then. It had only been a month. Didn't she have the right to take some time to get over losing the love of her life for the second time?

Without bothering to dry it, she piled her hair on top of her head in a messy bun and put on some well-worn sweats that hung off her body. She hadn't been able to eat lately. She sighed and headed to the kitchen to reheat some chicken soup Megan had made for her when she was here a couple nights ago.

Her sisters have been taking turns checking in on her. A part of her wanted to be left alone, but she wasn't doing a very good job taking care of herself, so she was grateful for her sisters' fussing.

Angie took the bowl of soup to the dining room table and sat down to eat. She swirled her spoon around and around to let it cool a bit.

She missed Joshua so much. She desperately wanted to see his handsome face. But would she still want to see his face if it was shadowed with accusation and resentment? She didn't know.

She wished she'd been braver and confessed her love to him sooner. But he had seemed shocked and appalled when she told him. They'd agreed to keep love out of the equation, but their relationship had been real. They had cared about each other and understood each other. Didn't that count for something? And even without the words, she had loved him. Had he not felt it? Had he not returned the feeling in some way?

No. Even if she'd told him she loved him before the secret was out, he wouldn't have been able to love her back. How could there be love without trust? There was never any hope for them. Maybe it was for the best that he'd broken her heart now.

The soup had turned cold before she even tasted it. Suddenly, she couldn't force herself to swallow a single spoonful. She pushed back her chair and went to lie down on the living room couch, her slippered feet scuffing the floor. She couldn't stand being alone with her thoughts, so she turned on her favorite classical music station. The music soothed her like nothing else could and her eye lids grew heavy. Sleep would be a welcome escape. She began drifting off...

"We have a special guest for you today. We know who the anonymous composer A.S. is. But now we get to meet the man who discovered A.S.'s true identity."

Angie sat up so quickly that a pang of dizziness swept through her. The man, a journalist for a small magazine, explained how he'd been searching for A.S.'s identity for the past couple years. She stopped listening when he went on about stumbling upon a shell corporation and a business account. And there it was. Proof that she wasn't the one who had leaked his identity.

If he still had doubts about her involvement in leaking his secret, Joshua would soon learn that she wasn't the one who sold him out. Then what? Would he regret doubting her? Would he regret casting aside her love as though it was an inconvenience to him? It didn't matter. None of it mattered.

It was too late.

Joshua dug the heels of his palms into his blurry eyes then refocused on the computer screen in front of him. It was close to the end of the day and weariness bore down on him. He'd come into the office at seven in the morning even though he'd been there until 2:00 a.m. the night before. Cleaning up the issues following his unveiling as A.S. had taken time away from his duties at Riddle, and a mountain of work awaited him.

He'd done an interview with a trusted local news station to tell the story of his journey as a composer and corporate executive from his own perspective. There was no point in hiding from the media at this point. It was better to face them on his own terms to stem any rumors or speculations. Any remaining questions should be resolved once the interview aired.

The screen blurred in front of him and he rubbed his tired eyes. The grueling hours weren't strictly necessary, but work distracted him from thinking about Angie. He missed her so much. It was as though he was deprived of something essential to his life, to his survival.

He gave in to the urge to check his phone again. No missed calls. It was foolish to wait for her call, but he couldn't help himself. What did he expect? That Angie was going to see the new string trio he wrote and immediately understand that he loved her? And call to tell him she loved him, too? He huffed a humorless laugh.

There had been no creative block this time. The music had come to him as naturally as a breeze blowing through the trees. He'd been immature to think that music and Angie existed as one synergetic force—that losing her meant that he would lose his music, too. He understood now that his love of music was his alone. Nothing could take it away from him except for his own stubbornness. Perhaps he had been grasping at whatever excuse he could find to stop himself from falling in love with Angie. But that had been a hopeless cause from the start.

It was his denial of his feelings for Angie that had par-

alyzed him from composing the first string trio. He had
bound and gagged his soul so he wouldn't have to admit
that he loved her. How could he have composed like that?
Music was born from his soul after all. Once his soul was
freed, the music had flowed through him.

But so did the anguish. He hardly ate or slept, guilt and
regret plaguing him day and night. He wanted to run to
her right now and beg for her forgiveness. But now was
not the time. She had to focus on the Chamber Music Society's first performance of the season and the premiere
of the new piece. Nevertheless, it took all his willpower
to stop himself from running to her, and he didn't know
how much longer he could last.

Meanwhile, he did everything he could to be worthy
of her love. First was rewriting the string trio. What he'd
written before had been good, but it wasn't the best that
he could give her. She deserved his best. And this new
piece was his love letter to her—his apology, his hope
for a second chance. The music had begged to be written. Begged to be hers.

He'd also volunteered to conduct one of his own pieces
with the chamber orchestra on opening night. The Chamber Music Society was so important to her, he wanted to
help make their season a success. It had the added bonus
of making him even busier than he was now. Rehearsals
would take three to four hours out of his day until the
performance two weeks from now. Maybe he would be
so exhausted that he could sleep for a few hours at night.

Joshua desperately hoped he was doing enough to make
Angie give him a chance to talk to her. All he wanted was
a chance. Nothing he said might convince her to forgive
him—fear struck through him at the thought—but he had
to try. He had to show her that he trusted her and loved
her with all his heart.

A glance at his watch told him that he needed to leave

for his first rehearsal with the chamber orchestra. He hadn't conducted since his college days, but he knew what his music should sound like. He was confident that he would be able to work well with the orchestra. His only fear and hope was that he might run into Angie. All members of the Chamber Music Society were rehearsing at the performance center in preparation for the opening night.

He reread the email he'd been composing to Nexus before he hit send. Then he grabbed his suit jacket off the coat hanger and walked out of his office.

"Oh, good," Janice said. "You're leaving on time for once."

"I'm just stepping out for a few hours. I'll be back later this evening."

"You're going to burn yourself out working those outrageous hours," his assistant chided.

"I'm fine." He gave her a small smile. "I'll see you tomorrow."

Joshua made good time to the concert hall and walked in with excitement unfurling in his stomach. To hear his music played in front of him by a live orchestra, one that he was conducting, no less, would be exhilarating. It still amazed him how not having to hide his identity as A.S. anymore gave him so much freedom.

He stepped on stage with his heart beating hard in his chest. The dark wooden panels of the stage and the deep burgundy chairs filling the auditorium made everything all the more real to him. He'd stayed on the outskirts of the classical music industry for the past few years, and he was finally stepping into the middle of it.

The members of the chamber orchestra welcomed him with resounding applause. He bowed deeply at the waist, showing his appreciation, before taking the podium.

"I'm honored to be in front of this amazing orchestra." There was more applause. "It's beyond exciting to finally hear this piece played live the way I heard it in my head as I wrote it."

When he picked up the baton, the orchestra readied their instruments and gave him their full attention.

The music they made together filled him with awe and humility. He never appreciated his decision to become a composer more than he did at that moment. And the darkness that had wrapped around him when he lost Angie lightened slightly. But his joy would only be complete if he was able to share moments like this with her.

When the rehearsal was over, he chatted with a few members of the orchestra out in the hallway, adrenaline still coursing through him. Then time stopped. Because when he looked up, he saw Angie standing a few steps away from him.

Her eyes widened in her pale face and she gasped. She'd lost weight and had dark circles under her eyes. He blamed himself for that. Even so, she looked so beautiful that heat prickled behind his lids. He wanted to run to her. Fall on his knees and beg for his forgiveness, but her sisters stepped protectively in front of her.

"Angie…" He took a step toward her.

"Mr. Shin," Megan cut him off. "Fancy meeting you here. Oh, wait. How could I forget? You're the famed composer A.S. I guess it isn't that much of a surprise."

Angie's gaze found his, then skittered away. Then her lips firmed into a determined line and she met his eyes again. She put a hand on her sister's arm and walked up to him. But she stopped just out of his reach. He clenched and unclenched his hands, forcing himself to stand still.

"Hello, Joshua." Angie's voice was distant but polite.

"Angie." He searched for something he could say to her. Anything. "I hope the new string trio meets your approval."

"It's a beautiful piece. We're practicing hard to do it

justice." She turned around to include her sisters in the statement.

"Speaking of practice—" Chloe stepped up and grabbed Angie's hand "—we should get going."

Without a backward look, the Han sisters walked past him into the concert hall. Steeling himself, he stumbled out to the parking lot and collapsed into his car. Seeing her only made him miss her more. The coldness in her eyes shot fear through him, but had he expected anything different? He had hurt her, but he would make it up to her.

They belonged together. He would prove it to her.

Fourteen

The first performance of the season always carried with it a special kind of anticipation that was felt by both the performers and the audience. It was a reunion after months apart. That anticipation was doubled this season because this was the first performance since the pandemic. The thrill of seeing each other was marred only by a certain nervousness about breaking the ice and getting comfortable with each other again after being apart for over a year and a half.

The Hana Trio was premiering Joshua's composition later in the program, and in the meantime Angie and her sisters stayed backstage, watching the chamber orchestra. The orchestra members were seated and ready, and their conductor took the podium. Slowly, the buzzing chatter of the audience quieted down, and anticipation built to a fever pitch in the ensuing silence.

As the first notes of the season resounded through the concert hall, chills ran down Angie's arms, a rare smile lifting the corners of her mouth. It happened every season, but the beauty of the music filled her with gratitude after the long absence.

Angie and her sisters erupted into applause along with the audience when the orchestra finished its first piece. Their fellow musicians had played beautifully and Angie was so proud of them. They worked hard and it showed.

She felt a tingling warmth on the back of her neck and knew that Joshua was standing behind her. He was there to conduct the next piece—his own composition. News of his special appearance had caused tonight's performance to sell out in record time. In a way, it was his debut in the music world. They had never seen him before.

It should feel incongruous that he was also the new CEO of Riddle Incorporated, but this version of him—both CEO and composer—was who he was meant to be. Despite her heartache, she was relieved to hear of his appointment as Riddle's CEO. She had been afraid that the revelation of his secret identity would give his rival an edge over him, but Joshua had done it. He would carry on his family's legacy just as he wanted.

But Angie still didn't know why he was going out of his way to help the society. He had to be busier than ever. Perhaps, it was his way of assuaging his guilt for breaking her heart. Well, that was his business.

Although she was trembling inside, she put a cool, professional expression and turned to face him.

"Joshua."

He looked unfairly handsome in his tuxedo, but she kept her gaze glued to his eyes.

"Angie," he said formally, and nodded at her sisters, who reluctantly acknowledged him.

When he made no move to walk past them, Angie figured he was nervous. They might not be lovers anymore, but they were fellow musicians. She wanted to help him. "Good luck out there."

Joshua's eyes widened in surprise, then a ghost of a smile appeared on his lips. "Thank you."

He finally walked past them, but looked over his shoulder at Angie for a long moment before taking the stage. Angie's heart stuttered at the longing in his eyes. No, she was just imagining things. There was nothing between them anymore. Even so, she walked closer to the curtains so she could watch him on the podium.

Silence fell over the audience again as Joshua lifted his baton. His movements weren't as practiced and artful as the conductor before him, but he moved with a natural grace and passion as he led the orchestra in his composition. She had heard this piece played many times over, but it sounded new and thrilling under his guidance. So this was how he heard the music in his head. Watching him conduct his own music felt like an intimate look into his soul. The audience was captivated, and she was with them. It was a performance she would never forget. When Joshua exited the stage through the other side, she pulled herself out of the trance.

"Girls, we're up," Angie said to her sisters. Pride filled her heart as she prepared to go out on stage.

She and her sisters were dressed in sapphire blue tonight. Angie wore a strapless, floor-length silk gown with an empire waist and a full, flowing skirt. Megan's asymmetrical one-shouldered dress hugged her figure and flared out midcalf like an inverted blossoming flower. Chloe had chosen a cap-sleeved, A-line dress with a sleek bodice. All the gowns were rich in color and simple in design. For a finishing touch, all three sisters wore identical black ribbons around their waists.

"We got this." Chloe shuffled her feet, wearing her

game face, which was adorably incongruous with her formal gown.

"We're going to blow them away." Megan smiled with glowing confidence. "Let's go."

The three of them stepped out onto the stage. The auditorium was packed, and Angie's pulse quickened with adrenaline and anticipation. Playing live in front of such a big audience thrilled the performer in her. She and her sisters bowed to the applause and took their seats.

Vibrant silence descended in the auditorium once more and it was the Hana Trio's turn to fill the room with their music. Megan raised her bow, and Angie and Chloe followed suit. And at Megan's nod, everything fell away and the music took over.

Maybe it was her desire to do the music justice, or maybe it was seeing Joshua bare his soul while conducting his piece, but overwhelming tides of emotion crashed into Angie and flowed through her fingers as she played. More than ever, she and her sisters played as one—as *hana*—and the sound they produced was stunningly harmonious.

When the final note played out, Angie and her sisters lowered their bows together. Thundering applause broke out and the audience jumped to their feet in a standing ovation. She and her sisters exchanged glances filled with awe and joy, and stood from their seats to take their bows. The applause continued even as they left the stage.

Still holding their instruments, they gave each other one-armed hugs, laughing and wiping away happy tears.

"I'm so proud of you," Angie said.

"I'm proud of us," Chloe chimed in.

"Me, too." Megan pulled their youngest sister to her and smacked a kiss on her cheek.

They put their instruments away and returned to listen to the rest of the program. The chamber orchestra played its final piece and the curtain closed. The backstage was soon awash with a sea of performers, conductors, directors and the society's board members. As colleague after colleague congratulated Angie and her sisters, she couldn't help but scan the crowd for a glimpse of Joshua. But he was nowhere to be seen.

What had he thought of their performance? Was he satisfied with the premiere of his new work? She hoped he was happy, and rightfully proud. If the audience's reaction was any indication, the piece was destined to be another success.

"Girls," Janet called out, walking across the room with her arms wide open. She pulled all of them into a group hug. "You sounded sublime. You made that string trio come alive."

"Thank you." Angie hugged her mentor back, glad to have made her proud.

Her sisters left to join the merry throng, and Janet continued, "I want to thank you for everything you did for the Chamber Music Society. Without your help, we would never have gotten A.S. to collaborate with us."

"You should thank him. I really didn't do anything," Angie said quietly.

She could hardly believe that it was only a few months ago that she barged into Joshua's office to coerce him into composing a new piece for the society. They had come so far from then, but now...it was all over. All her energy suddenly drained out of her.

"Angie, are you okay? You've gone pale," Janet said, holding her gently by the arm.

"I think I should call it a day. Everything turned out beautifully, but it's a lot," Angie said with a strained smile. "Can you let my sisters know that I left early to rest?"

"Of course, my dear." Her mentor studied her with worried eyes. "Drive safe."

Angie pulled her cello by her side as she walked to her

car, hardly noticing her surroundings. She and Joshua had no reason to meet again. Everything they'd agreed to was wrapped up neatly with a bow. Searing pain dug into her chest and she could hardly breathe. It was really over.

When she got to her car, she hefted her cello into the rear and lowered herself into the driver's seat. She headed home, holding herself together. She wiped impatiently at the hot tears on her cheeks, struggling to keep her misty eyes trained on the road.

Would they still have been together if his identity hadn't been revealed? Maybe. She wouldn't have had the courage to leave him on her own. Then what? Would she have settled for their arrangement as long as she could be with him, even though it lacked true commitment? No. Their relationship would've ended sooner or later.

Being with him made her happier than she'd ever been. They had real affection and respect for one another. But that wouldn't have been enough. She deserved to be loved—wholeheartedly and without reserve. If he couldn't give that to her, it was better that it ended now rather than later.

Taking in a shuddering breath, Angie clenched her jaw to stop the tears from flowing. Her limbs felt leaden and she couldn't wait to get home. She just wanted to collapse into bed and sleep until she stopped hurting.

She drove past the front entrance of her apartment building to the attached parking garage, but screeched to a halt when she saw Joshua's tall form lit by the dim light of the entryway. Rolling down her window, she shouted across the street, "What are you doing here?"

"Can we talk?" he yelled back, running down the stairs toward her car. "I just want to talk."

Angie continued into the parking garage; she didn't want cars backing up behind her. What was he doing here? He wanted to talk? Talk about what? He was probably here to apologize for believing she could have revealed his identity. Should she give him that? Forgive him for not trusting her? Did she want to take that weight off his conscience?

She parked and walked down the corridor leading to the lobby and the main entrance. Joshua was leaning limply against the wall outside. His head and shoulders drooped low, as though they were too heavy for his body. Everything about his body language told her he was dejected…devastated.

Confused…and yes…worried, Angie rushed to open the door. "Joshua?"

His head shot up at the sound of her voice. At first, his expression was disbelieving, then something bright and vulnerable, like hope, lit in his eyes. "Angie. You drove away. I thought…"

She felt herself reacting to the light in his eyes, but shrank back in fear. She didn't want to feel hope for something that could never be. She wrapped her heart in another layer of armor. "Why are you here?"

He took a step closer to her and she flinched. The fragile hope in his expression seemed to dim a little, but he drew himself up and said in a determined voice, "I want us to talk."

"What's there to talk about? We've already said everything we could say to each other."

"That's not true. I… I have things left to say to you." His Adam's apple bobbed as he swallowed. "Things that have to be said."

What was the harm of one last talk? It broke her heart to see him, but never seeing him again was going to hurt more. If she let him in, she would at least be able to spend a little more time with him before they said goodbye forever.

"Fine. We can talk in my apartment." She stepped back and opened the door wider for him to come through.

They walked silently to the elevators, then down the gloomy hallway. Once they were inside her apartment, the space suddenly felt too small with Joshua's tall, broad body occupying it. Their formal attire seemed out of place in her cozy living room, but she sat down on the sofa and offered him the seat on the other end.

He sat and swiped his hand down his face. He looked haggard but still achingly handsome in his tux with his bow tie undone and hanging from his collar. Despite his insistence that they talk, he sat staring wordlessly across the room.

She wasn't impatient for him to start. Taking her time, she drank in every detail of his face and body. Being wrapped up in him had made her feel so safe and content. Would she ever find that with someone else? It seemed impossible now, but she had to hope that there would be happiness in the future for her.

"I'm sorry," he said, his voice breaking. "I'm so sorry, Angie."

"You're sorry?" Her voice rose as dormant anger awoke in her. "So that's why you wanted to talk. You want me to assuage your guilt."

"That's not true…" He reached out to her in entreaty but she evaded his touch.

"Isn't it?" Tears prickled behind her eyes, but she refused to cry in front of him. "You thought I was the one who revealed your identity. And when I told you I loved you, you cast my words aside like you found it offensive. Now you want me to *absolve* you of that?"

"You deserve my apology a thousand times over but I don't deserve your forgiveness. I hurt you and that's something I have to live with. But please listen. All I want is a chance to explain…a chance to make it up to you." His whole body stilled and his eyes seemed to will her to look at him. "I love you, Angie."

"You don't love me, Joshua." Something between a sob and an incredulous laugh tore from her. "How can you love me when you believe I betrayed you? How can there be love without trust?"

"But I do trust you. And I know you'd never knowingly hurt me," he said in a rush, as though he was afraid that he was running out of time. "I relived every moment of our horrible fight and forced myself to *feel* everything. I forced myself to face the truth. Angie, I never believed you betrayed me. Not even for a second."

"Stop. Just stop." She wanted to plug her ears and stop listening. The hope that filled her was so terrifying... If that hope shattered, she wouldn't be able handle it. "You and I are finished. You made sure of that."

Joshua knelt on the ground in front of her and grasped her hand. She didn't pull it away, but she turned her head to the side.

"In the last few months, you showed me in so many ways that you loved me. You helped me get through my creative block with faith and patience, and you truly cared about my grandfather and played for him from your heart. Someone like that would never have revealed my secret to the world. You're incapable of doing something so selfish and calculating."

"None of that matters now." She jerked her hand out of his grasp and glared at him. "Your sudden change of heart only came after you found out who revealed your secret. You don't really trust me. Believing me now that you have concrete evidence of who betrayed you doesn't mean anything."

"I never believed you betrayed me. Please. My love for you isn't a *change of heart* and it has nothing to do with the bastard who exposed me," Joshua implored. "I only stayed away until now because I didn't know whether you would be able to forgive me. I didn't want to cause you more turmoil while you were preparing for tonight's concert."

"Trust goes both ways. Why should I trust you now?"

His eyes jumped around the room in a panic then light dawned on his face. "The new string trio. I wrote that for you before I found out who leaked my identity. I wrote that for you as soon as I realized I love you."

The tears she'd been holding back flowed down her cheeks. She was so confused. So lost. A vise gripped her heart and she couldn't take a full breath.

"Think, Angie. When did you receive the new piece from the Chamber Music Society? You got it before that bastard came to bask in the limelight, right?"

It was true. She received the new string trio just before the journalist came forward. Joshua had to have written it prior to then. But what does the new string trio prove?

"I was blocked because I was denying my love for you. How could I compose when I was lying to myself? I was able to compose the first string trio with your help, but it was still missing something because the lie held me back," he explained as though she'd spoken her question out loud. "Once I admitted to myself that I loved you, I knew I had to write you a new piece—one that was worthy of you. Unleashed from my lie, I was able to pour my everything into that music. That string trio is my apology, my love letter and my hope for our future. It is my soul. Surely, you felt that."

Angie covered her mouth as a sob broke through. She felt it all. She didn't allow herself to believe it, but the music had spoken to her. "If you love me, then why? Why did you push me away like that?"

"I was afraid. Fear held me back from admitting my love for you. Fear made me believe that you would inevitably leave me. I thought I could protect myself from more hurt if I pushed you away. I'm so sorry for letting you walk away believing that I didn't trust you. That I didn't love you." He grasped her arms and stared into her eyes. "I love you, Angie. More than life. Please give me a chance to make it up to you. I'll make you happy with everything in me."

She cried freely now, sobs wracking her body. He meant it. She felt it in her bones. He loved her.

"Please don't cry." He hesitated for a moment before he gently pulled her into his arms. "I can't take it. Please."

"I want to believe you." She wrapped her arms around his neck and hung on tight. He had found the courage to trust her with his heart again. Now she had to find the courage to accept his love. "No, I do believe you, but I'm so scared."

"I'm scared, too, but we can do this together. We're meant for each other. How else could I have fallen in love with the same woman twice?" He cradled her head with his hand. "I loved the girl you were and I love the woman you've become. You're the only one I've ever loved. Angie, you're it for me."

And he was the only one for her. She took a shuddering breath and leaned back to look into his eyes. "I love you, too. I never stopped loving you."

"Say it again," he whispered as though he might awaken from a dream. "Say you love me."

"I love you, Joshua." Her soul rejoiced at being able to freely say those words to him. Because he was hers. Hers to love. She cupped his beautiful face in her hand. "Tell me you're mine."

"I'm yours. Yours alone. Yours forever." His eyes roamed her face, filled with wonder and happiness. "I'm never letting you go again."

"Promise?" Her smile glowed from the depth of her.

"With all my heart." He smoothed her hair away from her face—his touch reverent. "I want to spend a life time with you if you'll have me. Will you marry me, Angie?"

"Yes." Her breath caught in her throat and tears filled her eyes again. The happiest tears. "I'll marry you."

Joshua cradled her face between his hands and kissed her with aching tenderness. She kissed him back with her heart singing, sealing their promise of forever.

* * * * *

MIDNIGHT SON

BARBARA DUNLOP

For my fabulous sister-in-law, Melinda

One

"You'll just have to learn how to be rich, Sophie," my friend Tasha Gillen stated as if it was the easiest thing in the world.

We were standing on the breezy deck of a house for sale just north of Seattle. The bright blue Pacific Ocean spread out in front of us, edged by a steep slope of jagged rocks. The deck held a cozy cluster of rattan furniture with burgundy cushions, slatted teak side tables and a brick barbecue nook. Behind us, a high wall of glass fronted a lavish great room.

"What would I even do with six bathrooms?" I was single and feeling that singleness more and more each day.

Last year, my three closest girlfriends had been single right along with me. But they weren't anymore, none of them, and it was hard not to feel abandoned.

"You don't need to use them all at once," she said, her tone telling me I was being obstinate.

It wasn't on purpose, but she wasn't wrong about my attitude. "I can't see myself rotating through them."

"You're going to have guests, Sophie."

"Who? All my best friends have new lives."

Tasha, Layla and Brooklyn had all fallen in love, gotten married and relocated away from Seattle.

"You're playing the sympathy card?" Tasha chided.

"A little," I admitted.

Deep down, I was happy for my friends. I truly was. But they'd always been my support system, and my life had taken a very odd turn. I couldn't shake the feeling I was scrambling to catch up.

I'd helped create a new technology last summer. Called Sweet Tech, it produced fancy desserts for high-end restaurants. It was very successful—far more successful than any of the creators had ever imagined.

With the help of Tasha's husband, Jamie, we'd sold the patent to a Japanese company for a whole lot of money. The deal included royalties, which meant the checks just kept coming and coming. Having all that money turned out to be trickier than I'd expected.

"Poor little rich girl?" Tasha asked with a lilting laugh to her voice.

"Yes," I said.

She'd hit the nail on the head.

"I'm all alone," I complained. "I'm at loose ends. I'm bored."

I didn't have a job. I didn't feel productive. I didn't have any reason to go anywhere or do anything, and that was more than a little unsettling.

Tasha turned to gaze at the house again. "This would be a great place to be alone and bored. It's stunning."

I turned to take it in again. "I find it daunting."

"Don't be such a chicken."

"I'm not afraid of it." I wasn't—at least not exactly.

"You're intimidated by it," she said, and she was right.

"How would I even keep it clean?" Doing the floors alone would take an entire day.

"Sophie, you get people for that."

I laughed at the thought of getting "people." I mean, there was embracing the wealth, and then there was going full-on pretentious about it.

"You really do suck at being rich," Tasha said.

"Yeah? Well, it sounds like you've gone completely over to the dark side."

Tasha and her economist husband, Jamie, had tapped into some genius-like investment abilities and were making a ton of money in the stock market.

"I never said *I* had people," she said.

"You have people," I countered, certain of it.

She'd tossed the idea out way too casually to not be doing it herself.

"Okay, I have a couple of people. The point is you can afford a nice house like this. You can afford to live on the waterfront. I know you love the waterfront."

"I do." I did. And this house was pretty much my dream.

"You can do whatever you want now, Sophie. You should do it."

"But what *is* it?" I didn't quite keep the desperation out of my voice.

Sure, I could do whatever I wanted. Trouble was, I hadn't figured out what that was. And I'd tried pretty hard.

I'd donated to charity. Because if you had any kind of a soul at all, that's the first thing you did with an influx of unexpected money. Our local literacy organization, the hospital and the animal shelter were grateful for my support. They'd sent me thank-you letters and toasted me at parties.

But it wasn't a day-to-day gig. They didn't need me to help run things. And even if they did, I didn't have expertise in health care or teaching or animal care for that matter. I hadn't even had a pet since I was six and my bunny, Snuggles, died.

It was just me and my mom while I was growing up, and her job as a nurse didn't pay all that much. That meant we rented. She told me apartments were a lot easier to find if you didn't have a pet. So, Snuggles was my first and last pet.

"You're not going to find a small house on the waterfront," Tasha injected into our paused conversation. "The property is way too valuable."

Our house-hunting efforts had definitely proved that correct.

This was the tenth waterfront house we'd toured this week, and it was a showplace like all the rest. But I had to admit I really loved this one, even if I would have to draw myself a map to keep from getting lost between the master bedroom and the kitchen.

It was hard to wrap my head around the fact that I could buy it on a whim—just whip out the old checkbook and write down a number with a whole lot of zeros from a bank account with even more zeros.

"Maybe I could live in the garage suite," I said. "Rent the rest of it out to a family with five kids."

Tasha spread her arms. "And give up the deck?"

"I do love this deck."

Anybody would love this deck. It ran for sixty feet in three sections across the front of the living room, dining room, den and the master bedroom. Beneath it, on the lower floor, a giant games room opened to a patio with a pool and hot tub. You'd get shade down there on hot summer days, plus privacy.

"The place comes furnished," Tasha said.

I wasn't sure if that was a plus or a minus. "I already have furniture."

"You have a sofa, a kitchen table and a bed."

"It's a great sofa."

I thought about my comfy leather sofa—how long I'd saved up for it, how I'd thought such a fine and expensive piece of furniture would last me for decades.

That was one of the things about unexpected money. It obliterated most of your previous life efforts. I could buy ten leather sofas now, or a hundred leather sofas. Or I could just move into a place like this where a professional decorator had coordinated the sofas, armchairs, tables and everything else.

"Can you see yourself living here?" Tasha asked. "That's the real question. Does rich Sophie see herself sipping morning coffee on the deck or curled up in front of the stone fireplace reading a book?"

I could see that. Trouble was I couldn't see anything else. I couldn't just read and drink coffee for the rest of my life.

"I thought about park beautification," I said.

"Excuse me?" Tasha was clearly confused by my swing in topics.

I tried to explain. "After the charities, I thought about getting involved in the community. City beautification is a big thing right now. It turns out I can adopt a park."

"Or you could buy a house," Tasha said.

"And just stand around inside it all day long?"

"It's a house, Sophie. You do the same things as you do in your apartment right now, only better, bigger, more beautiful and very comfortable."

"You like gardening more than I do," I said, casting my

mind back to the park adoption website. "I'm really not crazy about gardening."

I did enjoy being in gardens. They were beautiful and they smelled so nice. But I didn't particularly like digging around in the dirt. I didn't see the appeal of that.

Tasha glanced over her shoulder at what served as the house's yard. "Those rocks down there look pretty low maintenance to me."

"I meant in the park."

"Why are we still talking about a park?"

"Because buying a house is the easy part. I'm thinking about what else rich people do. Now that I think of it, *you* should get involved in city beautification. You're the gardener. And you have time on your hands. You'd like the park thing."

"I'd also like the library thing."

That made sense since Tasha had a degree in library science.

"I joined the library board," she said.

"Really?" I don't know why it surprised me. It was a perfect fit.

"We're starting an outreach literacy enrichment program into elementary schools," she said.

"See, I need to find something like that."

"You will. You'll get the hang of being rich."

"Maybe," I said. I wasn't convinced. "I've got *all* this money."

Tasha smiled. "So, buy a house. Buy *this* house. I can tell you love it."

It was true. I did love it. Its size made me twitchy, but I found I didn't want to leave. I wanted to stay right here and enjoy it. I supposed that meant I should.

"And then what?" I asked.

Tasha shook her head in sympathy. She looped her arm around me and gave my shoulder a squeeze. "It's too bad you don't have a few impoverished relatives."

"So, they could come and live with me in this big place?" I said it as a joke. But I wasn't joking.

If I had any family, I'd definitely help them out somehow.

It would be great if I had siblings or cousins, or maybe some nieces and nephews who needed a good college education.

But my mom had been adopted and an only child. Her parents were dead now, and she hadn't known anything about her birth history or her adoptive parents' extended family.

On my dad's side, well, she'd told me he was a one-night stand. She'd been pretty up-front about it. He was a married pilot with the Australian Air Force.

They'd met at a hospital in Germany, where she was on a six-week assignment. He'd flown relief supplies for the UN in Bosnia and had suffered a head wound when his plane came under fire, and he was forced to crash land. His copilot hadn't been so lucky and had died.

My biological father had been far away from home, injured and despondent. My mom had comforted him in his grief. They'd spent a weekend together that she swore she never regretted—especially because it gave her me.

"Have you ever looked?" Tasha asked.

I struggled to remember the conversation thread. "Looked for what?"

"Your family."

"I really don't think there's anyone out there to find."

I had absolutely no intention of messing up my biological father's life.

Still, for a moment I pictured myself as an amateur sleuth digging into my heritage. Come to think of it, sleuthing might be fun. Maybe my rich future was in solving mysteries. I could set up a command centre in the games room. There was plenty of space down there.

"Go to one of those family history websites," Tasha said. "Take a DNA test."

It took me about half a second to decide it was a good idea.

"No harm in finding out," she continued. "If they look dangerous, you don't have to contact them."

I felt a surge of excitement. But behind it came a healthy dose of reality. Something like a fifth cousin twice removed—

which was who I'd most likely find—wasn't exactly close family.

Still…

I was on a plane to Alaska—Anchorage to be precise. I was in first class because Tasha told me that's what rich people did. At first, she'd told me rich people would charter a private jet.

Seriously? First class was perfectly fine, thank you very much.

It was more than perfectly fine. It was champagne and orange juice, white linens, hot towels, delicate croissants with apricot jam and feeling guilty about the people squished into the coach seats fine.

It had turned out I had a first cousin, well a *likely* first cousin. We were a 13 percent DNA match. According to the website, that was very significant. His name was Mason Cambridge. He was thirty-five years old, born in Alaska, and he worked for an Anchorage-based company called Kodiak Communications.

I'd looked him up and found a few photos. He didn't have much of a social media presence, although the local newspapers had a few articles about him attending civic events. I was guessing it didn't take all that much to gain notoriety in a place like Alaska.

I'd found his physical address, but no phone number or email.

I knew I could probably track him down through Kodiak Communications, but I'd decided I wanted to meet him in person.

If he was going to send me packing, I'd rather have a short face-to-face conversation with my only known relative. Better that than a cryptic email or phone call brushing me off.

I knew I was taking the chance of being disappointed, of wasting a long trip. But it wasn't like I had a whole lot of other things to do with my time.

The purchase agreement on the new house wouldn't clear escrow for a few more days. And Tasha was back in LA now.

I might as well have an adventure.

As the plane started its descent, I was feeling sufficiently full, sufficiently pampered and more than sufficiently nervous about showing up unannounced at Mason Cambridge's house.

I rented a car at the airport and discovered Anchorage was a whole lot bigger than I'd expected—with a towering downtown, sprawling suburbs, plus green spaces and mountain vistas. If it wasn't for the GPS, I'd have gotten lost in the maze of streets.

The route eventually took me south of the city and soon the houses disappeared. Trees closed in from the hillsides to the east. From the west, waves from the inlet lapped the shore.

I saw a fox in the grass beside the highway. Then I saw a moose. When I saw two bears cross the road in front of me, I nearly pulled a U-turn and headed back to the airport. There wasn't much traffic on the stretch of road, and I had a momentary vision of breaking down and having the little SUV attacked by rogue grizzlies.

But then I came to a gravel road, and the GPS told me to turn. I was grateful the rental clerk had given me a four-wheel drive.

The road was smooth enough, considering it was gravel. But it was a winding climb through towering spruce, fir and birch trees. I started to picture Mason Cambridge as a mountain man with a grizzled beard and buckskin clothing.

He hadn't looked that way in the two newspaper photos. But maybe he dressed up to go to town. It was possible he spent most of his life traipsing around in the bush, only shaving and showering for monthly forays into Anchorage for supplies—I was guessing maybe beans, bacon and hardtack.

Then I crested the hill and came out of the trees. The gravel road ended and turned to smooth pavement.

I was surprised, shocked really, to see an expansive lush lawn dotted with tidy flower beds and sculpted shrubs. The odd pine tree rose around the edges, blending with the surrounding forest.

In the middle of the yard was a house so big it took my breath away.

Made of huge, polished logs with towering windows, peaked roofs and impressive stonework, it sprawled across the lawn two stories high, stretching out in two separate wings. It looked like a five-star hotel. In fact, I wondered if it was a five-star hotel. There were no fewer than ten vehicles parked out front.

I pulled in and parked at the end of the row.

It was possible Mason Cambridge lived in a hotel. It was odd, but definitely possible.

I set the brake and shut off the SUV.

I slung my purse over my shoulder and opened the driver's door, stepping outside.

There was a chill in the fresh-smelling air. A breeze caught me, blowing my hair into my face. I wished I'd thought to put it in a ponytail or a braid. It was too long to be loose in wind like this.

As a temporary fix, I raked it back and held it at the base of my neck as I crossed the parking lot.

I had to fight the feeling I didn't belong here. The place had a hushed air about it that didn't invite random interlopers. If I had to guess, I'd say it catered to the very rich and the very privileged.

I might have money in the bank now, but I couldn't pull off rich and privileged. My jeans were from a department store, and my purse had been on sale for twenty dollars. I didn't even want to think about my ankle boots. They were scuffed brown leather with low blocky heels. They'd seen a lot of miles. But I'd expected to need practical footwear in Alaska.

I owned my fair share of high-heeled pumps and sandals, but they were all back in my apartment in Seattle.

The place seemed to grow bigger as I got closer. The porch was at least thirty feet wide, five steps up leading up to an oversize set of wooden double doors.

I climbed the stairs and stared at the doors for a minute, wondering if I should knock or just walk in.

If it was a hotel lobby, nobody would hear a knock.

If it was a private home, it would be insufferably rude and probably illegal to just walk right in.

I thought about it and decided if it was a private home, the door would be locked.

That made sense.

I liked the analysis.

Conversely, if the door was unlocked, it was a hotel lobby.

I pressed my thumb on the latch.

It gave.

I pushed a little, and the door swung easily open to the entry. Beamed ceilings soared out over a beautifully appointed lobby.

I stepped inside. Beyond the entrance and beyond several groupings of cream-colored leather furniture, I took in a wall of glass that revealed amazing views. To the west, I could see over the cliffs and down to the ocean. South and east, a grassy meadow stretched for what looked like miles. I saw a fence line and squinted closer to eye brown animals dotting the grass.

"Can I help you with something?" The voice was deeply masculine.

"Yes," I said, giving myself a shake and closing the door behind me.

When I met his gaze, my heart took a funny beat and my lungs suddenly tightened in my chest.

He took a few steps toward me, looking like a jungle cat, all smooth motion and fluid limbs, with an arresting stare that was assessing me as—I don't know—prey?

He was darkly handsome with tousled hair, intense blue eyes, a Mediterranean tan and a whisker shadow covering his square chin. Tall, with broad shoulders and a confident stance, he was everything a woman might expect if looking for perfection.

His brow rose in a question. "Help you with…?"

"I…uh…"

He waited, while I felt more awkward by the second. I mean, it was maybe seven or eight seconds altogether, but they sure seemed long.

"I'm looking for Mason Cambridge," I finally said.

"Is Mason expecting you?"

"No. Is he here?"

"Not at the moment."

"But he lives here." I looked around again.

Mason Cambridge had to be very wealthy to live in a hotel like this.

It didn't seem like he was going to need my money for anything.

That was a small disappointment, but he was too old for college anyway. So, I couldn't have sponsored him in that.

"This *is* the Cambridge house," the man said.

It took a second for his words to sink in.

I felt a rush of mortification. "This isn't a hotel?" Oh, man. I'd just walked right on into a private home.

"Are you looking for a hotel?" the man asked.

"I'm looking for Mason Cambridge. I didn't mean to walk in on you. I thought..." I was looking around again and realizing this didn't really look like a hotel lobby. There was no check-in desk, no reception or bell staff anywhere.

"What do you want with Mason?" the man asked.

I wasn't about to explain myself to a stranger. "Do you know when he'll be back?"

"None of your business."

Neither of us were about to win any etiquette awards here. But I was entitled to my privacy, and I had a legitimate purpose in looking for Mason.

"If you met him at a bar—"

"I did *not* meet him at a bar." I knew who was losing the etiquette battle with that crack.

"At a party?" the man asked.

"Why does your mind immediately go there?" I challenged.

He looked me up and down. His expression told me he liked what he saw. He didn't even try to hide it.

Wow. No manners whatsoever.

"Because you're his type," the man said.

"I'm not his type." I paused. "At least... I mean... I've never met him."

The man gave a calculating smile.

"What?" I asked, puzzled.

"I'm glad to hear he doesn't have dibs." There was a glow of appreciation in his eyes.

"Seriously?"

He thought he could flirt with me?

He shrugged. "So, shoot me."

"Would you please just tell me what time Mason will be back? I'll go away and try this again later. I'll knock next time, I promise."

The man's smile widened. He was enjoying my embarrassment. "Sometime later today."

"Fine," I said.

"Where are you staying?"

The question took me aback.

"In case Mason wants to call you. You don't strike me as an Alaskan. I'm Nathaniel Stone, by the way."

"Sophie Crush. I'm not an Alaskan."

"Are you staying at the Tidal, the Mountainside?"

"I haven't decided." I supposed I could have made a hotel reservation before I left Seattle. But I hadn't considered that Anchorage would be such a hotbed of tourism that I couldn't find a place once I got here.

"Then I'd recommend the Tidal. Or if you're on a budget, the Pine Bird is nice."

I choked back a laugh at that, thinking about my recent conversations with Tasha. No, I wasn't on a budget.

"Something funny?" he asked.

I shook my head. "Not at all."

"Random laughter? I'd feel obligated to warn Mason if you're…pulling some kind of prank…"

"I'm not…pulling some kind of prank. And I'm not on a budget. I'll try the Tidal."

"Good choice. What do you want me to tell Mason?"

It was a fair question. I tried to frame something innocuous to say. But then the door opened behind me, and Nathaniel's focus moved there.

"Oh, good," he said to whoever had entered. "You're early. Mason, Sophie Crush is here to see you."

My stomach fluttered in anticipation. I took a swift bracing breath and turned to find another fit, good-looking man standing in the doorway.

"Hel…lo," he said, drawing out the word like it was a compliment.

"She won't tell me what she wants," Nathaniel said.

Mason gave a carefree grin. "I don't care what she wants." His gaze met my eyes. "The answer is yes."

I knew I had to nip this flirtatious thing in the bud. If I didn't, we were both going to be very embarrassed.

So I just came out with it. "I'm your cousin."

Mason's expression froze.

"What?" Nathaniel asked from behind me.

After my revelation, they hustled me into a private room.

I presumed it was the den, since most of the small mansions I'd viewed had dens. They tended to be decorated with bookshelves, writing tables and oversize chairs, with warm light that beamed against gleaming wood-paneled walls.

This one was no different, and Mason closed its door behind the three of us.

The ceiling was lower than in the great room—it was twelve feet high instead of twenty-four. I sat down in an armchair facing a set of windows that overlooked the pretty front yard and the forest beyond.

Outside, everything was fresh and green. The air was crystal clear, the sky blue with a few wispy clouds. I didn't see any more wildlife scampering around the lawn, but it felt like something interesting could emerge from the forest at any moment. Alaska felt surreal—like I'd wandered up to the edge of the earth.

I was sitting on one of four brown-and-butter-yellow plaid armchairs. Mason was across a low glass-topped table from me. Nathaniel was next to him.

I couldn't help checking out Mason's features and comparing them to mine.

His chin was different, square where mine was narrow. His nose was bigger, but in the ballpark of the same straight shape. His eyes were lighter brown. Mine were espresso dark. His hair was almost black, full and thick to my golden brown.

If I had to pick one thing, I'd say his lips looked familiar. There was something about the way he smiled and their shape when he talked.

"Can I get anyone a drink?" Mason asked.

"Seriously?" Nathaniel put in with an edge to his voice.

"Well, *you* sure look like you could use one," Mason said to Nathaniel. He looked to me. "Sophie? We have wine, red or white. Or whiskey if you need it."

"I'm not the one who's been shocked by the news," I said. "I'm fine. I don't need anything to drink."

"Whiskey, Stone?" Mason asked Nathaniel as he rose. "I'm having one. Personally, I am a little shocked by the news."

"Fine," Nathaniel said.

It was clear they weren't thrilled to meet me. They'd obviously had no idea that I might exist, which got me to thinking through the possible relationships.

If the genetic connection was on my mother's side, she might have been a shameful secret who was adopted out years ago and kept under wraps all this time. If it was my father's side, then maybe he wasn't an Australian air force officer. Maybe he was a black sheep that the family had shipped off to Australia years ago over a scandal. And now I was coming back to haunt his family.

The possibilities were endless, really. And some of them could be bad. It might be best for me to leave before I caused any real trouble. I didn't want to cause any trouble.

Mason dropped ice cubes into two heavy glasses. Then he poured the whiskey from a bottle at a wet bar.

Nathaniel was glaring at me.

I tried not to look back while we waited.

He seemed more disturbed by my appearance than Mason did.

That got me wondering who he was and how he fit into the family. His eyes were deep blue, and he looked nothing like either of us.

"Does the test say for sure that we're cousins?" Mason asked as he sat back down.

"She could be making the whole thing up," Nathaniel said.

"In this day and age?" Mason asked him. "It won't take long to prove it one way or another."

"She can do a lot of damage along the way."

"I don't want to do any damage," I felt compelled to say. "I thought this might be good news, fun news."

"Fun for you," Nathaniel said. "Announcing you're a long-lost cousin to the owners of the biggest telecommunications company in Alaska."

The statement took me by surprise. It was the first I'd heard about the family owning anything, never mind Kodiak Communications. But that certainly explained the huge house. It also meant nobody in the family would need my financial assistance… Ever.

I tried not to be disappointed by that. "I didn't know they owned it."

Nathaniel coughed out a laugh of disbelief.

"We can give her the benefit of the doubt," Mason said to him.

"I'm not here to cause you any grief." I said to Mason, ignoring Nathaniel.

"So, cousins for sure?" Mason asked.

"I could be your great-aunt or you could be my great-uncle based on the common DNA percentage. But given our ages, first cousins seems a whole lot more likely."

"*First* cousins," Mason said and seemed to ponder.

"That's what the report said." I didn't have anything more to add.

Maybe I should have gone for the deluxe DNA package. It hadn't seemed worth the extra cost at the time, since I was only looking for the basics.

"What report?" Nathaniel asked. "From where? Who did it? Do you have a copy?"

"Stone," Mason said in a warning voice.

"If this is a shakedown," Nathaniel said back.

I stood. "Listen, I didn't do this to cause trouble for anyone." I looked at Mason. "I just wanted to meet you. I've met you. Clearly, I'm not a happy surprise, so I'll just head on back to Seattle before—"

"Don't," Mason said.

"Mason." Nathaniel turned Mason's name into a warning.

"Please sit down," Mason said.

I found myself looking at Nathaniel. I wasn't seeking his permission, but I was gauging his mood.

His brow was furrowed, and his mouth was turned down in a frown.

Okay, mood gauged.

"Ignore him," Mason said.

Nathaniel's voice sounded strangled. "You know what this will—"

"Sending her away won't change anything," Mason said. "We have to protect the family."

Mason gestured to the armchair behind me. "Please."

"I want to do the right thing." I truly did.

I didn't know what I'd expected to find in coming to Alaska—maybe to be greeted with open arms, to find a big, cheery extended family sitting around a kitchen table sharing pot roast, a fiftysomething aunt who baked sugar cookies, a jovial uncle who told rambling stories. I realized my imagination had a distinct Norman Rockwell bent to it.

"Sitting down is the right thing to do." Mason looked sincere.

I sat.

"My mother was an only child," Mason said. "My father only has a brother, Braxton. I take it you're in your late twenties?"

I nodded.

"Then logic says you were conceived while my uncle Braxton was happily married to Aunt Christine. That's the only way I can see where I end up with a first cousin."

"Could your mother have had a brother?" I asked Mason.

"Definitely not. She lived in Alaska her whole life. Everybody knew the family."

"A secret half brother?" I asked, covering all the bases.

"That would make you a half cousin. The DNA percentage would be different."

"Do we really need to walk through hypotheticals?" Nathaniel asked, his tone revealing frustration. "Do you want money? Is that it?"

"Stop it," Mason barked at him.

Nathaniel's suspicions revealed his own nature, since dishonest people always looked for dishonesty in others. So, mood noted and ethics noted.

"Let's find out what she wants and get on with it," Nathaniel said.

"Don't judge me by your standards," I responded.

His eyes narrowed and his jaw went tight.

"She's got you there," Mason said. Then he took a swig of his whiskey.

"I'll write you a check right here and now," Nathaniel said.

I stood. "Well, see, that's the fatal flaw in your logic. The *very* last thing I want is money."

Before I could make a dramatic march from the room, the door swung open.

I turned to see a fiftysomething man filling the opening.

He was tall with a distinguished bearing and a stern expression. He wore a charcoal blazer over a white dress shirt. His streaked gray hair was combed back from his forehead, while his face was shadowed by a short graying beard.

"What's going on here?" he asked in a commanding voice.

Both Nathaniel and Mason came to their feet.

"Uncle," Mason said with a nod.

"Hello, Braxton," Nathaniel said.

Braxton's gaze shifted to me. His eyes were just like mine—espresso dark.

"And who's this?" he asked.

Two

Braxton's penetrating gaze bore down on me. He obviously expected an answer.

"This is Sophie Crush," Nathaniel said.

There was a beat of silence in the room.

"And?" Braxton prompted, clearly looking for more information.

I thought I should let Mason take the lead. But he didn't, and the silence stretched.

"I'm from Seattle," I said, stepping forward to offer my hand. "It's nice to meet you... Braxton?"

"Braxton Cambridge," he said as we shook.

His hand was broad, slightly callused. His grip was restrained, as if he knew his own strength and didn't want to take a chance of hurting me.

"Sophie Crush," I repeated.

"She's here to see Mason," Nathaniel said.

Braxton looked past me to the other two men. "Is there something I should know?"

"No," Nathaniel quickly said.

I let my hand go lax, and Braxton let it go as I glanced over my shoulder at Nathaniel. I didn't appreciate the way he'd beat Mason to the answer, and I let my expression tell him that.

"Yes," Mason answered Braxton.

Nathaniel gave him a glare. "Can we not wait—"

"I think we've waited long enough," Mason said.

"I'm not having fun here," Braxton said in a dark voice.

"Braxton, you should sit down," Mason said.

Braxton looked me up and down. "Is she pregnant?"

"Why does everyone go there?" I asked.

Mason looked confused.

"Nathaniel thought I was your one-night-stand."

Nathaniel frowned. "I never said—"

"You *strongly* suggested," I reminded him, and he shut his mouth.

"Nobody's pregnant," Mason said. For a moment he looked like he was going to add something more, but he didn't.

"Business?" Braxton asked, voice still gruff.

"No," Mason said.

"Depends on how you define *business*," Nathaniel muttered.

"I told you this is not about money," I shot back, losing my patience. "It's not *nearly* about money." Then I calmed myself. To Braxton, I said, "This can all end in two minutes with me walking out the door and never coming back."

Braxton's complexion looked a little darker now than it had a few seconds ago.

"That's not how this is going to end," Mason said.

"She's made a perfectly reasonable offer," Nathaniel said to Mason.

"Somebody start *talking*!" Braxton all but shouted.

Another silence took over the room.

"Sit down, Uncle," Mason said.

With a huff of impatience, Braxton marched to the nearest chair.

Nathaniel dropped down next to him in the chair I'd just vacated.

I took Nathaniel's chair and Mason sat back down in front of his drink.

"Sophie is my cousin," Mason said.

"Is what she *claims*," Nathaniel finished.

"Based on a DNA test," I added so that Braxton would have the entire picture.

Braxton's gaze jumped from Mason to Nathaniel and finally to me.

It took him a moment to speak. "*Who* are you?"

"Sophie Crush from Seattle. My mom was Jessica Crush. That was her maiden name too. She never did get married. She was a nurse, trained in the military."

Braxton looked to Mason. "What *is* this? Does Xavier know about this?"

"We just found out ourselves," Mason said.

"Sophie showed up half an hour ago," Nathaniel said. "Out of the blue."

"From Seattle." For some reason I felt compelled to repeat that.

"My dad doesn't know," Mason said. "At least I *presume* he doesn't know." He looked over at me for an answer.

"I don't think he knows." At least as far as I knew, nobody did.

"This makes no sense," Braxton said. "Who…" He thought for a minute. Then his expression turned to a very dark scowl. His tone was a near roar. "She's *lying*."

That was it.

I was done.

I came to my feet and slung my small purse back over my left shoulder. "It's been—" I almost said nice "—interesting meeting you," I said to Mason.

I gave Nathaniel a curt nod.

"I'm not a liar," I said to Braxton, who was now very red in the face. "But I can see that it's better for you if I am. So, goodbye, all."

I started for the door.

"Stop!" Mason cried out, coming to his feet. "This is ridiculous. Making her go away won't change anything. If she's my cousin, I want to know."

"She's not your cousin," Braxton said.

"Are you positive?" Mason asked him.

I paused with my hand on the doorknob. I didn't have to turn around to know Braxton had risen to his feet. I could hear it in his voice.

"I was *never* unfaithful. *Ever*," he said.

"Then how do you explain Sophie?" Mason's tone was reasonable.

"She's lying, obviously," Nathaniel said.

"Stone, you don't know that for sure," Mason said.

"Well, *you* should know that for sure, *nephew*," Braxton said.

"There's a simple way to prove it," Mason said.

I turned back. "You're welcome to a copy of the DNA test. But I'm still leaving. I didn't show up here to get in the middle of a family fight."

"You *caused* the family fight," Nathaniel said.

"Shut up, Stone," Mason said.

"I'm not about to trust her DNA test," Nathaniel said.

"I can tell you 100 percent it's a fake," Braxton said.

"She can take another one," Mason suggested. "If you're willing," he said to me. To Braxton he said, "Pick a doctor, pick a clinic. Find someone or something you trust."

Braxton's expression relaxed. He seemed to contemplate this for a second and then sent me a sly smile. "Sure." He paused, seemingly waiting for me to back down.

I was a little surprised at his confidence. Given that I wasn't making any of this up, he had to know there was at least a small chance he was going to get caught. Where was his confidence coming from?

"Okay," I said, mostly because I was warming up to Mason.

Braxton's eyes narrowed, like he was trying to guess my game.

I stared straight back. I wasn't playing any game.

"Let me talk to Sophie alone," he said.

Here it came. The bribe. But there wasn't an amount of money in the world that would buy me off. Then again, I wasn't here to ruin his life. Maybe we'd agree to pretend he paid me off, and I'd go away quietly.

It would be a shame not to get to know Mason. But the cost might be too high.

"Out," Braxton said to Mason and Nathaniel.

It took a minute for the two men to leave the room.

"Do you always order them around like that," I asked as the door shut behind them.

"What's your game, Ms. Crush?" Braxton asked.

"No game. I just wanted to meet my cousin. All I had to go on was the percentage DNA match. That's all they gave me.

I didn't get the deluxe package. Maybe I should have. Maybe it would help us all understand—"

"Please, stop talking."

I did. Mostly because I didn't have much more to say, but also thinking he was one seriously short-tempered man.

He peered closely at me. "We both know how this is going to turn out."

I nodded.

"So, what do you want? What did you hope to gain?"

"Nothing."

He gave a cold laugh. "There's no point in being coy. We're alone."

I wasn't being remotely coy. "I only wanted to know."

"Know..." he asked in a lilting tone as his gaze narrowed on me. "Whether or not I'd write a check no questions asked?"

He was ridiculously far off base.

"No," I responded in the same lilting tone. "Whether or not I had a cousin." I paused. "Funny, before I got here, I wondered if Mason might need some money. I know that sounds stupid now. But I thought maybe he might have kids who needed a good education, like I could set up a trust fund or something."

"You're good."

I was getting tired of correcting his assumptions, so I didn't answer.

"I mean, you're *really* good. Cool as a cucumber. Let's do that DNA test."

"You're sure?"

There was nothing about this man's attitude that said he was prepared to find out he was my father.

My father.

I stared at him for a full minute, letting that thought sink in.

Braxton Cambridge was very likely my biological father.

Nathaniel had deputized himself DNA test coordinator, reaching out to Braxton's doctor, who he obviously trusted. Fine by me. I'd already trusted an anonymous website that probably subcontracted to a lab somewhere offshore.

We were back in the great room now, waiting to decide our next move. Nathaniel was in a corner talking to the doctor's office. Braxton stood alone, still scowling as he sipped on a single malt in a heavy cut crystal tumbler. I'd turned down an offer to join him. It hadn't seemed very sincere. Mason seemed to be texting someone.

I looked around, taking in the decorative log beams, the three-sided, glassed-in fireplace next to the sofa grouping and the view outside through the many, many windows. The house—mansion, I supposed you'd have to call it—was magnificent. It was many times larger than any of the houses I'd viewed in Seattle.

The great room opened to a formal dining room with a dramatic oblong-shaped oak table with a patterned burl inset of red-hued swirls. The table was surrounded by eighteen upholstered, high-backed chairs with carved wooden armrests that echoed the pattern of the table.

Through a stone archway and up three stairs, I could see partway into a vast kitchen with cream-colored countertops and banks of red-toned wood cabinets.

I moved closer to the back windows and realized the brown animals in the distance were horses. A couple dozen of them, and they weren't all brown—white, black, chestnut. They looked beautiful down there dotting the huge paddock.

"He can fit us in tomorrow morning," Nathaniel said, pocketing his phone. "But it's going to take a couple of days for results."

"Just give me the address and time," I said to Nathaniel. "I'll be there."

"Nine thirty. It's at Laurel Street and East Tudor, in the Burge Medical Building."

"Great. Can you also point me to the Tidal Hotel?" I was relieved to have this initial meeting over with.

It hadn't gone at all the way I'd expected. I was tired now and hungry. And I was a little bit emotionally exhausted. All I wanted was to kick off my boots, fall back on a soft hotel

bed and order up a big burger and fries from room service.
I'd earned it.

Mason looked up at me from typing his text. "What? The
Tidal?"

"Nathaniel recommended it."

"Stone, what are you doing recommending a hotel?"

"She didn't have a reservation," Stone said.

"She's not going to a hotel."

"Mason." There was a warning in Braxton's low tone.

"She's staying here," Mason said with finality.

"Bad idea," Stone said.

I agreed with Stone. That was unsettling. "I'm going to a
hotel." I wasn't a fan of awkward situations, and this fit all
the criteria of *awkward*.

"She says she's going to a hotel," Braxton echoed.

"No, she's not," Mason said. "She's family."

Stone scoffed out an inarticulate sound.

"I happen to know she's not," Braxton said.

"I happen to believe she is," Mason said, staring levelly
at his uncle.

"I happen to have two functioning feet, an SUV in the
parking lot, a valid credit card and free will," I said, making
my move. "I'm going to a hotel."

Braxton stifled an obviously reluctant smirk.

"You don't think she's family?" Mason asked Braxton with
an arch of his brow.

"I know what I did and what I didn't do," Braxton said.

Mason fell into step with me as I headed for the door. "We
have empty guest rooms here. They're comfortable and self-
contained." He jabbed his thumb over his shoulder. "You'll
barely have to look at those two."

"It's very kind of you to offer."

"No," Mason said. "It's selfish of me to offer. I want to hang
out. I'm curious about you. Uncle Braxton can go downtown
and hide at the office if he wants, and Stone can fly off to
check on Kodiak's infrastructure on the North Slope. But you
and me, we're staying here and getting to know each other."

"She's not your cousin," Braxton said.

"She's a stranger and probably a con artist," Stone said.

"I'm not a con artist," I said back, reaching for the door handle.

"Then you know you're my cousin," Mason said, his tone quietly triumphant.

He was right. I did know that. Unless there'd been some colossal, bizarre mix-up at the DNA lab, there was a 99.65 percent chance Mason was my cousin.

"Don't you want to get you know your cousin?" he asked mildly.

I hesitated.

"Great," Mason said. "I'll show you upstairs."

"But—" I hadn't made up my mind yet.

"Stone, go get her suitcase." Mason gallantly offered me his arm. "Is your vehicle unlocked?"

I didn't take the arm. "Are you always this bossy?"

"It's a genetic thing. Aren't you bossy too?"

"This is unacceptable," Braxton said.

"I'm not bringing her suitcase inside," Stone stated.

"You'd rather show her upstairs?" Mason asked Stone.

I couldn't help but grin at Mason's antics. But I shook my head. "It's better all around if I go to a hotel."

Mason leaned in. "It's only better for *them*. It's better for me if you stay. And it's better for you if you stay. I'm a fun and interesting guy. You should get to know me."

I believed him. And I had to admit, he had me curious.

"Stone," Mason said, obviously taking my silence as acceptance, thereby prompting Stone on the suitcase.

"Fine," Stone ground out. "But I'd like to go on the record as being opposed to this."

"Noted," Mason said.

Braxton smacked his tumbler down on a table and stalked out of the room.

"You don't know him yet," Mason said as he watched his uncle depart. "But that was a yes."

Stone scoffed out an inarticulate sound.

"That didn't sound like a yes to me," I said to Mason.

"It wasn't a no. By default, it's a yes."

"Is that how it works?" I was skeptical that Braxton meant anything remotely like that.

"That's how it works."

"He doesn't want me here."

"That's not it." Mason looked my way again. "He doesn't want it to be true."

"I'm kind of sorry it is." I was. I had no desire to upend Braxton's life. He might be abrasive and grumpy, but I didn't mean him any harm.

I considered heading back to the airport and disappearing, forget taking a new DNA test. Did I really want Braxton in my life?

"Well, I'm sure not sorry," Mason said.

"It's not true," Stone said.

I couldn't keep my annoyance at him to myself any longer. "Why would I agree to a new DNA test if I knew it would come back negative?"

He gazed at me for a moment. "I'm trying to figure that out."

"The answer's not obvious?"

"It's obvious to me," Mason said.

I was still looking at Stone. "You don't want to hedge your bets here? A little bit? Even if it's just to save face later on?"

"No."

I gave a shrug. "Okay."

I wondered if he was the kind of guy to apologize when he got something wrong. He didn't look like that kind of a guy. He looked proud, determined, also honorably loyal to Braxton if I was being honest about it.

I'd obviously upended his life too. I couldn't help but wonder why.

And then it hit me. Just because he wasn't listed in the family history website, and just because his last name was Stone, didn't mean he wasn't a Cambridge.

"Are you related?" I asked him.

"To who?" Stone asked.

"Braxton, Mason, me?"

"No," Stone said in a flat tone. "No relation."

"But you live here?" I'd assumed he did from the first moment. But now it occurred to me that I might have had that part wrong.

Stone's jaw went tight. He looked offended by the question.

"He's very close to the family," Mason said. "And he's a vice president at Kodiak Communications. Plus, it's a big house. We have to fill it with somebody."

Calling it a big house was an understatement. And calling where I was standing a bedroom was a misnomer too.

It was a suite, palatial and high-ceilinged with exposed beams and banks of windows along two walls. It had a king-size four-poster bed with a thick mattress that I'd have to hop to get up on. The windowed corner held a conversation area with a sofa, two plush, cream-colored armchairs and a couple of glass-topped tables. A marble gas fireplace took up most of one wall, while a dressing and closet area led into a massive bathroom with a huge tub, a separate shower and dual sinks.

The floor was natural wood highlighted by a plush, forest green area rug. I gave in to the temptation to pull off my ankle boots, curling my toes into the thick luxury. I dropped my purse on a cushion-covered window bench and wondered what to do with myself until dinner.

There was a knock on my bedroom door.

"Come in," I called, expecting it to be Mason.

The idea of curling up in the conversation corner and getting to know him a little bit was appealing. I had questions about his father, his family, Alaska—and maybe what it was that made a guy like Stone tick, since it was easy to see Mr. Stone was going to make my stay here as uncomfortable as possible.

The door swung open.

Instead of Mason it was Stone, and he was carrying my suitcase.

Somehow, I'd forgotten the impact of his good looks and solid frame. I was struck all over again by his confidence and intensity. He made the doorway look small, and he held the suitcase as if it was a bag of feathers.

"Here?" he asked, pointing to a little bench at the foot of the bed and walking that way in obvious anticipation of my answer.

The single word heated my chest. He didn't change the room temperature. It was more like he changed the atmosphere, electrifying it somehow.

I took a reflexive step back to give him room, taking a second to find my voice. "Sure. Yeah. Thanks."

He placed the suitcase on its back, then turned to face me.

His bright blue eyes zeroed in, observant, encompassing, like the rest of the world had just disappeared and there was only me. I didn't know whether to be flattered or unnerved.

"You're smart," he said, but it sounded like sarcasm. "You have to know you've only got a couple of days to pull off whatever it is you're trying to pull off."

"Because the DNA test will come back negative?" I didn't bother hiding my own sarcasm.

"I've known Braxton for nearly twenty years. I've never seen him lie."

"Therefore, I'm the one who's lying?"

Stone didn't miss a beat. "Yes."

I caught the logical fallacy, even if Stone didn't. "Maybe he lied about being a liar. Maybe he's really good at lying."

Stone's deep voice went deeper still, menacing. "You come into his house and insult him? You have a lot of nerve."

I gave my hair a defiant toss. "I know what I know. That's all. And it's pointless to keep arguing."

He moved closer. "Just tell me what it'll take. I can help you. *I'm* the guy you want to deal with on this."

"I'm not looking for money."

He shook his head in rebuttal. "It's the only thing that makes sense."

"It's the one thing that doesn't make sense." I wanted to

put a firm and final end to this line of thinking. I didn't like arguing at the best of times. I liked it even less with Stone.

I turned my back and unzipped my suitcase. My laptop was tucked under a couple of pairs of jeans, and I lifted it out.

"Showing me your bogus DNA results is not going to help," he said.

"I'm not showing you the DNA results."

It was a beat before he spoke. "Then what are you doing?" He sounded genuinely curious.

Balancing the laptop on one arm, I booted up and called up the East Sun Tech website.

I heard, then felt Stone move to look over my shoulder. My finger faltered on the trackpad. I could feel his heat, smell his outdoorsy scent. His nearness made my skin tingle in a wholly unfamiliar way.

I gave myself a shake and clicked on the link.

"There," I said as the picture came up.

"What's this?" His arm brushed mine and the tingle increased a thousandfold.

I had to struggle to keep from sounding breathless. "That's what we sold. To East Sun Tech. Me and my friends."

He lifted the laptop from my arms for a better look.

I let it go.

"I don't get it," he said.

"I used to work in a restaurant." I shifted so I could look at him.

He seemed puzzled.

"East Sun Tech sells it now. Through suppliers and distributors all over the world. We get royalties." I could see that he still didn't understand. "Money, Stone. Lots of money. They send it every month, and I don't know what to do with it all."

I wasn't sure why I'd added that last part. Except that it was true. It's what had brought me here, so the thought that Stone could offer me a bribe to make me go away was laughable.

"You're rich?" he asked.

I took my laptop back. "I'm…" I was about to say *com-*

fortable or use some other euphemism for wealth. "Yes," I admitted. "I'm rich."

I set the laptop down on the little bench.

"Then what's this all about?" he asked.

I straightened, uncomfortably close to him now, barely six inches from his chest. It was unnerving, but I refused to be the one to back off.

We stared each other down.

His eyes went from sapphire to cobalt, and his voice lost its edge. In fact, he sounded puzzled. "What are you after?"

I thought about the answer to that. I hadn't found what I'd expected in Alaska, not by a long shot. But I was here, and now there was something I wanted.

"The truth," I said.

"Well, isn't that noble of you." With every breath, he seemed to get just a little bit closer, daring me in some way.

I lost the thread of my response.

He leaned in another inch, and my focus locked on his lips.

They were sexy lips. Sexy lips and a sexy man in a sexy room.

This time, I was the one who moved closer, tipping my chin, tilting my head. I wasn't doing it on purpose. It was just happening.

The air was still and woodsy crisp. The room was silent, not a whirr, not a buzz, completely silent.

Stone brushed my cheek with the pad of his thumb.

I closed my eyes and let the sensation rush through me, down my neck, over my breasts through to the pit of my stomach.

Oh, wow. All that from a touch?

I sucked in a breath, and his lips touched mine, closing over me, moist and hot with rich hints of aged whiskey.

I kissed him back, parting my lips, coming up on my toes, snaking my arms around his neck as his hands closed over my waist.

It was a sexy kiss, a fantastic kiss. His mouth was tender, mobile and skilled. When his tongue touched mine, I moaned. Desire bloomed in my core, flowing into my limbs.

He broke the kiss for a heartbeat, then came back, deepening it, curving our bodies together, his firm chest coming flush against my breasts, his thighs intermingling with mine.

I wanted to tear off our clothes and tumble onto the bed.

I was giving it serious thought, when a bang sounded in the hallway.

I froze.

He pulled back a little and so did I.

We both blinked at each other.

"Uh…" I started, struggling to catch my breath, not knowing what my next word would be.

"I didn't mean…" He looked as baffled as I felt.

"That was probably a bad idea." I took a step back, separating our limbs and our bodies that were erotically entangled even though we were fully dressed.

"Probably?" he asked with an edge of astonishment. Then, as if he'd just remembered it was there, his hand fell from my waist, breaking our final touch. "That wasn't what I meant to do."

"You accidentally kissed me?" I shouldn't have been amused. This was absolutely not a time for amusement. I schooled my features.

"I'd planned to appeal to your sense of honor and integrity."

"By bribing me?"

"No. Bribing was plan A. Appealing is plan B."

"Oh. Okay. Well, appeal away." I waited.

"Braxton is more fragile than he seems."

My eyebrows rose in surprise. "*That's* your argument?"

"He's been hurt in the past."

I wasn't buying the story. "Other secret offspring have come back to haunt him?"

Stone's expression turned grim. "No. He lost a daughter. She was killed in a car accident along with his wife. She was his only child. She was nine."

I reframed my impression of Braxton, not completely, but a little bit. It was a heartbreaking story.

"I'm sorry to hear that."

Stone gestured up and down my body. "So, you can see

why you, coming forward with this claim of yours has affected him."

"That had to have been years ago." It was tragic, but it didn't change anything about my situation. I wasn't making a false claim to manipulate Braxton.

"You never forget a child."

"You have children?" I asked.

Stone wasn't wearing a wedding ring, and he had kissed me like there was no tomorrow, but that didn't mean anything.

Stone looked shocked by the question. "No."

"Then you're not exactly an expert." I wasn't hard-hearted, but I also didn't want to walk out before I learned the truth, whatever it might be.

I didn't want to walk out on Mason either. Whatever Braxton might be feeling, Mason had made his perspective crystal clear.

Stone looked affronted. "It doesn't take an expert to know people love their children."

I couldn't argue with that, so I pivoted. "You don't think Braxton deserves the truth? You don't think I deserve the truth?"

"I think you already know the truth, and I think Braxton deserves to be left in peace. If money won't do it, then tell me what will."

"Nothing. I'm here. I'm taking the DNA test. It'll show what it shows."

Stone searched my expression for a long time, clearly trying to figure out what made me tick.

I wanted to ask him what he saw, but he turned and left.

Just as well. There was a whole lot of volatility between us, and the situation didn't need any more complications.

Stone avoided me for the next two days. Braxton did the same. Mason was a gracious host, although he was busy working a lot of the time. Our conversations were shorter than I'd expected and hadn't moved much past polite chitchat.

I knew he'd attended college in California, and his sister,

Adeline, was still in Sacramento at Cal State working on a PhD in urban development. His younger brother, Kyle, was in Alaska but off visiting some smaller communities in his job with Kodiak Communications. So I had two more cousins—well, if things turned out as expected.

As the hours and days went by, I tried to forget about kissing Stone. I wasn't very successful, especially when I caught glimpses of him coming and going.

To distract myself, I wandered down to the horses. Mason had told me the family had a sideline, leasing horses out to wilderness tourism operators. It was a holdover from their great-grandfather, and a good use of agricultural land, which was in short supply in Alaska. There were also tax breaks, apparently. I just thought the horses were beautiful. Oddly, I missed Snuggles all over again and thought I might like to get a pet for my new house in Seattle. Not a horse, but maybe a puppy.

On the third afternoon, the DNA tests were finally delivered to the mansion.

Braxton still seemed convinced he'd be vindicated.

I considered the possibility there was a liquor-fueled hookup in his past that he'd honestly forgotten all about. I also wondered why my mother might have come up with such an elaborate story about my biological father being a married soldier from Australia.

Maybe she didn't want me to go looking for Braxton. Maybe there was a really good reason for that. Yet, I'd shown up in his life anyway. I hated to think Stone might have been right. Maybe I should have walked away that very first day.

It was too late for that.

We'd assembled in the den, door closed, wet bar at the ready.

I caught Stone's gaze on me and looked away. I wasn't quick enough to keep our kiss from blooming in my mind or to stop a rush of heat blasting over the goose bumps on my skin.

We each sat in one of the plaid chairs around the square coffee table.

Braxton watched me closely as he sliced open the sealed manila envelope. "You want to make a dash for the door?"

"I'm good." If there'd been an honest mix-up and I was totally wrong, I'd apologize, head back to Seattle and chalk this up to a very weird life experience.

It would mean I didn't have any blood relatives, at least none I'd be able to find. But I could deal with that. I'd be taking possession of my new house in a few days. I could visit some local dog breeders and spend some time deciding on a puppy.

Braxton pulled out a sheaf of papers and started to read aloud. "Results of DNA test…blah, blah, blah." He was clearly scanning his way down the top sheet.

Then he stilled.

His expression changed.

He blinked.

"Uncle?" Mason prompted.

Braxton looked at me. "It's impossible."

Stone rose like a shot and walked behind Braxton to look over his shoulder.

He looked at me. "How did you…"

"So, it's true!" Mason was obviously delighted.

"This isn't *right*," Braxton bellowed, his face going ruddy. "I did *not* cheat on Christine. Not *once*. Not *ever*. I *loved* my wife."

"It's in the past, Braxton," Mason offered.

"It's *not* in the past," Braxton said. He peered suspiciously at me.

Stone was looking suspicious too, like he thought I'd somehow messed with the results. For such a great kisser, he could sure be a jerk.

"I don't even know what lab they sent it to," I answered Stone's unasked question.

"Good grief," Mason said. "She didn't fake the test."

Braxton flipped the page, reading further. "There has to be an explanation."

"A party?" I asked, voicing the best idea I'd come up with.

He glared at me.

"Maybe when you were young, something you don't remember?"

"Don't you dare suggest I cheated on my wife in a drunken stupor."

I realized how it sounded. "That's not what I…" Well, it was what I'd meant. But there were a limited number of explanations here.

"Were you ever injured?" I asked. "Medicated? Were you in the military? My mom was a nurse."

"I was *not* in the military. I was *not* medicated out of my mind. I am fully aware of every hour of my life thus far. I *did not* cheat." Braxton rose from his chair and slapped the DNA results down on the table.

"What about a relative," Stone asked. "A secret brother or half brother somewhere who—"

"It says I'm her *biological father*." Braxton headed for the bar.

If someone offered, I thought I would take a drink this time, wine, beer, bourbon—anything really.

"A twin?" Stone asked.

Mason sounded highly skeptical. "A secret twin?"

"Could happen," Stone said.

"Sometimes the right answer is the obvious answer," Mason said.

Braxton turned. "Are you calling me a liar?"

"I'm pointing out that the scientific evidence says you're Sophie's father," Mason said. "And Sophie's a wonderful young woman. I want you to stop and think about that for a minute."

Braxton looked confused.

"Uncle. You have a daughter."

Braxton's horrified gaze went to me.

Mason kept talking. "However it happened, whatever the explanation. *You have a daughter.*"

"I'm sorry," I told Braxton. I truly was. Right now, I wished I'd never come to Alaska.

Stone was right. I might not know Braxton's story, but he was obviously desperate to have it stay a secret. And, looking back, my mother had tried to help him.

I needed to respect what she'd tried to do. I came to my feet. "I'll get out of your way."

"Oh, no, you don't." Mason rocked to his feet and reached out, linking his arm with mine and sidling up. "I have a say in this too."

"I didn't mean for it to happen like this," I told them all. "Don't worry. I'm not going to say a word to anyone."

"But it did happen," Braxton said. "There's no stuffing the genie back in the bottle."

"I'm going to figure this out," Stone said with determination.

"I've never been that drunk," Braxton said as he tossed back a couple of fingers of something amber. But he looked more bewildered than angry now.

He poured himself another.

"Kyle will be home tomorrow," Mason said. "And we have to call Adeline."

"Whoa," Stone said. "Let's not get ahead of ourselves."

"We're not ahead of ourselves," Mason said, pointing to the DNA results on the table. "It's been confirmed."

"It doesn't have to leave this room," I said. "I can catch a flight back to Seattle and—"

"Haven't we been through this already?" Mason asked me. "You're staying."

"That was only while we waited for the results."

"I'm not giving you up just yet." He waved a hand in Braxton's and Stone's direction. "Forget about those guys. You're my newfound cousin. This family's not so huge that we can afford to ostracize one of its members."

Despite the complexity of the statement, Mason's words warmed me. Since my mother's death, I hadn't had a single blood relative. Whatever happened after this, I felt like I'd always have one in Mason.

I swallowed. "Thank you."

Stone's expression faltered.

"You should stay," Braxton said.

Stone looked at Braxton in shock. *"What?"*

Braxton didn't bother repeating himself.

"What will you tell everyone?" Stone asked.

"We don't have to tell them anything," Mason said.

"Maybe you could come to Seattle for a visit," I said to Mason. If he came to me, we could get to know each other without causing local gossip.

"Did you ever donate to a sperm bank?" Stone asked Braxton.

Braxton drew his face back in a grimace. *"No."*

"Just considering all the possibilities."

"These two are not going to chase you out of Alaska," Mason said to me. Then he paused. "Wait, do you have a job to get back to?"

I found myself locking gazes with Stone.

Then I shook my head. "No. The world pretty much spins without me right now."

"Perfect," Mason said. "You can meet Kyle tomorrow."

Three

Kyle turned out to be a near carbon copy of Mason. He was a year younger, a little taller and a little less polished, but had essentially the same features.

"Wow," he said, reaching out to touch my shoulders. "Look at you?" Then he pulled me into an encompassing hug. He rocked me back and forth in his arms, laughing.

I was shocked at his exuberance, but I managed a light hug back.

He drew away to gaze at me again. "I can't believe you even bothered with the test. She looks exactly like Braxton."

"No, she doesn't," Stone said, frowning where he was sitting at a big central island.

We were in the kitchen making fancy morning coffee at an elaborate machine built right into the wall. A basket of fragrant scones was set out on the counter. The sun was high and had been up since the two-hour twilight ended around three thirty this morning. I was glad for the blackout curtains in my bedroom.

"That's because you're not looking for it," Kyle said. He cocked his head sideways. "Get a load of that beautiful mouth."

Stone's frown deepened.

"Braxton doesn't have a beautiful mouth," Mason said from his perch at the central island.

"Sophie has the beautiful version," Kyle said.

He crossed to the coffee maker, where Stone was retrieving his full cup. "So, did we offer her a job?"

"She doesn't need a job," Stone responded.

"I won't be staying that long," I told Kyle.

"We're still hashing that part out," Mason said, taking a sip of his mocha.

"I just bought a new house in Seattle," I said as Kyle punched the buttons on the coffee machine.

It was new news to Stone and Mason, and they both looked over at me in surprise.

"It's right on the water, and I'm really looking forward to getting moved in." I carried on talking to Kyle, ignoring their stares, Mason's curious and Stone's still suspicious. "I'm moving out of my apartment, so the extra space will be great."

I wanted Stone to know I had a good life outside this newly found biological family.

"I'm going to get a puppy," I added for good measure.

"You seem almost as chatty as me," Kyle said as he lifted his brimming cup of what looked like a smooth latte.

"Not usually," I said.

He raised a brow. "That wasn't a criticism. I was thinking it must be genetic, *cuz*."

I smiled at that. I couldn't help it. Kyle was easy to warm up to. "Why don't you tell me about you?"

"Happy to. Middle child, as I'm sure you know. I work for the family firm. I head up operations. Stone takes care of technical. And Mason's client relations."

I hadn't known their exact positions in the company, so that was interesting.

"I just got back from the Kodiak Communications facility in Juneau," Kyle continued. "Hey, Stone, you should get them to walk you through the new security infrastructure. It's amazing."

"I saw it a few times under construction," Stone said.

"Well, it's a sight to behold now that it's operational. Fly over in the Cessna. You'll be home by dinner."

"I told Kirby I'd give a hand moving the horses," Stone said.

"For Radcliff Tours?" Mason asked.

Stone nodded. "Two dozen this year. They're booked solid."

"I'm heading to the lower forty-eight for a job fair in the morning," Kyle said. He looked my way. "It's in Seattle if you want to come along."

"Come along?" I asked, confused.

"The King Air's not as fast as a commercial jet, but it's

nicer to fly private. I'll be there overnight, so if you have anything that needs doing. Or you can pick up a few of your things." He looked completely serious.

Kyle was offering me a flight to Seattle on a private airplane. I couldn't help thinking Tasha would be proud.

"She can buy whatever she needs here," Mason said.

"I don't need more things," I said.

"You might as well get comfortable." Kyle shrugged.

"You'll need a second pilot," Stone said.

Kyle looked surprised by that. "I can fly single."

"It's better two with crew."

"Are you hoping to abandon me there?" I asked Stone.

Kyle looked from me to Stone and back again. "What did I miss?"

"Stone's worried about Braxton," Mason told him.

"Why?"

"Have you done the math?" Mason asked his brother.

Kyle paused. He looked at me. "You mean…"

"I'm twenty-seven," I said.

Kyle's eyes widened. "Ohhh…"

"Yeah," Stone said. "Ohhh…"

"That's a surprise." In fact, Kyle looked much more than surprised. He looked perplexed. His expression told me he didn't think Braxton would cheat on his wife.

"I *am* going to figure it out." Stone folded his arms over his chest.

"It doesn't fall to you," Kyle said.

"Somebody has to step up," Stone muttered.

When the coffee chat broke up, I wandered through the cavernous house, debating Kyle's offer and wondering if I should take it and say goodbye to Mason. I'd found what I came for, and there was little reason to prolong the stay.

I ended up in a small library off the entry hall in front of a cluster of family photos stretched across the wall behind a desk. I recognized Mason and Kyle as young teenagers. The photo was taken on a trail, and they were on horseback.

I guessed the man between them was their father, Braxton's younger brother, Xavier, who I'd yet to meet.

Younger versions of the two boys were in another photo of what looked like a picnic. The little girl with them on the blanket had to be their sister, Adeline.

I took another step and came to a photo of a woman and a different young girl. They were crouched in a field of wildflowers, yellows and oranges and purples. It was a bright sunny day, and they were both grinning at the camera. They had to be Braxton's late wife, Christine, and his daughter, Emily.

My breath clogged in my chest for a moment.

Emily was wearing a fancy blue dress with a matching headband over her light brown hair. Christine was beautiful, and Emily was adorable. Next was a close-up portrait of Emily, obviously taken on the same day. She was still wearing the blue headband, and the bright sunshine beamed sideways off her smiling face. Her fingertips were touching a little necklace.

I moved closer. The necklace charm was the stylized letters *EC* inset with what looked like little diamonds in the gold. Emily, for sure. I took in her eyes, her nose, her chin. I could swear there was something familiar about her.

It hit me hard then. She was my half sister.

My chest got tighter still, and my throat thickened with emotion. If she'd lived, I would have had a half sister. That would have been wonderful.

"There are photo albums somewhere." Stone's voice came from behind me.

I swallowed the emotion, not yet trusting my voice.

Stone stood beside me, looking at the pictures. "I still can't believe he's lying."

I looked up at him. "So, I must be lying."

He gave a shrug to that. "I can't see what you'd be lying about."

I supposed that was the closest he'd come to saying he'd been wrong. I couldn't see any reason to belabor the point. So I turned my attention back to the photo in front of me.

"Emily looks really happy here."

"She was a happy kid. It was a few months after this was taken…" He reached out to brush his finger across the glass.

"That she died?" I knew she'd died when she was nine, and she looked to be about nine in the photo.

"This was her birthday," he said. "August 15."

The strangest feeling washed over me, like a breeze through the still room that blew straight to my bones. "That's—" I couldn't finish.

Stone waited a moment. "What?"

I could feel his gaze on me, and I looked up. I had to force out the words. "My birthday is August 15."

We stared at each other in silence.

"You're twenty-seven," he said.

I nodded.

"Emily would be twenty-seven."

I struggled to process the information. It meant something, something huge and unfathomable.

I leaned in and looked more closely at the photo of Emily. She still looked familiar.

"Where were you born?" Stone asked in a hushed voice.

It occurred to me then. Emily had my mother's eyes. She had my mother's smile.

"Not here," I said. I shook my head hard. I couldn't accept what we were both thinking. "My mom was working on a military base in California, north of San Francisco."

It was another beat before Stone responded. "Emily was born in California."

"No." I took a step back from the photo.

"You're Emily," Stone said on a note of amazement.

"No," I repeated.

"And Emily was you."

"That can't happen." I felt angry with him for saying it out loud. "It couldn't happen. It didn't happen."

"Sophie."

"No! My mom was my mother. I was her daughter." My hands started to tremble, and my knees felt weak.

"Are you—"

I closed my eyes and swayed.

He braced my shoulders with a strong arm. Seconds later he was wrapping me in a hug, a firm one, like he thought I might collapse or bolt or something.

I didn't fight his support. I scrunched my eyes closed and buried my face in the crook of his shoulder, wanting to shut out the world and hide in the dark just as long as I could.

But I couldn't hide from my own thoughts. They boomed.

"This isn't happening," I whispered. My throat had closed in, and my voice sounded raw.

"It's going to be okay," he said.

"It can't be true. There are protocols, security features, fail-safes." From what I knew of modern hospitals, it was all but impossible to mix up babies.

"It explains the paternity," Stone said.

"It erases my *life*."

"No, no, no," he said. "You're still you. You'll always be you."

I didn't feel like me. I suddenly didn't feel like anyone. "You don't know anything about me." I was angry with Stone, mostly because he was available.

"You're right," he said. But he continued to hug me close.

I leaned into him like an anchor.

"Hey, Sophie, I wanted—" Mason cut off the words.

I opened my eyes and looked to the doorway.

Stone turned his head too.

"What are you...?" Mason asked, his voice baffled as he took us in.

Stone looked down at me, a question in his eyes.

I nodded. This wasn't something I could keep a secret.

"We need to talk to you," he said to Mason.

"What the *heck* is going on?" Mason asked. He took in my stricken expression, and his frown deepened. "Stone, if you did something—"

"I *didn't*," Stone said. "Can you close the door?"

Mason closed the double doors behind himself, still peering suspiciously at Stone.

I thought about speaking up in Stone's defense. But I didn't trust my voice.

His arm at my waist, Stone guided me to a chair at a square table.

"Talk," Mason said to Stone. His voice had a hard edge.

"We just figured something out," Stone said, sitting as well.

Mason watched me closely, looking worried.

"It's shocking," Stone warned. "You should sit down."

"Spit it out," Mason said.

"It's Emily and Sophie."

Mason's gaze shot to Stone at the mention of Emily's name.

My heart thudded hard in my chest. The more Stone talked, the more real it felt.

"They were born on the same day," he said. "Both in California."

Mason didn't react.

Stone waited for a moment, and then Mason's eyes widened to round.

"They were switched at birth." Stone's voice was low and serious.

"We don't *know* that," I blurted out.

"We do know that," Stone stated with certainty. "It's the only explanation that makes sense."

Mason stared at me. "You're Emily?"

"No!" My answer came out more sharply than I'd intended.

"She's still Sophie," Stone said. "But the genetics aren't what we all thought."

Mason dropped into a chair. "Wow."

My mind started racing with the implications. I wanted to talk to my mother. I wanted to hug her. I wanted to tell her how much I loved her, and that I didn't care what some stupid DNA test said.

Then I wanted to call the hospital and demand their records so I could figure out who had made such a colossal mistake. They deserved to answer for what they'd done.

And then the worst hit me, the terrible truth.

It should have been me all those years ago. I should have

been in the car with Christine on that icy road. I should have been the one to die.

"Emily should be here," I said awash in guilt.

Both the men looked at me in confusion.

"I should be dead."

"Don't, Sophie," Stone said, reaching out his hand.

I resisted the urge to take it.

"You can't think like that," Mason said. "It was a horrible, horrible mistake."

I rose from the chair and walked back to the picture on the wall. I looked at Emily's eyes, her smile, the little cowlick in the front of her hair.

My mother, my wonderful, funny, compassionate, intelligent mother, never even got to meet her baby daughter. Instead, she got me.

I felt Stone's broad hands close around my shoulders. "It'll be okay," he said softly.

It didn't feel like it was going to be okay.

"We have to tell my uncle," Mason said from where he was still seated.

"Tell him what?" Braxton's voice interrupted.

I turned to see his imposing form fill the doorway.

Mason came to his feet. "We think there's been a mix-up," he said to his uncle.

Braxton's attention went to me. "She confessed, did she?"

"No," Stone said.

Braxton took a few paces toward us. "How'd you do it? *What* did you do?"

"Uncle," Mason said in a pleading tone.

"Don't uncle me. I deserve an explanation."

"You do," Stone said.

I knew I should speak up, but my throat hurt, and I didn't have the first idea of where to start.

"So?" Braxton said, coming to a halt a few feet away, eyeing me up and down like I'd turned right back into the enemy again.

"Sophie is Emily," Mason blurted out.

I wished people would stop saying that. It physically hurt me to hear those words.

Braxton's expression went blank.

"Switched at birth," Stone said, obviously deciding to throw it right out there.

Another beat of silence passed.

"No," Braxton said. He vehemently shook his head. "No."

I empathized.

His reaction was the same as mine.

His precious Emily was obviously as important to him as my mother had been to me. It was horrifying to have that suddenly ripped from your life.

"She's not!" Braxton said, staring at me with a cold accusation.

He seemed to think it was my fault.

Maybe it was my fault. I mean, I couldn't have stopped myself from being switched in the hospital, but I could have stayed away from the family history website. And when I learned how upsetting my existence was for Braxton, I could have walked away. I could have pretended to be a con artist so the Cambridge family could go right back to normal.

"They have the same birthdate," Mason said. "They were both born in California. And you made it abundantly clear you didn't cheat on Aunt Christine."

"No," Braxton repeated, but there was less power in his denial.

"I'm sorry," I managed.

"Don't do that," Stone said to me. "This screwup had nothing to do with you."

"It had everything to do with me. Why didn't I just stay quietly in Seattle?"

"That wouldn't have changed anything," Mason said. He moved closer to Stone and me. "It wouldn't have changed a thing. Besides, we're your family. There's no question that you belong here."

I didn't belong in Alaska.

I stood alone on the Cambridges' back deck, gazing out

at the horses and the surrounding wilderness. I wasn't sure I belonged anywhere.

I felt an urgent desire to go home. But home was my apartment, and I'd already given up the lease. The movers had started packing and would unload the moving boxes at my new house in just a few days. I couldn't go back now.

At least I'd have my own things in the new house, my keepsakes and my photos. I was going to pull out all my childhood albums and photo collections and stare at them for a few hours to remind myself of my mom and my life.

The breeze freshened around me. It was midafternoon now, high summer, and the sun was doing a lazy circle in the sky. It was never straight overhead I'd discovered, but it never quite set either. The north felt like an alien world. It was impossible to wrap my head around the idea that I might have grown up here instead of in metro Seattle.

I thought about going to visit Tasha or Layla and Brooklyn in order to feel normal. Better still, I could get them all to meet me somewhere. I was sure they'd do it, especially if I told them what had happened. They'd rally around me if they knew.

A spa would be nice—a girls' weekend at the spa like we used to do, mineral pools, massages and pedicures—and wine, plenty of wine.

I heard the French doors open behind me.

I didn't turn. I didn't care who it was. In fact, I hoped if I ignored them, they'd go away. I didn't really want to see anyone right now.

"Sophie?" It was Braxton's voice.

I tried to steel myself, but I wasn't remotely ready for whatever he might have to say. My emotions were too close to the surface, and I didn't trust myself not to tear up.

He came up to the railing a few feet away from me and leaned against it.

A horse whinnied in the distance. Chickadees chirped from the trees as a gust of wind rustled the poplar leaves and a few fluffy clouds inched their way across the clear sky.

"You okay?" he finally asked.

I almost laughed at the question, partly because it was so absurd, and partly because Braxton's gruff, guttural voice made it sound like he resented having to ask at all.

I wondered if Stone and Mason had forced him to come out here and talk to me.

I faced him, bracing my hip on the rail. "You don't have to do this."

"Do what?"

I waved my hand toward the house and the people who'd obviously sent him. "Pretend you care."

He took a step closer to me. "You don't think I care?"

"Why should you care? I'm a stranger. We're strangers."

His bushy brow went up. "You're my daughter."

"No, I'm not." I let out a chopped laugh. "I mean, I am. But I'm not."

His deep chest rose with an indrawn breath. He was a sturdy man, tall with broad shoulders and a very deep chest. His striking presence had me thinking about genetics.

I was sturdy, slim, but not fine boned. And I'd always been more athletic than my mom. I'd assumed I got it from my dad. Which I had. I knew that now.

"Right." His flat response resonated in the big outdoors.

I didn't know where we were supposed to go from here. I had no interest in a heart-to-heart talk with a callous stranger. I hadn't even wrapped my own head around this reality.

But he didn't leave, and the silence was growing less comfortable by the second.

"Did Stone and Mason make you do this?" I asked.

"Do what?"

"Come out here, talk to me, make… I don't know, a connection or something."

Braxton gave a ghost of a smile. "No."

I digested that for a moment, not sure whether I believed him. I decided to let it slide. "Okay. So, what do you want?"

"Believe it or not, to see if you were all right."

"In what way?"

He shrugged his wide shoulders. He was clearly uncomfortable, and I had to give him credit for sticking it out this long. I wasn't making it easy.

"I thought you might be upset," he said slowly, as if he was feeling his way through the statement. "Maybe angry? Confused?"

"Confused," I said, finding something to agree with him on. "Definitely confused."

He gave a nod. His voice went lower, quieter. "Me too."

We gazed at each other for a long minute.

Braxton broke the silence. "I can see Christine in you now."

I wasn't sure I believed him. Only a few hours ago he was disavowing me, and now he could see the family resemblance?

"I wasn't looking for it before," he said, as if he knew what I was thinking. "I hope you understand why I wasn't looking. I knew with absolute certainty that I wasn't your father."

Truth was, I did understand his perspective now. There hadn't been a drunken party in his past, no injury with mind-addling pain medication that made him forget about a one-night stand with a pretty nurse. All along he'd known he was right, but I kept pressing and pressing.

Served me right for what I found out, I supposed.

"I need to go home," I told him honestly.

He looked disappointed. "If that's what you want."

"I have a life out there." I thought again about Tasha, Layla and Brooklyn. They were the closest thing I had to family since my mom died.

"You could stay a little longer," Braxton said, sounding almost hopeful.

I shook my head. "I need to get my feet under me, get centered, think about what all this means."

"You could do that from here."

I needed something familiar, something from my past to cling to while I reframed my world. I'd come to Alaska hoping to find a cousin. Instead, I'd lost my mother.

"You expected to find family here," Braxton said.

"Not like this." I took a shuddering breath, struggling to control my emotions. "She was my *mother*."

Once again, the outdoor sounds echoed around us under the massive sky.

"I had one child." Braxton shifted his focus to the horizon, and his voice sounded far away, drawing my sympathy. "My wife, Christine." He swallowed. "I mean, your mother."

Something twitched inside me and wanted to erupt in a protest. Christine couldn't usurp mother, not so easily, not just like that.

"She nearly died giving birth to Emily." Braxton seemed to gather himself. "I mean to you. Her blood pressure skyrocketed, and her kidneys very nearly shut down. After that... well, we didn't dare have another child. But then I lost them both. It was so sudden, and they were both so young." He turned his head, and his eyes focused on me. "But here you are. Here...you...are."

"I'm not her." The world shifted beneath me, rolling like I was on the deck of a ship, and I gripped the railing.

"But you're you. And that's something. That's some kind of a miracle."

I didn't want to be a miracle. I didn't want that at all.

I only wanted my life to be mine again. The one I recognized.

I was packing.

I'd taken Kyle up on his offer of a ride to Seattle, and I didn't know when I'd come back.

I'd call Tasha as soon as I got home, because I was liking the spa idea more and more. I wanted to mentally check out from reality, somewhere warm and cozy with my dear friends and skilled massage therapists and a well-stocked wine cellar.

Maybe we could try Vegas again. Layla's and Brooklyn's husbands owned an elegant hotel on the strip. We could probably get a discount. Not that money was an object anymore.

There was plenty of space in the dresser drawers and closet in the guest room, but I'd been living out of my suitcase. I hadn't felt like I should settle in. Turned out I was right.

Now I dumped everything onto the bed and started resorting and folding.

Over my objections, Marie, a superfriendly fiftysomething housekeeper had taken some of my shirts and underwear away to wash them. I'd asked her not to bother, to just point me to the washing machine, but she'd laughed and told me to act like a guest, not a staff member.

I hoped she'd have them done before it was time to leave. If not, well, I figured I'd buy new ones when I got back to Seattle. At least it would give me something to spend some money on.

There was a knock on my open door.

"Yes," I called out.

I doubted it was Braxton. It would be ironic if it was Marie. But my money was on Mason. He'd probably talked to Kyle by now and wanted to convince me to stay.

I didn't want to hurt his feelings, but he wouldn't change my mind.

"You're packing." It was Stone who walked in.

"I'm packing." I confirmed the obvious, tucking a pair of jeans in next to my tennis shoes.

I wondered if Stone was still thinking about copiloting the plane with Kyle. I hoped not. It would be better to walk away from him here than be cooped up together in the air for a few hours and then say an awkward goodbye in Seattle.

Though we were both trying our best to ignore it, our kiss hung between us. I could tell by the way he looked at me, as if he was searching for an answer to a question.

I also couldn't forget how his arms felt around me in the den in those minutes after we'd discovered the baby switch. He'd been compassionate and comforting. I wouldn't have guessed he had something like that in him.

"You're leaving." His tone made the statement into an accusation.

"That's why I'm packing." I lifted a T-shirt from the bed only to realize two pairs of my panties were beneath it. I set it back down again.

It was silly, but I didn't really want him staring at the filmy silk and lace. He didn't need to know I liked mint green and pale blue.

"Braxton said he asked you to stay." Stone came farther into the room.

I turned to face him, ready to stand my ground but also protecting my privacy by blocking his view. "I prefer to leave."

He frowned. "Are you sure that's the best idea?"

"For me? Yes."

He looked like he was about to mount an argument.

I preempted him. "Come on, Stone. You've been desperate to get rid of me since I first showed up."

"He wants you to stay."

"I know."

"He doesn't ask for much."

I blinked in surprise. "Seriously? Braxton strikes me as a guy who asks for and gets everything his own way, always."

"It's a facade."

"I don't think so." I turned back to what I was doing.

Forget about hiding my undies. Whatever Stone saw, he saw.

He touched my shoulder. "Sophie."

I froze. The gentle pressure sent magnetic waves of warmth along my arm, down into my chest.

"It's my decision," I managed.

"Will you hear me out?"

I fought the urge to turn in his arms. "This isn't about you and me."

Silence followed my words.

"It can be," he said.

"Stone."

"Do you want it to be? Am I the reason you're leaving?"

I turned and his hand fell away from my shoulder. I missed it. No, I didn't. *Yes*, I did.

"*I'm* the reason I'm leaving."

"I know I wasn't as welcoming as I could have—"

His words surprised a laugh from me.

He frowned. "To be fair, I thought you were a con artist."

"To be fair, I'm not. You could have given me the benefit of the doubt at several points during the past few days."

"*That's* how people get conned."

The reaction gave me a peek into his psyche. "What happened to make you so cynical?"

"I was in foster care." His bald statement took me by surprise.

I didn't know what to say.

"You learn to be suspicious," he said.

"I...had no idea."

"Why would you?"

"I'm sorry." It sounded like a difficult way to grow up.

"Five foster homes in ten years. I'm not saying that to get your sympathy. Though I'll take it if it helps you stay." His self-deprecating quirk of a smile was disarming.

"Don't try to charm me," I warned him.

"Is it working?"

"No." I wasn't going to let it work.

"I met Braxton when I was fifteen," Stone said, sobering. "I was on the wild side back then. My friends and me were looking for fun, and to us that meant trouble. We climbed into one of Kodiak Communications cell tower compounds."

"You got caught," I guessed.

I could easily picture Stone getting into trouble back then. It was his cocky attitude, his defiant look, like he'd always run by his own rules and nobody else's.

"Not while we were in there," he said. "But we neglected to factor in the security camera."

"Whoops."

"We were young, not particularly good at crime. We used the satellite dish for target practice."

"You had guns?" I asked in shock.

"Slingshots. I had the best aim." He paused. "Took out over a thousand customers."

"What did Braxton do?"

"That's the thing. He could have thrown the book at me. I could easily have ended up in juvie. It would have derailed my life for sure."

"He didn't?" That surprised me. Everything I'd learned

about Braxton told me he didn't have compassion, didn't give second chances.

Stone shook his head. "When he found out about my history, all those foster homes, he made me a deal. I could live with him under 'house arrest' and work off the cost of the repair—a combination of laying data cable and shoveling horse manure. He said if I kept my nose clean and my grades up, he'd drop the charges."

"That was…" I couldn't find the right word: *generous, compassionate, noble.*

"He saved my life. Well, my future anyway. He gave me a home, gave me a job and funded my education. Everything I am, I owe to Braxton."

My opinion of Braxton shifted again. How could it not?

Braxton wanted me to stay so Stone wanted me to stay. Problem was, *I* didn't want me to stay. And my opinion counted too.

"I've got some thinking to do," I told Stone. "I need time and space."

"Think here," he said.

"It's not—"

"There's time in Alaska. There's space in Alaska."

"I'll come back later," I said.

His look of disappointment tugged at my heart. "Why don't I believe you?"

"Because you're cynical."

He gave me another half smile for that one. "People don't always do what they say they're going to do."

"He's my father." As I uttered the words, I knew for certain I'd be back. And probably sooner than I'd planned. I very much wanted to know my biological family.

"Why waste time?" Stone asked.

It was a good question. I didn't have a ready answer.

Four

"Staying or going?" Mason found me in the kitchen the next morning.

I was an emotional eater, and Marie had pointed me to a batch of lemon cupcakes that cook Sebastian baked, saying they were fair game for all.

I'd called Tasha last night, and I was still recovering from that and everything else.

She'd been stunned to learn I was switched at birth. She'd been alternately excited and sympathetic, also endlessly supportive and reassuring. Before the long call ended, she'd helped me pro and con the situation from every conceivable angle.

"Kyle says you're going," Mason continued as he came my way. "Stone says you're staying. Who's got it right?"

I set the cupcake on a little plate and licked an errant dab of vanilla icing from my thumb. I'd been contemplating taking two—they were small—but Mason's presence made me hesitate on my splurge. I set the glass cover back on the platter.

"Staying," I said.

Mason's shoulders relaxed. "Thank goodness." He rounded the big island and helped himself to a cupcake. "I didn't believe Stone when he said he'd talked some sense into you."

"Stone said that?"

Mason nodded and bit off half the cupcake.

I slipped up onto a stool at the island and shifted my cupcake in front of me, gazing at the fluffy buttercream and the swirl of sugared lemon peel, anticipating that first savory bite. Sweets were my weakness, that was for sure.

"Stone didn't have much to do with it." I was crediting Tasha more than anyone. Then again, if I was being honest with myself, the conversation with Stone had prompted me to call Tasha in the first place—instead of just getting on the plane. "He had a little to do with it. We had an argument."

"Stone can be hard-nosed."

I smiled at the understatement. "He said he wanted what Braxton wanted."

As Mason nodded, I took a bite of my cupcake, and my taste buds leaped with joy. The cake was moist and fluffy. The icing was sweet, the lemon flavor tart.

"Oh, wow," I said with a smile. "That's delicious."

"Sebastian is a treasure," Mason said. "You should try his burgers. Stone always wants what Braxton wants."

"He told me about being a foster kid and how Braxton helped him."

"He did?"

I nodded as I took another heavenly bite.

Mason looked thoughtful. "I'm surprised. Is that what changed your mind?"

I kept the discussion with Tasha to myself. "I realized I'd just end up coming back anyway. And, I'm here now. I might as well get to know you."

Mason looked happy. "That's good. So, what do you want to do first? Need anything? We could go into Anchorage. I'll show you around the town."

"I saw some of it when we got the DNA test."

"That wasn't the best part. We can stop by Kodiak's head office. You might rethink your interest in the business."

I finished the final bite of my cupcake. "Telecommunications? Not even remotely in my area of expertise." I didn't want Mason or Stone or anyone to think I was settling in here for the long haul. "Plus, my life is in Seattle."

"Message received," he said. He took another cupcake and perched on a stool across from me. "We could still do a tour of Anchorage."

"I'd like that." It would be fun to spend some time with Mason.

"Like what?" Stone asked as he walked in.

"A tour of Anchorage," I said. "I just told Mason I'd stick around for a few days."

"Only a few days?" Stone asked.

"Don't push her," Mason warned him.

"Don't manage me," I told them both. I pointed at Stone. "You didn't persuade me." I turned to Mason. "And you won't influence me."

"Not even if I'm super charming and fun, the best cousin ever?"

"I'm not here to have fun."

"You might as well have some fun," Mason said.

A diesel engine rumbled outside the house, and its backup alarm emitted loud beeps.

Stone's brow shot up, his attention going to the window. "They've started already?"

Mason grinned at me. "You definitely have to stay for the party."

Stone shifted over to the window and looked outside.

"Party?" I craned my neck to see what was going on, but the truck was beyond my field of vision.

"A week Saturday." Mason stood to go look himself.

I followed suit.

"The annual Kodiak Communications staff appreciation party," he said as a big green-and-white semi backed its way along a narrow driveway curving beside the vast lawn between the house and paddock. "Everybody comes. We have a massive barbecue, a band and dancing, plus trail rides and games for the kids in the afternoon."

Stone opened one of the French doors, and the three of us filed out to line up on the deck, watching. I stood between them feeling, the throb of the engine and listening to the high-pitched backup alarm.

I wasn't sure how I felt about attending a company party when I wasn't part of the organization. I'd feel like an interloper.

"What's in the truck?" I asked instead of committing.

"The tent," Mason replied.

"Once it's up, we'll get the sound system, tables, stage, a dance floor."

"You're building a dance floor in your yard?"

"For the dance," Stone said.

I shot him a look of impatience, catching the twinkle in his eyes.

"Ha, ha," I said back.

"It's a great party," Mason said. "If I was you, I wouldn't want to miss it."

"Bribery's not going to work."

"This isn't bribery," Stone said. "It's an opportunity."

"What would you even tell people about me?" I wasn't planning to stay that long, but the question had me curious.

"The truth," Stone said.

"Whatever you want us to tell people," Mason offered.

The thought of Braxton's friends and associates knowing about me felt weird.

"She's not a shameful secret," Stone said.

"She's entitled to her privacy," Mason said.

"I thought we'd keep it to family for now." I considered Tasha family, Layla and Brooklyn too.

I felt a sudden urgency to reach out to Layla and Brooklyn and bring them in on everything. I reached for my phone, but I couldn't make a call out here in the noise.

I waved my phone to indicate what I was doing before turning to the house.

"Hello?" A woman appeared in the doorway in front of me.

I quickly came to a halt, feeling slightly flustered. "Oh, hello."

She looked past me, obviously to where Mason and Stone stood. "Are you visiting… Mason?"

I didn't answer. I wasn't exactly sure what to say about myself.

"Stone?" she tried again, looking surprised by that.

"Neither," I said. "Well, both." I twisted my head to see if they were looking.

They were still watching the truck back up, so they didn't know we were behind them.

"I'm Adeline," she said.

I looked back in surprise. This was Adeline? I'd only seen her in childhood pictures. She'd grown up.

"Mason's sister," she added.

"I know. I'm…"

"Are you here on business? Kodiak stuff?"

"No." I looked back again, wishing either Mason or Stone would see us and join in. "It's…uh…a bit complicated."

Adeline looked intrigued. "You're with *both* of them?"

"Oh, no, not that kind of complicated."

"Adeline!" Finally, Mason's voice.

The truck engine suddenly went silent, and both Mason's and Stone's footsteps sounded on the wooden deck.

Adeline brushed past me, and I turned to see her hug her brother. Then she hugged Stone, rocking back and forth in his arms, a broad smile on her face.

"What are you doing home?" Mason asked.

"For the party," she said.

"You're early." Stone looked puzzled. He glanced over her head at me.

She linked her arm with his and turned my way. "Introduce me, why don't you?"

Stone nodded at Mason, obviously letting him take the lead.

"Adeline," Mason said in a serious tone. "This is Sophie. She's…" He looked to Stone, squinting in obvious hesitation.

"A complicated story," Stone filled in for him.

Adeline considered me with curiosity. "That's what she said."

"She's a long-lost relative," Mason said. "We have the DNA test to prove it."

"DNA?" Adeline asked.

"Sophie Crush." I stepped forward and offered her my hand.

"Cousin Sophie Crush," Mason said.

Adeline turned her head to Mason, clearly baffled.

I let my hand fall away.

Stone spoke up. "She and Emily were—"

"Sisters?" Adeline asked. "I don't get it. How does *that* work?"

"Switched at birth," Mason said. "Sophie and Emily were switched at birth."

Adeline reared back, and Mason steadied her.

"You're a girl." Adeline spoke giddily, reaching across the bistro table to squeeze my hand.

The four of us had taken a driving tour of Anchorage, walked a few streets, checked out some shops, then decided on the Moonstone Grill. The place was cozy and comfortable, with padded leather chairs and a big round fireplace burning in the middle of the room. I could feel the heat on my back.

She looked at Mason and then at Stone, who were on either side of her at the round table. *"Finally.* I've been outnumbered for years."

"Oh, you poor thing," Mason said with false sincerity.

A waitress had dropped off a round of drinks, chatting easily with Stone and Mason, who were clearly regulars. Adeline had ordered a martini, Stone and Mason a local beer on tap, and I went with a glass of merlot.

"You have to tell me everything," Adeline said to me.

It was easy to warm up to her. She was bubbly and friendly, insightful and funny. And her only reaction to me appearing in the family seemed to be delight.

I couldn't help smiling at her eagerness. "Everything about what?"

"What you do, where you grew up, what your family was like." She sat back in her chair. "Start at the very beginning."

"Can we order first?" Mason asked. "It could be a long story."

"We can talk and order at the same time," Adeline said.

"Sophie hasn't memorized the menu," Stone said.

"Get the pesto quesadilla," Adeline told her.

"You don't know what she likes," Mason said.

"Do you like yam fries?" she asked.

"I do," I answered.

She looked at her brother. "Who doesn't love chicken and pesto?"

"Someone with tree nut allergies."

I stifled a smile at their good-natured bickering. I'd watched Layla and her brother, James, do it most of my life.

Stone caught my look and rolled his eyes, grinning back.

"Sophie doesn't have allergies," Adeline asserted. "Nobody in our family has allergies." Belatedly, she looked at me. "Do you?"

"No allergies."

"See?" She nodded to Mason.

"I recommend the beluga burger," Mason said. "No actual beluga. It's beef on a homemade bun with their signature sauce."

They were both staring at me, and I felt like I was caught in the middle.

Stone opened the menu in front of me. "Maybe Sophie could choose for herself."

"I like the sound of the quesadilla," I said.

Adeline looked triumphant.

Stone arched a brow in my direction.

I wasn't staying loyal to the sisterhood. The quesadilla did look good to me. And I loved yam fries.

But I did dutifully glance down at the menu. A slice of banana cream pie instantly caught my attention. It was thick with whipped cream covered in what looked like white chocolate shavings.

"That one's my favorite," Adeline said, seeming to see where I was staring.

"So, we're having dessert?" Mason asked.

"It's a celebration," she said.

"That's champagne," he said back.

"Are either of you going to let Sophie talk?" Stone asked.

Mason and especially Adeline looked confused.

"She can talk anytime she wants," Adeline said.

"What's stopping her?" Mason asked.

"The two of you," Stone piped up. "She can't get a word

in edgewise." To me, he said, "Their conversational style is an acquired taste."

Everyone stopped talking then and stared at me.

"Oh, great," I said. "No pressure at all."

"Say something brilliant." Adeline grinned.

"Tell them about your invention," Stone said.

"You have an invention?" Adeline asked.

"What does Stone know about it?" Mason asked.

"You're doing it again," Stone said with a frown.

They both stopped talking and stared at me.

"It's a dessert-making machine," I said. "I worked with some brilliant friends to create it, and we sold the patent."

"To who?" Mason asked.

"What does it make?" Adeline asked.

"Delicacies," I answered Adeline first. "Very fancy and very precise with lots of cream, ganache and pastry. We sold it to East Sun Tech in Japan."

"Japan?" Mason looked impressed.

"I didn't sell it myself," I clarified. I didn't want to take the credit. "My friend Tasha's husband has contacts all over the world. He's my other friend Layla's brother, and I've known him for years. Without him, we'd probably still be tinkering in the garage and schlepping it around to local restaurants in Seattle, auditioning it."

The waitress approached us again, thirtysomething, petite with wavy brunette hair and round flushed cheeks. "Are you all ready to order?"

"I think we're set," Stone answered.

"The usual?" she asked him.

"You bet."

She turned to Mason.

He gave her a nod. "Cheeseburger and home fries for me."

"Extra fries," she said as she made a note.

Mason smiled.

She looked to me next, her blue eyes open and friendly. "What looks good to you…"

"Sophie," Adeline supplied my name. "She's our—"

Mason swiftly nudged his sister under the table.

"—visiting from Seattle," Adeline finished smoothly.

I was impressed with her recovery. "I'd like the pesto quesadilla."

"Welcome to Alaska, Sophie. I'm Janine. You want the yam fries with that?"

"Yes, please, Janine. I'm told they're delicious."

"You got some good advice there," she said.

"A quesadilla for me too," Adeline said. "Extra guacamole if you can."

"We can," Janine said. She sent a silent question my way, obviously wondering if I'd take Adeline's lead.

"Sure," I said. "Adeline seems to be the expert."

"Got it," Janine said. "Give me a shout if you need more drinks."

"Thanks," Stone said, gathering my menu along with his own and handing them over.

"You must come here a lot." I could see why they would. The ambience was laid-back and friendly, the decor was subdued and the seating more than comfortable.

"The DJ starts at eight," Adeline said. "Dancing if you want it."

I couldn't help a fleeting glance at Stone. Then my gaze caught Adeline's and she gave me a secretive smile.

I wanted to shout out *no*. That hadn't been what I'd meant at all. I didn't want to dance with Stone. I mean, well, sure, maybe it would be fun to dance with him. Although, who knew if a guy like him would even dance? But I didn't want Adeline to get the wrong idea.

"Ladies' room?" Adeline asked me, pushing back her chair.

"Sure." Perfect. I'd clarify things for her while we walked.

"So, Stone, eh?" she said before I could even broach the subject. She linked her arm with mine. "He's pretty hot."

"No."

"What do you mean no?"

"I mean, I didn't mean that the way it looked."

"Your moon-eyes at Stone?"

I whirled to try to face her directly.

Adeline tugged at my arm, redirecting me around a table. "Watch out."

"I did not make moon-eyes at Stone," I said, fearing I might have done just that.

"It was subtle. He didn't notice."

"Subtle moon-eyes?"

She laughed as we crossed the foyer to a small staircase.

I might be uncomfortable, but I couldn't help but like her. "It's not…"

"You think he's hot." She nudged her hip against mine. "Don't worry about it."

"We mostly argue. We don't see eye to eye on anything. He thought I was a con artist when I first showed up."

She went ahead as we started up the stairs. "Because you claimed Uncle Braxton was your father?"

I followed, and the aging stairs creaked under my feet. "I didn't know that part at first. I didn't even think that at first. All I knew was that Mason was probably my cousin."

"I can't believe Mason gave them his DNA. That's weird for him. Don't get me wrong, I'm superglad he did. Otherwise we'd never have met you."

"You're not…" I tried to figure out how to phrase my question. "I don't know, mad about Emily?" I had to think that Adeline and Emily had been friends growing up. The two families seemed so close.

"That was such a tragedy," Adeline said, stopping outside the ladies' room door. "We were years getting over it. But it wasn't your fault."

"I feel like it was…like it should have been me."

"Well, it should have been you. But then we'd have been just as devastated to lose you."

I thought about that. It made some sense.

"We can't change it, Sophie."

That was true too.

"Do you need the restroom?" she asked.

I shook my head. I'd just come along for the ride.

"Me neither."

We both turned and headed back down the staircase.

Adeline paused in the reception area. "I was going to offer to help get you together with Stone."

I lowered my voice, since the hostess was watching us. "I don't want help getting together with Stone."

"Are you sure? Maybe a little dancing later."

"No."

"He really is hot."

"Stone and me, not a good idea." The attraction was there all right, but so was the combustion, the exasperation and the complications. I didn't even want to get started on the complications.

Adeline looked puzzled now. "How can you possibly know that?"

I pressed my lips together as I tried to form a reasonable answer.

"Something already happened?" The expression on Adeline's face told me she was entirely too intuitive. She pulled me into an alcove where we had more privacy.

"Nothing happened," I said. It hadn't. Not really.

"Define nothing."

"Are you always like this?" I tried to deflect.

"Like what?"

"So...so..."

"Right?"

"I didn't say that."

"But you meant it." She gave her thick auburn hair a little toss. "I have a knack."

I couldn't argue with that. "For reading minds?"

Her green eyes lit up. "So, something *did* happen. I knew it."

I decided it was stupid to keep playing this game. "I kissed him. Or he kissed me. We kissed each other."

"And...?"

"And nothing. We stopped."

"Why?"

"Because we didn't mean to do it. We were fighting. He was trying to get me to leave Alaska, and I was insisting on finding out the truth."

She looked confused. "Wait. I thought Stone talked you into staying."

"He didn't talk me into anything. I don't know why he keeps trying to take credit for it. Yes, sure, *now* he wants me to stay. But back then he wanted me to get the heck out of Alaska and never come back."

"He always takes my uncle's side. They stick together, you know." Her expression turned more serious.

"Stone and Braxton?" I assumed that's what she meant.

"All of them. The Cambridge men. They never listen to a thing—" Her expression brightened again. "But that's irrelevant. I'm here for you if you want my help."

"I don't need any help with Stone." I'd finally gotten a certain composure about my feelings for him. I wasn't going to act on them. "I'm staying to get to know Mason and you and Kyle. I've never had cousins before."

She linked arms with me again. "You're going to love having cousins. At least, you're going to love having me as a cousin. And I'm going to love having you. Be careful of the guys though."

I was surprised by her warning. She seemed to have a great relationship with her brothers, at least with Mason. I hadn't seen her interacting with Kyle yet, since he'd headed off to Seattle.

"Why?" I asked.

"They're very strong-minded."

"I'm strong-minded too."

"Just watch yourself, that's all. I bet our food's almost ready."

I found myself agreeing with Adeline about strong-mindedness as I watched Stone and Kyle directing the yard setup for the Kodiak Communications barbecue. They both seemed to know exactly what they wanted.

The Cambridges' backyard was at least five acres. The gardeners had ridden around on multiple mowers this morning, trimming everything even. And there were still at least six of them fine-tuning the garden beds close to the house. A string of six horses stood along the fence watching the goings-on.

They'd erected a massive tent with a clear top, which I thought was a very nice touch. Its sides were open, and blue draping was being hung from the peaked ceiling alongside rows and rows of little white lights. Lights and some greenery also decorated the lattice pillars that camouflaged the tent poles. I could picture the final effect in my mind. It was going to be magnificent.

I watched some of the workers unloading tables from a truck trailer. They were rectangular, utilitarian. I knew you could spruce them up with tablecloths and centerpieces, maybe some candles and decent dinnerware. But they were less than ideal, especially given the beauty of the tent itself.

I approached a man who seemed to be in charge of setting up the dining area. He was fiftysomething, stocky, with a receding hairline. He wore navy pants and a crisp striped shirt with a blue tie and his sleeves rolled up. He was checking a tablet, and people came and went asking him questions.

I approached. "Good morning."

He gave me a nod. "Hello."

"I'm Sophie Crush."

"Michael Hume."

"Nice to meet you, Michael."

"Line that one up with the pillar. Six foot spacing," he called out to a pair of workers who were placing a table. To me, he asked, "Can I help you with something?" He didn't seem annoyed, just busy and distracted.

I got that. "Do you have a solid attendance estimate?"

He seemed surprised by the question. "Two hundred twenty-five."

I did a quick scan of the space. "Buffet or table service?"

Now he was looking a little less patient. "Buffet. And you are?"

"The person in charge," Stone announced from behind me. I hadn't heard him approach.

Michael saw Stone and his impatience vanished.

"I'm not trying to take over," I said to Stone. I wasn't sure why he'd spoken so firmly.

"I'm deputizing you," he said. "Sophie can take over the dining plans."

"Of course," Michael said to Stone. "I didn't realize."

"Neither did I," I said, trying to make light. I didn't want to get off on the wrong foot with Michael. I just had a few suggestions.

"She knows what she's doing," Stone said. "She used to run a restaurant in Seattle."

Stone was overstating. I hadn't been in charge of the entire Blue Fern restaurant, just the dining room service.

"What did you want to change?" he asked me.

I decided to plunge in. Hoping that Michael wouldn't react too badly to my ideas. "I was thinking round tables would work better than rectangular."

"Rectangular was the order," Michael said in a cautionary tone. "It's been the tradition for years."

"Do you have rounds available?" I asked.

"Yes, but—"

"Let's exchange them," Stone said.

"It'll take extra time."

"Is it reasonable?" I asked. "Costly?" I could picture the setup in my mind, and I liked the way it looked. I also knew the conversational flow of rounds was much superior to rectangles. But I didn't want to be obstinate about it.

"There'd be some overtime tonight," Michael said.

"Not a problem," Stone said. "We want it to be the best."

"Rounds would be best," I said.

"Done," Stone said.

Michael clamped his jaw but kept his tone on a professional level. "Rounds it is." He gave a whistle.

Everyone who was working looked up, and he paced toward them.

"I hope I didn't cause him too much grief," I said.

Stone shrugged. "We're paying him to get it right. And I trust your ideas. Anything else?"

"Did you ever consider table service instead of buffet?"

I could tell by his expression that he had not. "Talk to the caterer. It's Mel and Off-the-Land."

"*Me* talk to them?"

"We've never had a restaurant professional in the company before."

"I'm not in the company," I said.

"You know what I mean."

As two men passed by us removing the big tables, Stone canted his head toward the entrance. "Come on. I'll take you to see her."

I followed along. "Who?"

"Mel."

"Mel's a woman?"

"She is. You'll like her."

"Can you just do this?" I asked, glancing around behind us at the organized chaos.

"Mel won't mind the interruption. We're one of her biggest events of the year."

We were heading up the back driveway in the general direction of the garage.

"I mean use my ideas to change the party."

"You volunteered."

"All I said was round tables."

"And table service. It's all on you now, Sophie."

"Ha, ha."

We approached a pickup truck and Stone opened the passenger door. "You seem to like this kind of thing."

He was right. I did like this kind of thing. There was a reason I'd gone into dining room management. I got a kick out of planning dining experiences and an immense level of satisfaction out of seeing people have a good time.

"Hop in," he said.

"I thought we were going to see Mel?" I looked around for a car or van marked Off-the-Land.

"We are."

"She's not here?"

"She'll be at her restaurant in town."

I met his gaze. We were a couple of feet apart, but I could still feel his magnetism. I hadn't been thinking about it during our exchange, but for some reason it hit me all at once.

"You're going to drop everything and drive me into Anchorage."

The timbre of his voice was deep. "I am."

"Why?"

His gaze bored into mine, reigniting all the feelings I'd been struggling to keep at bay. "I think you know why."

"I don't." I dared to hope he'd say something flattering or complimentary, that he liked me or wanted to spend time with me or something like that. I wished I didn't feel that way, but I did.

"For Braxton," he said. "He'll like it that you're getting involved in the event."

Disappointment hit me before I could stop myself.

This was for Braxton, not Stone.

Five

I'd driven into Anchorage a few times now, and the trip down the highway that had seemed so long on that first drive from the airport felt shorter. At least it had on my last trip. Not so much this time, since I was stuck in the cab alone with Stone.

I knew he couldn't read my mind. He didn't know that I'd been deflated like a teenager with a crush back there. But I knew, and I really wanted this trip to be over.

Instead, the miles churned slowly past as we drove the winding road that followed the water's edge.

Something black flashed in my vision.

"Whoa," Stone said, cranking the wheel.

I was thrown his way. My seat belt snapped tight as I grasped for the armrest.

My brain sorted out the image, and I realized it was a bear. No, two bears. No, three—a mother and two cubs.

"Look out," I said reflexively, even though he could see everything I could see and was taking every possible evasive maneuver.

The ditch was deep on my side of the pickup, the rock face beyond it steep and immovable. There was a cliff on the other side down to the water, and I sure didn't want to go over that. I didn't know what we were going to hit, but we were going to hit something—if not the bears, then the mountainside.

But suddenly the truck righted. It rocked on its wheels, gravel spun from beneath us, and in an instant we were headed up a narrow side road cut into the hill.

"You okay?" Stone asked, slowing the vehicle.

I gave a jerky nod. "Fine. Startled. That was a bear." I craned my neck to look out the back window, but we'd gone around a curve on the narrow road and I couldn't see the highway any longer.

"That was a bear," Stone confirmed, bringing us to a full

stop. He put the shifter into Park. "You're not hurt? Did you wrench your neck?" He looked me over closely.

I stretched my neck back and forth, checking for pain or stiffness. "All good, I think. Does that happen a lot?"

"Occasionally. Usually it's moose that startle and run out in front of you. Bears seem to have more traffic sense."

"Good to know."

Stone gave a grin, a handsome, blue-eyes-lighting grin that, despite the situation, wormed its way to my toes. Why did he have to be so attractive?

"They can both wreck your car, flip it even and cause fatalities."

"I plan to be careful." I did—very careful driving from here on in.

Stone's reactions were faster than mine would have been.

"Good thing this road was here." If he hadn't taken the hidden turn, we'd have crashed.

"It leads up to Horn Lake," he said, nodding forward. "Really pretty green from the glacial runoff. You can ride horses up the back trail to get to it. We swam in it once when we were teenagers. Nearly killed us. But we were dumb back then."

"You, Mason and Kyle?"

"We pilfered a bottle from the whiskey cellar and drank it first."

"I guess you'd have to."

"Found out later it was a *very* expensive bottle, but that's another story. That night we dared each other to duck under the water. Once one of us took up the challenge, the rest had to put up or shut up."

"Who took up the challenge?"

His expression told me it was him.

"You had something to prove?" I guessed.

"Let's say I didn't have the genteel upbringing of Mason and Kyle. In my formative years, if someone dared you, you did it. It was the only way to keep their respect and keep yourself safe."

"That's sad." I couldn't help but feel sorry about his rough childhood.

"It's not sad. Mostly it was exhilarating. Plus, it worked. When I was younger, the other guys left me alone." He gave a chuckle. "That time it was worth it to see the expressions on Mason's and Kyle's faces."

"Exactly how cold was the lake?"

"Only a little above freezing. You can see the glacier where it runs off."

"Yeah?" I found myself looking up the road, curious about the site of Stone's youthful hijinks.

"You want to go see?" he asked.

My curiosity must have been obvious. "Would it take long?"

He pulled the transfer case into four-wheel drive. "It's a few miles."

"Do we have time?" I'd already interrupted his day.

"Sure." He pulled slowly ahead.

As we trundled along the narrow, rutted road, I found myself excited at the prospect of seeing Horn Lake and the glacier. First, it sounded beautiful. Second, I wanted to picture Stone, Mason and Kyle in their teenage years, having fun.

I'd attended parties and pulled a few silly stunts when I was in high school, but I had a feeling my antics were small-time compared to Stone and my newfound cousins.

The road became steeper, and Stone was forced to negotiate around big boulders. Trees crowded in around us as the truck rocked back and forth, tossing me around.

"Hang on," Stone said, indicating the top corner on my side as he wrestled with the steering wheel.

I looked up to see a handhold, and I grabbed it. "Thanks. Are you sure we can make it?"

He gave me a fleeting look of surprise. "It's easier on horses, but we'll get there."

"It's so rough." I'd never been on a road remotely like this before.

"This is nothing," he said. "You're not getting motion sickness are you?"

"No. I'm fine."

"Good. Just a couple more miles."

"A couple more *miles*?" I'd been expecting the lake to appear at any moment.

He flashed an unabashed grin. "We picked it because it was private."

"For your stolen moments of drinking."

"And swearing like lumberjacks, and a little making out on occasion."

I felt myself go hot at the image of Stone making out. I looked away before he could see a blush come up on my face. The last thing I wanted was for him to know I'd put myself in that particular image with him.

"Does it get worse?" I asked to change the subject.

"The road?"

"Yes."

"A little bit, right near the top. You kind of have to take a run at the last bit."

"Oh, good."

"It's fun."

"I can't wait," I said sarcastically, wondering what I'd gotten myself into.

We bumped our way around a few more bends, and then he pressed the accelerator. "Hang on."

I gripped the handle and reached out to grasp the back of the bench seat.

The truck went faster, rattling the frame, rattling my teeth. Then an impossibly steep embankment loomed up in front of us.

"We're going up *that*?" I asked as the truck shifted gears.

"I've done it dozens of times," Stone said. He was hanging tight to the steering wheel, his shoulders stiff and his back planted hard against the cushioned seat.

I closed my eyes, felt the cab tip up in front, heard the

wheels spin in the dirt, then for a second it felt like we were floating.

We came down hard, and I felt the shock up my spine.

"See?" Stone said as everything slowly stilled. "Wasn't that fun?"

My first glimpse of Horn Lake confirmed it was spectacular. Crystal clear turquoise water surrounded by lush forest, with a gleaming white glacier in the distance against a stark blue sky.

Stone spun the truck in a tight circle, so we were facing the road. His arms stretched across the back of the seat as he looked over his shoulder going in Reverse. He rocked us to a stop, put the truck into Park and set the brake. "Come and take a look."

He unfastened his seat belt, and I did the same, opening my door to slide from the high seat onto the dirt. Then I shaded my eyes to gaze at the view as we walked to the back of the truck.

He dropped the tailgate, giving us a high seat. "Boost up?"

"In a minute." First, I wanted to check the temperature of the water.

I crouched down to where miniwaves lapped the pebbled shore and dipped my fingers into the water. It was painfully cold.

"Ouch," I said, immediately pulling my hand back.

"Cold, huh?" he asked, stopping next to me.

I rose. "Freezing."

"Yeah, we were pretty wild back then. I don't know how long it takes to get to hypothermia in that temperature, but it can't be long."

"Are you saying you were lucky to live through your youth?"

"Now you see what Braxton had to work with."

I had thought about that a few times, wondering what kind of a man would take in a rebellious teenager who'd vandalized his property. It was admirable. There were obviously things about Braxton I didn't yet understand.

From a genetic perspective, it was encouraging. I might have inherited some of his short temper, but maybe I'd also inherited some of his hidden benevolence.

"Do you know why he did it?" I asked.

Stone shrugged. "It's still a mystery to me. I sure didn't deserve it."

"You're selling yourself short."

"I'm not. I was a little jerk back then. It took a long time for me to appreciate what he did for me. It took— Will you look at that." Stone pointed to the sky.

I followed his gesture to see a pair of huge birds floating in the sky.

"Golden eagles," he said. "That'll be a mating pair. They likely have a nest nearby."

I'd seen bald eagles from the house, but this was the first time I'd seen goldens. I watched them soar in silent circles above us, their wingspan impressively broad and silhouetted against the sky.

I moved my gaze back to earth and had to blink to adjust my vision from the brightness. "What were you saying?"

He crouched and splashed his hand in the water. "Are you up for a swim?"

"No way."

"You're sure? Ah, that's what I remember. Refreshing."

"About Braxton…" I tried to coax him, being curious about the relationship of the two men.

"What about Braxton?"

"You were saying something."

Stone picked up a handful of rocks and tossed one into the lake. "Only that it was tough at first. I went from an over-crowded three-bedroom foster home to…well, you've seen it."

"The Cambridge mansion."

He tossed another rock that made a long arc before splashing into the smooth water. "They gave me a bedroom bigger than my old backyard."

"Funny," I said, thinking about my own change in circumstance. I was an adult and had made my own decisions to get here. But both our experiences had been sudden and dramatic.

"Funny?" he prompted.

"My newfound wealth is a culture shock. I'm not saying it's the same thing as you went through. But my friend Tasha had to drag me out house shopping. I wanted something on the water. I love the idea of being on the oceanfront. But the houses there, they were all so big. Not mansion big, but too big for one person."

"You said you just bought a new house."

"I did."

"So, you found one you liked."

"With five bedrooms. What am I going to do with five bedrooms?"

"You'll figure it out." He threw the last rock, then dusted off his hands.

"That's what Tasha said."

"She sounds very smart." He gestured to the tailgate, and we made our way back. There, he gave me a quick boost, just a couple of seconds, but the ghost of his touch lingered at my hips.

"She is very smart," I said to distract myself. "She completely revamped her life, got married and joined the library board. She does a reading outreach program for kids."

He sat next to me. "Good for her."

I took in the sweep of the view, thinking about Tasha and Layla and Brooklyn. "All my friends seem happy being rich."

"You have nothing but rich friends?"

I didn't want him to get the wrong idea. "They didn't used to be rich. Believe me, we were all perfectly average. It happened sort of unexpectedly for each of them. You know, maybe it was easier with husbands. They didn't have to do it alone."

I pondered the theory for a moment. It might be easier with a partner. It made sense. You could talk things out, exchange ideas, get past the strangeness of it all together.

"Layla and Brooklyn married into money," I continued. "Twin brothers."

"Yeah?"

"Max and Colton were already rich, so they obviously knew what they were doing." Something big and black registered in my peripheral vision.

"They were also insulated from—"

The black thing suddenly moved, and I grabbed Stone's arm. "What's *that*?"

He took in my expression then jerked his head around. He immediately hopped to his feet in the truck box and pulled me up with him. "That's our bear."

I moved closer, sticking tight to Stone. Every sense came alert and I could hear my heart pounding in my ears. "What does it want?" My voice was a rasp.

"She's curious."

The cubs were moving around their mother. One of them came up on its hind feet and sniffed the air.

"Are they hungry?" I didn't really want an answer to that.

"Bears don't eat people." Stone paused. "Mostly anyway."

"Mostly," I squeaked in a whisper.

One of the cubs gave a cry.

The mother huffed and came up on her hind legs.

My eyes went wide. She was *huge*.

"Back up to the cab." He urged me that way. "Nice and slow, nothing sudden."

"Can she get us up here?" I asked, knowing it was a stupid question. The bear could probably hop into the truck box without breaking her stride.

As we backed into the cab, her ears went back and she huffed again. The two cubs rushed to hide behind her, and I couldn't help thinking that was a bad sign.

"I'm going to jump out on the driver's side," Stone said in an undertone.

"You're *leaving* me?"

"Can you follow?"

"Yes." I nodded rapidly. I'd follow him anywhere in a situation like this.

"I'll open the door, and I want you to dive inside as fast as you can. I'll be right behind you."

"Right. Got it."

The bear dropped back down to all fours and gave a deafening roar.

"Now," Stone said and put his hand on the side of the box, hopping over and grabbing the door handle.

I clambered over much less gracefully, scratching my belly and tearing my shirt. But I hit the ground feetfirst and lunged for the door, scrambling inside, aware of the bear charging around the back of the truck. Her feet pounded on the ground, sending out sharp vibrations.

Stone's hand pushed against my butt, shoving me unceremoniously forward. Then I heard the door slam behind him.

I dared to look and saw the bear rear up, her big paws going on the roof as she roared against the glass.

"Can she get in?" I managed to ask.

Stone started the engine. "We're not sticking around to find out."

The noise had seemed to surprise the bear, and it dropped away, giving Stone a chance to lurch forward. We bounced crazily down the incline.

I hadn't had time to put on my seat belt, and I fell off the seat, my knee hitting the floor.

"You okay?" Stone called.

"Good," I said. "Fine. Keep going."

He glanced in the mirror. "She's not following."

The ride got a bit smoother as Stone slowed us down.

"Can you get up?" he asked.

"Yeah. Sure." I shakily pulled myself up on the seat and reached for my seat belt, clicking it securely into place.

Stone pulled his own across his chest with one hand. "Can you help me with mine?"

I reached over. Our hands mingled above the mechanism, getting it sorted out in the right direction, then I clicked the seat belt in.

I rose and sat back, blowing out a breath. "Has that ever happened before?"

"Not here," he said. "Grizzly encounters are unusual."

"So, that was special?" I managed a shaky laugh.

"Very special." He glanced my way. "Seriously. Are you okay? Your adrenaline's still pumping, so you might not feel it yet."

He was right about that.

"I banged my knee, but it's just a bruise."

"Your shirt's ripped."

I pulled back the torn bit to look. "Just a scratch."

"You're bleeding."

"Barely." It was starting to sting now, but it wasn't a deep cut. I dabbed at it with the end of my shirt. "You?" I asked. "Any injuries?"

"None. Good cardio workout there for a minute." He laughed too. His sounded a lot less flustered than me.

We drove a few minutes more in silence.

"Thanks," I finally remembered to say.

He glanced at me again, his brow going up. "For putting you in danger?"

"For staying so calm, for knowing what to do."

"I'd never have left you in the box, you know."

"I know." I did know. I knew that now more than ever. I realized my hair was a mess, hanging over my eyes. When I smoothed it back, I saw my hand was shaking. It was the adrenaline coming out of my system.

"Hey," Stone said, his voice laced with concern.

Before I knew it, he'd stopped the truck, released our seat belts and drawn me into his arms. He felt solid, strong, incredibly reassuring, even though I knew we were out of danger now.

"You're fine," he said soothingly against my hair.

I nodded in response. "I know. It's just the adrenaline."

"Adrenaline is good."

"Especially around bears."

He chuckled. "Good for you, Sophie."

"Good for me what?"

"Bouncing back, making a joke, not turning all anxious."

It hadn't even occurred to me to get anxious. Not that there'd been time. Stone's reactions had been fast, smart and decisive.

"Thanks, Stone," I whispered again. I put my arms around him, hugging him tight in gratitude.

We silently held each other for a long minute, then his lips brushed my temple with the lightest of kisses. My chest went tight. My skin heated in reaction. My limbs tingled and I unconsciously arched my body against him.

He kissed me again, more firmly this time, making his way along my cheek, down and down. Then he pulled back a little. His palm cupped the back of my neck. He gazed into my eyes, his own full of questions.

I nodded in answer, and he tipped forward, kissing me full on the lips.

Joy rushed through me. I was thrilled to be alive, thrilled to be in Stone's arms. The wilderness around us was vast and energizing, and for the first time I didn't feel so much like a spectator in Alaska. I had a toehold on belonging.

Our lips fused, the kiss going deeper. Desire and arousal rushed through me. His shirt was thin cotton, and I could feel the heat of his chest seeping into my breasts.

He bracketed my hips, tugging me along the bench seat, easing me back until he was lying on top of me. His lips left mine, moving to my neck, planting hot, sexy kisses along the tender skin.

I shivered in reaction as his lips left imprints of arousal in a chain toward my chest. He popped the buttons on my shirt, and I held my breath, waiting for his touch on my breasts. My bra was thin silk, and I could feel my nipples tightening against the fabric, waiting more desperately for his touch as the seconds ticked past.

Then his mouth touched me, dampening the silk fabric, drawing the hard nub into the cavern of his mouth. It was the sexiest sensation I'd ever felt, and I gasped, arching, looking for more. He obliged, moving to the other breast.

I tugged at his shirt, dragging it over his head. I wanted to feel skin on skin, our bodies together. He ducked his way free and tossed the shirt aside. He pushed my shirt off my shoulders, trapping my arms with the final buttons.

He looked deep into my eyes, then teased my breasts again as he freed the last of my buttons. I all but tore off my shirt and impatiently ripped my bra over my head. Then I dived headlong in, pressing my breasts against his skin, wrapping my arms around his neck, kissing him deeply, letting my imagination run wild to making love, our bodies together, completing each other.

"Sophie." His voice sounded a long way away.

"Yes," I said. "Oh, yes." I reached for the snap on his jeans.

"Sophie," he said again.

"Stone," I said back. *Stone, Stone, Stone,* my mind echoed.

His hand covered mine, stopping my quest to release his zipper.

I looked up, more than a little puzzled.

His expression was tight, his lips drawn thin. His voice was a rasp when he spoke. "I wasn't thinking of this."

My brain was a muddle of confusion.

"We…" He scrunched his eyes shut.

He was saying no? He was saying *no*? We were one step away from paradise here. I didn't know about him, but passion like this didn't come along every day in my world.

"Are you okay?" I asked, stupefied. I might not be the most experienced woman in the world, nor a genius, but I could tell when a guy was into me, and Stone was very, very much into me right now.

He pushed my hand from his fly. "Not a good idea."

"No," I said. "It's a *great* idea."

"Sophie," he said, and his forehead dropped lightly against mine. He held it there.

"What?" I asked.

"We're reacting to the scare. It's a hormone thing."

I could agree it was hormones, but I wasn't agreeing with the rest. "We kissed long before that bear came along."

"We didn't do *this*," he said, drawing back to look. His gaze dropped to my bare breasts and stayed there.

"We wanted to," I said. At least I'd wanted to, and it sure seemed like Stone did too, even back then.

He picked my shirt up from the floor and pushed it against me, covering my breasts. "This is way too complicated."

The passion was rapidly disappearing out of me now. A woman could only stay hot for a guy so long while he was rejecting her. I shook out my shirt.

Stone looked pointedly away as I pushed my arms into my sleeves and did up the buttons. My bra dangled from the seat beside me, and I stuffed it into my jeans pocket. Then I smoothed out my shirt.

"There," I said, an edge to my voice. "Happy?"

He looked at me like I'd lost the plot. "No. Ticked off."

He was mad at me? Come on.

I turned in my seat, facing forward, tipping my chin, my body language telling him I was ready to go now. "You're the one who called a halt."

He drew back. "Not at *you*. At myself. At the circumstances." He moved back to the driver's seat, grasping the steering wheel. "You don't know who I am, Sophie."

"Yeah, well, you don't know who I am either. Is that a prerequisite to sex?"

"Yes."

I turned to give him a look of disbelief. *"Really?"*

His expression turned sheepish. "Not always. But in this case, yes. Yes, it is."

"Why?" I was genuinely curious. Our situation was complicated, sure. But we were both adults. We were entitled to make up our own minds about how we felt about each other. It was nobody else's business.

"You're his daughter."

"This is about *Braxton*?" A man I barely even knew was messing with my sex life?

"Yes."

I gave my head a little shake. "You won't touch me because of some warped sense of loyalty to him?"

"I touched you plenty."

"You do know I make my own decisions, right?"

Stone's knuckles went white as he gripped harder on the steering wheel. "That's irrelevant."

"I'm an adult, Stone. My personal life is none of Braxton Cambridge's business."

"That's my point. We're not going to tell him."

The statement took me by surprise. "Of course, we're not going to tell him. Why on earth would we tell him?"

"Exactly. And then I'd have a secret…from him. That's not the way I operate." He pulled his seat belt around himself. "Buckle up."

"Are you saying this conversation's over?"

"Yes."

I stared at his profile a moment longer. I wanted him, and he wanted me. I didn't see where Braxton had anything at all to do with it. But I sure wasn't going to beg.

"Sophie."

"Fine." I jerked hard and reeled the seat belt out. "Have it your way."

I was surprised when Stone turned toward Anchorage instead of back to the Cambridge mansion. I had no idea why he'd want to stay trapped with me any longer than absolutely necessary.

"We're still going to Off-the-Land?" I asked.

He brought up the truck's speed. "That was the whole point of the trip."

That had been the original point, but things had gone significantly off the rails since then.

"Nothing's changed," he said.

I felt like quite a lot had changed. "That's your perspective?"

"It's a fact not a perspective. You're going to meet Mel,

talk about ideas for the party, share your expertise, get yourself involved in the event and the family. Everybody wins."

I didn't feel like pussyfooting around. "This doesn't make you uncomfortable?"

"That I stuck with my principles? No, that never makes me uncomfortable."

"Well, I'm uncomfortable." I didn't like sitting here with a guy who'd just turned me down for a reason he had yet to explain.

"Get over it."

"That's your whole answer, *get over it*?"

"As you so aptly pointed out earlier, we're both adults. There's some sexual chemistry between us, sure, but we can handle it. We can make a choice whether or not to act on it."

That wasn't the entire point. But I was sure I wouldn't be acting on it again anytime soon. If that's how he wanted to play it…

"Fine." My tone was clipped.

"Good." He responded in kind.

"Tell me something about Mel." Now that it was settled, I was anxious to move on.

"Sure."

We took a turn at speed and I hung on to the handle to keep from swinging his way. The tires didn't break loose beneath us, so I assumed he knew what he was doing.

"Mel's great," he said, his tone returning to normal. "Smart, down-to-earth. She inherited the business from her dad, who inherited it from his dad. Off-the-Land has been in operation since the gold rush."

I couldn't help but be intrigued. That was a very long time to be in business. "Is it catering only, or do they have a dining room?"

"I guess you could call it a dining room. They have a seating area. It's casual. Their clientele tends to be working-class guys looking for a hot, filling lunch to either take out or eat in."

"I see." I'd expected the barbecue to be more high-end than this was sounding.

"What do you see?" Stone asked.

"Off-the-Land doesn't sound like what I was expecting."

"Which was?"

"Something a little more…"

"Posh?"

"Not posh." I reframed my expectations. "I guess it *is* a barbecue."

"Are you a snob, Sophie Crush?" His teasing tone surprised me.

I'd expected us to stay aloof with each other for a whole lot longer than this. "I'm not a snob. But the Cambridges have gone to a lot of trouble for this—the tent, the temporary dance floor, grooming the yard. It has to be costing a fortune."

"It's our way of thanking the employees. We're not going to skimp."

"So why the lowbrow caterer?"

"Did I say *lowbrow*?" He wasn't teasing any longer.

"No. But you made it sound as if—"

"Mel's cooking is amazing. I hope you're not going to act like this when we get there."

Now I was insulted. "Act like what? I'll be perfectly polite."

"And respectful."

"*Yes*, respectful. What do you think of me, Stone?"

He did a sweeping look at me as we drove past the first buildings in town. "That you're big-city."

"Seattle?" We were pretty laid-back in Seattle compared to, well, pretty much any other big city in the entire county.

"This is Alaska. We're grounded and hardworking. We take things at face value."

"Fine," I said. Then my tone turned sarcastic. "I'll be on my best behavior."

"Just don't have any preconceived ideas, is all."

"I don't have any preconceived—"

He shot me a look.

"You said it was rustic," I reminded him.

"Rustic can be good."

I was tired of arguing. "Fine. Sure. Rustic can be great."

"Say it with a little more enthusiasm." He was teasing again. It was hard to keep up with the man's mood swings.

"Rustic can be great," I said with sincerity. It helped that I believed it was true.

"That's the spirit." He flipped on his signal then and swung the truck into a big gravel-strewn parking lot.

A sign above the sprawling plain brown building read: Off-the-Land Restaurant and Catering, Est. 1898. The building didn't look like it had been around since 1898, but it did look like it had probably been in place since the fifties.

Stone parked the truck out front, and we both exited into a slightly dusty breeze.

We crossed a creaky porch and he pulled on a large raw wood handle. The door screeched open on rusty hinges, and he motioned me in.

The restaurant was dim inside; a few narrow windows let in some murky daylight. A dozen picnic-style tables were set out in two rows with a scarred bar stretching behind them. Two glass-fronted drink coolers stood behind the bar, bathing the area in fluorescent light. I could just make out a row of plain wooden bar stools pushed underneath.

There were no tablecloths, but each table had a tin coffee-pot stuffed with paper napkins next to a mismatched pair of salt and pepper shakers, a ketchup dispenser and a bottle of Tabasco sauce. I reminded myself of all the things Stone had said. It wasn't for me to be judgmental.

"Well, hello there, Stone!" A woman burst through a set of swinging half doors from the kitchen. She was tall, probably close to six feet. She had flaming red hair twirled up in a bun, an attractive face and a pair of gold-rimmed glasses perched on her straight nose.

"Hey, Mel," Stone replied.

Mel's curious expression turned my way.

"This is Sophie Crush. She's up from Seattle and helping with the barbecue."

"Nice to meet you, Sophie," Mel said, coming closer.

"Sophie used to be in the restaurant business."

Mel's expression faltered for a second. "You bringing in the big guns?" she asked Stone.

"Nothing like that," Stone quickly said.

"I'm just a friend," I added. "Visiting. I was watching them set up in the Cambridges' yard and got curious."

"Oh. What can I do for your curiosity?"

I hoped we hadn't got off on the wrong foot already. "I'd love to hear the menu."

Mel perked up. "Sure. Come on inside and take a look."

Slightly bemused, I followed her back through the swinging doors and into the industrial kitchen.

Stone brought up the rear.

Unlike the front of the restaurant, the kitchen was bright, modern and stocked with up-to-date stainless steel equipment. It was easy to see that half of it was devoted to meal preparation and the other half was set up as a bakery.

Three men were working on the kitchen side, two at a salad counter and one over the grill. Farther in the bakery, a woman removed a tray of tarts from the oven. They smelled delicious.

"You do your own baking?" I asked. It wasn't unheard of to combine both businesses, but it was unusual. Back at The Blue Fern we'd taken a daily order from a nearby bakery. They had their specialty, and we had ours.

"It's a significant part of our business," she said. "We go through sourdough like nobody's business."

"Bread?" I asked.

"And our hamburger buns." She gestured to a multitiered cooling rack. "Most of the baking goes out in the morning, but burgers are on the dinner menu and grilled sandwiches too. We serve them with soup at lunchtime. Fries are more popular for the dinner crowd, and the chili, my secret recipe. It travels really well for takeout."

"This is an impressive setup." I looked all around.

"For the Kodiak Communications barbecue, we'll have burgers, of course. But chicken burgers too."

"Breaded?" I asked, picturing fast-food chicken burgers.

"Grilled. They were popular last year, and a couple of people asked about adding pesto to the condiments. I think it's a good idea."

"I love that idea," I said. "Have you considered offering avocado?" It was another fresh taste that could liven up a traditional menu.

"I hadn't… But, you know, we could do a Tex-Mex version with guacamole and salsa."

"What about the classic T-bones?" Stone asked. "Baked potato, sourdough rolls, coleslaw."

"You're unimaginative," I said.

"We'll have all that, Stone," Mel said with a laugh. "Don't you worry."

"Another word for *unimaginative* is *hungry*," Stone said. "A slice of avocado's not going to do it for me."

"Don't forget about dessert," Mel said, giving him a playful tap on the arm. "Bumbleberry pie and chocolate layer cake."

"Some of your ice cream," Stone asked hopefully.

I couldn't help but think Stone and I would get along just fine on the dessert front.

"Mason put in a request for mint chocolate. We'll do a batch of vanilla as usual. It'll go with anything."

"You make your own ice cream?" I asked.

"Jack-of-all-trades," Mel said.

"I'd say master-of-all-trades," Stone said.

The baker slid a tray of tarts into the cooling rack below the sourdough buns.

"Are those the bumbleberry?" I couldn't help asking.

"Try one?" Mel asked.

"I sure will." Stone moved as she spoke, beelining for the cooling rack.

I couldn't help but smile at his enthusiasm.

"I'll get you a plate," Mel said to me.

"Got any ice cream?" Stone asked.

"You're shameless," I told him.

"She's used to me."

"I am that," Mel said. "You should have seen him as a teenager, a bottomless pit."

"I burned a lot of calories while I was growing."

"I hope he ate more than just tarts." I had to admit to feeling a little jealous at the thought of being able to indulge in all the desserts I wanted without fear of gaining an ounce.

"Her cake's good too," Stone said with a smirk.

Mel handed each of us a plate and a little fork. "Help yourselves. I'll get the ice cream."

"You have to try them with the ice cream," Stone said to me. "Especially when they're hot like this. You haven't truly lived until you've tasted one of Mel's tarts à la mode."

Mel laughed and bustled off to a walk-in freezer.

"I told you you'd like her," Stone said in an undertone, even as he transferred two tarts to his plate.

"I do like her." I settled for a single tart. A corner of the pastry flaked off on my plate, and the rich aroma filled my nostrils, rousing my salivary glands.

"All I've got is vanilla," Mel called out as she returned to us with a tub of ice cream in her hand. She set it down on the wide stainless steel counter, peeled off the lid and pulled open a drawer to extract a scoop.

"Sophie?" she asked, scoop at the ready.

"Absolutely," I said, feeling privileged at the chance to try such a delicacy.

She popped a scoop of the vanilla-bean-speckled ice cream next to my tart. Then she nodded across the wide aisle to a rolling stool. "Grab a seat."

Stone set his tart plate on the counter and retrieved three stools for us to sit down while Mel gave him a double scoop of the ice cream.

"Not joining us?" he asked her as she covered the tub up.

"I have to pace myself," she said. Her eyes twinkled in my direction. "I can't wait to see what you think."

I cut into the pastry and the deep purple berry mixture ran free. I combined the bite with the ice cream and took my first taste. The flavors all but burst in my mouth—tart berries with tender pastry and sweet cold vanilla. "Oh, my." I touched my lips with two fingers.

Stone took a big bite too and grinned at me.

"This is awesome," I told Mel. I was impressed with her skill. And for a moment I felt guilty about the money I was making from Sweet Tech. Our technology might turn out beautiful creations, but they couldn't compete with Mel's for flavor.

Her grin went wide. "Thanks."

"Truly awesome."

What was she doing hiding up here in Alaska? With a talent like hers, she could be making a fortune anywhere in the country.

"Did I steer you right, or what?" Stone asked me.

"My faith in you is renewed." A whole different kind of warmth rushed through me as our gazes met and held.

Six

The backyard could only be described as organized chaos. Mel had said she'd consider table service if I would be willing to put together a selection of six plated meals. She'd also need another kitchen tent connected to the dining tent where the additional staff could work.

Stone had shrugged off the cost, and I'd decided he had mastered being rich. The extra tent was going up now, and Adeline was sitting next to me on the deck watching the progress.

She was curled up in a deep cushioned all-weather chair, while I had my laptop balanced on my knees, not really thrilled about either potato salad or fries as an accompaniment to the chicken pesto burgers.

"Does Mel serve yam fries?" I asked Adeline.

"Not that I've seen."

"Do you think she might?" Yam fries would be a nice differentiator between the fresher chicken burger and the more traditional beef burger.

"Probably," Adeline said. "Hey, what's that?"

I glanced at Adeline, then looked to where her attention was focused. A group of workers were hoisting a tall lighting scaffold up above the bandstand.

"That's impressive." Hoisting the thirty-foot scaffolding looked tricky.

"Isn't he though?" Adeline fanned her face with her hand. "They don't build them like that in California."

I took in the six men working and zeroed in on a buff, square-chinned, dark haired man with giant biceps straining under a red plaid shirt. I had to admit, he looked full-on Alaska. "I thought California was the bodybuilding mecca of the country," I teased.

"Those muscles are for show. These ones are the real deal." She was smiling warmly now.

"For show?" I'd never heard of such a thing.

"They build 'em for style, every exercise calibrated to bulk up and give definition."

"And that's a bad thing, why?" I couldn't help but think about Stone.

I'd seen him without his shirt, admittedly it was through the fog of passion. But I saw enough of his washboard abs and defined pecs to know he was in fantastic shape. And I doubted his exercise was calibrated to do anything cosmetic.

"Look at that strength and power," Adeline said with a lilt to her voice.

I glanced over to see the red-shirted man vault onto the stage in one smooth motion. I had to admit, his physique didn't seem designed for show. "I take it you don't have a boyfriend in Sacramento?"

"No boyfriend." She continued watching the man work as she talked. "Broke up with a guy a couple of weeks ago."

"Was it serious?" I wondered if that could be part of the reason she'd come home early.

"He thought so. I didn't."

"Oh. Then I guess that's not the worst breakup a person ever had."

"He works in the Governor's Office. I met him when he gave an undergraduate lecture, and I sat in. I have to say, he's very good at the front of a room."

"Less so up close and personal?" I asked.

She gave a noncommittal shrug. "Politicians aren't my thing."

"Is he going into politics?"

"He's the chief of staff. At that level, they all have aspirations of running for office."

I hadn't known that. But I'd never known anyone who worked in a political office either.

"Is that why you came home?" I asked her flat out.

"No." She gestured to the mayhem of trucks and cranes and tents and crew. "I came home for this."

"You like chaos?"

"I like excitement. The lead-up is as exciting as the party. You must like it too, otherwise why would you work in a busy restaurant on a Saturday night instead of taking a nice steady office job?"

"I guess I like a certain level of excitement. Maybe that's why I'm not so wild about being rich. It's quiet, way too quiet."

"What's too quiet?" Stone appeared next to me. He looked out at the activity in obvious confusion.

"Sophie's life," Adeline said.

"I don't mean right this minute," I said.

"Glad to hear it." He levered into the chair next to mine. "How are the plated meals coming?"

I looked reflexively down at my laptop to find the screen had shut down. "I'm getting there. The trick is to be exciting and not too exotic. They have to appeal to a wide range of people but still have enough flavor and uniqueness to not be boring."

"Hence the idea of a buffet."

"Buffets are long lineups, your tablemates coming and going, people all eating at different times, cluttering up the dining room." I shook my head as I spoke. "Sit-down is much better, especially when the point of the event is to get people together who have something in common but don't get to socialize with each other very often. Sharing a good meal is wonderful for that."

"She sells it well," Adeline said.

"She does." Braxton's voice joined the conversation, startling me.

We'd seen each other since our private talk a few days back. But we were always in a group, and I still felt nervous around him, jumpy really.

"I hear you're making changes to the barbecue," he said. It was clear he was addressing me.

"A few things," I said without turning. "I talked them over with Mel. She has the final say, of course."

"I think it's a good idea," Braxton said. His voice was easy as he took the chair next to Stone. "The event could use some freshening up. And you have as much right as the rest of us to—"

"I wasn't asserting a right." I didn't want him to think I was taking advantage of my genetic connection to the family.

"Sophie," he said in a gentle warning.

I didn't turn, but he waited until I finally gave in and looked past Stone.

"I'm glad you're interested," he said, his eyes soft.

"I don't want to overstep."

"You couldn't if you tried. You're one of us now."

"It's not like they won't push back," Adeline said.

Braxton's look turned sharp on his niece.

"Oh, don't pretend," she retorted, seemingly unaffected by his silent criticism. "If you do something they don't like," she said to me, "they push back hard. If you've got the green light here, go for it, enjoy it."

"You're not helping," Braxton said to Adeline.

"She is," I said, still looking at Adeline. "Thanks. I think I will enjoy this."

Braxton huffed out a breath and rocked back in his chair.

I got the feeling he was less than pleased that I'd sided with Adeline. But Adeline looked thrilled that I'd stuck with her.

Adeline looked like she was having fun at the party. So did Braxton for that matter. He was circulating through the backyard crowd, greeting people like he was best friends with them all, acknowledging their spouses and children and receiving warmth and appreciation in return.

The dinner had gone over well, the table service seeming popular among the guests, who were more dressed up than I'd expected. Luckily, Adeline and I had taken a shopping trip into Anchorage, where she'd encouraged me to buy a kicky little rust-and-black dress with long loose sleeves over a pair of leggings to protect against the bugs that came out when the wind died down. She'd wisely advised on low wedge heels since we'd be walking on the grass.

Everyone had migrated out of the dining tent, and the band

was setting up on the low stage. It was still strange to see the sun high in the sky at nine o'clock. Alaskan summers had to be experienced to be believed.

Stone came alongside me. "Well, that went well."

"Mel is a real pro."

She'd hired dozens of extra staff for the plating and serving, and they'd pulled it off with efficiency and aplomb. The plated meals were well received, with tons of compliments for the chicken pesto burgers garnished with avocado. The entire cooking and serving staff had received a thunderous round of applause, orchestrated by Braxton, at the end of the meal.

"He's very good at hosting," I said, nodding to Braxton.

"His staff loves him. He makes a point of getting to know everyone who comes on board with the company."

"That's more than two hundred people," I said, surprised but seeing the evidence with my own eyes.

"It's a point of pride for him."

"I wouldn't have expected it."

"That's because you met family Braxton. Not many people get to do that."

"Family Braxton?" I was intrigued.

"There's family Braxton and business Braxton. Business Braxton is even-keeled, professional and impeccable."

"Where family Braxton can be…irritable and cantankerous."

"I was going to say *exacting*."

I turned my head to give Stone a look. "You can't bring yourself to criticize him, can you?"

"I'm just being accurate."

"You're being kind."

"I'm a kind guy."

"Ha!"

"When have I not been kind?"

"The day I first walked through the door."

His expression faltered. "Well, you know, I thought—"

"That I was trying to con Braxton."

"It sure looked that way at the time. And I didn't know you."

"You know me now."

He grinned like he'd just won an argument. "And now I'm kind."

"Now you're impossible."

He looked me up and down. "You look great by the way."

The compliment warmed me far more than it should. "Adeline steered me to this. She's got a great eye."

"It looks good on you." His gaze went warm on me, and it brought to life a shimmer of desire in the pit of my stomach.

"I thought we weren't going to do that," I said, feeling self-conscious. I knew he couldn't read my mind, but I was worried that he might see the heat in my expression.

"Do what?"

I tipped my head to gaze accusingly at him. "Don't play dumb."

"I've been rethinking," he said, his smile decidedly flirtatious.

"Rethinking *what*?" I wanted to make sure I understood. I had no desire to play games.

"Telling Braxton about us."

I was stunned to silence for a second. "You want to tell Braxton you're going to have sex with me?"

Stone laughed.

I shriveled a little bit in embarrassment.

He seemed to notice my expression. "Sorry."

"You're not nice," I said.

"I meant tell Braxton I wanted to take you out on a date. The rest, well, I'm not about to make any assumptions."

It wasn't much of an assumption, since I'd thrown myself at him on the seat in his truck. Still, I was puzzled by his change of heart. "Why?"

"Why do I want to date you?"

"Why are you willing to tell Braxton about it?"

He sidled a little closer. "Mostly because that's the only

way I get to take you out. I was thinking dinner, maybe a little dancing?"

I searched his expression. "Something's going on here."

"Enjoying the event?" Braxton asked.

I hadn't seen him arrive. I pulled back from Stone, realizing I'd been drawn closer and closer to him while we talked.

"Yes," I answered.

"Good. Good." His smile was wide and his voice hearty.

I couldn't help but think this was business Braxton.

"People enjoyed the new dinner format," Stone said.

"They did! Thanks for that, Sophie. It was a great addition. I know Mel really liked working with you."

Okay, this felt weird, like I was interacting with a fake Braxton.

The bandleader shouted a greeting into the microphone, welcoming the crowd and drawing everyone's attention.

"Ah, here we go," Braxton said, sounding pleased. "This is the best part of the event."

"Kodiak employees are a dancing crowd," Stone said.

I could see people surge toward the dance floor as the band started to play.

"Why are you standing here like a bump on a log?" Braxton asked Stone. He cocked his head my way. "Be a gentleman and ask Sophie to dance."

Stone didn't seem surprised by the suggestion. He also didn't miss a beat. He held his hand out to me. "Sophie?"

I did miss a beat. Was Braxton tossing the two of us together? Or was this just business Braxton being a good barbecue host?

Stone raised his brow as he waited for my answer.

"Sure." I wasn't about to be rude. Plus, well, I really liked the idea of dancing with Stone.

When he wiggled his fingers to encourage me, I got a little hitch in my breath. I put my hand in his and waited for the inevitable rush of heat from his skin up my arm and through to my chest.

We started for the dance floor, leaving Braxton behind.

"What was that?" I asked as we wove a path through the crowd.

People smiled and nodded at Stone, some of them tossed a hello his way.

"I have no idea," he said to me as he acknowledged the greetings.

"Was that business Braxton doing his duty?" I asked.

"I expect it was. I don't know what else it would have been."

"Okay," I said, still feeling unsettled. But we'd made it to the edge of the dance floor, and Stone turned me into his arms.

We merged in seconds, our rhythms matching, our steps in sync. I hadn't expected Stone to be such a smooth dancer.

"You're good at this," I said, gazing up, liking the view of him this close.

He smiled. "Lessons in high school."

"There's a lot of dancing in Alaska?"

"It's very popular. We're a fun-loving people. And indoor activities are big in the winter."

"I guess you must get bored with all that snow."

"Not bored. The daylight hours are short, but people cross-country ski, go snowmobiling, go ice fishing or just get out for a walk or a horseback ride."

"What about when it's cold?"

"If it's really cold, we stay inside. Hence, the dancing. But anywhere above zero, there's plenty to do without huddling in your house."

"It's the rain in Seattle that keeps us inside. We have umbrellas, but we mostly use them to get to the store or the gym. We like our parks when it's sunny, and the beach—beach volleyball is super popular."

"Do you get out on the water?"

"Not me personally. It's not like California, where the water's warm and you can surf the sandy beaches for months at a time."

The band wound the song down, and I paused, waiting to see if Stone would head off the dance floor.

He stilled but kept me in his arms.

I was content to stay.

"Sophie!" Adeline called from a few feet away.

The band struck up a slower song, and Stone moved us into the rhythm.

"Hi," I called back over my shoulder.

She gave me a delighted, knowing grin and waggled her brow at Stone, obviously remembering my admission of kissing him.

"What was that?" Stone asked.

"I don't know," I lied. "The Cambridges can be odd."

"You're a Cambridge."

"I'm not—" I stopped myself. I was a Cambridge. "Only by an accident of genetics."

"Only *completely* by genetics. You're as Cambridge as they come."

I fell silent as melancholy came over me. I softened against Stone, leaning into his strength as I'd done a couple of times before.

"Hey," he said. "What's wrong?"

I tried to put it into words. "Things are moving so fast."

"Life has a way of doing that."

I remembered that he'd been through his own rocky times. "It's like the past is fading and I can't seem to catch it. I don't want to lose it."

"You'll never lose it, Sophie. Your mom's always going to be your mom. I know my mom's always going to be mine." There was a hitch in his voice.

"Your mom?" It was the first time he'd mentioned her.

"She died when I was six—heck of a thing to learn on the third day of first grade."

"I'm so sorry." I felt terrible for bemoaning the twists and turns in my life when Stone's had been so much worse, so much more profound.

"It was bad," he said. "But it was a long time ago. I know now it wasn't her fault. It wasn't anyone's fault."

I tightened my hold on him, feeling an urge to comfort the young boy he'd been back then.

"It gets better," he told me. But his arms tightened around me too.

"My problems are nothing compared to yours," I said, feeling guilty for complaining.

"You've been blindsided, and it's only been a few days. You're allowed to feel confused and upset and angry."

"I'm not angry." It was true. I was sad and disoriented, but I wasn't angry. "Well, maybe with the hospital." I paused. "Then again, if they'd got it right, I wouldn't have met my mom, wouldn't have grown up with her, would have…"

"Don't go back to feeling guilty again," Stone said, his deep voice soft. "Nobody's fault, remember?"

"I know." I nodded. Intellectually, I did know that. And I could tell my emotions were slowly catching up.

Adeline was alone in the kitchen making coffee when I came downstairs. It was coming up on ten o'clock in the morning, but we'd all danced and laughed the night away, indulging in wine from the Cambridge cellar. My head felt a little woolly this morning, and I was looking forward to a shot of caffeine.

"Espresso?" Adeline asked. She was dressed in a pair of bright plaid flannel pajama bottoms and a worn lime-green T-shirt. Her auburn hair was half in, half out of a messy ponytail. Even with her makeup smeared, she still looked beautiful.

I'd managed to hold off the coffee craving long enough to comb my hair and dress in a pair of yoga pants and a loose-knit oversize sweater.

"Something smoother," I said. "Mocha?"

"Coming up." She pulled a cup from the cupboard and pushed a series of buttons on the machine.

"You're a lifesaver," I said, pulling myself up on a bar chair and leaning my elbows on the island.

"That was a blast," she said.

"It was," I agreed. I couldn't remember a more fun party. Aside from those who'd taken their kids home early, the

Kodiak Communications staff had danced, drunk and laughed into the wee hours. It was the strangest sensation trudging into the mansion at that time of night with the sun barely dipping below the northern horizon.

While my mocha brewed, Adeline sat down across from me and sipped her espresso. There was a twinkle in her eyes, an expressive display of emotion on a morning like this, I thought.

"You danced a lot last night," she said, then waited.

"I did." I stood up and rounded the island to retrieve my mocha. I took a sip before walking back to the island. It was delicious. "Yum."

"You and Stone looked like a pretty good idea last night," she said as I took my seat.

I couldn't stop my own smile of remembrance. "It was fun."

"And…" She leaned forward. "And…"

"And, nothing. We danced. The night ended. Most of us came back inside as a group."

"And…" she said, canting her head to the side to watch me closely.

"And I went to bed." I'd been exhilarated but exhausted.

Adeline leaned closer still, a look of expectation on her face.

"Alone." I took another sip of the mocha, a bigger one since it had cooled a little.

Her expression fell and her shoulders drooped.

I couldn't help but chuckle at her disappointment. The laugh hurt my head.

"Good morning, good morning," Braxton's voice boomed.

"Ouch, Uncle," Adeline said, pressing her fingertips to her temples.

"Serves you right." Xavier Cambridge, Adeline's father followed his brother, Braxton, into the kitchen. I'd met Xavier in passing last night as the party was getting underway.

"Good morning, Sophie," he said to me now.

"Good morning."

"You look a sight better than Adeline."

I wasn't sure I felt that much better than Adeline, but I didn't need to tell him that. "It was a wonderful party. I had a really great time."

"I hear you were the brains behind the sit-down dinner."

"Mel did all the work." I didn't want to take credit. The initial idea might have been mine, but Mel had jumped in, and she'd been the one to pull it off.

"Mel's amazing." Xavier beat Braxton to the coffee machine.

"Is Stone up?" Braxton asked.

Adeline shot me a look that had me wishing I could kick her under the table.

"I haven't seen him yet," I said.

Adeline shook her head and, thankfully, neutralized her expression. "Me neither."

"I was thinking of sending him up to the Seafoam Glacier installation," Braxton said.

Xavier looked confused. "This week?"

"No harm in getting a head start," Braxton said.

"You ticked off at him for something?" Xavier asked.

I stilled, listening, worried I might have done something last night that had annoyed Braxton. Did he not like the idea of me and Stone?

"No," Braxton said as Xavier handed him a cup of coffee. "It's not like it's mid-January. It's nice up there."

"It doesn't have to be Stone. You could send an engineer."

"Sophie." Braxton looked my way.

"Yes?" I found myself nervous. I didn't know what was going on, but Xavier seemed puzzled. And I'd seen business Braxton in action last night, so I knew he could cover his emotions when he wanted.

"You haven't seen anything outside Anchorage yet."

"Nowhere except here," I said.

"Kodiak Island is absolutely gorgeous this time of year."

"What are we talking about?" Stone sauntered through the opening from the great room, looking like he'd had a fine night's sleep, not showing a single sign of a hangover. He slid me a smile before looking at Braxton. "Something happen on Kodiak Island?"

"Seafoam Resort wants an upgrade."

"Already?" Stone asked, taking over the coffee machine as Xavier finished.

"They've added ten new chalets," Braxton said.

Stone paused, taking a quick look over his shoulder at Braxton. "You're really keeping up-to-date with them."

"Jack Nice asked me about it last night. They're going to some tourism shows on the Eastern Seaboard next month, and they want to offer video streaming and conferencing at the resort. It's a must-have for corporate customers."

"You can never have too much bandwidth," Stone said. He lifted his full coffee cup and turned back to us, taking a deep drink.

I saw a bit of puffiness around his eyes and decided he hadn't made it through last night completely unscathed. Somehow that made me feel better, more like a part of the gang.

"Why don't you take a run over there and make some technical recommendations."

Stone paused, his cup near his mouth, looking puzzled. He sent another quick glance my way. He was clearly confused too. "You need *me* to go out there?"

"It'll show them our level of commitment."

"I think upgrading their infrastructure will show them our commitment."

"Take Sophie along," Braxton said. His voice was blasé. Maybe a bit too blasé? Then again, maybe I was imagining things.

But there was a pause before Stone answered. "Yeah?"

"She's barely seen anything of the state. You can give her a flight-seeing tour along the way."

"I'd come along," Adeline said brightly.

It was clear from Braxton's expression that her offer came as a surprise.

"The scenery is spectacular," she said to me, enthusiasm

mounting in her voice. "Mountains and glaciers, usually lots of wildlife."

"It's settled then," Braxton said.

Stone looked thoughtful, dividing his attention between Adeline and Braxton.

"Sounds great," I said, since everyone seemed to be waiting for my response.

"Perfect," Adeline said as she hopped up from her seat. "We should go into town this morning," she said to me.

It was a quick change of topics, but that was okay by me. "What for?"

"To return your rental car. It's silly to keep it."

"We have plenty of company trucks," Xavier said. "You're welcome to borrow one anytime."

"Sophie doesn't need to drive a truck," Adeline said with a frown for her father. "We'll go to the dealer, find her a nice SUV."

"You want me to buy a car?" The idea seemed outlandish since I was only staying for a few more days.

"Kodiak will buy it," Adeline said brightly. "We can always use something new in the fleet. You just get to pick it out."

"I'm not going to—"

"That's a good idea," Braxton said in a thoughtful tone. "You need something to use while you're here."

I realized the Cambridges operated on a whole different wealth level than I did, but impulsively buying a new vehicle for someone who'd rarely even be here seemed preposterous even for the überrich.

I downed some more of my coffee to jump-start my brain.

"And you should pick out a new bedroom," Braxton said to me.

"Huh?"

"You're in the guest section of the house. You need to settle in somewhere more permanent."

"I'm a guest," I said. "And I'm heading home soon."

"You'll be back, won't you?" Xavier asked. "If nothing else, you and I have only just met." He looked around at the group. "We all want you to feel comfortable while you're here."

"I'm perfectly comfortable." I polished off the coffee but was still feeling woozy. I didn't want another one right away. For some reason I thought a stack of pancakes might help.

"We want to make it easy for you to visit as often as possible," Xavier said. "You shouldn't have to clear out your stuff every time you come and go."

It occurred to me then that I was taking up space that they might want for other guests. I didn't want to get in the way. "Whatever works best for you."

"Come on," Adeline said to me, moving toward the shortcut to the main staircase. "I'll show you what we've got."

I couldn't stop myself from taking one more look at Stone as I was leaving. His expression was still thoughtful, but it didn't give me a clue about how he was feeling.

Adeline waited until we were halfway up the big staircase before speaking, and even then she whispered. "Why was Uncle Braxton sending you off with Stone?"

"I don't know," I whispered back.

"He's up to something," she said as we came to the top of the stairs.

"What makes you say that?"

"Braxton never does anything without a reason. Neither does my father. The two of them have been plotting and scheming their entire lives."

"Is that why you offered to come along? To figure out what he was up to?"

We'd made it to the top of the stairs and had turned a corner in the hallway. "I mostly wanted to see how Braxton would react when I offered. He seemed to be orchestrating the trip—throwing the two of you together. I thought he'd make up an excuse why I couldn't go along."

"He didn't," I said.

"I know. I suppose I could have read it wrong."

I couldn't help but smile at that. "Maybe it's what he says it is—he simply wants me to like Alaska."

"Maybe…" She seemed to think hard. "I don't have all the pieces yet, but I know my uncle and my father. There's always more going on than meets the eye." She opened the door to a bedroom. "I vote you take this one. It's next door to me."

I looked around as I stepped inside the room.

It was hard to believe, but this suite was even bigger than the one I had now. It had a beautiful sitting alcove with a bay window that looked out onto the back of the house. To top it off, there was a balcony between the alcove and an identical alcove jutting out from the room next door. Below, I could see dozens of workers taking down the stage and the tents. I opened the door to the balcony and heard a backup alarm against the throb of a diesel engine.

"It's usually much quieter than this," Adeline joked over my shoulder.

"It's almost as big as my old apartment in Seattle."

"We want you to like it here," she said.

"I do like it here." I stepped onto the balcony, inhaling the fresh air and gazing at the now familiar view over the paddock to the mountain peaks.

If Braxton's secret plan was to make me like Alaska, he was well on his way to succeeding.

Seven

It was hard to believe it was possible, but Stone looked even sexier dressed in a flight suit than he did in blue jeans.

We were going up in a Cessna float plane, and I was excited. I'd never been in anything smaller than a commuter jet. I'd sure never taken off from or landed on water.

The blue-and-white Cessna was moored at a small wooden dock on the edge of Lake Hood. We'd arrived in a pickup, then the three of us lugged boxes and coolers and duffel bags from the truck to the dock. Leaning in through the open door, Stone had carefully stowed it all in the back, surrounding a single second-row seat next to the open door.

When he came through the door, he had a small duffel in his hands. "You'll have to hold this in your lap," he said to Adeline.

"I can take it," I offered. There was no reason why it had to default to her.

"You can't have it up front," he said. "It'll interfere with the flight controls."

Just then, another truck came to a stop on the laneway along the shore.

"It's Mason," Adeline said as Mason hopped out of the cab and gave us all a wave.

"I hope he's not thinking he'll come along." Stone scanned the tightly packed goods through the windows of the plane.

Mason came down the rise balancing a big box in his hands.

"What's up?" Stone called out.

I stepped to one side on the dock to give them both some room.

"Seafoam just called it in. They need to replace three extinguishers."

"What's the weight?" Stone asked. He took the box from Mason and hefted it to check.

"Ninety-seven pounds even."

Adeline shot her brother a frustrated look. "Are you kidding me?"

"You've been bumped," Stone told her.

Adeline shook her head, then slanted me a warning look.

I could see the wheels were turning on her suspicions, but I couldn't see this as a plot. Sometimes things just happened.

"Well, you two have a good time," she said in a flat voice.

"It's not like you haven't seen the sights before," Mason said to her.

"I know. I wanted to hang out with Sophie. She's fun. Not like you lot."

Mason and Stone both chuckled at her frustration.

I felt bad for her. "I could—"

"No," all three of them said at the same time.

"You're not staying here with me," Adeline said.

"You're not trading places," Stone said.

"You're going to have a great time," Mason said.

I gave up trying to be noble. "Oh… Well, okay then."

Stone hoisted the box onto the remaining back seat and settled the small duffel on top of it. Then he wrapped a strap over them both and fastened it down.

He repositioned the front passenger seat. "You're going to step on this," he told me, pointing to a small metal outcropping. "Hang on to the handle here. It's high, but I'll steady you from behind."

"Okay," I said, squaring myself with the door.

"We can talk when you get back," Adeline said.

I smiled. I was sure I'd hear theories about Braxton and Xavier, but I liked talking with Adeline. She was smart and funny and always a lively conversationalist.

I lifted my foot and reached up for the handle.

Stone bracketed my hips with his hands to steady me. He gave me a boost as I pulled myself up, ducking my head, twisting at the waist until I was sitting in the compact copilot's seat.

"Good?" he asked me.

I nodded.

He reached under the front of the seat. "Pull forward."

Just like a car seat, this one moved on rails, bringing me closer to the windshield and the controls.

"Keep your feet away from the pedals," he said. "They'll move. The door opens this way—pull up on the handle and push out." He demonstrated. Then he guided my hand under the seat. "There's a life jacket here if we go into the water."

"Excuse me?"

"It's a floatplane, Sophie. We'll be on the water."

"But not *in* the water."

"Not on purpose. But that's what the life jacket is for."

"This is not reassuring."

"Accidents do happen."

"Have you ever had one?"

"Not in a floatplane. A couple of hard landings on a bush strip, but nothing for you to worry about."

I wasn't really worried. Stone projected confidence and professionalism that put me at ease.

He disentangled a multistrap safety belt from beside my shoulder and put two straps over my chest. "These go in here." He inserted two small metal latches at my waist. "Then push like this. If you have to unbuckle, you just pull up on this. Got it?"

"Got it."

He tugged down on each of the straps and I felt securely lashed to the seat. Then he handed me a bulky headset with a microphone, and I put it on.

"Close to your mouth." He positioned the microphone. "Or I won't be able to hear you." His voice was muffled through the headset, but I understood. "All good?"

I nodded, the weight feeling strange as I moved.

Stone stepped back, and I noticed Adeline and Mason were still standing on the dock.

I smiled and waved to them again as Stone closed the door and cast off the ropes holding us to the dock.

Adeline snapped a photo.

I was glad she was memorializing my flight. I knew I'd be happy to have a picture of this adventure.

Stone went to the front of the plane and somehow crossed the floats, sliding down the far one before opening the pilot-side door and levering himself inside. He flipped some switches and moved knobs and levers, starting up the engine with a very loud roar. The plane rumbled beneath us as it bobbed in the waves.

Stone put on his headset, made some more adjustments, talked to the tower through the radio, and then he brought up the engine revs and we were moving out onto the lake.

"All set?" he asked through the headset with a grin.

"I am," I said back.

I was struck again by how sexy he looked in the khaki and green flight suit with a Kodiak Communications logo on the shoulder. A matching well-worn baseball cap shaded his eyes above a pair of sunglasses.

I wore sunglasses too, having been warned it would be bright in the sky.

Stone revved the engine further, turned the plane, made some more adjustments and sent us skimming along the waves. The plane went faster and faster until we tipped to one side. The movement startled me, and I held on. Then the second float lifted from the water, and the engine speed suddenly changed. The nose went up and we were floating on a cushion of air.

I looked out the side window as the shoreline and truck got smaller and smaller.

He banked the plane, so I was staring at the earth out my side window.

"Nice, huh?" His voice in my ears startled me.

"Nice," I agreed. It was stunning.

As we climbed higher, I could see the tall buildings of Anchorage. There were white-tipped mountains in the distance, and the ship-dotted water spread out far and wide. We headed for the ocean while Stone exchanged choppy information with the control tower.

"How long is the trip?" I asked after the tower went silent.

"Depends," he said.

"On...wind speed?" I gave it a guess.

"On how much you want to see along the way."

"Is there something I should see?"

"Many, many things."

"Then I'll let you decide." I settled back in my seat while Stone flew us off into the blue Alaskan sky.

Compared to commercial jets, we flew low and slow, making the detail of the world below us crisp and clear. We left the buildings of Anchorage behind and flew over the freighters and ships in the harbor before crossing a forest dotted with scattered lakes and populated with moose and caribou and even a few grizzly bears.

"I like the bears a whole lot better from up here," I'd said.

Stone had laughed at that.

We crossed a vast stretch of water to get to Kodiak Island. Then we followed an inlet, circling down to a long beach and a red-roofed log lodge surrounded by a bunch of smaller buildings. I could see a dock with two big floaters and assumed that's where we were aiming.

I got a little nervous as the water grew closer. Then we hit it with a jolt and immediately bogged down and slowed. Stone revved up the plane and turned us to the dock. As we lumbered up alongside one of the floaters, he stripped off his headphone and unbuckled, cracking his door open.

Then he shocked me by hopping out, quickly rounding the front of the plane across what I realized was a wire between the airplane floats before leaping onto the floater, a rope in his hand. He tugged the rope tight.

I sucked in a breath of surprise and relief. We were there.

I removed my headset and fumbled my way out of the safety belt. By the time I got everything sorted out, Stone was opening my door and offering to help me down.

I slipped a little on the foot peg and he grasped me tight, turning and setting me down on the floater. I held on for an extra second, getting my legs stabilized as it rolled with the waves.

My hair blew around my face and I grabbed it up at the base of my neck, wishing I'd thought to put it in a ponytail.

While Stone finished securing the plane, I gazed at the beach and a second floater, where two big metal fishing boats were moored.

"Hello, Stone," a man's voice called from the top of a long ramp from the shore. It split at the bottom and connected the two floaters.

"Hey, Ray-Jay," Stone called back. He opened the back door of the plane and began hauling out the cargo.

I wanted to help, but it wasn't obvious what I should do, and I didn't want to get in the way.

"How's the fishing?" Stone asked.

Ray-Jay came onto the floater. "Fantastic. We're having a great year for salmon and cod, a few rockfish, which is nice."

"Lots of reservations?"

"Still booking up a couple of years in advance."

Stone grinned. "That's what you want."

Ray-Jay looked me over. "Hi, there. I'm Ray-Jay, general manager of Seafoam Resort."

"Also the owner of Seafoam Resort," Stone put in. "This is Sophie Crush."

"A special friend of yours?"

"A special friend of the family."

Ray-Jay's expression grew interested. "Oh, in that case, it's *very* nice to meet you, Sophie Crush."

He was about six feet tall and looked to be in his midthirties, weathered and fit, his hair a little unkempt and his beard growth a few days old. He was a good-looking man, dressed in tan canvas utility pants and a green buttoned shirt with the sleeves rolled up.

He stepped closer, offering me his hand, and I shook with him, finding his grip strong and his palms calloused. He might be the manager of the resort, but it was obvious he did a lot of physical work as well.

"Stand down, sailor," Stone growled at him.

"What stand down?" Ray-Jay looked at my left hand. "I

don't see a ring. So, what are you, Sophie? Single, in a relationship, engaged to some dude who couldn't be bothered to buy you a diamond?"

"Uh…keeping my personal life private," I answered in a teasing tone.

Stone chuckled.

"Ouch," Ray-Jay said through his own laughter.

"We've only just met," I told him, happy to keep it light and joking. "Give a girl a chance to get to know you."

"That's not a no," Ray-Jay said.

"It's a no," Stone said. "We're only here for the afternoon." He turned back to his unloading.

"I sometimes get to Anchorage," Ray-Jay said to me. At the same time, he moved toward the open door of the airplane to help Stone.

"I live in Seattle," I told him.

My response seemed to stump him for a moment. "Seattle's an awfully long way away. Have you considered relocating?"

"She's not moving to Kodiak Island," Stone said. He climbed partway into the plane and handed a box out to Ray-Jay.

"We have the biggest spring salmon in the world," Ray-Jay said.

"Stop," Stone said. "You're annoying her."

"Am I annoying you?" Ray-Jay set the box down on the floater.

"You're amusing me," I told him honestly.

He gave a wounded groan.

Stone laughed from inside the plane as he pushed several boxes to the open door to Ray-Jay.

"That's not a bad thing," I said to Ray-Jay. "You have a good sense of humor. I like that."

"She likes that," Ray-Jay said to Stone, pulling out box after box and setting them down in a neat pile.

"She's brushing you off," Stone said.

"You don't think I know that? I'm not stupid when is comes to women. But she likes me. I'll take that."

I moved closer to the plane. "Can I help at all?"

"Nope," Ray-Jay said.

"We got this," Stone said.

I took a step back to clear the path.

"I'll call the boys to haul it all up to the lodge," Ray-Jay said. He pulled out his phone while Stone hopped down from the plane and shifted the last of the cargo to the floater.

"I feel quite useless," I said to Stone as he moved to my side.

"I didn't bring you along so you could work." He lightly touched the small of my back, urging me toward the ramp. It was fairly steep, and the beach came halfway down the dock, so I guessed the tide was out.

There was a double rope handle on either side of the ramp and the floor was rough, like sandpaper that gripped the bottoms of my hiking shoes. The wind was still brisk, so I used one hand on the stiff rope and kept the other around my hair.

We came to the top and crossed the dock, bringing us onto a lush green meadow. A well-trod gravel path led to a gleaming log building, two stories high with a peaked roof and towering windows. It had a deck along one side overlooking the ocean and a tall stone chimney sticking out the top.

"This is really nice," I said, in awe that something this magnificent had been built in the wilderness. I'd seen from the air that there was no road access.

"Hungry?" he asked me.

My nose picked up the scent of fresh baked bread. "I am now."

"Good. Marianne will give us lunch, and then I've got some work to do."

"Anything I can help with this time?" I asked, hopeful, as we started up the path, a hundred yards or so to the main building.

"Got a background in data transmission or satellite tech?"

"Economics Degree from UW."

"Yeah?" Stone seemed impressed.

"Please don't tell me that surprises you."

"You don't seem like an economist."

"Not smart enough?" I'd admit there hadn't been an opportunity to demonstrate my business skills in Alaska.

"Not nerdy enough. You need a pair of glasses, a different color hair, maybe eyes that don't sparkle like you're up to something all the time."

"My hair is plain brown. And I'm not up to anything." Nobody had said that about my eyes before.

He seemed to study my hair. "It isn't brown. It's caramel with highlights of copper and gold. Haven't you ever seen it in the sun?"

I wasn't exactly buying his exotic description. "That sounds both expensive and delicious."

We came to a short staircase the led to a pair of double doors with big, multipaned windows. Stone touched the small of my back again. It was featherlight, gentlemanly. Even though I was perfectly capable of safely walking up a flight of stairs, I kind of liked it.

His fingertips were warm against my sky blue T-shirt. I knew there was an inch of bare skin between the shirt and my jeans, but he wasn't touching me there. I wished he would. I'd like to feel his rough fingertips brushing my bare skin.

A second later, he let me go, leaning around me to push open one of the wooden and glass doors.

It was nearly as bright inside as out with a wall of windows and multiple doors to the west side leading out to the deck. The floor was polished wood, gleaming a warm red and yellow. A reception desk and sitting area were at the front, with a comfortable-looking restaurant behind a partial stone wall.

"Stone!" A stocky woman of about fifty rushed forward. Her cheeks were rosy, her hair neat and short, and she was wearing a black double-breasted tunic over a pair of gray slacks. She all but launched herself into Stone's arms and grinned as she gave him an enveloping hug.

"I heard you fly in." She smacked him on both shoulders as she let go. "Welcome back." Her attention then shifted to me.

I stepped forward, offering my hand. I wasn't usually into

someone with that level of exuberance, but I found myself quickly caught up in Marianne's. "Sophie Crush. I'm up from Seattle, visiting the Cambridges."

She gave my hand an enthusiastic shake. "Nice to meet you, Sophie Crush. I'm Marianne. Welcome to Seafoam Resort."

I took another scan of the rooms surrounding us. "I'm blown away by all of this."

She smiled with what looked like approval. "Not what you expect out here, is it?"

"I don't know what I expected. Smaller for sure and more rustic."

"We get clients from everywhere. It's their trip of a lifetime, and we don't want to disappoint. The fishing is world-class."

"I saw the boats," I said.

"They just got back for lunch. Oops! I need to get back to the kitchen." She stepped away. "Make yourselves comfortable. It's clam chowder and salmon burgers today with chocolate cherry torte."

I loved the sound of chocolate cherry torte, and I hoped the bread I was smelling would be a part of the meal. Then I thought I might have to hike up a mountain or something after lunch to counteract the caloric intake.

The meal was every bit as delicious as it sounded. The buns were fresh baked, dense and chewy around flavorful salmon that Marianne said had been caught earlier in the morning. The dining room had filled up with a group of fishermen from New York City and another group who said they were from Berlin. Everyone ate hearty and seemed to be in a jovial mood.

They cleared out quickly after lunch, apparently heading back out for more fishing. Stone told me the staff processed and quick-froze the catch on-site so the guests could pack it home on dry ice and enjoy it all year long.

Stone and Ray-Jay left on four-wheel ATVs to drive up to a satellite station, while I spent the afternoon alone, happily wandering along the beach and around the property. I found a sunny spot on the sundeck, where an attendant offered me a pair of binoculars.

I counted twelve bald eagles, saw countless birds and squirrels in the trees and even saw a deer and a fawn in the distance. To be fair, it was the friendly attendant who pointed out the deer and helped me train the binoculars on it. But I was still thrilled with the experience.

It was after five when I heard the ATV motors and watched Stone and Ray-Jay return them to a garage down the beach from the lodge. I'd discovered the garage, some sheds and equipment buildings tucked along the rocky beach east of the main lodge. On the west and south sides, the prettier parts of the property with a sandy stretch of beach, there were self-contained chalets dotted along the waterfront and among the trees.

I'd learned from a brochure in the lobby that guests could rent hotel rooms in the main lodge or they could choose more privacy with a two-or three-bedroom chalet. Gourmet meals, including wine and top-shelf drinks, were complimentary with either option. The Seafoam Resort was five-star all the way.

From where I sat now in a deep wooden Adirondack chair in a gazebo in front of the lodge, I watched Stone and Ray-Jay make their way up a dirt path.

Stone smiled when he saw me and gave me a wave.

I waved back.

Ray-Jay said something to Stone, and they both laughed.

I tried not to feel self-conscious. There was nothing that said they were talking about me. It could have been about anything.

"I hope you had a nice afternoon," Ray-Jay said as they approached.

"See everything?" Stone asked.

"I think so," I answered. "I saw a deer and a fawn."

"Good time of year for that," Ray-Jay said. "Did you get up to the river?"

I must have looked confused.

"The Seafoam Glacier River." Stone pointed up the mountain behind the lodge.

"We have a wildlife viewing platform over the valley."

"I saw them from the deck."

"You should take her up there," Ray-Jay said. He glanced at his watch. "It's a little early though—a lot more to see late in the evening."

Stone came inside and sat in the chair across from me. "Sound good to you?"

"It does." It sounded like fun.

"We can stick around and go up this evening."

I was surprised we had that kind of flexibility. Then again, it wasn't like it would get dark later.

"I'll let them know," Ray-Jay said as he headed for the lodge.

On the water below us, a couple of resort workers were scrubbing the floaters with long-handled brooms and big buckets of soapy water. They called back and forth to each other as they worked. Above us, a raven cried out, circling with three others above the rolling waves.

Stone stretched his legs and leaned back in the chair. He'd taken his flight suit off and wore a light T-shirt and a pair of black multipocket utility pants. He looked completely at home in the wilderness, tough and seasoned, although I knew he was only thirty-four.

"Do you travel to many installations?" I asked, picturing him flying all over Alaska in all kinds of weather.

"Not so much anymore. I've got a big crew now, so I stay in the Anchorage office most of the time. I miss it though. It's nice out here."

I remembered Adeline's suspicions about this trip. "Do you have a theory on why Braxton sent us?"

"I do," Stone said easily.

My curiosity perked up.

"It's not rocket science," he said. "He wants you to see some of Alaska."

There was a distinct contrast between Stone's interpretation of Braxton's motives and Adeline's.

"This particular part of Alaska," I probed. "Today, with you?"

"Why not this particular part of Alaska? It's a jewel in the crown, don't you think?"

"You don't think that's all it is?" I wasn't sure why, but I couldn't completely discount Adeline's perspective.

Stone considered me for a moment.

A gust of wind ruffled his dark, slightly unkempt hair, and I was reminded all over again that he was pure sexy.

"He feels guilty," Stone said.

"Because he was so suspicious of me?" Maybe a sightseeing trip was Braxton's method of making up for that.

"Sophie, really?" Stone's tone and expression told me I was missing something simple.

I shrugged my shoulders and gave my head a little shake.

"Braxton left the hospital with the wrong baby. He left his own daughter behind."

"Oh." I hadn't thought about it from that angle.

For a split second I was glad my mother had missed all this. She might have felt the same way about leaving Emily behind, and that wouldn't have been fair. It wasn't her fault. Which meant, by extension, it wasn't Braxton's fault either.

"He's trying to make up for lost time," Stone said.

I felt a pinch of guilt. "I'm not making it easy, am I?"

Stone leaned forward in this chair. "It's not up to you to make it easy. Fact is, it's more his fault than yours, so he's the one who has something to make up for."

I shook my head while Stone spoke.

"None of this is on you, Sophie. No way, no how."

"It's not on him any more than it's on me."

"That would be a nuanced debate. Point is, he *thinks* it's his fault, so he's trying to make amends."

For the first time, I felt sorry for Braxton. Stone's words had a ring of truth.

"What should I do?" I was half wondering, half asking out loud.

"Nothing." He gestured with his hands to the scenery around us. "Enjoy."

He made it easy to feel better. I was enjoying myself. And Stone was a big part of the reason why.

It was well past eight o'clock when Stone pointed me to a four-wheeled ATV outside the resort's main garage.

"I thought we'd walk up," I said, thinking of the apple pie Marianne had served for dessert. It had come with ice cream and a slice of aged cheddar cheese. I'd eaten both.

"It's five miles," Stone said. "Distances are long around here."

Five miles uphill.

Stone swung his leg over the ATV and settled at the front of the long seat. "Hop on." He pointed behind himself. "Look for the footrests." He started the engine. "You can hang on to the back rack...or to me."

I saw his grin in profile. I put a hand on his shoulder and swung my leg over the seat, settling to get comfortable and finding the footrests.

The rack behind me did provide a convenient handle, so I hung on there. Snuggling up behind Stone and wrapping my arms around his waist seemed too intimate for the situation.

"Ready?" he asked.

"Ready."

He pulled ahead with a little lurch, turning us to go around the garage before picking up a dirt trail. We bumped a little on the uneven ground, but as we picked up speed the wind felt nice on my face. Earlier, Marianne had found me a hair fastener, and my high ponytail was much better than loose hair in the wind.

The fishermen had seemed tired during dinner, mostly settling into the lounge with their phones afterward or heading back to their rooms and chalets. Nobody else was interested in the trip up to the viewing platform.

The sky was still awash in sunshine, and moss-covered spruce trees towered above us as we climbed. Then we emerged from the trees onto the slope of a wildflower meadow covered with crimson fireweed, yellow poppies and blue lupine against the lush green grasses. Color flooded off in every direction.

We skirted a tiny glacier lake, then bounced our way over a rock-strewn trail, rounding a cliff face before we came to the platform. Railed and gated, it jutted out over a river valley about fifty feet below.

Stone pulled the ATV in a tight circle, parking it next to the gate, pointing down the hill. He shut off the engine, and the quiet boomed around us.

"Do you think we scared everything away?" I asked, taking in what looked like a deserted valley bottom as I climbed off the ATV, making room for Stone to dismount.

He left the ATV, flipped open a latch and pushed in a gate. "They won't have gone far."

We walked onto the platform, where chairs were arranged in two groups facing the valley. There were six covered spotting scopes set along a narrow ledge with a row of cupboards below.

"Is it dangerous around here?" I asked, taking in the eight-foot chain-link fence on the trail side. It gave way to a much lower wooden railing out on the platform.

"It's mostly to give the tourists a sense of security. The bears aren't all that interested in us."

"Will we see more bears?" I looked around, deciding this might be my favorite way to see bears. It had been fun watching them lumber through the meadows from the airplane. But this vantage point would bring us much closer.

Stone removed the covers from two of the spotting scopes. "It's best to pick a spot and scan slowly."

I moved up to one of them.

"Pick a reference point up the river, then move your way down. This is the focus, and you can move it with the little lever here."

I moved my eye close. "It's all black."

"You have to take off the lens cover."

Light suddenly appeared in the scope.

"Oh. Thanks." I tried again, focusing, and I could make out an amazing level of detail on the shrubs and rocks and rushing water.

I scanned as Stone had suggested but didn't see anything that moved.

"Take a look here," Stone said, stepping back from his scope.

"What did you find?" I was already standing up to have a look. I squinted into the eyepiece. "A deer?"

It was a whole lot bigger than the deer I'd seen from the resort sundeck. Its head was crowned with an impressive rack of antlers. It bent forward to take a drink from an eddy on the river.

"That's an elk," Stone said.

"Is it big, or does it just look big from here? Wait." A rush of excitement went through me. "There's another, and another."

"They're fairly big, up to seven hundred pounds."

"That's plenty big. Are they grumpy?"

"They can be if you bother them. We're not going to bother them."

I moved back to my own scope. "How can I find them?"

"Go ahead and use mine. Watch for a while."

That didn't seem fair. He was the one who found them.

"Go ahead." He motioned. "I'll see what else I can find in yours. I've done this before."

I took the invitation because I was quite fascinated by watching the animals. But when I looked back, they were gone. "They left." I tried not to sound disappointed.

"Are you sure? Look closely."

I looked again, focusing, waiting. And then I saw a big brown shape. "Whoa."

"You see them?"

"I see what scared them."

"A bear?"

"Yes. No. Three bears." I watched as a big bear, a slightly smaller bear and a cub walked into the water, nosing around.

"Sow and a cub?"

I realized I was hogging the view and stepped back. "Go ahead."

"I'm good. You're having fun. Keep watching."

I hesitated.

"Seriously. I want you to have fun."

I tilted my head, squinting at him in mock suspicion. "Is Braxton paying you?"

"He is, but not to do this."

It was the first time that thought had entered my head. Why *was* Stone doing this?

I sobered. "I hope you know you don't have to be my tour guide."

"I know that."

"I mean, really."

"Really." He moved a little closer, and his voice turned hushed. "I like it when you're happy, Sophie." His gaze softened on me then. Or maybe it was the sunlight that had softened on his eyes. Everything suddenly felt softer, more intimate.

He moved closer still. He was going to kiss me, and I smiled at the idea.

"Happy," he repeated. His hand came up to my neck, fingers slipping against my hairline. He bent his head, put his arm around my waist and drew me forward.

"Happy," I echoed.

Our lips met, and just like it had all the times before, passion sizzled through me. I parted my lips. My arm slid around his neck. I leaned against him, pressing my other palm against his chest, feeling his strength and the echo of his heartbeat.

Our kiss grew deeper, and his fingertips found the seam between my shirt and my jeans. He touched my bare skin, and my whole being sighed in contentment. His hand splayed on my back beneath my shirt. Our thighs pressed together, and my back arched in desire.

He drew back ever so slightly, separated from me, then gave me a brief tender kiss on my swollen lips.

"Happy," he said, smiled and brushed my cheek.

"Happier," I said.

He stepped back farther. "You want to keep looking for animals?"

I was feeling far too restless to watch the elk and bears. "I'm done."

"Okay." He slipped the covers back on the scopes and we walked over to the ATV.

I didn't know what happened next, and I wasn't bold enough to ask. The last time I'd propositioned him, he'd turned me down flat. I didn't want to do that again.

He climbed onto the seat and started the engine.

When I climbed on behind him, he reached back, took my arms and drew them around his waist. I leaned in, snuggling up to his back, feeling his warmth, settling my hands on the flat of his stomach.

"Ready?" he asked.

I was beyond ready.

Eight

The ride back seemed disappointingly fast, much faster than the trip up. I gazed a little bit at the scenery, but mostly I focused on Stone. His shoulder was solid beneath my cheek, and the muscles of his stomach flexed as he steered the ATV around curves and obstacles, down steep slopes and through small creeks.

The sun was dipping below the horizon when the red roof of the resort came into view below us. But instead of taking the trail to the garage, Stone veered off on a little sideroad, coming to a halt in front of a pretty chalet.

I waited until he turned off the motor before lifting my head. "Are you picking something up?"

The windows were dark, and there were no signs of movement in the building. It was dead quiet and looked deserted.

"Can you hop off?"

"Sure. Are we walking to the dock?" I was a little tired, but I was up for it.

He turned on the seat and dangled a key from his left hand. "Ray-Jay gave this to me earlier."

I took in the key, then looked at the chalet. "We're staying?"

His eyes had a glow as he rose to his feet. "Yes."

"Together?"

"Well, there are three bedrooms if you're not—"

I stepped unhesitatingly up and grasped the front of his shirt. "I *am*," I said and kissed him.

He kissed me back, hard and deep, smiled, then kissed me again. "Good. Because I am too."

Hand in hand, we crossed the porch. The light was shadowed inside the chalet, dusk coming in through wide picture windows. I had a vague impression of two sofas, a fireplace, some landscapes on the walls and a kitchen nook at the back. But my attention was on Stone, his dark eyes, his strong sexy face, his fit body that I was already wrapping in my arms.

He kicked the door shut behind us, his breathing deep as he stripped off his shirt.

I did the same, thinking there was no point in waiting around on this. For good measure, I unhooked my bra and tossed it aside. Then I met him chest to chest, wrapping my arms around his neck, kissing his mouth. This time I knew we weren't stopping.

"Oh, man," he whispered between kisses. His warm palms splayed across my back. Then they rubbed and wandered, skimming beneath the waistband of my jeans, coming around to my stomach, moving up to my breasts.

"Oh," I groaned. "Yes." I tipped my head back and felt the sensation ricochet through me. Desire pooled at my core because Stone was magic.

I felt my way over his firm shoulders, his sculpted pecs, along his washboard abs until I came to the waist of his pants, the fabric stiff and ungiving.

He cupped his hands under my rear and lifted me up.

My legs went naturally around his waist and our connection amped up my passion even through the layers of clothing.

He was moving then, walking forward, taking me backward until I felt a table come in beneath me. That freed up his hands, and he stroked my face, brushing back my hair and tenderly kissing my lips.

We stayed that way for a long time until he reached between us and unfastened my jeans.

I found the button at the top of his pants and did the same. Our gazes stayed glued to each other as we both shimmied out of our remaining clothes. And then we were naked and pressed back together.

Our kisses grew deeper. His hands roamed my body, and mine roamed his, touching, feeling, caressing as his breath quickened, and I could feel the deep thud of my heart pounding in my chest.

His caresses grew more intimate, and my need pulsed to life.

I scooted forward against his hand. My back arched and I moaned his name.

"Now?" he asked, the question more a growl than a word.

"Oh, yeah. Now is good. *Now*."

It felt like he smiled, but my eyes were closed so I didn't know for sure.

Then he was with me, and we were one, and he thrust against me while his hands kept working their magic, finding spots I didn't know existed, pushing my passion to higher and higher heights.

The air grew hot around me, the rustle of leaves rose in volume.

Stone kissed my neck, then my shoulders, then my breasts. His labored breathing told me he was as into me as I was to him. It made me smile just as he returned to my mouth.

"Good?" he asked me, a smile in his own voice.

"Great," I told him. "So...very...great."

"Good," he said with a distinct shade of satisfaction. His thrusts become harder, faster, more insistent.

I gripped his shoulders as my body tightened into an endless spiral, colors flaring behind my eyes and an ocean's roar rushing through my ears.

"Stone," I gasped as the world contracted and pulsed within me.

"Sophie," he groaned in satisfaction, cupping my body, holding me tight and fast.

It felt like forever, but my breathing slowly grew shallow. Lethargy took over my limbs. It was good that Stone was still holding me, because I felt like I might melt into a puddle on the floor of the chalet.

I blinked my eyes open. They focused, and I looked around at cream-colored leather furniture, a rich burgundy rug, lovely oil lamps and vases, and a well-stocked bookshelf.

"Nice place," I said.

Stone chuckled, vibrating against me. The movement shouldn't have felt sexy, but it did. I had absolutely no desire to leave his arms, and my hold on him tightened.

He gathered me closer. His voice was muffled against my hair. "I like it here. I like it a lot."

When he drew back it was to run the pad of his thumb across my cheek.

I sighed, my face tilting for more.

He crossed my lips, and they tingled. They were thoroughly kissed but I still wanted more, so I kissed his thumb.

He paused for a brief second, then he kissed my mouth.

Passion stirred inside me, surprising me, and I reflexively squirmed against him.

He smiled against my lips. "You think?"

"Can we?"

"Oh, we can." He slanted his lips over mine, his tongue toying with me.

A bubble of passion grew and tightened inside me as waves of desire rose once more toward a crest.

We eventually found our way to a bed, a huge, soft, four-poster with a thick mattress and six fluffy pillows. We snuggled onto clean, crisp sheets.

Then we slept in each other's arms, waking in the morning when activity started outside around the resort. I wished we could stay longer on Kodiak Island, but I knew that was impossible. We were already late getting back, and I hoped it hadn't caused problems for anyone. Stone did have an important job, and I expected he'd been missed.

Marianne's breakfast was wonderful, and I stuffed myself again on her homemade bread, this time with wild blueberry jam. I raved so much about it that she offered me a jar to take back to Anchorage. I happy accepted the gift, looking forward to sharing it.

We eventually made our way back to the floater. The fishing boats were already out on the water, so it was quiet on the shore. Stone stowed a few things in the back of the airplane, but the load was a whole lot lighter this time, and the flight more direct.

Stone had left his truck at the Lake Hood base, so it was a quick trip back to the mansion, where Adeline was waiting to meet us.

"What did you think?" she asked, linking her arm with mine and steering me away from Stone.

"It was fantastic," I said.

"Pretty place, isn't it?"

"Yes, and delicious. And I loved the flight."

At first, I thought we were heading for the kitchen, but we took a right out onto the deck and closed the doors behind us.

The backyard was quiet again, barely a sign there'd been a party there just a couple of days ago. A gardener was at the far end on a ride-on mower. I'd discovered that grass and everything else grew incredibly fast in the long daylight hours of summer.

I'd have to tell Tasha about that phenomenon. Although after last night, the fast growing season in Alaska seemed like the second or third most interesting thing I had to share. I found myself smiling with the memory.

"Okay, now you really do have to tell me," Adeline said.

I realized she was watching my expression.

"Tell you what?" I put off my answer for a minute. I'd already decided I wasn't keeping it from her. I wasn't embarrassed about sleeping with Stone. Plus, she'd already guessed we were attracted to each other.

We stopped at a little furniture grouping in the sunshine. The cushions were hot, but they felt good, and a little breeze kept the air fresh.

"Spill," she said, kicking off her sandals and curling her legs beneath herself on the big comfy chair.

I did the same. "We saw moose and bears and caribou from the plane." I was teasing her, but it was pretty fun to watch her expectant expression.

"And…"

"And Kodiak Island is fabulous. You've been there, right? The food was off-the-charts. If I'd stayed much longer, I'd have gained five pounds."

"And…"

"And we went up to the viewing platform, saw a grizzly bear scare some elk."

"And…" She leaned toward me.

"And." I paused. "Yes, we did."

Adeline let out a little shriek, and I quickly glanced around to make sure nobody was in earshot.

"I knew it," she said in a whisper. Then she leaned closer still. "Give me all the details." She hesitated. "No, wait. Don't give me details. That would be weird. It's Stone we're talking about."

"I wasn't going to give you details."

She leaned back in obvious satisfaction. "I knew you were into him big-time."

She didn't know the half of it. Stone and I were positively combustible.

Adeline took on a pained expression and groaned. "Oh, man, your face. I so wish you could give me details."

We heard a door open and both looked over.

"I'm glad to see you back, Sophie," Braxton said as he and a younger man came out onto the sundeck. "Did you have a nice time?"

"The trip was wonderful." I didn't dare glance Adeline's way. "We saw all kinds of wildlife from the air and on the ground too. The Seafoam Resort is amazing."

"Stone said it was a success."

"You talked to Stone?" I was definitely not looking at Adeline now.

"I did. He says we can have the Seafoam Glacier installation upgraded in plenty of time. Sophie, this is Joe Breckenridge," Braxton said.

"Hello, Sophie. Nice to see you again, Adeline." Joe Breckenridge was tall with dark hair and a nice smile.

I guessed he was in his midthirties, in good shape, looked intelligent, was dressed quite formally for what I'd seen of Alaskan men, wearing charcoal slacks and a steel gray sports jacket, his white collar open without a tie. His boots were practical though, sturdy brown hikers that looked like they'd seen a few miles.

"Joe." Adeline's response was curt, her tone anything but welcoming.

"You'll stay for dinner," Braxton said to Joe, clapping him on the shoulder.

"That's a tempting offer," Joe said. But his focus remained on Adeline as if he was trying to figure something out.

It was going to be my turn to pump her for information on this one.

"Not at all," Braxton said. "I appreciate you taking the time to talk in person while you're here in town."

"I wouldn't want to miss one of Sebastian's meals."

"He'll be happy to hear that."

"Sophie and I have dinner plans," Adeline said.

I shot a glance her way, immediately realized I looked puzzled and switched to a neutral expression.

Braxton's jaw tightened, but his voice remained even. "Can you postpone them?"

"We have a reservation."

"Change it."

"It's at The Big Edge, Uncle. You know how hard it is to get in there."

Joe extracted his phone from his inside jacket pocket. "I can help you out with that. What's a good alternate date."

I could see the offer threw Adeline, so I jumped in to try to save her. "I'm not sure how much longer I'll be staying."

That got Braxton's attention. "What? This is the first I'm hearing about you leaving."

"My house," I said, grabbing the first excuse that came to my mind. I figured I could back off on it later. "I have to get down there, at least for a while to get moved into the new house."

Braxton's eyes narrowed in suspicion, but he didn't call me on it. He turned his attention to Adeline, pinning her with the same glare he'd given me when I first announced the DNA results. "Please don't be rude."

"I'm—" She folded her arms over her chest and let out a huff. "Fine. We'll cancel."

Joe smiled, seemingly oblivious to the undercurrents, which was impossible, so he was faking it. He tapped something on his phone. "What day and time?"

Adeline didn't answer, still scowling.

"Friday," I suggested. "Seven o'clock." I figured there was no way he'd get a table, so we'd at least be off the hook for dining at The Big Edge, wherever that was.

"Hello, Rhonda," Joe said into the phone. "This is Joe Breckenridge calling. Can you possibly give me a table for Friday at seven?" He waited for a moment. "Sure. On the deck if you've got it, near the fireplace?" He paused again. "Yes, I will. Thanks." He disconnected. "Done."

I was shocked. Who was this guy?

"He's a Member of Congress," Adeline said after Braxton and Joe left the sundeck. "You want a drink? It's only two, but we could have a mimosa, pretend it's part of brunch."

"As in the United States Congress?" I asked.

Adeline came to her feet. "Yeah, that Congress. You want a scone or something to go with it?"

"Sure," I said, standing. "He's pretty young to be in Congress."

"His family owns the biggest ranch in Alaska. They've been here for generations. Joe went to Harvard Law, and he thinks he's the stuff."

We started across the sundeck to the kitchen.

"He's a lawyer?" He did strike me as the lawyer type.

"That's how some get into politics."

"You don't like him." I stated the obvious.

"I don't really know him."

I wasn't buying it. "Come on, your reaction to him was extreme."

Adeline stopped with her hand on the kitchen door handle. "Sophie." Her tone was patient with just a touch of exasperation that I didn't think was directed at me. "Here's the thing. Braxton and my dad want influence across the state and beyond. They have enormous plans for Kodiak Communications, and they want to launch a family dynasty along the way. Who better to pull into the fold than a congressman?"

A light bulb flashed on in my brain. "Oh."

She opened the door wide. "Yeah, *oh*. Mimosa?"

"You bet." I followed her into the kitchen, leaving the door open and letting the fresh air follow us inside.

From one of two double-doored refrigerators, she pulled out a pitcher of orange juice and a bottle of champagne.

I took a moment to marvel at the kind of household that had random bottles of champagne just sitting in the fridge for anyone to use. It was a good label too. I recognized it from working at The Blue Fern.

"Glasses are third cupboard from the end." Adeline pointed.

"He's not your type?" I asked as I extracted a pair of stemless champagne flutes. They were beautiful blown crystal, with a heavy base and a tapered oblong shape.

"He's a politician."

"That's a dealbreaker for you?"

"Yes. And even if it wasn't, or even if he was just a plain old lawyer, I'm not going to let my dad and his scheming brother get away with programming my life for their advantage. There's a reason I've spent nine years at school in California."

I held up the glasses. "These?"

"Perfect."

I pushed the cupboard closed with my elbow. "So, you're not there for the love of urban planning?"

"I do love urban planning. And I really like California. I like Alaska too, but coming back for too long has its problems. As you just saw." She popped the cork on the champagne bottle, and it flew into the air, hitting the ceiling then bouncing off the counter before settling on the tile floor. She scooped it up.

"Are you sure it's all about you?" I set down the glasses and poured orange juice into each of them.

There was dry laughter in Adeline's voice as she wiped the

errant bubbles from the outside of the bottle. "Oh, I'm sure. My dad and Braxton are bulldogs, not particularly subtle."

"How does Joe feel about it?"

"I'm the daughter of a prominent businessman, in the technology industry no less, who was born and raised in Alaska and is of marriageable age. I know how to dance and how to schmooze and I dress up decently for formal occasions."

"You'd look beautiful on formal occasions."

She had the kind of leggy figure that looked great in absolutely everything. Plus, her auburn hair was dramatic, and her green eyes were unique. If I was Joe, looking for a great Alaskan political bride, Adeline would be my first choice.

"I'd do it if I was him," I said.

"Do what?" She topped up each of our glasses with bubbly champagne.

The drinks looked delicious. And there was a basket of fresh cranberry scones on the counter.

"Marry you if I was Joe," I said as I took one of the mimosas and helped myself to a napkin and a scone.

Adeline laughed so suddenly, I thought she might spill her mimosa. "*You*, I'd marry."

"Then again, we're cousins."

"Good point." She shrugged then, heading for the door. "But we've wandered way off topic."

She was right about that.

As we found our chairs again, the horses whinnied in the distance. A small herd of them galloped across the extended paddock, and I wondered if something had scared them. I'd asked Stone if bears bothered them, but he said they were safe in a herd.

"You're not really leaving soon, are you?" Adeline asked as we sat down.

"I haven't given it much thought lately." I realized it was true. I had settled in at the mansion, staying focused on the day-to-day instead of planning very far ahead. Maybe because nothing was calling me from Seattle. "My best friends, all three of them, moved away from Seattle last year."

"Do you miss them?"

I set the scone on the low round table in front of us and took a sip of my mimosa. It was delicious. "I do, especially Tasha. The other two, Layla and Brooklyn got married first to twin brothers."

"Really?"

"Yeah, it's a little strange seeing the four of them together. I can't tell the men apart until they hug or kiss their wives."

Adeline laughed and broke off a piece of her scone, popping it into her mouth.

"But they're really happy. Tasha and I were left behind, so we spent a lot of time together last year. But then she took up with James, Layla's brother, and they moved to LA."

"So, you have friends in LA?"

I nodded. Then I took a bite of my scone, and it melted in my mouth. "These are fantastic. How does Sebastian not own his own restaurant?" The chefs I'd met in Anchorage so far were beyond impressive.

"Because we pay him so much to stay here."

"Really?"

"I don't know the exact figure, but whenever he muses about expanding his horizons, the family panics, and somebody ups his salary."

"I don't blame you. But I hope he's happy."

Stone strolled through the open kitchen door. "Hope who's happy? Me?"

Adeline rolled her eyes. "Sebastian."

"Why wouldn't Sebastian be happy?" he asked, taking one of the chairs in the grouping.

"I thought he might want to open a restaurant," I said.

Stone stared at me for a second. "Are you trying to steal Sebastian?"

"What? Me?"

"Are you going to open a restaurant."

"No."

"Here in Alaska?" he asked.

"I said no."

"That's a great idea," Adeline said. "But maybe you should do it in California. You know, to be closer to your friends." She gave a cunning smile. "Sacramento is nice."

"Don't you try to steal Sophie," Stone warned her.

"I'm not a trading good," I answered back.

"It's up to Sophie," Adeline said. "But Sacramento is a whole lot warmer than Alaska in January."

"You both know I'm not opening a restaurant, right?"

"We'd outbid you for Sebastian anyway," Stone said. "Any more of those scones left?"

"In the basket," Adeline said.

Reminded, I savored another bite of my scone while Stone went to the kitchen to get one for himself.

"Does he know I know?" Adeline whispered while he was gone.

I shook my head.

"Okay," she said. "Mum's the word."

It wasn't a deep dark secret. Then again, I'd prefer it if the entire family didn't discuss my sex life.

"I see Joe's here," Stone said as he sat back down. He'd poured himself a mimosa as well. "The three of them are holed up in the den."

"Some coincidence," Adeline said.

"That they're in the den?" Stone asked.

"That Joe Breckenridge showed up right now."

Stone grinned. "He's a decent guy. You should give him a chance."

"Not on your life."

"Are you in favor of matchmaking?" I asked Stone, a little surprised that he knew and a little surprised by his acceptance of the interference in Adeline's life.

He shrugged. "There are all kinds of ways to meet people."

"I'm not chattel," Adeline said, clearly annoyed.

"You're having a knee-jerk reaction," he said.

"To being paraded in front of a suitable match for the convenience of the family corporation?"

"It's more than just that."

"Whose side are you on?" I asked Stone. Adeline clearly wasn't interested in Joe. Why would anyone want to push her there?

"There are no sides," he said. "Just a family who loves her and a man who's attracted to her."

I squared my shoulders. "What about a woman who knows her own mind?"

"Yeah," Adeline said, pointing to me. "That."

"I'm only suggesting you—" Stone turned to include me in his answer "—*she* give the guy a fair shot."

"He's a congressman," Adeline said, her tone laced with disgust.

"And I'm a vice president." Stone took a drink of his mimosa.

I really didn't get the comparison.

Adeline came to her feet. "Want another scone?" she asked me.

"No, thanks. I'm good." They were delicious but filling.

As she walked away, I opened my mouth to ask Stone why he was pushing Adeline.

"Hey," he said, interrupting my question, shifting closer, his smile soft, his blue eyes warm and welcoming. "How're you doing?" It was as if our debate had never taken place.

"Fine." I gave in to his change in mood because I didn't really feel like arguing. Plus, I was fine, very fine with warm memories of Stone from last night and this morning.

"You want to do something?" he asked.

"Like what?"

"I don't know. Head into town, dinner, dancing."

"Are you asking me on a date?"

"Yes, I'm asking you on a date. Want to go on a date?"

Adeline's footsteps sounded on the deck as she made her way back to us.

"Sure," I said quickly before she arrived.

"Sophie still needs a new vehicle," Adeline said as she sat back down. "It really is silly to keep that rental car."

I hadn't wrapped my head around that idea yet—

buying something that would sit idle for so long. I did intend to come back to Alaska for visits. But I didn't know when, and I didn't know for how long.

"Sophie's used to a different kind of lifestyle," Stone said.

"A lifestyle without cars?" Adeline asked as she sat down. "Do you take transit, or surely you don't Uber it all over Seattle?"

"I have a car at home," I said.

"A normal lifestyle where people have to save up to buy things like cars," Stone said.

Adeline looked confused. "She doesn't have to pay for it herself."

"I can easily pay for it myself." I could pay for it with this week's royalties alone.

She shot Stone a look of incomprehension. "So, what's your point?"

I decided to be blunt. "I'm having trouble getting used to being rich."

"You mean getting used to being a Cambridge?"

"Sophie has her own money," Stone said. "A lot of money."

"Recently," I clarified.

"Oh, right, the invention," Adeline said.

"She worked for every penny. The dessert machine, Sweet Tech, was very valuable."

"That's fantastic!" Adeline rocked to her feet. She reached down and polished off the last of her mimosa. "Then let's head down to the dealership. This is going to be fun."

Nine

Adeline had ushered me into a luxury car dealership while extolling the value of long-term comfort, looks and quality over short-term price savings. Stone had brought up the rear, agreeing with everything she said. In the end, I'd decided on a midsize metallic blue crossover that, I had to admit, I absolutely loved. Coached by Adeline, with Stone dismissing each of my objections, they'd talked me into taking one that was already on the lot and loaded with options and extras.

I'd driven it back to the mansion with Adeline in the passenger seat, arriving in time for the dinner with Joe Breckenridge.

Her bedroom was next door to mine, and we shared the balcony. Since we both liked fresh air, we kept our balcony doors open much of the time and had taken to going back and forth that way.

She breezed into my room. "What do you think?"

I finished pulling a sweater over my head and looked at her.

She did a twirl in a bright white pullover blouse with fine mesh on the upper chest and cap sleeves. It was snug and silky over a pair of black skinny jeans with a pair of midnight blue leather boots. Her earrings were gold and chunky, and her makeup looked brighter than normal.

"What are you doing?" I asked.

"What do you mean?"

My sweater was deep purple with a bit of sparkle to it, three-quarter sleeves and over a pair of blue jeans. I'd planned to wear flats.

"You're all dressy."

She looked down at herself. "Not that much. We're eating in the formal dining room."

I checked myself out. "Should I change?"

"You look great."

I decided I'd at least wear some boots with heels and re-brush my hair. "Are we going formal because he's a Congressman?"

"Because Dad and Uncle Braxton think the sun rises and sets on him. And I don't want any grief from them later on for supposedly shirking my family duty."

"Then I'm at least changing my pants." I popped the button and unzipped.

I'd brought some black pants with me that would work, plus a pair of tapered heel ankle boots. And I was definitely upgrading my earrings.

"They won't fuss about you," she said.

I took the pants from my bottom drawer and slipped them on. "So it's the matchmaking thing?"

Adeline gave her hair a toss. "They'll pretend it's something else, like a lack of respect, yada, yada. But I know what's really going on."

"Uh-huh." Sophie was starting to think Adeline was protesting a little too much. She watched me for a moment. "I don't suppose there's someone at the table *you* want to impress."

I couldn't keep myself from smiling. "I don't think he's fussy about what I wear."

"If anything at all," she said with a gleam in her eyes.

"It's dinner," I said in a mock rebuke.

I brushed out my hair and switched my gold stud earrings for a pair of smooth purple crystals dangling in braided silver. Then I pulled on the boots and did my own pirouette.

"We look amazing," Adeline said.

"We'll definitely dress the place up."

"Make sure you sit beside me. I don't want to get stuck in the business talk all night long."

"Were you ever interested in the family business?" Other than Adeline, all the members of the family were intimately involved in Kodiak Communications. She seemed to quite studiously avoid it.

"Never."

"Why not?"

"I'm not technologically inclined. I'm not interested in being on the sales force. And, most of all, I'm not going to spend the rest of my life under my father's thumb."

"Is he really that bad?" My impression of Xavier so far was that he was a lot like Kyle, easygoing and carefree.

"Passive-aggressive."

"How so?"

"He makes suggestions on what I should do, where I should go, how I should feel. And if I don't take them, he frowns."

"Frowns?" That didn't sound so bad to me.

"Then he makes them again…and again. Then he reframes them, thinking he's being sneaky. Oh, and he always brings Braxton in on pressing me, plus Mason and Kyle. I don't think my brothers are malicious about it. They just listen to his logic—which is always well planned out by him and Braxton—and then they ask me why I'm being so stubborn." She opened the bedroom door to the hallway.

"Give me an example," I said as we started for the dining room.

"Joe Breckenridge."

"I already know about him. What else?"

"University of Alaska instead of California. My major. My prom dress. My prom *date*."

"Did they try for Joe?" I joked.

"Joe came later. They didn't know he'd rise like he did, otherwise…" She pulled an exasperated expression.

We laughed together as we came to the bottom of the stairs.

The formal dining room was at the front of the house off the great room. Its dramatic oblong table was usually surrounded by eighteen comfortable chairs. It was shortened tonight and set up for eight. Braxton and Xavier were talking alone, while Stone, Mason and Kyle engaged Joe in what looked like a lively conversation while they sipped something amber in heavy crystal glasses.

"Ah, *there* they are," Xavier said.

Something in his tone had me glancing at Adeline. Were

we being rebuked for tardiness? I hadn't known there was a set time for the dinner.

Adeline gave my forearm a surreptitious squeeze.

"Welcome, ladies," Braxton said. He came partway to greet us. His gaze on me, he pulled out a chair. "Please," he said.

It was pretty clear I didn't have a choice of where to sit.

Xavier had done the same thing directly across the table. "Adeline?"

"I was going to sit next to Sophie."

"Don't be silly," Xavier said smoothly. "Sebastian has it all planned."

Adeline gave me a knowing look as we separated.

I sat down on the springy seat and Braxton gallantly pushed in my chair.

"Thank you," I said over my shoulder.

Stone took the seat to my right, closest to the head of the table, while Mason sat on my left. Joe sat down opposite Stone and Kyle settled across from Mason. Braxton and Xavier took the ends of the table that had been set to fit the gathering.

A man in a suit jacket—I guess I'd call him the head-waiter—immediately emerged from a side door. He was followed by eight others in black slacks, white shirts and vests. It struck me as overkill, significant overkill.

The headwaiter spoke up. "Good evening, everyone. To-night's dinner will be honey Dijon scallops, followed by a charred citrus salad. Pan-seared halibut with plum and cucumber, accompanied by wild mushroom risotto will be the main course, with a crème brûlée for dessert. For the red to-night, Sebastian suggests a 2007 Napa Cabernet Sauvignon from Chateau Black. For the white, a 2013 Hilltop Vineyards Chardonnay."

I was growing hungrier by the second.

"Ladies?" Braxton looked to me first. "Red or white?"

"Red, please." I suspected either of them were going to be spectacular.

"White, thank you, Randall." Adeline said.

Randall gave a subtle hand signal and a waiter stepped

up behind Adeline. It took me a second to realize another waiter had stepped up behind me and was reaching past to fill my wineglass. Another waiter deftly removed my white wineglass.

I'd always thought The Blue Fern had offered gracious service. But these guys had us beat by a mile.

"Gentlemen?" Xavier asked.

Around the table, each of the men stated their wine preference. Stone went with red. Joe and Adeline were the only ones drinking white.

I leaned closer to Stone while several waiters poured, keeping my voice low. "Is this how the rich do it?"

"Sometimes," he replied in an undertone.

"It's unnerving."

"Just roll with it."

"How's the family, Joe?" Xavier asked as the waiters all finished and withdrew.

"Dad's good," Joe answered. Then he smiled. "Mom's on him to let the ranch manager take over more work so they can travel, but I don't think he's interested."

"He should think about it," Braxton said. "Family has to come first."

I took a first sip of my wine. It was fantastic.

"I'll tell him you said so," Joe answered with a wry smile. "But I doubt it'll do any good."

"Your sisters?" Xavier asked.

"Patty's pregnant again, and Elaine's dating a guy from Texas."

"You have sisters?" I asked Joe. I don't know why, but Joe had struck me as an only. Maybe that was me listening to Adeline's opinion.

"Just the two of them, no brothers though. Elaine's Texas guy is from a ranching family."

"Your dad will be happy if that works out," Xavier said.

"And we all know *that's* important," Adeline said, stopping the conversation.

"I don't have any sisters or brothers," I put into the silence.

"These new cousins are who I have now, of course, and I'm super excited about that." My words beat Adeline's for stunned silence, and I quickly realized my mistake. I swallowed. "I assumed you'd told him."

"Why?" Mason asked in obvious surprise.

"Are we telling people?" Braxton looked pleased.

"Close friends and family," I answered hesitantly. I'd already told Tasha.

Joe sent a warm smile my way.

Adeline frowned.

"I'm immensely honored to be included in that group." Joe looked to Braxton. "What is it you didn't tell me?"

Braxton set down his wineglass and sat up straighter, squaring his shoulders. "Sophie—" he gave me the warmest smile I'd ever seen "—is my daughter."

Joe kept a straight face, but I could see the shock in his eyes.

"We better tell him the whole story," Stone said.

Joe looked to Stone, but it was Mason who spoke up. "Emily and Sophie were switched at birth."

"At the hospital," Stone added. "It was a terrible mix-up that we only just figured out."

Now Joe peered at me, assessed me. "You're…"

I raised my glass. "Part of the family."

"She sure is," Braxton said in an overly hearty voice. It lent credence to Stone's assertion he was feeling guilty.

Kyle raised his glass my way. "Welcome, Sophie."

Everyone followed suit, and I felt extremely self-conscious.

Stone gave me a squeeze on the thigh. "Just go with it," he whispered again.

I was also rolling with my new SUV, sitting in the driver's seat with the thick owner's manual in my hands. I was in part simply marveling that it was all mine—since I'd never owned a brand-new vehicle before. But I was also having fun learning how everything worked, like how to add Bluetooth to the sound system and adjust the seat heaters. It was plenty warm now, but if I came back to Alaska in the winter, I was going to appreciate having a hot back and a toasty rear end.

The passenger door opened, surprising me. I looked up to see Braxton.

"How do you like it?" he asked, bending to peer inside.

"I like it a lot." I'd promised myself to be more patient with him. I didn't hold him responsible for the hospital mix-up, and the situation was clearly difficult for him too.

He gestured to the passenger seat. "Do you mind?"

"Sure," I said, and he slid inside, closing the door behind himself.

"I'm learning about the heated seats," I said to keep the moment from becoming silent and awkward.

"You'll like those. Have you tried the remote start?"

"I did," I admitted. I'd played with it a few times, shutting the SUV on and off from across the driveway.

"You'll like that in the winter too. We can clear out a spot in the garage for you."

"There's no need."

"Happy to do it. Saves you from having to brush off all the snow."

"Okay. Thanks." I told myself to be gracious. Maybe I would be back in the winter. And who wouldn't prefer to park in a garage at thirty below?

He affectionately patted the blue dashboard. "Were you thinking about taking it out for a spin?"

I nodded. That had been my plan. "Would you like to join me?"

"I'd like that." He looked pleased by the invitation.

Though I still wasn't sure of my feelings about him, I knew spending some time alone together was a good idea.

I took a breath and pressed the start button. The engine revved right up.

"Sounds good," he said.

I hadn't yet got used to the size compared to my compact car, and the SUV felt large as I pulled down the driveway toward the road.

But it was smooth on the gravel, and very quiet inside. It was a little too quiet with Braxton sitting next to me. So I tuned in a local radio station, glad I'd looked up how to work the sound system.

"I pulled out a few photo albums for you," he said as I turned left on the road.

"That was nice of you."

"I thought you might like to see some more pictures of your mother."

I chafed a bit at the description and felt my jaw go tight.

"Would you rather I called her Christine?" he asked kindly, obviously attuned to my expression.

I would, and I told myself to be honest with him. "When I hear the word *mother*, I think of my real mother... Sorry, I mean, the mother who raised me."

"Don't apologize. Christine it is then."

"Does that bother you?" I glanced his way but couldn't read his expression.

"It's not about me," he said, but his gaze stayed forward, staring out the windshield.

I could acknowledge her as the stranger who was my biological mother, but that was as far as I could go right now.

"Have you been down to the marina yet?" he asked.

"On Lake Hood?" I assumed he meant the one next to the floatplane dock.

"There's a smaller one at the marine park," he said. "It's just up ahead, through the lookout."

I shook my head. I could see the lookout coming up.

"We have a sailboat moored there if you're interested."

I'd never been sailing, but what I'd seen of the sport looked like fun.

"I wouldn't mind taking a look." I'd admit to feeling more comfortable with a focus and a destination than to driving aimlessly along making conversation.

"Turn into the lookout," he said.

I slowed my speed and hit my signal, even though there

was nobody else on the road to see it. Then I pulled into the big gravel semicircle.

"Straight through," he said, pointing ahead.

I hadn't seen it from the main road, but there was a narrow road leading out the opposite side of the pullout.

"It's better if you use four-wheel drive."

"Is this a test of me or the SUV?" I asked in a joking tone.

"It's not a test. The road's just bumpy and steep."

I shifted the knob to four-wheel drive.

The road twisted through the fir trees and the underbrush. I slowed my speed, avoiding the worst of the boulders and potholes.

Soon, the road leveled off and smoothed out. We took a sharp turn and the forest disappeared behind us. We'd come out at a beach, more a marina than a park, with a rocky shore, a small parking lot and a grid of docks berthing about forty different boats. They ranged from twenty-footers to something that looked like forty or so feet. Some had sailing masts, others were obviously pleasure yachts. I didn't see any fishing boats.

"You can park anywhere," Braxton said.

I pulled to the edge of the lot where I thought I'd be out of the way of other traffic.

"You sail?" I asked as we started for the dock.

I was guessing he must. Sailing took a lot of skill and practice, but who better than rich people to have the time to learn? Not to mention the money for lessons and upkeep of a sailboat.

The breeze was brisk by the water, but I'd learned to pack a hair tie everywhere I went, so I pulled my hair into a snug ponytail. It was a warm day, so the wind was refreshing against my bare arms.

Braxton settled a ball cap on his head. "Do you sunburn?"

"I tan pretty easily."

"That's good. This way."

We crossed the gravel patch to a dock that led out to the rows of wharfs. I speculated on whether the Cambridges owned a little dinghy for day fun in the waves or something more exotic and luxurious.

As we kept walking, the answer became obvious. The *Emily Rae* was the biggest sailboat in the marina. It was gleaming white with a long center mast, dual benches on deck that wrapped around the helm. There was a man on board wearing white slacks and a pale blue shirt.

"Morning, Mr. Cambridge," the man called out.

"Morning, Wade. This is my daughter, Sophie."

If Wade had a moment's pause at meeting a full-grown daughter of Braxton's, he didn't show it.

"Good morning, Ms. Cambridge," he said.

"It's Crush, but Sophie's fine."

"Then good morning, Sophie. You're welcome to come aboard."

There was a small gangplank connecting the sailboat to the dock, and he held out his hand.

I was more than happy to take a tour. I'd never been on a sailboat before.

"Do we have time?" I asked Braxton. My morning was clear, but he was a busy man.

"All the time in the world," he said, looking happy that I'd agreed.

He followed me on board, and the boat rocked gently on the waves beneath our feet.

"Any trouble with motion sickness?" Wade asked me.

I shook my head. "Never have."

"Good." He shaded his eyes and looked across the bay. "It's not too bad out there today."

Out there? I felt a shimmer of excitement at the prospect of skimming over the bay.

"It's only a quick hop to Fiddler's Point," Braxton said to me.

"There's a pretty trail on the island if you'd like to stretch your legs," Wade added.

"Am I keeping you from something?" I asked Braxton.

"Not a thing."

Wade grinned.

"What can I do to help?" I asked him. I didn't know much about sailing, but I knew it took work to crew the boat.

"You can enjoy the ride," Wade said. "Let me get you a life vest. Do you have sunglasses?"

I didn't. I hadn't planned to go far. "No."

"No problem. We've got spares." He disappeared, ducking his way down a short staircase middeck.

"This is amazing," I said to Braxton, looking around at the shore, the surf and the few other boats skimming past. Seagulls swooped and cried above us, while the wind whistled past and the waves slapped rhythmically against the hull.

Braxton's gaze was soft. "I'm so glad you like it."

Wade returned with three black-and-yellow life vests plus a white baseball cap and a pair of sunglasses for me.

We shrugged into our outfits and buckled up.

Braxton handed Wade his phone. "Can you get a shot of us?"

Wade took the phone and motioned us into the center of the deck in front of the mast.

I braced myself in case Braxton wrapped an arm around my shoulders, not sure how I'd feel about a hug from him. But he didn't. Instead, he took half a step back and shifted behind my shoulder to better fit in the frame. Wade then snapped a couple of quick shots, handed the phone back to Braxton and deftly cast us off.

We chugged out a fair distance using a quiet motor before Wade and Braxton let out the sails. In mere moments Wade was back at the wheel and we were skimming faster and faster across the waves. The boat canted to one side, but I felt perfectly safe hanging on to the rails.

The wind blew against my face, water spraying up, cooling me in the warm sun.

Braxton sat down next to me.

"Do you sail yourself?" I asked, thinking my earlier assumption could have been wrong. Maybe the rich didn't have to learn how to sail, since they had the money to hire people to do it for them.

"Sometimes, more when I was younger. Now, Stone, Mason and Kyle are the keeners."

"Stone sails?" As soon as the question was out, I realized my mistake. I should have included Mason and Kyle in the question. "I mean, as well as flying floatplanes."

"Flying and sailing use a lot of the same principles," Braxton said, making a motion with the flat of his hand in the breeze. "A sail is just a wing of a different nature."

I hadn't thought of it that way before. But I could see what he meant. I gazed up at the bright sail billowing in the breeze. "It pulls instead of lifts."

He looked pleased. "That's right."

"Do you spend a lot of time on the water?" I asked.

He seemed at peace out here.

"Not as much as I used to do." He closed his eyes and seemed to savor the motion. "I miss it."

"It's very calming."

"It is on a day like this," Wade noted. "But we have some rough ones too. Days when the weather changes on a dime. Then it gets adventurous."

I checked out the few clouds, the breeze through the trees on shore and the roll of the waves. "Is it going to change today?" I wasn't sure I was ready for adventurous.

"Probably not," Wade said.

"The forecast is good," Braxton said. He opened his eyes. "It should be smooth sailing." He seemed to appreciate his own joke.

It was such a typical dad joke, so I smiled with him.

"Can I look below?" I asked, still curious to see what was down there.

"By all means," Braxton said. He rose and gestured for me to go first down the narrow stairs.

I ducked my head and blinked my eyes to adjust them to the change in light, pulling off my sunglasses to improve my view. It was compact down here, but it looked efficient, streamlined and gleaming clean.

Royal blue benches curved around the perimeter. There

was a dinner-height table in between them, a tiny sink and kitchen area directly beside me, and a door to a berth at the far end. There were narrow porthole windows on each side.

"Head's through here," Braxton said, tapping a door opposite the kitchen. "Twin berths behind us. We can sleep six, well three couples. The beds aren't the biggest in the world."

"So, you could do a multiday trip?"

"Sure can."

"This is impressive."

"It's compact, but we've got a lot of use out of it over the years."

"It's bigger than I expected." I scooted around the table and took a look inside the front berth. It seemed like it would be better for kids than adults with the way it narrowed at the foot. You'd have to snuggle up close to your sleeping partner to get two adults in there. I thought briefly of Stone and smiled.

I took a look at the aft berths next. They were bigger and looked comfortable. I couldn't help but wonder if I might have a chance to take an overnight trip someday. My thoughts went to Stone again and curling up with him while the waves rocked us.

When we went back up into the sunshine, we were halfway across the bay, heading straight for a spit of land on the opposite shore.

"Is that Fiddler's Point?" I asked.

"That's it," Wade answered as Braxton sat down.

I noticed a woodgrain walkway around the bow of the boat. It was narrow but surrounded by a thin railing. I pointed. "Okay to walk up there?" I pictured myself leaning into the wind at the tip of the bow.

"Sure," Braxton said. "Hang on to the rail. But if you fall in, don't worry. We'll circle back and pull you out."

I checked his expression to see if he was joking. I couldn't tell, but I wasn't afraid of falling. The rail looked sturdy, and we were steady on the water. I grasped the smooth wet rail and stepped up.

"She's a natural," Wade said behind me.

I liked the idea of being a natural. Maybe I'd learn the basics of sailing someday. Maybe Stone would teach me. He'd suggested a dinner date, maybe it could be a sailing picnic instead of a restaurant meal.

I made it out to the bow and steadied myself in the triangle of the rail. The wind was fresh, filled with salt spray and hitting my face head-on. I grinned and gazed at the shore as it came closer and closer.

Wade called out to me. "I can dock here if you'd like to walk up to the waterfall."

I was intrigued but still worried about the time. I turned and made my way back, hopping down to join Braxton on the bench seat. "You're sure I'm not keeping you from anything?"

"I'm enjoying myself," he answered. Then he gave Wade a nod and rose to help.

My phone pinged in my pocket, surprising me, since cell service was spotty outside Anchorage. I would have guessed we might be too far offshore.

I checked, expecting Adeline, but it was Tasha.

Can you talk? was her message.

Call you later? I responded. I'm on a sailboat.

With that Stone guy?

With Braxton.

Interesting... Hope it goes well! Later!

I signed off with a thumbs-up emoji and tucked my phone back into my pocket.

The boat lurched as we touched against a rather broken-down wharf and rocked side to side.

Wade hopped off with a rope in his hand and quickly tied us off.

He came back and lowered the gangplank, and we all stepped off.

"We won't be long," Braxton said to Wade.

"Take your time, sir."

We left the wharf and picked our way across a rocky beach before heading up a wide dirt pathway under a pretty canopy of trees. We were in dappled shade, and the air turned a few degrees cooler.

I could hear a roaring sound as we walked. "Is that the waterfall?" I asked.

"We're almost there," Braxton answered.

Just then, we rounded a bend and came to a picturesque little pool. It was surrounded by a beach of flat, smooth stones. The water was bright green, and a high waterfall fell on the opposite side, about fifty feet away, boiling the water into a white foam.

The faintest hint of spray reached us.

"Wow," was all I could say as I stared. Talk about a natural wonder.

"We'd bring the kids here when they were little," he said with a wistful tone and a faraway look in his eyes.

"Did Emily like it?" I asked, guessing that's where his thoughts had gone.

He nodded, then he bent down and picked up one of the stones. He slung it sideways, expertly skipping it over the water, five, six, seven times before it disappeared into the waterfall.

"You must miss her," I offered softly.

"Every day."

"I'm so sorry."

He shook his head. "None of this is remotely your fault." He gazed around. "But I wanted to show this to you. Because—" He shrugged his broad shoulders. "I don't know. I feel like you missed out on so much."

I could tell this was a special place for him, but I didn't know what more to say.

To my relief, his expression changed.

He looked meaningfully down at the gravel beach, a little grin growing on his face. "Give it a shot."

"Yeah?"

"It was a favorite pastime."

"Okay," I agreed with a grin of my own.

My first effort was a flop, and he chuckled. "More to the side, crouch and give it a little bit of an upswing."

He demonstrated, and I tried again.

I had more success this time, and by my tenth rock I was making it almost to the waterfall.

"I can see why you love it here," I said.

"It's a hidden gem. The looks of the wharf scares people off, so nobody's been inclined to upgrade it."

"Helps keep it a secret," I guessed, feeling like I was part of a secret society.

"We should head back," he said with a sigh, his expression turning sad for a moment. "I do have a conference call at noon."

"Thanks for showing this to me," I said, softening toward him even more.

"Anytime." He smiled again, and the wistful expression was back. Then he lobbed a final rock into the pond.

Ten

"He took you to Fiddler's Point?" Adeline asked from where she leaned on the doorjamb of my open bathroom door.

I'd showered the salt spray from my hair and changed my clothes.

"It was great," I said over the sound of the blow-dryer.

Stone had suggested dinner tonight, and I thought I might ask him about going sailing someday.

"We used to go there all the time when we were kids," Adeline said. "Have they rebuilt the dock?"

I shook my head. "Braxton said it was a disguise."

Adeline flashed a grin.

"We skipped rocks," I offered.

"That's a time-honored tradition." Adeline fell silent.

In the mirror, I caught a pensive expression on her face and shut off the blow-dryer. I turned to her. "What?"

"He's really pulling out all the stops with you." The wheels were obviously turning inside Adeline's head.

I knew she was perpetually suspicious of Braxton's motives. "Stone says Braxton feels guilty."

Adeline's eyes narrowed.

"For mixing me up at the hospital," I elaborated. "Like he should have recognized one newborn baby from another after only a few hours."

"Braxton's not motivated by guilt. I don't say that to be mean. He's just a very complex man."

"Complex, sure, but he did bring home the wrong baby daughter." I surprised myself with my blasé delivery of the statement.

The guilt angle seemed entirely plausible to me. It also struck me that he was trying to make up for lost time. Today had been fun in the end, but it had sure felt forced at the beginning.

Adeline nodded, although she didn't look completely

convinced. But then she smiled. "Enough psychoanalyzing. What's up for the rest of the day?"

"Stone wants to go into town for dinner."

Adeline brightened. "Yeah? Where? Moonstone's? I'd be up for some dancing." She shuffled a couple of steps, then did a twirl.

I was pretty sure Stone was planning on it being just the two of us.

"I've got the perfect dress for you to borrow," Adeline continued, heading out of the bathroom.

I followed.

"Either the teal green with the little lace insets or the butter yellow off the shoulder," she said. "Hmm... Maybe not the yellow, maybe the basic black instead. It's got a little swirl in the skirt. The yellow's not the best if we're going to be eating. Oh, and I've got a *ton* of shoes you can pick from—some a little big for me, some a little small. We'll find you something."

She sounded so enthusiastic, that I didn't have the heart to tell her she couldn't come along. And why shouldn't she come along? Stone and I could still dance together. Dancing would be romantic.

"Sophie?" Stone's voice sounded outside my bedroom door as he rapped gently.

"Come on in," Adeline called out.

He did.

"I hear we're going to Moonstone's tonight," Adeline said. She glanced at her watch. "Sophie and I should start getting ready for that."

Stone shot me a look of confusion.

I gave a helpless little shrug in return.

"Moonstone's sounds good to me," Mason said appearing in the doorway behind Stone. "I'll let Kyle know."

I fought off a laugh at Stone's expression, but I didn't see how we could back out now. There was no choice but to roll with it.

By the time we all got ready and assembled in the front hall, it was coming up on seven. I'd gone with the teal dress, liking how the subtle lace on the bodice and at the midthigh hem gave a layered look to the fabric. Adeline went with the black. We both agreed yellow was too much of a risk, although it had looked amazing when she modeled it.

Stone wore casual slacks and a nicely cut sports jacket, while Mason and Kyle went with dress shirts alone. They all wore ties and looked very handsome. I had a feeling our table would get a lot of attention from the women in the room once the dancing started.

"What's happening here?" Braxton asked, looking us all up and down as he marched in from the great room.

"We're heading into town," Mason answered for the group.

"Did I miss something?" Xavier came up on us from the opposite direction, a newspaper under his arm.

"They're going to town," Braxton said. There was something meaningful in the look he gave his brother.

"Bit of a problem with that," Xavier said, moving forward.

"What problem?" Kyle asked.

"Family meeting tonight," Xavier said.

"For *what*?" Adeline asked, clearly frustrated.

"All of us?" Kyle asked.

"Just the three of you." Xavier's glance took in each of his kids.

"Not Stone?" Mason asked.

"It's an estate planning issue," Xavier said.

"Tonight?" Kyle seemed dumbfounded.

"Why tonight?" Mason asked.

"It can wait," Adeline said.

"The lawyers need it first thing in the morning. Filing issue."

"Are you serious?" Mason asked.

"Wouldn't be saying it if I wasn't serious." Xavier shrugged.

I looked at Stone, and he gave me a half smile. I could see what he was thinking. It was back to just the two of us.

I couldn't say I was massively disappointed in the turn of events, but I felt sorry for Adeline, Kyle and Mason, since they'd dressed up and were raring to go. But I'd take Stone alone any night of the week.

Braxton clapped Stone on the shoulder. "No need to mess up your plans."

Adeline gave a slow turn of her head to stare suspiciously at Braxton.

"Shall we?" Stone asked me.

"Sorry, guys," I said to the other three.

Kyle waved me off. Mason rolled his eyes. Adeline was the only one who looked truly bothered.

"Lesson time," Stone whispered as we made our way out the front door.

"Lesson on what? Tell me you didn't put Xavier up to that."

Stone looked genuinely surprised. "I did not. I wouldn't undermine Mason and the rest. Why would you think I'd do that?"

"Because you just said this was lesson time."

"Not a lesson on scheming. A lesson on being rich."

"Is that what we're doing?"

"You wanted to learn how to be rich."

"At Moonstone's?" I liked Moonstone's a lot. It was a great place. But it wasn't exactly upscale snooty.

"I still have a reservation for two at The Big Edge."

"Is that the snooty place?"

"It's gracious and classy—and very expensive."

"Then bring it on." I did want to hear Stone's take on being rich, since he hadn't been born with a silver spoon in his mouth. He'd barely been born with a spoon at all.

He steered me to a black SUV and opened the passenger door.

We left the SUV with the valet and crossed a pretty front porch covered in latticework, flowers, subtle white lights and glowing antique lamps positioned in a row along the floorboards.

"Step one," Stone said.

"Open the door?" I asked.

"Cute." He opened it. "Tip the valet well. He's probably putting himself through college, plus he'll take really good care of your vehicle."

"Is he putting himself through college?" I asked as I stepped over the threshold. Stone obviously knew something about the young man since he'd called him by name.

"As a matter of fact, he's in engineering. We may end up hiring him at Kodiak when he graduates."

We entered a small, plain foyer, and Stone pressed the button for an elevator.

"We're going up?" I asked.

"We're going up."

The panel pinged and the button light went out as the elevator door slid open. Stone followed me inside, and it closed again.

"Alone at last," he said and slipped an arm around my waist.

All of me sighed in pleasure at his touch.

He moved so we were chest to chest. As the elevator rose, he cradled my cheek with his palm and placed a tender kiss on my lips. "I've missed that."

"Me too," I admitted, leaning into him. "Me too."

As we came to a smooth stop, he smiled and turned, keeping one hand loosely around my waist as we walked into the restaurant foyer.

"Good evening, Mr. Stone." A smartly dressed hostess stepped from behind a polished wood counter to greet us. She was tall, willowy with very long brunette hair. Her smile for Stone said she found him attractive.

Who could blame her? He was spectacular.

"Hi, Kristy," he replied. "How are you doing tonight?"

"I'm very well, thanks." She retrieved two leather-bound menus. "Your usual table?"

"Please."

As she turned into the dining room, I leaned close to Stone. "Is she in college too?"

"I don't know for sure. But I think she's a little old for college."

He was probably right. I'd have guessed she was in her late twenties.

We followed her through a subtly lighted dining room. It was Alaska rustic but in the finest of ways, polished wooden beams outlining wide windows with the glowing lights of the city beyond. The tables were well spaced, each with a mini antique lamp in the center with its light flickering a soft romantic yellow. The service entrances were disguised and well away from the dining area. The music was subtle, and the temperature perfect.

Kristy led us to a round table in a little alcove next to the windows.

The white linens were pressed. The silverware polished, and the china was fine white and gold, everything positioned exactly right.

Stone pulled out my chair, and I sat on a soft cushion, nestled in a curved wraparound back.

"Thanks, Kristy," he said as he moved to his chair.

If I hadn't been looking for it, I wouldn't have seen him slip her a folded bill. I knew hostesses at The Blue Fern were supported by the waitstaffs' tips. It was rare for them to receive tips of their own. I wondered if it was different in Alaska, different in an establishment this upscale or different because it was Stone.

"Does everybody do that?" I asked him.

He settled into the chair around the table curve from mine, both of us facing the window.

"Do what?"

"Hand out tips to everyone who moves. How much did you give the valet?"

"Enough," he said with a little smile.

"I'm supposed to be learning here."

Stone reached out and took my hand.

My attention shifted to his touch, and I almost forgot the question.

"This is a nice place," he said.

"I agree."

The Blue Fern was special, and I could tell this place was a leap above it.

"People come here often."

"Because of the food?"

"Because of the contribution to the local economy. The Big Edge charges high prices and pays higher wages, creating plum food sector jobs in Anchorage." He paused. "Don't get me wrong, it's not completely altruistic. I enjoy fine food and fine service. It's a happily symbiotic relationship."

"You have a nice evening and leave behind as much money as possible." That certainly made sense from a local economic perspective.

He rubbed his thumb across the back of my hand, raising goose bumps. "Go to the head of the class."

I struggled to keep my attention on the conversation instead of focusing solely on his touch. "Well, you gave me the CliffsNotes up front."

"I did."

"I don't know what we're going to do with the rest of the evening," I couldn't help teasing even as I glanced down to where he held my hand.

The waiter arrived, and Stone withdrew his touch.

"Good evening, Mr. Stone, ma'am."

"Good evening," I replied.

"Nice to see you again, Richard," Stone said.

"Can I start you off with a cocktail?"

Stone looked to me.

"Does the bartender have a specialty?" I was feeling adventurous, plus I thought it was a good way to order an expensive drink.

"Indeed, he does. The Clear Glacier Martini."

"I'll try it," I said.

Stone gave me a knowing smile. "Same for me."

"Coming right up." Richard left the tableside.

"See, you catch on fast," Stone said with a smile.

"So, I did just order an expensive drink?"

"You did, and it's one of my favorites."

A second waiter arrived with a fragrant basket of rolls, setting them down with a flourish, then placing our cloth napkins in our laps before using silver tongs to put a roll on each of our bread plates.

"I try not to be the dead end." Stone tore his roll in half, and the delicious fragrance intensified.

"The place where the money stops circulating," I said with a nod. "My real problem is how to keep it moving on a large scale. I bought the biggest house I could reasonably live in by myself. And it's some of the most expensive real estate in greater Seattle. I just bought a new vehicle here. I suppose I could buy a new car in Seattle, but that's where my imagination ends."

"In smaller economies like Alaska, jobs are the best way to keep the money train going."

"Kodiak Communications hires locally?"

"Anytime we can, and we support scholarships for hard-to-find skills."

"I don't want to open a business." The most obvious choice would be a restaurant. But I wasn't interested in getting back into that area, especially not as an owner. They were truly 24/7 operations. Plus, I felt like I should be moving forward not backward.

"Then find someone who does."

"You mean a partner?" I took a bite of my roll. It was sweet and tender, the butter flavor bursting in my mouth. It was all I could do not to moan in appreciation. "These are fantastic."

"The head baker studied in France."

"Well, he…or she…sure learned a lot somewhere."

"I mean invest in a business," he said, digging into his own roll.

I'd never thought of myself as a venture capitalist, but maybe I should have. "That's what Jamie's company did for Sweet Tech, provided us with start-up capital."

"And that sure turned out well."

Our drinks arrived in chilled stemless martini glasses, crystal clear, just a touch of condensation and garnished with a swirl of lemon peel curving over the rim.

"I like it already," I said.

"Have a taste," Stone said, waiting for me.

I did. It was smooth, fresh and light. "Oh, yeah."

"Perfect," Stone said to the cocktail waitress.

I took another sip. "Braxton took me on the sailboat today."

Stone sipped his martini. "I heard."

"From Adeline?"

"From Braxton. It's been a while since he was out on the water."

"He took me to Fiddler's Point." I watched Stone's expression in the glowing lamplight, wondering if he'd question Braxton's motives like Adeline had.

But he didn't react at all. "It's nice out there. Good destination for a short trip. Had you ever sailed before?"

"No."

"What did you think? Some people don't like the motion."

"I was fine with it. I liked it a lot. I'd go again." I let the idea hang, thinking my hint was suitably subtle.

Hand on his glass, his smile widened. "I'll take you anytime."

"Braxton said you sailed."

"So that *was* a hint."

I lifted my glass for another sip. "Maybe."

"So, you're up for another date?" This time it was Stone gauging my expression.

"*Maybe*," I said on a teasing note. I let my eyes tell him I was completely up for another date.

He took my free hand with his. "Not that this one has to end anytime soon."

"Are we stretching it into dessert?"

"Dessert's a good idea. But we're sitting on top of an illustrious boutique hotel."

I reflexively glanced at the floor.

Stone leaned in and lowered his voice. "And we can stay here just as long as you like."

I liked. I truly did.

We opted for dessert in a hotel suite, ordering a bottle of champagne and a tray of decadent chocolate truffles.

The room service beat us to the suite, so while I toed off my shoes—well Adeline's shoes, black high slim-heeled pumps with inset crystals around the peekaboo toes—Stone extracted the champagne bottle from the ice bucket, removed the foil and popped the cork.

The living room had a modern feel to it, sleek leather furniture, warm cream-colored walls and a deep burgundy rug in front of a long glass fireplace set between the living room and the bedroom. A gas fire flickered low inside. The curtains were open on a floor-to-ceiling window overlooking the city.

My teal cocktail dress was pretty but not super comfortable, so I checked the bathroom and found a plush white robe, exchanging it with the dress and tightening the sash.

When I walked back into the living room, Stone froze in place, a glass of champagne in each hand. "You…look…"

"Comfortable?"

"Sexy. Beautiful. Desirable." He came my way. "How do you expect me to drink champagne while you're dressed like that?"

"Because it's very fine champagne." I took one of the glasses from his hand and took a sip. "And those truffles look like they're to die for."

I strolled to the dining table, where the truffles were set out on a silver tray. Their chocolate shells were beautifully colored, swirls of gold and purple, deep blue and ruby red. I went with a mottled purple, brought it to my lips and bit down.

I could feel Stone watching me. I felt sexy under his gaze, aroused by passion but in no hurry to rush through it.

"Oh, that's good," I said, turning to share my expression of bliss.

He joined me, and I held out the other half of the truffle. "Taste?"

He took the chocolate in his mouth, sucking on my fingers.

Desire shimmered through me, increasing, intensifying as he drew closer, kissing me with his sweet mouth, easing me against him, letting our heat mingle.

I felt him remove the champagne glass from my hand. I didn't know where he put it, and I didn't care, because he tugged on the sash of my robe, unfastening it, pushing aside the fabric, slipping his hands inside the folds and wrapping his arms around me.

I tipped my head and kissed him more deeply.

His palm slipped around my waist, moving up, covering my bare breast.

"The champagne can wait," he growled.

I agreed. Everything could wait. There was nothing in the world more important than making love with Stone.

He scooped me into his arms and headed for the bedroom, tossing back the covers and laying me down on the cool crisp sheets.

I waited there in anticipation, watching while he stripped off his jacket and tie, his shirt and slacks. His gaze stayed fixed on me until he was naked. Then he knelt down and slowly peeled my panties down my thighs, my calves, over my ankles.

His kissed his way back, taking his time, pausing at my belly, my breasts, my neck and my lips. And then he was on top of me. Our kisses and caresses turned to a tangle of arms and legs.

We were together again, and the waves and pangs of passion I was coming to love swept between us. I didn't want it to end, but the force was unstoppable. We climbed higher and higher, holding out and hanging on until the last second when we cried out our passion and crested together in waves of unremitting pleasure.

I felt myself drop back to earth in stages.

Stone's weight pinned me down, hot with a sheen of sweat between our bodies.

The sheets were cool where I stretched out my arms but warm right under me.

We were sideways on the bed with a ceiling fan above us. Its blades were still, but shimmers of heat from the gas fireplace wafted our way. The orange light flickered on the walls and reflected off the massive window.

Stone rose on his elbows to look at me.

I gazed back. I didn't have anything to say. I didn't feel the need to speak.

"You're amazing," he finally said into the silence.

I couldn't stop myself from smiling in absolute joy. "You're not so bad yourself."

"I mean it, Sophie. This is…" He shifted to one side. His fingertip traced my face. "I've never felt like this before."

I hadn't either. I didn't know what to make of it. I knew I was falling for Stone. I was falling fast and hard and maybe irrevocably. But I didn't have any context for my feelings.

I turned my head to look at him. "I've never felt like this either."

"Good," he said. Then he leaned forward for a tender kiss.

For some reason, it nearly brought me to tears. Emotion clogged my chest. I couldn't seem to talk, so I wrapped my arms around his neck and held him close for long minutes.

"Thirsty?" he whispered in my ear.

"Sure." I couldn't think of anything better than to lie here in bed and sip champagne.

He eased back from me and rolled to his feet, walking naked into the living room and returning with the champagne and the truffles as well. He set a glass on my bedside table, and I pulled up to sitting, arranging the pillows to lean on. There were eight of them, so I tossed a couple across the room to get them out of the way.

Stone laughed at that and climbed in the other side, setting the truffles between us.

"I'm glad we kept our priorities straight," he said as he took a truffle then popped it into his mouth.

"Was there ever any doubt?" I asked.

"That the minute we found ourselves alone together we'd hop into bed?" He finished my thought. "No. No doubt about that."

We looked at each other and smiled. Whatever else was going on here, the sex was fantastic. Why wouldn't we want to do it as soon and as often as possible?

Stone's phone rang from the pocket of his jacket tossed on an armchair beside the window.

"You should get that," I said.

"They'll call back."

"You sure? You don't even want to check?"

"I'm sure. No, I don't want to check. I want to lay here naked with you and drink champagne."

"Good choice."

"Thank you, ma'am."

"Do you think *ma'am* makes me sound old?"

Stone cocked his head in astonishment. "What? You're nowhere near old."

"The waiter called me that too."

"He was just being polite." Stone paused. "I was being amusing."

"Oh." I struggled to keep a straight face. "I didn't get that."

He nudged me with his shoulder as I reached for a truffle, making me fumble.

"Hey," I admonished him. "Don't get between me and my dessert."

"You have a sweet tooth?"

"Big-time. You?"

He shrugged. "I like rich more than I do sweet, like dark chocolate and cream."

"Well, buck up, man. These are pretty sweet."

He lifted a red swirled chocolate to size it up. "I know."

"Or back off and let me eat them."

"All of them?"

"Maybe not *all* of them. We can order you something else."

"I'm manly enough to make the sacrifice." He popped the chocolate into his mouth.

His phone rang again, and he heaved a sigh.

"Better check," I said. "It might be important."

"Nothing's more important than you."

"Maybe a cell tower blew up or got struck by lightning. Maybe the whole Alaska grid is down, and they need you to do disaster coordination."

"Then how are they calling me?"

"I don't know." I nodded to the sound of the ringtone. "Ask them and find out."

He rolled his eyes at me but went for the phone.

"Yeah?" He paused and looked my way. "Can that question not wait?" He listened, then frowned. "Right." He gave me a shake of his head, then pointed to the bedroom door.

I nodded. It did seem like something had gone wrong.

He left and closed the door behind him.

I sat for a second, finishing another truffle. But then I remembered my own phone was in the en suite where I'd left it when I put on the robe.

I retrieved it and called Tasha.

"Finally." She sounded happy as she answered.

"Sorry about that."

"Are you still sailing?"

"No. No. That ended earlier today. I got caught up with Adeline, one of the other cousins."

"I remember."

"Then... Stone and I decided to go out for dinner. I mean, well, we were all going to—"

"You're with Stone?"

"Yes."

"Right now?"

"Uh-huh."

"What are you doing talking to me? Hang up already and get back to the hunk."

"I didn't say he was a hunk."

"I have access to social media. You don't think I did a search on him?"

"Okay, yeah, he's a hunk. He's also in the other room on a call."

Tasha's tone changed. "I thought you were out for dinner."

"We were. We kind of still are. But we moved dessert to a hotel suite."

"Way to go, *Sophie*." There was a smile in her voice. "So, you like him a lot."

"I do." I plopped my head back down on the pillow. "I'm… I don't know… Thing is… I mean, he's just so…"

"Oh, my." Tasha sounded amazed.

"Yeah."

"You've fallen hard."

"I don't know what hard feels like, but this is something. I wish you could meet him. You'd see what I mean."

"So, bring him home. We'll come to Seattle for a visit." There was a muffled sound in the background on Tasha's end of the phone. "It's Sophie," she called to whoever was with her. "There's a guy." Then she was back to me. "Jamie says hi."

"Tell him hi back." I pictured introducing Stone to Tasha and Jamie. They'd like him. I knew they would.

The bedroom door opened, and Stone reappeared in all his naked glory.

"Gotta go," I said to Tasha.

She laughed at me. "You bet."

Eleven

Stone and I barely stopped at the mansion the next morning, just long enough to change into casual clothes. From there, we went to the marina and hopped on the sailboat. Wade wasn't working, but Stone sailed us off for a glorious day together.

We headed along the shoreline while Stone taught me the basics of sailing. I was klutzy, but we laughed a lot. Then we stopped at a little village, ate lunch and bought some baked goods for the boat. We bought some souvenirs, silly out-of-season things like mittens and scarves to help clear the inventory of a little store. Then we loaded everything into the sailboat, heading for home, stopping for a tryst in a deserted cove before docking back at the marina.

Adeline was in my bedroom minutes after I got there.

"You two stayed out all night," she said.

I couldn't keep the satisfied smirk from my face. "We did."

I expected a grin in return and was surprised when she frowned instead.

"What?" I asked her.

"Last night was a setup." She plunked down on the end of my bed.

She had me confused. "A setup how?"

"My dad didn't need to keep us here last night." She waved a dismissive hand through the air. "I mean, sure he had some document, and he made a big deal about the fact that Braxton had a new heir now."

I stiffened. "An heir?" I didn't like the sound of that. "You don't mean me."

"Sure, I mean you."

My buoyant mood slipping a little, I sat down on the other end of the bed. "I'm not Braxton's heir."

Adeline blinked at me in obvious disbelief. "Yeah, you are."

"I'm not. I mean biologically, sure. But I'm not interested in inheriting anything from him." Deciding I was his heir seemed way over-the-top at this point. We were barely getting to know each other.

"Braxton's going to do what Braxton's going to do," Adeline said. "But that's not my point."

I thought it was a pretty important point.

"We're years," she continued, "I mean *years* away from any of that mattering. The idea that Mason, Kyle and I had to stay home last night to deal with it is ridiculous. So, you know…"

I tried to read her expression. "I know what?"

"It was definitely a *setup*, Sophie."

"*What* was a setup?" I felt like we were going around in circles.

"Last night. You and Stone. Braxton's throwing you together with Stone."

"Stone was the one who asked me on a date."

Adeline was nodding to herself. "It's all starting to come together now."

"Stone asked me out a couple days ago," I explained. "It was all planned before last night." As the words came out, I realized that sounded like she'd been unwelcome. "Don't get me wrong, I didn't mind the idea of you guys coming along."

Adeline came to her feet and took a couple of paces. "Braxton loves Stone like a son. And now here you are, his daughter." She held her palms open as if her conclusion was obvious.

"You're saying Braxton wants me to get together with Stone."

"*Yes!* I was vaguely suspicious before, but now I'm positive."

I didn't want to burst Adeline's bubble, but if Stone and I weren't attracted to each other, there was nothing Braxton could do to force the situation. We were attracted to each other, but it had absolutely nothing to do with Braxton.

"You do know Braxton has no control over my emotions, or Stone's emotions, or anybody's emotions for that matter."

She returned to the bed and sat back down. From her faraway expression, I wasn't sure if she'd heard me.

"He needed the rest of us to stay home so that you two could be alone together."

"What if he did?" I wasn't really seeing that it mattered much.

Adeline peered at me as if I was missing some important point. "That's his superpower."

"Superpower?" I was thinking of Stone now, and the options for declaring he had a superpower—intelligence, looks, sense of humor, strength, compassion. The list was long.

"Braxton's superpower. My dad's too. They have a way of making you think it's all your idea."

I fought the urge to laugh at that. "It takes more than ESP to get me into bed with a man."

"But you did go to bed with Stone."

"I did."

"I rest my case."

I still struggled not to grin at the absurdity of her theory. "I slept with Stone because I like him. I like him a lot."

I was beginning to suspect I liked Stone more than just a lot, but I wasn't ready to share that detail with Adeline, at least not yet and definitely not during this conversation.

"I can see now that Braxton wants little Stone and Sophie babies to perpetuate his dynasty," she continued as if I hadn't spoken. "I can only imagine he's over the moon at the thought of it."

"It's not Braxton's decision," I pointed out again.

I might like Stone a lot, but it was far, far too early to think about making babies with him. I pushed the idea firmly from my head.

Adeline leaned forward. "All I'm saying is don't lose yourself."

"I'm not losing myself. How would I be losing myself?"

"This." She waved her arm in an arc. "It's always been so big."

"The place is huge." I had to agree with that.

"More than just the house," she said. "The family, the dynasty. It's easy to get swept up in the drama and grandeur of it all. Braxton wants you to stay in Alaska for his own reasons. But don't forget who you are."

I wasn't sure how to take that. "I know who I am."

Okay, so I might not have figured out everything about being rich Sophie. But I wasn't about to fall into line with whatever Alaskan plans my biological father might have for me.

Braxton might want my life to work out the way Adeline described. But he couldn't force me to do things I didn't want to do.

"I've insulted you," she said, looking contrite.

"No, no." She hadn't, not really.

She couldn't know me well enough to realize I was clear thinking and emotionally grounded. I'd always been grounded. It might be my personal superpower.

"I'm sorry," she said.

I reached out to squeeze her hand. "You have nothing to be sorry about. You're watching out for me."

She squeezed my hand in return. "You're my cousin."

I smiled at that as I let her go, feeling really good about our relationship.

"We women have to stick together," she finished.

"We will," I agreed, meaning it.

She paused then. "I do know you're smart. I do know you're logical. Just promise me you'll keep your head in the game."

"I'll keep my head in the game."

"And don't take anything at face value."

I started to smile again. "I like Stone," I repeated. "I like him a lot, and it has nothing to do with Braxton."

She looked like she wanted to say more, but she pressed her lips together instead. "Spit it out," I told her.

She shook her head. "I've said too much already."

"We're cousins," I pointed out. "We share."

She took a breath. "Just make sure…" She hesitated again. "Make sure you put yourself…your wants, your needs first. Don't get swept away by the family's aspirations."

"I can do that." I knew I could. I wasn't about to let Braxton or anyone else mess with my head.

I headed downstairs for dinner, my path taking me through the great room toward the kitchen and the informal dining area where the family usually ate. I couldn't help looking forward to seeing Stone, but I warned myself to keep my expression neutral. I didn't want Braxton or anyone else to guess at the off-the-charts chemistry between us.

I heard Stone's voice first, deep and resonant from the den. His words were indistinct, but I felt the vibration right down to my toes and instinctively moved closer.

Braxton answered him back. "I don't think you are, Stone. I really don't think you are." He sounded annoyed, like he had back that first day I'd met him.

The surprise slowed my steps.

"I've done everything you asked." There was an edge to Stone's voice too.

"You're dragging your feet. You don't think I can't see you're dragging your feet?"

"We're not making widgets here."

I took a backward step. I didn't know what they were fighting about, but it was none of my business.

Braxton gave a cold laugh. "She already likes you."

I paused. She?

"I'm not pushing any harder." Stone's voice was resolute.

"I'm not asking you to push harder."

"That's exactly what you're asking me to do."

"I'm asking you to see the opportunities, exploit the opportunities."

"Exploit?" Stone asked.

"Maybe that was the wrong word."

There was a beat of silence in the room.

"You're too impatient," Stone said.

I glanced to the staircase then, knowing Adeline was still up there. Her earlier words echoed, and I was horribly afraid

I was the "she" in question—the one who liked Stone and wasn't being properly exploited.

"You're telling me this is the best you can do?" Braxton asked.

"I'm telling you to *back off*."

"We're on the clock."

"She's always going to be your daughter."

I felt my knees go weak.

Braxton's voice softened. "But she's not always going to be here."

"Under your control."

"Available. You know how these things go. Close the deal, Stone. Close it now."

They were silent for a long while.

"I owe you." Stone's voice had turned low and thick. "I will always owe you. For what you did, for what I did, for what you forgave, but I have my limits."

A whimper escaped me, and I put my fingertips to my lips. The last thing I needed was for them to catch me listening.

I couldn't let them discover me out here.

I couldn't face either of them ever again.

"You owe me," Braxton agreed as I took a step back, poised to flee.

"But I won't lie to her," Stone said.

I almost laughed at that one, a hysterical laugh, a desperate laugh. It seemed like Stone had done nothing but lie to me all along.

He'd done everything Braxton asked. He'd just said so himself. And it was obvious Braxton had asked him to snare me in a romance.

An image of lying naked in Stone's arms came up in my mind—naked and smiling, as if all was well with the world.

I ruthlessly tamped it down.

"Just one more step," Braxton said.

"Not right now. Not like this." Stone was emphatic.

"The grandchildren," Braxton said, a catch to his voice. "*My* grandchildren."

"I'm not saying never."

I pressed my fingertips harder against my lips. Did Stone think stringing me along even longer was somehow an answer? Did he plan to keep wooing me until…until I—

My breath left my body, and my heart sank to my toes.

"You can't let this chance slip past," Braxton said.

A voice shouted inside my head as I backed farther away. I would *not* fall in love with Stone. Not now, not ever.

Stone spoke again, but his voice was indistinct as I made it to the staircase. I rushed silently up and into my room, pulling my suitcase out of the closet and opening it on the bed.

I grabbed shirts and jeans and underwear out of the dresser drawers, tossing them haphazardly into the case.

"Sophie?" Adeline walked in through the open balcony door. "What?" Her eyes widened as I tossed my toiletries into the suitcase and zipped it shut.

"You were right," I told her, stopping for a deep breath. My lungs hurt. My chest hurt. My throat felt raw and dry.

"About what?" she asked, looking stricken now.

"Everything. Him, them." I gestured vaguely out the door. "I have to go. Now. Right now."

"Oh, no." She took a step closer, reaching out to me.

"I overheard." My voice quaked. "Them." My emotions were a jumble, and I was afraid to try to sort them out.

Adeline drew me into a hug. "I'm so sorry."

"He was pretending all along, Adeline." I pulled back. "They were planning, scheming about a future for us."

She rubbed my upper arms. "They can't help themselves."

"I have to go." I backed away.

"I know."

"Stone lied straight to my—" I couldn't finish. I couldn't put into words how badly I felt betrayed. I slung my purse over my shoulder.

"Wait," she said. "How did Stone—"

"I should have listened to you." I pulled the suitcase from the bed and started for the door. "I'll text. I'll call." Maybe

Adeline could visit me in Seattle, or I could hop down to California. It wasn't like money would be an object.

"Sophie, wait—"

But I couldn't wait any longer. I had to get out of here before I ran into Stone.

"You're going to love it here," Tasha said with patently forced enthusiasm.

We were sitting in my new living room on unfamiliar sofas picked by a decorator to coordinate with her choice of landscape paintings, everything positioned to highlight my new million-dollar water view. It was obscured by a downpour right now, but the rain suited my mood.

Tasha and her husband, Jamie, had flown up from California this morning as soon as I told her why I'd left Alaska. Jamie had braved the rain on a wine and pizza run an hour ago. We were drinking merlot from my old wineglasses. At least those were familiar and a little bit comforting.

"Eventually," I dutifully agreed with her statement.

"I can talk to you about heartbreak," Jamie said, resettling himself in one of the armchairs. "And humiliation." He was referring to the day his bride, Brooklyn, had left him at the altar. He then sent a smile Tasha's way. "And about getting your happily-ever-after when you least expect it."

"Too soon, honey," Tasha said with a meaningful look toward me.

"Yeah," Jamie agreed. "Sorry, Sophie. Just go ahead and drink up. There's another bottle if we need it. I also picked up a few pints of mocha almond fudge."

"You're the best," I said, managing a smile. I'd been teary-eyed most of the day, but talking things out with Tasha had helped, and Jamie had been empathetic too.

There was a sharp knock on the front door, and we all looked at each other in surprise.

"No one knows I live here," I said.

"A neighbor?" Tasha guessed.

"In this rain?"

"Maybe there's some kind of emergency. I'll go check." Jamie rolled to his feet and headed for the foyer.

I heard the door open. Then I heard Stone's voice. It was unmistakable.

Tasha caught my shocked expression. Her eyes went round. "Is that *him*?"

I reflexively pressed my back against the sofa. "Make him go away."

"You bet I will." Tasha was on her feet and crossing the room.

"Wait." I stopped her.

She turned, and we stared at each other for a moment.

I didn't want to see him. Did I?

"Sophie?" Jamie appeared. "He's insisting—"

"Please hear me out," Stone said to me. He'd followed Jamie into the living room.

Jamie turned to face him, folding his arms over his chest, widening his stance as he blocked Stone.

"It's okay," I said to Jamie, secretly relieved to have the decision taken out of my hands.

Maybe this confrontation had to happen. Maybe it would help me to move on.

"You sure?" Jamie asked over his shoulder.

"I'm sure."

Jamie stayed put for a second longer, then, seeming reluctant, moved to one side.

Stone's gaze met mine. Energy shot between us, storming my emotional barriers, bringing back every glorious minute we'd spent together.

"Can we talk?" he asked, glancing around like he wanted some privacy.

"Say it here." I didn't trust myself to be alone with him.

He looked at Jamie's scowling face and then at Tasha, who was obviously more than ready to jump to my defense.

He heaved a sigh of capitulation. "Adeline told me what happened."

I managed an indifferent shrug. It wasn't like he didn't already know what he'd done. Adeline didn't need to clue him in on that.

He took a couple of steps toward me, glancing sidelong at Jamie. "You walked out."

I nodded sharply.

Adeline might have clued him in, or maybe he'd made an educated guess. But his guilty expression said he knew that I knew.

"You should have come talk to me."

I raised my brow. "Seriously? So you could lie to me some more?"

He canted his head. "So I could tell you the truth."

I gave a cold laugh. "What truth?"

"That when you walked out that door, my heart left with you."

I wasn't about to let him get away with that statement. "We both know that's not true."

"Sophie, you don't know how I feel."

"I know what you did. I know what you want. I know you *owed* Braxton."

He drew up straight. "This isn't about Braxton."

I came to my feet. "From what I overheard, *everything's* about Braxton."

Stone's voice stayed level and calm. "You don't know as much as you think you do."

"I know enough." The jig was up already. I couldn't figure out what he was doing here. It wasn't like I'd fall for his lies all over again, swoon and fall into his arms.

"I'll leave Alaska," Stone stated.

The words stopped me cold.

"We can stay in Seattle," he continued. "Or we can go someplace else, anywhere you want."

I didn't believe him, not for a second. Braxton would never let that happen, so it had to be another trick, another way to manipulate me.

"How would that work?" I pressed, forcing him to admit it was a ruse.

He looked baffled for a second. "The usual way."

I wasn't letting him gloss over whatever it was he was saying. "What's the usual way?"

"I stay here." He looked around himself. "Or we buy a house someplace else. I'm very employable in the tech sector. We'd have options."

Now I was the one who was baffled. Was Stone offering to give up his life in Alaska for Braxton's dream of grandchildren?

What then?

Would we take the kids to Alaska for occasional visits? I doubted Braxton would be satisfied with that arrangement.

"I need you, Sophie," Stone said, reaching into his pocket.

"For what?" I was trying, but I wasn't seeing his endgame here.

He produced a small velvet box and popped it open to reveal a solitaire diamond. "Forever."

For a split second, my heart took him seriously, and I wanted to throw myself into his arms. But then I remembered Braxton's plea to Stone: just one more step.

This was obviously that step.

I squared my shoulders, forcibly hardening my heart. "You'd actually *marry me* to make him happy?"

Stone looked aghast. "This isn't about him."

"Everything's about him. It's been about him from minute one."

"Sophie, no—"

"Give it up, Stone. You were caught out. It's over."

Stone's voice got deeper, more determined. "Okay, yes, I'm loyal to Braxton. And yes, he threw us together. And I let him. But I liked you. I liked you a lot."

"Well, wasn't that lucky for you."

"Sophie."

"Don't Sophie me. What kind of man—"

"You were *there*," Stone blurted. "Do you think I was *faking* it?"

His reserve seemed spent. Instead, he seemed to be running

on pure emotion. In answer to his question, I didn't know. I would have bet not. But I hadn't seen the con coming either.

"I *owe* Braxton," Stone said, his jaw tight. "More than I can ever repay. And, at first, that was part of my motivation."

"I know he took you in." Knowing what I did, I couldn't truly blame Stone for his gratitude to Braxton.

"Took me in?" Stone gave a hoarse laugh. "That's not the half of it. He let me *stay*."

I already knew the foster care story.

"After I killed her," Stone finished flatly.

My knees went weak, and I gripped the back of a chair.

"It was my fault Emily died," Stone said with cold, hard finality. "I was supposed to drive that day, but I was goofing off with my friends. Christine hated driving on the icy roads. She hated—" He seemed to stagger for a second.

My heart went out to him. "Oh, Stone."

"And then you showed up. And it was a second chance. He asked for my help, at first just to keep you there so he could get to know you. But then he saw us together, and he thought about what might be. He started picturing grandchildren." Stone paused, but none of the rest of us broke the silence. "It was the first time in eighteen years I'd seen him truly, unreservedly happy."

"You can't marry me for Braxton." I didn't care how much Stone owed the man.

"I'm not marrying you for Braxton. I want you for me. I love you, Sophie. I've loved you since we faced down that bear."

"I don't believe you." How could I? He was faking it for Braxton, again for Braxton. Everything was for Braxton.

"Do you love me, Sophie?"

"No." My lie was quick and sharp.

Stone stared at me a minute longer. It felt like he was daring me to tell the truth. But then his expression changed. He looked defeated. He snapped the ring box shut, turned and walked out the door.

It closed behind him to silence, nothing but the rain pounding on the roof, splattering on the deck outside.

"That was…" Tasha was the first to speak.

"He seemed…" Jamie looked at Tasha.

"It was like that the whole time," I said.

They both looked at me, clearly puzzled.

"Adeline warned me not to trust anything. They are the most complicated family."

"All families are complicated," Jamie said.

Tasha nodded. "Jamie's sister married his ex-fiance's husband's twin brother."

"Complicated," Jamie said with a nod.

"That was different," I said.

"Different how?" Tasha asked.

"Max was in love with Layla."

Jamie's gaze turned to my front foyer. "That guy… I'd say that guy's got it very bad for you, Sophie."

As Jamie voiced it, I knew it was true and my heart sank.

Stone had just proposed. He'd told me he loved me. He was loyal to Braxton, sure. But I knew about their scheme. Why would he still lie about loving me?

"Oh, no," I said out loud.

"Go," Tasha said.

I rushed for the door, out into the rain, where my blouse was instantly wet to my skin.

Stone was still there in the driveway, standing still, staring at the door of his rental car.

"Stone?"

He looked my way, his expression stark.

I kept moving forward. "I lied, Stone. I'm sorry. I love you. I love you so much."

He stared a moment longer, as if he didn't quite believe I was real.

Then he swallowed and opened his arms. I launched myself into them, feeling their strength close around me, feeling the warmth of his chest and the cool of the rain, on my head, in my hair, dripping down my face.

He kissed me hard, spinning me around. "Oh, Sophie."

He set me down slowly, then he reached into his pocket. He got down on one knee, ignoring the puddles, ignoring the driving rain. "Sophie, please, will you be my wife, have kids with me and make me the happiest man in the world?"

"Yes, Stone, oh, yes!" My heart sang with joy.

He rose, grinning, and slipped the ring on my finger. I stared down at the wet diamond sparkling under the drive-way lights.

He looked past me and gave a nod. "Your friends."

I turned to see Tasha and Jamie, arm in arm, their smiles beaming at our happiness.

"We want to hear about the bear," Tasha called.

"Later," I said and flashed the ring.

They gave a cheer as I turned into Stone's arms.

"I'm a little afraid of that guy," Stone said into my ear.

I laughed at the thought of Stone being afraid of anyone or anything for that matter.

"We should go back to Alaska," I said.

"We can go anywhere you want."

"I want to spend time with Adeline and Mason and Kyle."

"And—" Stone hesitated. "Braxton?"

I gave a deep sigh. "Families are complicated."

"I don't know what that means."

"It means Braxton is my father, even if we do need to work out some boundaries."

"He'll be so thrilled to see you. He's heartsick about chasing you away."

"I'm sorry I bolted so fast."

"Don't be sorry."

"I should have stayed and fought…for us, for you, for my complicated family."

"You don't have to fight for me," Stone whispered, wrapping me close to his chest and his heart. "I fight for you. I love you, and I'm yours forever."

* * * * *

COMING SOON!

We really hope you enjoyed reading this book.
If you're looking for more romance, be sure to
head to the shops when new books are
available on

Thursday 3rd February

To see which titles are coming soon, please visit

millsandboon.co.uk/nextmonth

MILLS & BOON

THE HEART OF ROMANCE

A ROMANCE FOR EVERY READER

MODERN

Prepare to be swept off your feet by sophisticated, sexy and seductive heroes, in some of the world's most glamourous and romantic locations, where power and passion collide.

HISTORICAL

Escape with historical heroes from time gone by. Whether your passion is for wicked Regency Rakes, muscled Vikings or rugged Highlanders, awaken the romance of the past.

MEDICAL

Set your pulse racing with dedicated, delectable doctors in the high-pressure world of medicine, where emotions run high and passion, comfort and love are the best medicine.

True Love

Celebrate true love with tender stories of heartfelt romance, from the rush of falling in love to the joy a new baby can bring, and a focus on the emotional heart of a relationship.

Desire

Indulge in secrets and scandal, intense drama and plenty of sizzling hot action with powerful and passionate heroes who have it all: wealth, status, good looks…everything but the right woman.

HEROES

Experience all the excitement of a gripping thriller, with an intense romance at its heart. Resourceful, true-to-life women and strong, fearless men face danger and desire - a killer combination!

To see which titles are coming soon, please visit

millsandboon.co.uk/nextmonth

LET'S TALK

Romance

For exclusive extracts, competitions
and special offers, find us online:

 facebook.com/millsandboon

🐦 @MillsandBoon

📷 @MillsandBoonUK

Get in touch on 01413 063232

For all the latest titles coming soon, visit
millsandboon.co.uk/nextmonth

JOIN US ON SOCIAL MEDIA!

Stay up to date with our latest releases, author
news and gossip, special offers and discounts, and
all the behind-the-scenes action
from Mills & Boon...

 millsandboon

 millsandboonuk

millsandboon

It might just be true love...